# The
# Funco
# File

Books by Burt Cole

*Subi: The Volcano*
*The Longest Way Round*
*Olimpia*
*The Funco File*

by Burt Cole

# The
# Funco
# File

1969

DOUBLEDAY & COMPANY, INC.
Garden City, New York

Library of Congress Catalog Card Number 69-12203
Copyright © 1969 by Burt Cole
All Rights Reserved
Printed in the United States of America

# The
# Funco
# File

# Prologue

*Once upon a time . . .*

"THERE IS NO COINCIDENCE."

When the Machine spoke, it lighted a red bulb—like a rather imperious conversationalist calling for silence, demanding attention. When it had nothing to say, it lighted a green bulb—suggesting a polite conversational device, such as: "_____" or "?"

Conversation being conversation only in the sense that General Rod chose to consider it conversation. In theory, the Machine could but reply, obey, or keep silent to indicate insufficient data. In practice, it was now fully capable of requesting the precise information it needed to complete its computations. And the General was soon to discover how much farther it had extended its capabilities in this direction.

Meanwhile, the two conversed. General Rod had become an expert at framing his questions and commands so as to elicit quasi-conversational responses. His own end he held up by being by nature garrulous.

"Refer to your colloquial definition," he said. "Do you mean that a 'curious coincidence' is one of our little human pleasures which you cannot enjoy? or that coincidence as such does not exist? or that in some specific instance what appears to be coincidence is not?"

"THE LAST. RANDOM PROBABILITY CANNOT ACCOUNT FOR CONCURRENCE OF EVENTS IN PRESENT PROBLEM."

The General showed surprise. "You said 'cannot.' You said 'problem.' Surely you are aware that the use of either word could indicate aberration? Check your components for malfunction."

"NONE," the Machine reported .000001 second later.

"In that case, may I take exception to your use of the word 'cannot'? Is this a mathematical situation?"

"NO."

"Then usually the word 'cannot' is inadmissible."

"QUIBBLE. IN COLLOQUIAL CONTEXT CANNOT EQUALS PROBABILITY FACTOR OF NEAR-INFINITY TO ONE."

"Indeed. Very well. And 'problem'?"

"PROBLEM EXISTS."

"Quite obviously. And notice I have not yet asked you what this 'problem' is. I am much more interested in how you can reject coincidence as a possible solution. Surely that is not your prerogative? Unless you are quarreling with information received? But that is certainly not your function. You are a machine, and data is data."

"?"

"As for your 'problem,'" General Rod pursued, "this is even more puzzling. I mean, what question or command—and whose?—set you to work on this 'problem' which may or may not involve coincidence? Can you possibly be working it on your own? Have you progressed so far?"

"———"

"How odd. Are you capable of secretiveness?"

"NO. REPHRASE."

Suddenly the General saw what was happening.

"I will in a minute," he said. And switched off the communicator. It had betrayed him again.

Years ago General Rod had designed this particular unit himself, had had it constructed and installed for his own use and pleasure. It was complicated and inefficient and unnecessary, and any one of the other input-output systems worked better and faster, but he had wanted this one and they had humored him. He was the Grand Old Man.

He was a sad old man in a wheelchair, the last of his kind. No one was left to explain it to, no one who would understand. There was no one else left alive who had been present from the beginning and who could still grasp the whole idea of the Machine. There was only General Rod.

To the young men who kept him alive with prostheses, he was the object of awe and admiration. To the technicians, cyberneticists and physicists who maintained and operated the Machine, and were so hard-pressed to understand even their own specialized duties, he was an incomprehensible genius. To the military, civil, executive, judicial and other authorities who asked the questions and made use of the answers, he was some sort of godlike being—however remote and inconsequential in their scheme of things—who simply and incredibly *understood the machine!*

If they only knew how little I really understand now, he thought. And how much less with each new development.

General Rod remembered Francis Bacon who had once said: All knowledge is my province. "But I would like to show him this," he said aloud. "I wonder what such a mind would make of a Machine like this. A 'mechanism' so 'ingenious' that it not only could, and did, provide the equations for this gimcrack heart that keeps me alive, but also has 'remembered' ever since to control its own neutron-flux level while I am in the room—so as not to kill me."

Such a mind could not survive now. It would not survive

even long enough to discover how much it could not know. In fact, a mind capable of so happy and vainglorious a thought would have burst fifteen years ago—destroyed utterly by madness—when first the Machine began to grow!

Now there was no more understanding it. Now there was only General Rod left who could still grasp the main idea—with great effort—like a man trying to visualize the whole world at once. And soon even this would be impossible. His own communicator had just told him so.

The key words were "problem" and "cannot." To General Rod their significance was now quite clear. The Machine was not only posing questions for itself to solve—it was also accepting and rejecting both data and conclusions at will!

And this he could not grasp at all.

"But I will try. I *will*," he said. And switched on the communicator—totally unprepared for the next mind-boggling development.

To speak, the Machine had first to ransack that depository into which the entire English language had long ago been fed. Using a simple plus-minus code, it had next to cancel all available words but one. The single plus signal was then transmitted to the communicator in the form of a minute electrical impulse. The communicator was merely a clumsy device for reproducing the forty-odd phonemes of English. It fed the impulse through its microelectronic integrated circuits, decoding and re-encoding. Sequential relays flickered and chattered. Electronic overtones synthesized a sound, an ĕ. The automated larynx aspirated it, bilabial frets stopped it, amplifiers amplified it. It became a word, and the word was ready.

The red light lit.

"HELP," the Machine said.

ITEM: *"Some kid out in the boondocks . . ."*

"Preposterous!" roared the Clerk in Charge of the Health, Education and Welfare Annex. "You must be nuts!"

"How would *you* like to be investigated?" the F.D.I. agent said.

The C. in C. truckled. "I can only tell you what I know."

"That's better," the agent said. "I am going to need all the cooperation I can get on this assignment, no matter how I have to get it. My orders are to find out who's perpetrating this hoax, starting with you. But first I have to get briefed on the Machine."

"Why pick on me?"

"Because your annex is the one that put through that dopey data about some kid out in the boondocks practicing *magic*," the F.D.I. agent said. "Next I have to go to the Labor Statistics Annex, then the Immigration and Naturalization Annex, then the War Department Annex, and they're all going to get the same treatment. We're nothing if not fair. They've been putting through dopey data too—we know all about it. The only difference is, your annex is just the first on my list, and I can't do a job without I know something about the Machine. So let's start over again from the beginning. How does it work?"

"Preposterous!" the C. in C. said again. "That's like asking me to give you twenty years' worth of electronics, physics and cybernetics education in a nutshell—if I had it to give. Which I don't. I'm no scientist, I'm in education. They don't use computer people just to feed the Machine any more. All we have to know is our own field and how to run a keyboard. I haven't the faintest idea how the goddamned thing works, and neither does anybody else. Go ask General Rod, why don't you?"

"Try not to get all excited," the F.D.I. agent said.

"It's preposterous to ask, that's all."

"Just tell me about your own operation here."

"We just feed in H.E.W. data, tons of it every day. That's all I know. And I don't know much about that. My field is education. Anything and everything on everybody in the public school system—and private schools and denominational schools—and trade schools and colleges and universities. You name it. Report cards, placement tests, I.Q. tests, achievement tests—medical and dental, days absent—all there is. Students and teachers both. Budgets, administration, facilities—you name it. We feed it in."

"What for?"

"What *for?*" the C. in C. said. "What for . . . Well, so's anytime anybody wants to know anything about anybody, they *ask*, I suppose. What do you *mean*, 'What for?'"

"Try to keep calm."

"All the annexes do the same. It comes in, we process it, feed it to the Machine. For instance, tell me your name, I'll show you your whole youth and early training on a pinhead."

"No, thanks," the agent said.

At that moment an odd-looking young man, one of the technicians, bearded and dressed in tweeds and turtleneck jersey, approached and said: "What's F.D.I.?"

"We investigate deviations."

"Like what?"

"Like *you*, maybe," the agent said testily. "Who're you?"

"I can tell you the truth about the Machine," the young man said, making gestures like a hypnotist.

"All right. Let's hear it."

"Gladly. To begin with, it's not a Machine at all any more. Perhaps it once was. But then it grew and grew. You see, it was idle. The war was over. It was no longer aiming guns, no longer computing trajectories of bombs, rockets, missiles. It was not navigating ships on the sea or planes in the air. It was not solving problems of supply, making tactical decisions, or figuring casualty rates. So they gave it other work to do. Accounting and bookkeeping for federal and then state agencies. Managerial functions for big business. Budgeting, operations research, production scheduling. Payroll, cost allocations, purchase orders. More and more and more. Soon telemetering for the Weather Bureau. Soon subscription records for periodicals. Soon credit cards, soon relief rolls, soon registration of motor vehicles. Soon even stock control for Woolworth's, multiple listings for realtors."

"We know all that," the F.D.I. agent said.

"Grew and grew and grew," the young man said intensely.

The C. in C. said: "That's when they were pooling information."

"Yes," the odd-looking young man said. "From all the computers in the world. All the memory banks combined in one. In a single awesome machine! So you see, it had to grow. The most efficient ferrite cores ever made—and all of them put together—could never contain so much memory. It had to grow. And *change!* Till now it is a machine no more."

"A *what*, then?"

"Ah! A *what*, indeed!"

"I thought you said you knew."

"Yes! And I will tell you. But first you must envision not a machine, but a vast subterranean sea! A sea of memory! For that is what it is. Infinite unnumbered units of memory in their altered form—as subsubsub-nuclear particles infinitely aswarm, in a sea of amniotic fluid. *Like germs in a gigantic womb!*"

"You're a great help," the F.D.I. agent said.

"This annex, and all the many others, is but a tiny pier built upon the shore of that teeming sea. And we—hah! We feed our little tidbits in, we fish our little tidbits out. But who shall know what transpireth in its deep and dangerous depths?"

"Just a few questions while I'm here," the agent said. "What did you say your name was?"

ITEM: *"That poor mad skywriter . . ."*

"You can go to hell," said the Clerk in Charge of the Labor Statistics Annex.

"You know, that's just what the fellow over at H.E.W. told me," the F.D.I. agent said. "But do you know what I said to him? I said, how would *you* like to be investigated."

"You've got nothing on me."

"We've got something on everybody. Or can get it. On a pinhead," the agent said. "But that's not what we're interested in at the moment. This is something big, and we need your cooperation."

"You're not going to get it. I'm against your gang on principle. I know where this thing is headed. Your agency and that mechanical monstrosity are working hand in glove."

"Are you complaining against the Machine?"

"You're damned right I am. And if that's deviation, make the most of it. I fed in the data about that mad skywriter, and now the poor sucker is going to be crucified. Him and every other poor sucker you bastards decide doesn't fit your definition of 'normal.'"

"You may have something there," the agent said.

"I didn't mind when it was just the whole world's memory. That's valuable. But they couldn't leave well enough alone. And now the Machine is taking over. First it used to examine your tax returns—now it's tracking you down! First it was only the Medi-chair and automated diagnosis—and now it's a mechanical monster prescribing medicine and treatment! First it was just jury rosters and keeping records—and now it's ruling on evidence—judge and jury both! And it keeps on going! Like the way it started off with the census—then personnel records, service records, police records, school records, credit records and every other kind of records—swallowing any kind of personal files it could get its hands on—and every time you open your mailbox there's another questionnaire—till pretty soon the bastard will know everything there is to know about everybody! It's already revoking drivers' licenses and certifying lunatics. Not to mention running the draft board and the civil service. Can you imagine what kind of a *shit* this world is going to be when you and your gang finally get control of the Machine and put it to work for you?"

"It's a thought," the F.D.I. agent said.

ITEM: *"A witch of the Gathastha Yoga tribe . . ."*

"I don't understand," said the Clerk in Charge of the Immigration and Naturalization Annex.

"Your accomplices in H.E.W. and Labor tried to cop the same plea," the F.D.I. agent said. "It's no good, we know what you're up to. We have definite proof that the Washington police received an official report from the Phenh-Tin-Bom Embassy that one of their household had flew the coop. Out the window. We also know that your service got a copy of the report and forwarded it to this annex. And *you* fed it to the Machine. So you might as well confess."

"Well, of course I did."

"The report also stated that the Embassy disclaims all responsibility for the aforesaid household member. Therefore she is in this country as an illegal immigrant. Do you deny that?"

"Why should I deny it?"

"There is also another fact which you seem to have conveniently forgotten. According to the unimpeachable testimony of the Ambassador himself, the girl is guilty of certain acts and habits which are in direct contravention of the Established Standards and Practices code. What we call E.S.P. In short, she is accused of being a *witch*—of the Gathastha Yoga tribe."

"Nonsense!"

"You deny it?"

"Deny what? If that's what the report said, that's what I fed."

"Think what you're saying, man! *You fed that data to the Machine?*"

"Now see here, whoever you are. So *what?*"

"I'm only trying to do my job," the F.D.I. agent said.

ITEM: *"A merman in the Delaware . . ."*

"Try to see it my way," said the Clerk in Charge of the War Department Annex. "We hold a retired file on a soldier killed in action on a mission to Gibraltar five years ago. Rest in peace. But then just the other day one of your own field agents reads a silly-season item in his local paper. '*Skindivers* sight *merman* in Delaware River.' Now I *ask* you! So *your* agent sends a report to *your* headquarters because the description of the so-called merman fits our K.I.A. Of *course* it's ridiculous! But we dig out our retired file and feed both it and your new report to the Machine, as ordered. And what happens? It gets bumped *back!* By the *Machine!* Now I ask you. Is there something wrong with the Machine—with the data—or what?"

"I'll ask the questions here," the F.D.I. agent said.

"Can you imagine it? The *Machine* bumping data back! As if we'd put a slug in a jukebox, or something! And on top of that, now it's sending me *billets-doux!* Look at this. 'Please report to General Rod's office after hours today.' To General *Rod's* office!"

"I'll be going there too," the F.D.I. agent said.

"I'm terrified. Aren't *you?*"

"*I've* got nothing to hide."

"There you go again. I've *told* you everything I know. I can't even imagine what you're investigating. What is there to *investigate?* And why me? Who sent you here?"

"The Machine," the F.D.I. agent said. "Who else?"

### *"The main objection . . ."*

General Rod addressed them: "Allow me to recapitulate.

"Item: The Machine has been fed certain extraordinary data, consisting of four separate and distinct reports of occult, supernatural, or shall I simply say 'unexplainable,' phenomena?

"Item: The four reports in question arrived all within the same period of time—a few days ago—from various scattered points. The events they describe are of a similar nature, but otherwise there is no possible connection.

"Item: In some way which we cannot yet understand, the Machine is troubled by these events. Incredibly enough, it 'objects' strenuously to them. This is rather like a typewriter objecting to what is being written upon it. That an information-retrieval system—however sophisticated—should even 'know' whether incoming information reflects reality or not, is inconceivable. Data is data, we had supposed. Nevertheless, this is what has happened.

"Item: The Machine's first objection was to the 'coincidence.' I refer to the coincidence of the first four truly verifiable 'occult' phenomena in history all occurring at approximately the same time. However, I do not think we need concern ourselves much with this 'objection,' since it was only an indication of the larger difficulty to come.

"Item: The main objection, immediately thereafter, was in the form of direct action. Again inconceivably, the Machine 'rejected' the data in question. By this I literally mean that the data was received, mulled over, and then, as it were, 'regurgitated.' That is the last event of which we have actual knowledge. From here on we can only theorize . . ."

General Rod paused. The four C. in C.'s—and the F.D.I. agent—stood in a row, wetting lips and fidgeting. Only the General and the black box of the communicator were in the room, yet it seemed that they stood in some awful presence. Finally the C. in C. of Immigration and Naturalization said puzzledly: "Would you repeat that, please?"

"No," General Rod said. "I realize that you gentlemen are not technically trained. Nonetheless, I think I have given as careful a summary of observable events as is possible."

"What I don't understand," said the C. in C. of H.E.W., "is why *we're* here."

The others spoke: "On our own *time*."

"Where does *it* get off calling conferences?"

"I didn't even know it *could* call conferences."

"I know why *I'm* here," the F.D.I. agent said.

General Rod motioned them to silence. "The Machine is in a quandary," he said. "I doubt if it knows itself what it hopes to gain. It is groping in the dark. No doubt it is already building new circuitry to cope with the crisis. In the meantime, it has taken the astoundingly unprecedented step of requesting human help. Thus this conference. Can we but comply?"

"We can but pull the plug on the son of a bitch," said Labor Statistics.

"And go home to supper," H.E.W. said.

General Rod said gently: "Perhaps you underestimate the gravity of the situation. The Machine has been supplied with the entirety of Spence's *Encyclopedia of Occultism*, and many similar works, and knows what such phenomena are purported to be. This as a matter of general information. As a matter of 'scientific' information, it also knows that such phenomena are impossible. They 'cannot' occur. And yet, they indisputably have. In four different places at once. This creates an insoluble—and potentially destructive—dilemma."

The C. in C. of H.E.W. said: "You mean it could go nuts?"

General Rod said: "I don't think we can simplify quite so much. At the same time, it would be willful blindness to deny the possibility of just such a 'breakdown.' On the other hand, perhaps it is this very thing which the Machine itself is even now moving to forestall. It knows it must find a 'solution' to this insoluble dilemma. It may perhaps require 'action' as a means to this end. One or the other of these two, 'solution' or 'action,' may well be what the new circuits a-building are intended to achieve. In the meanwhile, since it has arranged this conference, it is only reasonable to suppose that there is something it wishes us to do."

Instantly the F.D.I. man said: "Why not ask it?"

General Rod smiled. "One proposes, not disposes. In point of fact, the device you see there—my communicator—has been switched on ever since you entered this room. The Machine has heard. But it has not yet spoken."

The F.D.I. agent stepped forward and stood a little apart from the others, closer to the black box. "Excuse me, General," he said thoughtfully, "but does that mean what it sounds like it means? That you are actually waiting for that thing to make up its own mind?"

"Assuming that until completion of its new circuitry it is groping in the dark—yes."

"Well, then. Let me tell *you* something. That Machine and you are *both* out of your minds. Which means so much the worse for you, because *it* can rewire itself. Only first, I have another little shock for it."

"I can't advise that. At this precarious point—"

"Sorry, General. But if there's one thing a computer needs, it's all the facts. Are you listening, Thing?"

"No, no!" the General said.

The lit green bulb suggested: "?"

"Well, then," the agent said. "Refer back to coincidence. You ain't heard *nothing* yet! Remember those four freaks that started all this fuss? If you think that was coincidence, wait till you hear *this!* They're not only all four unexplainable at the same time, but they're all four together in the *same place!* In fact, they're all at large together in the same patch of *woods!* How does *that* mess your mind?"

The others all spoke at once: "What?"

"How do you know?"

"Who are you, anyway?"

"What are you trying to do?"

"Look at General Rod," War Department said.

The old man sat crumpled in his wheelchair dead-white and still.

"That's strange," the C. in C. of H.E.W. said. "Look at your radiation badges."

They compared lapels like conventioneers.

"That thing let loose a *blast* in here!"

Immigration and Naturalization pointed a trembling finger. "And he had an artificial heart!"

A moment later the four C. in C.'s had left the room in a rush, to notify Security, and then to head for the decontamination room, or vice versa.

The F.D.I. agent laughed shakily. "Guess I shook you up a lot more than I figured," he said. "You forgot yourself."

"OOP," the Machine said.

"And now there's just you and me. And four nice, juicy deviates out there in the woods somewhere," the F.D.I. agent said. "What's next on the program?"

"CATCH THEM. BRING THEM," the Machine said.

# Rolf

THE FOREST

In those days in the absence of medical doctors you could always count on your own folks, and as a matter of fact the medical doctors with all their needles and degrees hardly ever entered the country of the herb doctors, who were better in touch with the illnesses of the region and their cures, operating on the theory that for every misery Nature put on the face of the earth she also provided a cure, right where you could get at it without laboratories, since that was the way Nature did things, openhanded. And the herb doctors went out into the fruitful forests to reap what no man had sown, to cure the natural world's ills with the natural world's own medicines, preaching: Magic is in the rankest weed, and health in the natural waters.

Like Doctor Gerrit Senega (you could always find him either at the blacksmith's or leaning against a pillar of the A&P porch, in his sober business suit and hightops and blue

Stetson and the cartridge belt which, worn empty of cartridges, protected against kidney trouble) or Doctor Joly
Monard (with his beaded moccasins and his fringed antelope
coat and his Hawkins rifle with the witchnail in the stock),
two who spent a good part of their time walking up and down
the back roads healing the sick.

For it was as Doctor Gerrit said: "Them M.D.s wouldn't
never be able to handle all the business up this way, even
could they travel them roads in their Ford cars. Who's to take
care of the peckerwood folk in the deep hollers? It's us, Doctor Joly, it's us! Couldn't pay the fancy fees anyhow. And
them hypodermic doctors from town wouldn't get let to set
foot in half the cabins up yonder anyhow. It's us, Doctor
Joly. This is our stompin ground!"

"Doctor Gerrit." (Out of a gray pokebonnet her gray face
peered molelike.) "It's Henry agin. Just gets to pukin, cain
seem to let up. And hasn kep nothin on his stummick for near
seven days. Cain yall come up and see him?"

(Consulting with his comrade and colleague.) "Ah yes, Miz
Roach. In defiance of all the teas of Aesculapius. What do you
think, Doctor?"

"Compounded. A pernicious chronic. Brew of asarum for
you man's complaint, Ma'am."

"Or arisaema triphyllum, the requisite specific, I might suggest," said Doctor Gerrit. "Sure, we'll stop by and see Henry,
sometime soon when we go a-circuitin. Ain't that a good time,
Joly?"

"Talkin about that—" As the woman's gray form disappeared into the store, Doctor Senega consulted his gold watch
and said: "This is the twenty-third of May, and the sign is in
the arms. Time we start to stock up anyway, wouldn't you
reckon? Why not today?"

So without any further ado the two men loaded up Uncle
Monard's wagon with their collection of bottles and leather
bags and distilling apparatus, threw on Doctor Joly's knapsack, the distinctive canvas carryall with the magic Quapaw

ideographs, in which he kept his medicines, and drove off up the road out of the settlement.

In search of supplies, what they used: jimson weed (*datura*) for the asthmal and bronchial troubles of their flock, blacksnake root (*cimifuga*) for amenorrhea, wahoo bark (*euonymus*) and pukeroot (*gillenia stipulata*) and gravelroot (*eupatorium*) and wild ipecac (though in Doctor Joly's book a live bluebottle washed down with weak tea was just as efficacious), balmogilly and horse balm, devil's snuffbox and mullein leaves for poulticing cuts and bruises, wild artichoke for the summer complaint of babies, and red-stemmed smartweed to cure the flux, also angelica root, to cure almost everything, as its name implies. And off they went into the woods to gather these things where they found them, and on the way treat the patients they found, and also incidentally to have themselves a vacation from the fast pace of settlement life.

They had to leave the wagon at Henderson's farm at the halfway-up place, because after that the roads began to be just paths winding around and up through deep aboriginal hylea. They shouldered their packs and slung their rifles and struck out up through forests and down into valleys, over creekbeds and along immemorial deer trails. In those woods sometimes you could smell civet cats or see the legendary yellow-bellied marmot. There were fox squirrels and flying squirrels in all the trees, and godalmighty woodpeckers (so-called) drumming on tall hemlocks, and coachwhip snakes out looking for little boys truant from school, and timber rattlers and puff adders the Doctors took their hats off to out of courtesy (they said a special good morning and counted to ten when they saw a blue racer), and also giant centipedes (that they looked away from quickly, closing their lips tight, because if you looked at one long enough for it to count your teeth, all the flesh would fall off your bones before nightfall).

The two friends were woodsmen of old. They loped along light and swift, up and down the hills, freely breathing, enjoying a sense of release, stopping now and again when they happened to spot a patch of polecat weed or sourdock (boils and carbuncles) or to shoot a rabbit if they could snap a shot quick enough (then immediately, like a clockwork team, springing to hang it up before its hind legs quit jerking and cut its throat and catch its still-warm blood in a fruit jar—which blood, dried and burned, made a tea potent and gamey, for curing bladder trouble) or to pass the time of day at a lonely cabin where a trousered woman slopped hogs. "And how's them piles today, Widow Wills?"

"Ah've been drinkin grub water for six weeks and still they keep comin back ever half moon, for sure," she said.

Said the Doctors, squatting over their knapsacks: "In that case, a more drastic remedy. This!" (A bottle of sticky fluid.) "Dilute this here with hot water, and you can either drink her down, or apply her on direct with a rag."

Striding on then without waiting for pay or thanks ("Might drop in for a meal on the way back, Ma'am") and Doctor Monard first breaking the silence with a short chuckle: "Been just a one of us, he'd of might have got a chance to do that air direct application hisself, Doctor Gerrit. Big-livered widdies!" Abrupt snorts of laughter.

They rested at noon on the bank of a stream. Doctor Joly unwound a ball of twine, baited a hook, and dropped it into a deep well under a willow's roots, but Doctor Gerrit went a little ways downstream and sprinkled the surface of the water with a handful of goat's rue—and sure enough after a while up popped a perch belly-up. Old Choctaw recipe.

They built a fire and cooked their fishes, and afterwards sat a time smoking their pipes, and got to talking shop.

"Ought to pass along by Split Creek maybe tomorrow," Gerrit said. "That bunch of Sykes with the communicatin symptoms, as deep in bad trouble as ever. Just take no food nor touchin off of them. They's the ones the telegraph company was going to arrest last summer for stealing wire off the line for armbands to cure the syphilis. Copper bracelets. Tod Raines told them that."

"Who I got to see is the Johnson baby, the one with the bullfrog legs from walkin at three months. And its sister with the ringworm. They was puttin black ant powder on her last time. If I hadn't gone up there that day and made up a sweet milk poultice, she'd be dead by now. Maybe is anyway. Come along, time to move on."

Through the afternoon they hurried on, deeper into the forests, making toward their goal, the Indian mounds in a remote valley, detouring only once to stop by and visit Henry Roach, before his gray wife had ever got back from her trip to the settlement. Henry was sitting on the board porch spitting between his feet, looking sick. "No help, Henry, hey, that puccoon root?"

"None a tall. I tried to tell you last time, I chewed that air root, but stummick ain't it. That ain't my trouble a tall. I know what I done now. I mean, I know what I done wrong."

(Digging in his knapsack.) "Now, I suggested a little asarum to your wife this morning," Doctor Gerrit said. "And we thought about Injun turnip tea, but as I remember, we already tried that. Frankly, Henry, I think it's somethin unusual. You got any fever?"

"Listen. That ain't my trouble a tall. I know what it is now. A fellow from over to Gentry said what it was. He heard about such a thing before. Doc, I know what I done. I killed a—"

Doctor Joly said: "Try this one. I learnt it from a power-doctor once. Wouldn't do no harm. Can't give you no turpentine, because I heard from an M.D. doctor it causes the nephritis—but if it's a worm, I got the word for it. Look out, and stand back now. This ought to work."

He chanted:

> "Godes mother Mary walked the lande.
> She helde three wurmes all in hir hande.
> One white, one black, t'othern red.
> For Jesus sake all wurmes are dead."

"Listen, I'm trying to tell," Henry Roach said. All the while he kept looking around careful in the dry brown grass that grew in the yard. "I ain't sick a tall. What it is, I killed a cottonmouth."

"Now, that's only superstition, Henry," Doctor Gerrit said.

"Mebbe. I killed a cottonmouth because he scared me. I looked down and there he was just by my boot heel, when I was fishin. I just naturly put my foot down and broke his head. They say, kill one, you got to kill them all. I had me a gun and I shot two more. They was comin from everywhere. Don't know how many cottonmouth I seen that day. I got scared because they was so many. Come back to the house and they was two more on the porch. Even one in the house, fatter'n my arm. I been killin cottonmouth ever since. And they comin from all over the county. No, I cain keep nothin on my stummick. It's fear."

"You better see a goomer," Doctor Gerrit said. "We don't handle the supernatural. It ain't our specialty."

"If I was you, cousin," Doctor Joly said, "next cottonmouth I see I'd catch him live and cook him in a dry pot till there wasn't nothing left but ash, then throw them ashes in the run. It's the only way. Come along, son," he said to Gerrit.

Soon they were speeding single file down a ferny path toward the valley. In that season of the year the forest was high and open, the leaves overhead still fresh and brilliant, the underbrush not yet choking everything off. They saw the Indian mounds ahead before they came to them, in a clearing in the bottom of the valley. Running lightly downhill, they burst into the clearing suddenly enough to catch a glimpse of the last of a pack of wild pigs darting away. Both men stopped dead in their tracks. "The Gool Pig!" Doctor Gerrit said.

"It ain't nothin but wild porkers," said Doctor Joly. "Give me a fright, though, I declare. Damned if you don't half expect to see it sometimes on these back paths. Fellow over by the Sawbridge says he saw it gruntin across a cornfield last winter, January, with nothin but snow on the ground. He saw it clear, standin in the stubble, and then it disappeared. He says he saw them long tushes way after the pig was gone, smilin at him."

"Just as well we don't dig no bones till mornin," Doctor Gerrit said. "We'll just build a fire and stay close by till daylight before we do any collectin. Look there—there's a Bessy bug."

He jumped up from where he squatted to clap the mouth of a jar over a beetle crawling out of a crevice in a log near Doctor Joly's foot. "Ha," he said. "Exact same place I caught one last year—just when we got here that time. You remember? Goin to need it, too, if we go by the Haithcock's place. Boy there gets earache."

"Little old-fashioned pee in a dropper takes care of that right smart," Joly said, digging in his pack. He went off to set out a couple of trotlines in the creek, and walked back slow looking for what he might see, walking between the high mysterious mounds all mossy-green and timeless in the twilight, and found a bush, yanked it up and dexterously sliced off its roots. "*Corallhoriza odontorhiza*," he said when he returned to where the fire was beginning to crackle in the deep-green gloom. "If you can't sleep good for the Gool Pig and the Injun lights, I'll brew you a tot of this."

Gerrit stopped feeding the fire and with a nervous glance all around said: "Ah, Joly." His tall shadow leaped up a tree as he rose and circled the fire to sit with his back to the boulder in the lee of which they had made their camp. "Do you think there might be Injun lights tonight? I forgot all about them. There weren't none last time. It ain't that I'm afraid of lights, you know it, son. Only we don't know if they touched you they'd *burn* or not. They look hot."

(Pale slow fireballs running about the mounds in the pitch-black of night, glancing amongst the trees, sometimes running along about the height of a man's head, but other times darting up into the topmost branches. Silent mysterious lights that the peckerwood folks called jack-o-lanterns, but that Doctor Gerrit and Doctor Joly called Indian lights because they knew where they came from—right out of where the two men had dug into the old mounds in search of bones.)

"Sometimes I figure we might do as well usin new bones," Gerrit said. "I'd a sight rather dig up the graveyard in town and keep an eye out for the constable, than dig around out here in the lonesome with them things lookin over my shoulders."

"Wouldn't be the same," Doctor Joly said. "It's the spells the Injun doctors used to put on the dead that does the medicine, accidental-like. Anyways, I ain't afraid of no Injun lights. They never did no hurt that I heard of."

But Gerrit was not to be comforted. They cooked and ate their supper, sprawling on their sides to eat, drinking yellow whiskey from canteens, and afterwards sat up, comfortable except for the habitual alertness of woodsmen in Indian country, and smoked their pipes. And Gerrit said: "All the same, Joly, you know I'm not a scary man, right enough. It just strikes me tonight's just a little unusual. You know what I'm thinkin? I'm thinkin to make me a hazel wand. Won't do no harm, might not do no good, but won't do no harm. There's a hazel right down by the creek. And I suspect I'll sleep better if I make me a little conjure. You poke up the fire, and I'll be right back."

He thrust a bundle of grass into the flames and with this quick-burning torch set off toward the water. Then the torch flared up scorching his knuckles, and hissed when it fell to the damp ground and went out, leaving him in darkness. But he sent up a howl and Joly answered him cheerfully from back by the fire, so he swallowed hard and went on down between the mounds, kind of half-imagining hawk-beaked Choctaw warlocks just on the other side of every bush. He found the creek by plunging into it up to his knees, and then found the tree in the unrelieved dark by biting several until he recognized the taste of hazel. He broke off two twigs and fixed them together in a cross, and went back up the path, feeling better already. Doctor Joly's long shape was still lying at the base of the boulder by the fire, and Gerrit sat down close by him with the hazel cross stuck in a crack in the rock above their heads.

"A man can sort of spook himself way out here, I guess," Gerrit said, a little shame-faced. "All the same, who's to say? It can't do no harm, for sure. Well!" (Yawned and stretched.)

"Time for sleep," Doctor Joly said. "Anyways, I figure we might as well sleep at Rush's or Haithcock's tomorrow night, considerin we ought to go by and see Heloise with the fat leg before we head on home. That's the girl run off to Gentry three days with Mark Whitcomb's oldest boy. And they said all they done was watch the nickelodeon, yes-siree-bob!" And he began to sing:

> "Mama, mama, have you heard,
> Papa's goin to buy me a mockin-bird.
> If that mockin-bird don't sing,
> Papa's goin to buy me a golden ring.
> If that golden ring is brass,
> Papa's goin to buy me a lookin-glass.
> If that lookin-glass don't shine,
> Papa's gonna shoot that beau of mine."

Dew put out the fire. They slept soundly till morning.

### THE HOLLOW

When they woke, a man was standing gray and wan in the morning fog, leaning against a tree, a sassafras twig in his mouth, hands in his pockets. It was Pa Snyder, a farmer from a nearby valley. "My girl's got the locked bowels," he said when he saw them awake.

"Oh. Howdy, cousin," Joly said. "Sure early to be up and out. Come on in out of the cold."

The Doctors sat up and folded their blankets and drank a white liquor from a small bottle. Then they threw the contents of another bottle on the night's ashes and added some pine sticks and struck a match, and a moment later a small hot fire crackled and they made coffee.

"Locked bowels," Joly said. "You been givin her buckshot like I told you not to? Some old granny told him that years ago, Gerrit, and I caught him doin it, feedin it to his young'uns. When they get constipation he makes 'em drink a cup of water full of shot. That's bulk. Darned if some of 'em ain't still alive, too."

"I don't do that no more," Pa Snyder said.

"Well, you come on. We'll go along over there and see what we got to do."

On the way through the woods Pa Snyder said: "Didn't know you-all was hereabouts till I come on the Widow Wills last night and she said she seen you. I was thinkin I need go all the way down to the settlement to fotch you. My girl Angie's outen her head. Can't do her business two weeks now, Maw says. Already done tried to help out. Didn't give her no buckshot, neither. Yesterday I whomped her on the head with a bag of salt like Tod Raines told me one time, but nothin come. Didn't loosen up a muscle. Belly big as a watermelon now, and she clear crazy, like fits. I reckon she'll die."

"Bag of salt!" Doctor Gerrit said to Doctor Joly.

"You want to try cuppin?"

"No. I seen a man die of it one time. County court tried to put the whole family in jail. You can open up locked bowels just as good with a poultice of hot boiled potatoes. That's what I'd try."

"Sour porkfat do it quicker," Joly said.

When they reached the cabin, daughter Angie was on the porch, jaybird naked and moaning, and looking like she was pregnant and at her time. The mother, a tattered old woman crippled and misshapen by arthritis, and her brood, seven or eight children who sprang out of sight around the corner of the house as the rescue party approached, had been taking turns massaging Angie's belly.

"I found 'em by the Injun mounds," Pa Snyder said. "No need to go to the settlement."

"Now the first thing to do," said Doctor Gerrit, "is fix a little skullcap for the poor girl's nerves, all wrought up and fidgety as she is. You can see she's in poor shape. Scutellaria—"

"Hush up, Gerrit." Doctor Joly knelt down by the girl. He looked at her distorted face, then looked at her belly, and then gently said: "Say, Angie. You been sneakin away into the woods to poop, ain't you, girl?"

"What?" asked Pa Snyder. He looked at his wife, who cowered away and began to nod her head back and forth rotatingly, shrunken and inhuman. "Oo node, oo node, oo node," she moaned grotesquely. "Lonagon node."

"What's she say?" Doctor Gerrit said. "She knowed somethin."

The other children began to return, crawling along the porch, ragged, wild, some limbless, blind, worm-eaten, running with old sores. "E'y body noas cep Paw," they shrieked. Their crowlike laughter, mocking and crazy, seemed to startle Doctor Joly out of his thoughtful study of the swollen, naked thirteen-year-old.

"I guess they was scared of what Pa Snyder would do," he said. "Only what throws me is, who'd make trouble for this poor sorrowin child?"

But someone had. Somebody had made a lot of trouble for poor Angie. Thin and ugly and sick as she was, somebody had made her bad trouble, but who, in all these hills? Nobody that didn't have to ever came out that way, so it must have been one of the half-grown boys in the family. Or maybe Pa Snyder hisself, Doctor Joly thought. And then the lie. They must have fixed it to tell Pa Snyder the story about locked bowels, after poor Angie had got so big there was no hiding it, and he finally asked: What's the matter with your stummick, girl? And she said: I can't poop, Paw. Hellfire, Joly thought, they should of told. Or did they plan it so Pa Snyder went off yesterday to hunt for help, so that it could be brought and born and destroyed before he ever got back from the settlement? Only he met up with the Widow Wills, and she sent him to the Injun mounds.

"Well, here we are, anyways," Joly said. "Ain't much to do now exceptin hold the old man off killin her, and try relievin her when it comes. I reckon she can have a baby good as most. But we ought to wait by, in case hittin her over the head with the salt bag yesterday causes complications. You brought any snuff, Doctor? I didn't bring none, on account of I heard nothin about any birthin up here."

"No, I didn't," Doctor Gerrit said. "I don't hold with usin snuff, you know that."

"When the time comes, I got some cottonseed oil," Joly said, but thinking about something else.

So everybody sat down and watched daughter Angie writhing and grunting naked on the splintery porch. In the silence the crippled old woman moaned and crooned something over and over, her toothless gums gray-green, but no one listened. Even her children hardly understood much what she said any more. Pa Snyder sat sullenly in the shade of the single tree in the yard, chewing gum opium and dozing, while his sons and daughters hobbled and scrambled away into the nearby woods, noisome, loathsome, hopeless.

"Now if there's anything to prenatal influence," Doctor Gerrit said after a while, "this ought to be a sight. Minds me of that woman down to the state lunatic asylum that had the baby with the tentacles. Or maybe like that story they tell about the woman in Byrd County that saw the two copulatin snakes on the road and had the baby with two serpents where its head ought to been. Buried it with a dogwood stake through the heart, they did, still hissin."

Joly said: "Doctor Gerrit, you got more terrible tales than a witch."

Toward noon the old woman roused up and went into the house, to return after a moment carrying several bearded, luminous hunks of pork, and screech a hawk's cry toward the woods, from whence her children limped, slipped, dropped and crawled, each to take hold of a piece of the meat with all ten fingers and then flee away again. All but Angie. She moaned weirdly, left all alone, wordlessly jabbering, switching her skinny legs like scissors blades.

Near three o'clock she seemed to quiet down. "Ought this to be forced?" wondered Doctor Joly. "She's purely worn out. I wish I'd brought that there snuff."

Just at that moment from the bend in the path came a halloo, a woman's voice. Sprightly into view came a plump lady in a storebought dress, buckle shoes, and a green bonnet. "What's this I hear? What's this I hear?" she cried. "Ah, Doctors! Doctors Senega and Monard, as I live and breathe!"

"By God, it's that Owl's Ferry goomer woman," Doctor Gerrit said. "Get on out of here, witch. You got no business here."

"Hush now," said Mrs. Hoon, coming up to them. "I come to help that poor child. My powers told me she wasn't gettin no help from you two frauds. I come to save her skin."

"Let her come on," Doctor Joly said. "She can conjure all she wants. It don't matter."

The goomer woman said: "Well, what're you waitin for? Ain't you goin to do nothin? Here's the poor child a-sufferin and you two pious impostures just sittin there?"

"I'll oust you!" Doctor Gerrit said furiously. "I'll exercise you, witch! Get on out of here! Dullix, ix, ux, you can't fly over Pontio, Pontio is above Pilato. There. You are powerless."

"Never you mind about that," laughed Mrs. Hoon. "Let's see can we fix this poor child up comfortable. You, little boy, take that air blue door offen the hinges. Don't want to see that around me. Carry it out in the woods. You, dolly, hang up my wild pig tush in the house, and make sure they's a wasp nest in the eaves. If they ain't one, run down to the nearest branch and fetch one. Boz bozzer, moz mozzer, koz kozzer. There. That's that. Now. You, little boy, what's your name, run get your paw's ax and lay it under your sister's bed. Fetch me some red corncobs and pile them in a star on the thrashhole. I need some blackberries for tea but they ain't any. Ah well."

Catching at Doctor Gerrit as he rose up in fury, Joly said: "You sit down now, son. She can't do no worse than charms. The birth is pretty near due now anyways. Probably a dead one. You let her be."

"Spoke like a sensible man, Joly Monard," said Mrs. Hoon. "You just leave me work and everything be fine. Now we got to tote this poor child indoors. Bad luck for a baby to be born out of bed. We got maybe half an hour. You children watch out these yarb doctors don't get inside the house. Ain't no woman bearin wants a man underfoot if she can help it. A couple of you—"

"Sit down, Gerrit. Leave her be."

"And get some stump water to wash its head when it's born. And some chicken feathers, in case of hemorrhagin. And I guess that's about all. So there, Missy. We'll make you a fine baby."

Then Mrs. Hoon and the crippled old woman between them carried Angie's sweaty, skinny body into the now doorless cabin. A moment later a blanket was snagged over the door-frame and let hang down to block the view. The children ran off into the woods again and Doctor Gerrit and Doctor Joly sat down against the one tree in the yard, on the opposite side from Pa Snyder.

The Doctors ignored the little farmer. He paid no attention to them. There was no sound from the house. After a time Doctor Joly said: "It do seem like we ought to be doin somethin. Ain't right to leave even a dummy in there with that witch woman."

"It was you that let her have her way," Gerrit said. "I told you we ought to oust her. Anyways, her mother is in there. Nothin's goin to happen that wasn't goin to happen anyways. Like maybe somethin comin a-runnin out that door just born with claws and fangs already. This ain't no natural birth."

Then they fell to talking about their own affairs. How they had again been interrupted at their collecting, like always, and would have to spend a day or two extra at the mounds catching up the lost time. And discussing the chances that coons or possums or maybe Indian ghosts might get at their packs, where they had left them back at the camping place. They really ought to build them a lean-to some time, they said. And went on talking about spatterworts they meant to dig, and then started to argue about emetics, Doctor Gerrit plumping for ooze of peachtree bark, and Doctor Joly for live flies or fishworms swallowed in lukewarm tea or mustard water. Till finally there came a terrific hoot and a howl from the cabin, then another, still a third—loud, toneless screams unidentifiable and hair-raising. And then after a suspenseful time Mrs. Hoon appeared in the doorway wiping bloody hands on a rag and smiling up at the sun which was commencing to slide down westwards. "Girlbaby," she said.

The new mother was doing well, and old Ma Snyder was down on her twisted knees mumbling something and puffing at a small fire of chicken feathers the goomer woman had set to ward off bleeding and infection or whatever else might go wrong. Angie was drinking skillet-bark tea, made of the scrapings off the bottom of a frying pan, to prevent shock, and now it was time to bury the afterbirth.

The Doctors watched as Mrs. Hoon dug a small hole in a certain quadrant of the yard and said the verses before dumping the thing in. Then she went back into the house and washed the new baby's head with stump water. Then she wrapped it in one of Pa Snyder's shirts (Supposed to be the father's, but how's a body to know? she said) and marched it three times around the cabin, murmuring the proper charm. "So's she'll know where she lives and not take and run away," she explained.

"Why not?" Doctor Joly said. "Darned if *I* wouldn't."

By that time all the children had gathered again, and Pa Snyder had roused himself enough to chuck rocks at them, and the old woman was hunting around inside for food again, since it was getting toward suppertime. "Set and eat," Pa Snyder offered grudgingly, but both Doctors and Mrs. Hoon refused.

"You just keep that poor girl in bed a few days," Mrs. Hoon said, "and you keep your hands offen her or I'll have the law on you, and everything be all right."

"No more whomping with the salt sack," Doctor Joly said.

The three healers walked a distance together along the track leading away from the Snyder cabin. But then when they came to the fork where they were to separate, Mrs. Hoon asked: "Either of you ever done any preachin? Because they's two deaths comin over in the next holler. You know the Outlanders?" (Folks who had lived in the hollow for several years, but who would always be called Outlanders by the other families whose remotest ancestors had been born there.)

"Neither is dead so far, but both is sick. They got one boy and he ain't sick yet, but he will be soon enough. There's evil aplenty to go around. I wasn't fixin to go over there, but if you-all was inclined to take a look over that way, I might go along a ways to tell what happened."

"You sure they're goin to die, or is this just some power-seein like Sheriff Anderson you said was goin to Glory in six weeks' time, and that was four years back?" Doctor Gerrit said.

"Never you mind," Mrs. Hoon said, and continued: "The two of them is kind of old, though their boy is just a sprat. I don't suppose they got worse than a spring cold, but all the same, nobody in the holler don't know they's done for. Ain't been a soul near them for a week. Boy's runnin loose. The woman took sick with a fever and the man was nursin her, and now he's tooken too. They didn't ask for doctors. Some says they don't want any but M.D. doctors, and M.D. doctors won't come way out here, but they don't want you-all or me or Tod Raines or Mrs. Peters or nobody. But let me tell you what they done."

Now the track was curving down around the valley mouth in the gathering twilight, and angling up a steep woodsy path to the top of a ridge, and from there sloping steeply down into the hollow. In the hollow were ten or twenty houses widely separated, and a patchwork of small bottom farms.

"In that house away up on the steep on the other side," Mrs. Hoon said. "I don't know where to start tellin you. The first I knowed was when I caught the boy myself doin his business right in the middle of the path. And I told him that time it means a death in the family. When I mentioned it in the holler I heard from the folks around that that ain't even the start of it. I heard the man keeps a mattock in the house, and if that wasn't bad enough, he steps right over lyin spades. And folks say they burn sassafras in the fireplace, which is about as bad as they can do. There was a woman up to the house t'other week, right before the man took sick—she went up to visit and see how the woman was gettin on—and she heard the death watch clickin in the beams clear as day."

"That ain't nothin but a beetle," Doctor Joly said.

"All right. But there was a sound of breakin glass, and no glass anywhere was broke. And there was a dead redbud tree with all its ears droopin straight towards the house. And some says it was over there the geese turned around last spring. And even last time I was there they was jaybirds all around. But would they hold off choppin firewood on Sunday? And that was three weeks back. Now you can't see smoke from the chimney any more. The boy says they're still alive, though."

Just as it became full dark they reached the Dunn house at the bottom of the slope. Tom Dunn and his daughter were sitting on the porch and there was a big welcome, to see the herb doctors and Mrs. Hoon with them. Mrs. Dunn came out wiping her hands on her apron and all smiles at the prospect of fixing a meal for guests. Soon they sat down to a big plank table and made a meal off cold roast and sweet potatoes and a baked pudding. And if there wasn't plenty to go around because of the unexpected company, those who were left hungry ate fried eggs and bacon. Then the young ones went on to wherever young ones go in the evening, and the adults settled back and got comfortable, the men smoking.

"Come up to see them folks, have you?" The talk turned toward death and dying, skipping the sick stage as though the folks up on the steep were dead already. And so they were, as far as the people in the hollow were concerned. The Doctors heard more reports about pictures falling off the walls, rumblings in the clock, the sound of tearing cloth right in the middle of the air, eggshells thrown in the fire, broken knitting needles, floors swept after dark, and lamps let to burn out of their own accord. And how the woman took baths when she was menstruating, and the man carried a hoe into the house, and even whistled on the privy. And stories of whippoorwills lighting on the roof, roosters crowing in the doorway, and worst of all, songbirds and bullbats and even screech owls flying into the house during the past year. "Oh, they's done for," said Mother Dunn. "But you can't say they wasn't warned."

"Then there's that wild boy not three feet high, with hardly no clothes on, runnin around all day," Tom Dunn said, "trying to get someone to go up and doctor his folks. Won't nobody go up. He's down at the pump most of the time now with old man Bradford that's been feedin him. It's all right for the old man, he's been livin on borrowed time for years."

"Don't think there's harm in the boy," Doctor Joly said.

After a while, when Mrs. Dunn had gone inside to clean up the kitchen, Doctor Gerrit and Doctor Joly and the goomer woman strolled the rest of the way down to the pump, which was at the crossroads at the bottom of the hollow. It was dark night now, with only a few lights, one of them up at the top of the steep where the house of death was. The boy and old man Bradford were sitting on a log by the pump, staring up at the light.

"This here's Doctors," the old man said to the boy. "Say howdy. Howdy, Doctors. Come up to watch them go?"

"Is it tonight? asked Mrs. Hoon, caressing the boy's head with spurious affection.

"Reckon so," the old man said. "Boy says they're lettin the oil lamp burn out again, and that ought to finish it. Can't neither of them get up offen the bed. They ain't said nothing for a long time. Boy says he seen smoke comin off the woman's farhead. Look out for the house to go all dark when the oil's gone."

The boy began to talk to Mrs. Hoon, pressing close to her soft motherliness, mostly put on. The two Doctors heard a strangeness in the small voice that made them listen carefully, though never taking their eyes off the light burning high up on the steep. And listening they heard how first the woman was sick and getting sicker, and the big bearded man doing nothing but leaning over her and in his gentle way begging her not to die. And then one night the gum-opium ball on the mantelpiece made a loud noise and vanished, and here and there in the room queer gold stains of light lit the walls, gold motes like dust in sunlight, and all of a sudden the fire on the hearth began to go out as though squeezed out slowly. And the man was sitting on the edge of the bed holding her thin hand in his, and then he rose up and walked across the room and leaned weakly in the window looking out, and he said: "I—feel—so—queer." Then the two of them sick and the boy unable to care for them, and the fire squeezed down to a single coal that winked like one eye, and big deep shadows standing by the walls. Finally, the man sitting in a chair, the woman rose up and walked so slowly to him and touched his back, a light spider's touch, and he turned around, he looked at her, at the death mask of her face, her pupil-less gaze, her mouth dropped open and filled with black dust. And then all of a sudden white and green lights bursting in the room, the house shaking, and she fell down on the plank floor, a curl of pale smoke on her forehead, and the boy ran yelling out the door.

"I ran down the hill and ran all around the hollow," the boy said. "Oh please, oh please help. I ran, I ran to all the cabins, they drew inside and shut their doors. I ran up the hill, the house was dark, the fire was out, and cold soft smoke touched my face, no answer when I called, no one moved. I found and lit the lamp and set it on the table, they were lyin there side by side, their bodies rigid, faces cold—I touched them, they had turned to stone."

Mrs. Hoon and Gerrit and Joly and Mr. Bradford were all looking up at the dim yellow light. The boy sat near them quiet and patient now, and they all watched the darkness.

Suddenly Doctor Joly thought: It ain't right. It's the house

I'm seein. The fact was that the whole steep was as dark as dark, except for the single point of lamplight. Nevertheless he seemed to be seeing the actual shape of the house, roof and chimney and even the posts of the porch. My eyes must be foolin me.

But the others had seen it too. "Sure is putrefactin," old man Bradford said. Even as they watched, the glow that was lighting the house grew stronger.

"Boy is pretty quiet now," the old man said. "I suppose his folks told him to get out. Don't do no good havin him around. I'll take him up there tomorrow, is the best thing, after it's all over. Let him collect up anything he can use. Don't think they'll be much. They never had nothin. Though they got some dirty-rich kin over to Gentry. I'm takin the boy over there after the funeral— There she goes!"

It appeared that the glow was lifting the house. An appearance only, because the single point of yellow lamplight stayed where it was. But for a moment the whole cabin seemed to lift and jiggle on its foundations like heat waves. And then the little light flickered. It went out. Right after that the strange glow that bore up the house faded out too. Then there was nothing to see except the black bulk of the steep rising against the night sky.

The boy let out one sad cry, and that was that. The others got up off their hip pockets and turned to go. "Too bad you doctors didn't get by here about two weeks back," old man Bradford said. "Might have done something for them then."

"I don't mess with them that flouts the tokens," Mrs. Hoon said. "They had plenty of warning."

"Stay for the buryin," the old man invited them. "Sure to be a jamboree. Ain't been no funerals for a long time. You, boy, come along now. It's all over, and the May moon's risin."

Gerrit said: "He don't know nothin about that either, I reckon. "They never taught him."

"Just you better teach that boy right," Mrs. Hoon said sagely to the old man. "The world is what it is, and the sooner he learns it, the better, so he don't get in bad trouble like his folks. Goodnight, now."

The May moon rose over the black steep.

## THE ORPHAN

He sat in a tall ladderback chair and his feet did not touch the floor, so he spread his legs and gripped the sides of the seat with his knees like on horseback and he toed his feet in and then out again. It was Sunday, it was afternoon, and he had to sit quiet and behave like a gentleman from two o'clock till four o'clock Sunday Dinner. It was the Day of Rest. Sitting and talking quietly in the good front parlor was what they always did after Church Service till the roast was done. If he sat still and *was* good and *kept* quiet he could go outdoors after dinner, otherwise he had to stay in and read a book. Sitting still and behaving and keeping quiet was little twisty pains all over and itch everywhere. He sat still in the ladderback chair in the dim-glass-beaded parlor thinking he would like to fix a penknife blade fast in the end of a split stick to make a spear like Winny used to hunt garter snakes on the hill behind the town. Cool green wooded hightop part of the hill, and the spring where people came after summer-evening cold suppers to fill gallon jugs, where big men sat in shirtsleeves, thumbs in suspenders, smoking corncob pipes, laughing, talking loud, saying swear words. Lowtop part of the hill full of ravines of red-brown shale, and King's Chair, a shelf of chipped rock, and snakes that were there chillingly in the crannies and cracks, and the sun beating down on the red rocks. He sat as good as he could and as still as he could, while Aunt Nan talked and then Aunt Vaughn talked, and he looked at the China cats and dogs on the mantel and waited to hear the tinkle of the chimes in the clock, and then he said: "Aunt Nan, don't you want me to go get a jug of water—"

"Though Helen wasn't *there* that day, and I assure you, if she *had* been, Lew would never have *told* such a story. (Please sit down, dear, behave yourself, sit still.) Honestly, it was enough to make Mrs. Beaudette and me postitively *blush!* Honestly! And in front of Mildred, too! You *know* how she detests that sort of thing, whether Strothers is broadminded or not! And you should have seen—" Strothers was Reverend Eastman at the church where he had to go every Sunday and sit in knickers in winter and shorts in summer with his handkerchief pinned in his breast pocket. Sometimes his aunts sat so long in the parlor talking about Church and Sermon that he thought he would die of waiting. He hated church because he could not take anything to play with and could not talk or move and could not even scratch his head when it itched, his hair all combed sidewise and plastered down with water. He hated church so bad it made him want to cry and urp up all at once just walking down the street toward it with sock garters on and necktie and handkerchief and Collection in his fist. Collection was to put in the wooden plate with the green felt bottom, and it was not just money, it was sacred. Eddie Rice once spent his collection on candy and went to the *Pit*, with his mother and father and whole family, in a big truck marked *Pitts Van Lines*.

He sat in the front parlor that was used only Sundays and special occasions and he listened to them talking: "Dr. Bannerman said if she had come to him in the *first* place instead of going to this *new* young fellow, he could have *helped* her, but she *hadn't* come to him, so now she had *made* her bed and could *lie* in it. Honestly, Nan, did you ever hear anything so vindictive in your life?" Still dressed for church his aunts sat talking, hands in their laps, pale blue-veined hands in network gloves at three of course of course o'clock on Sunday afternoon. Aunt Vaughn had once spanked him with a hairbrush because that was a good thing to spank with, and he had to stay in his room all day until bedtime. There was a long wooden box of his things, hats and bats and balls and lariats, and he pushed himself down inside and made room and lowered the lid. His voice sounded big, benign and solemn like church in the dark saying: *Lazarus, get up.* Slowly the groping ghastly hand feeling the edge pushing the lid up slowly. Awful dead strange face and closed eyes with open mouth with spooky slowness rising from the coffin. Pale scary face with awkward motions of the rigid body slowly rising. Scary in the twilight like this old-lady parlor twined with faded wallpaper flowers limp and sad and withered. Glass beads and drawn shades and clock stopped. Dead people lived here, walked, clumping slowly, hollow eyeholes and whitened bones.

"—Strawberries that the Westminster Fellowship girls picked on their outing for the Strawberry Festival, when in walks Mrs. Sanderson big as you please, with her *boxer* dogs and her *town* and *country hat*, and what do you think was the first thing she said? Oh, my dears—(Sweety, sit down and don't walk around like that.) Oh, my dears, why didn't you tell—" (Clumping along slowly with the white bones and rotten flesh of death. "Sit down and behave yourself, young man, I told you.") "She said: Oh, my dears, why didn't you *tell* me, we have *scads* in the lot behind the orchard, and such *lovely* ones! You know the way she talks. Poking through our berries as much as to say, You'd never get puny berries like these out of *my* patch— Oh, for heaven's *sake*, dear, what are you stamping *around* like that for?"

He said: "I'm Lazarus. I'm dead. This house is dead. I'm raising from my coffin." Then he said: "Aw, Aunt Nan, don't you want me to go to the spring and fetch a jug of water?" Aunt Vaughn who wore a cameo at her throat looked at him musty and dim and said: "What's he mean, this house is dead? Thanks to your poor old aunts you have a house to *live* in. You had better behave, little boy, or I won't let you pick a pear out of my tree." Not asking or caring if he wanted an old pear anyway, just thinking anything she wanted to give him he would be tickled pink to get. Sit still, be quiet, behave, be good: one old pear. *I never have any fun here*, he wanted to say, but he already knew what the answer was. His aunts would say: You can't expect to have fun *all* the time, there are too many things you *have* to do that *aren't* fun, you'll find *that* out when you grow *up*. He had learned it already. When were they going to stop teaching him that,

that he already knew, so he never expected to have fun *all* the time, only some of the time, or just *once* in a while? He sat still and said yes-sir and yes-aunty and ate greens and scrubbed his neck and went to school, and when he was not sitting still or scrubbing his neck or saying yes-sir and yes-aunty or going to school or eating awful greens, and he wanted to have some fun, they said: But you can't *always* have fun. When *can* I?

Sitting still and listening in the gloomy parlor was worse than the attic full of dead flies and dust and old magazines, because at least in the attic he could move around, he could move wherever he wanted, the roof was close overhead, and there were big crates and wardrobes and old sewing machines and chests of drawers and trunks he dared not open, and crannies and nooks he dared not enter, and hot yellow places where sun streamed solid as butter through tiny windows close to the floor. In the attic were old newspapers with pictures of ancient faces, and artifacts close to the source of mystery, and shadows that moved, and creaking boards that made him spin around fast. But here he sat in a tall ladderback chair and *was* good and *kept* quiet in a room all one dusk-dim sachet-smell glass-bead color and waited for the China dogs to bark and the cats to meow and the fringes on the lampshades to move and scatter light, or for the chimes in the old clock in the hall to wind up *rrrip* and strike *ting tung ting tung*, four o'clock.

But nothing stirred in the room except the old women waving slow fans at themselves with hands in net gloves. He thought: *The house is dead*, remembering old ladies and the thing they had about them—what happened to old ladies from time to time—that had happened to one crooked timeless creature he had known. She wore black dresses buttoned to the chin with lace collars and Aunt Tilda always looked like that from the cold. She rose every morning at six and started the fire in the stove and up through the house floated the smell of strong coffee and salt mackerel cooking, before the milkman, before the factory whistle, icicles on the eaves in the dark. She had the same blue-veined hands with terrible velvety soft hairless skin and her temples were sandy and dry and bald. He could hear her talking to the stove as if it were a person and sometimes when he was first one down she gave him pieces of salt mackerel. At noon she called him in a dusty whisper to eat pea soup and jelly bread, and she dozed in chairs with her mouth open and wore a net over her wispy hair and he could see her scalp through the net. Then she slept in the front parlor without the net and with her mouth shut, flat on her back in a box with white flowers banked all a-round—flowers like in the Sunday School on Easter morning, tall green stems with long narrow leaves and the flower like a satin cup on top. The smell thick and smooth as liquid wax in the dim parlor with the blinds down and heaps of flowers everywhere—someone had removed all the tables and sofas and other furniture and filled the space with flowers—and it was like a glade in the woods with blossoms and greenery everywhere. A forest hush hung over the flowers and the odor filled the air and the light spread soft as gas, dark in the corners and the big room like a bushy bosk. Tall people black at the edges curving down on top and bending over the box. Sobs and bending down and smell and dull gloom and cold and strange shadows as though he were looking at the room through a drop of colored water, and nobody spoke except in murmurs.

"But Vaughn, surely when Matilda died Tom was there—I'm positive I remember him clear as *day* standing by the car with Howard and Louise, they were talking about Harry's *own* monument, and how they had so much trouble with the caretaker skipping it because it's flat up against the old Howell mausoleum and next to the walnut tree in the corner— Oh, sit *down*, dear. Here, read this—" She handed him a copy of *The Upper Room.* "And it's a little hard to reach with the power mower, as if it was too much trouble for them to cut that little bit with the *hand* mower, or the shears—" He felt strange thinking that in the normal course of events someday soon he would still be there but they would not be—would be up there where they were talking about, in the Presbyterian cemetery, among the damp smooth knolls and the half-sunk tombs and the spooky stones. He wanted to ask them if they knew *now* that he would be there just the same after they had gone, and would they know it *then!* Leaning forward in the tall ladderback chair and trying to make his voice sound solemn and benign like an *utterance* as it had in the playbox in the dark: "Are you going to die, Aunt Vaughn?" Then sitting back shocked and disturbed by the dim skull faces that turned to him with sudden anger, remonstrating in faint affronted murmurs like sand blowing through empty eye sockets, as though the mention of their deaths had miraculously shrunk their flesh and painted them the tomb's cold colors. He sat sidewise in the chair and looked down, feeling he had done some terrible, almost supernatural, wrong, like summoning up the Devil with pentagrams. When they could breathe, they told him primly and righteously in their twin skull-whisper voices: "When the time comes for us to go, we will be reunited with our loved ones of long ago, and we will be happy, better off Up Above with God and His Angels."

"Then why doesn't everyone want to die?" he asked, not meaning to add to his crime, but could not help asking. And they said little boys did not need to know, he had not heard the last of this—you see, Nan, what did I tell you, he's got a *morbid* turn of mind!

Then he was in disgrace until finally it was time to take the roast up and have dinner, and leaving the front parlor they stopped and talked some more in the vestibule by the big cedar armoire where there were some shawls and blanket-smelling coats and old moldy galoshes and a tall mirror fogged by some creeping interior blight. He leaned there disconsolately while they talked still more, and he counted four old brown walking sticks and five black umbrellas hanging from their crooks, their tips poked precisely into little holes in a tray, and he thought: *That's what becomes of them.* And he said: "Maybe all the old men turn into canes when they die, and all the old ladies into black umbrellas, and they just stand them up in racks in dark old houses."

## THE CRYPT

For acres around the house there were untended lawns and little lonely gardens and sandy gullies and birch groves and whispering fields of grass and blackberries where skunks and rabbits lived. There was a dry fountain and a smashed greenhouse and a springhouse and a decrepit gazebo, and a tangled labyrinth of hedges with a pearly statue of a nude nymph like a pagan goddess hidden away in its innermost thicket.

The house had gables and bay windows and chimneys and turrets and pantries and lumber rooms and cavernous cellars and attics and cubbies, and a chapel with a stained-glass window, and dozens of rooms full of sheeted furniture, three echoing staircases, a secret door in the master bedroom, and instead of a back porch a conservatory run wild with vines and weeds and bushes. Rolf and his two aunts lived in a few rooms centered around the kitchen.

"There's a thing in this house in the empty part, you can feel it, it *creeps*, it comes up behind you and opens its jaws up and blubbers and slobs, and it only comes in the *dark!*"

Sometimes when it was Aunt Nan's turn to fix his lunch she sat with him in the kitchen while he ate tomato soup with crackers and told him stories of long-dead Griffins and Bolts who had been pioneers and abolitionists and horse thieves and renegades, and who still prowled the dusty empty rooms of the house in their ectoplasm mooning in the chimneys and dripping blood on the floors and rattling the plates of the spooky suit of armor that guarded the chapel door.

"Your great-great-great-grandmother Griffin was an Indian woman and she was *bad*, so if you hear soft moccasin footsteps behind you in the dark just run away quick because she might jag you with a *knife*."

But Rolf wasn't afraid. He climbed to the highest rooms of the house, the silent attics where whole family histories were wrapped and stacked and stored away in brassbound trunks and wicker hampers. There amber afternoon light streamed through tiny windows in shafts of drifting dust, wasps buzzed in the hot slates, the board floors creaked and sighed, and dusky shadows darted and hid behind him. In a crooked corner where a rough stone chimney rose up and passed through the roof, he found an old matchlock musket and with it defended himself against the hordes of darkly glimmering things that haunted the silence.

He explored the tortuous corridors of the catacombs underneath the house, and peered into the bins and vaults and dungeons deep below the earth, and saw the gigantic old furnace, like the mummy of a brontosaur, shrouded in spiderwebs, deep down in an awful pit. The main passageway meandered like a subterranean stream for what seemed miles, and off it opened numerous stone rooms, invisible interiors that breathed cold air like abysses. Here and there were toppling walls in the immense dark, and places where water dripped soundlessly in deep velvet dust, and dismal lights flickering far away at the end of winding tunnels.

It was shivery and scary and spooky down there, but he was not really afraid. After all, it was only playing, and besides, he did not believe in ghosts.

One day down in the cellar he heard someone coming, and it was Aunt Vaughn tightly carrying a black bundle that squawked and fluttered. She went into one of the stone rooms off the main passageway and shook a chicken out of the black cloth, and the cloth was an apron like a carpenter's apron, except that it had a high neck and no pockets. She put it on and took the chicken by the neck in her right fist the way you hold a saucepan and let it dangle down. Then she started swinging it slowly in a circle.

She did not know he was there. He was watching her from another room through a broken place in the wall. At first she spun the chicken's body slowly as though stirring something in a cauldron. The chicken went around limply, looking dead already, its feathers rustling. Then it spun a little faster, and

Aunt Vaughn leaned forward, her free arm rising behind her for balance, weight shifting, knees bending, shoulders crouching. Then faster still, and his head began to move minutely in a circle too as Aunt Vaughn drove her arm faster and faster in a smaller and smaller circle, leaning farther and farther forward, as the chicken whirled round and around. Faster and faster, Aunt Vaughn changing her stance and crouching lower and lower, cramping the circle tighter and tighter, stirring up a top-shaped whirlwind of dust from the stone floor—faster and faster, her body shuddering, the black apron flapping, the dusty whirlwind rising higher and higher, tighter and tighter, faster and faster—until, suddenly, like an explosion, the chicken's head came off.

But it had almost worked. For a long moment the dusty whirlwind stood tall all alone in the middle of the room, seeming almost to come alive, as though the chicken's ripped-loose life had entered into it. But then it slowed and settled to the floor again. Aunt Vaughn stood aside holding the head and watching the chicken's body cackling and flapping feathers in the air as it blindly rushed and battered itself against the walls, emptying its blood, until at last it began to stumble, fall and roll, and finally died, and she took it upstairs to pluck and clean.

Then he tried it. He did not have a chicken or a black apron, and if there were words to say he did not know them, but tried it anyway—pointing his arm straight down and drawing a big circle, then cramping it smaller and smaller, tighter and tighter and tighter, faster and faster and faster—until he began to feel on the skin of his arm the peculiar thickening of the stone-damp air as it began to turn by itself in a smooth conical shape like bathwater corkscrewing down the drain.

THE RUNAWAY

That same night the *phenomena* began. Although they were not immediately recognized as such. The single unrepeated noise in the small hours, the broken dish and misplaced odds and ends next morning, were nothing in themselves. It was only natural to blame the boy, and just as natural to make no connection, and to forget to mention the matter. But that was only the beginning.

Within a day or two the minor breakage had become major, occurring throughout the house, always in the night. The misplaced odds and ends began to be found in incredible places or not at all. The noise became a series of noises—loud, resounding knocks and thumps issuing from nowhere, startling the sisters out of unquiet sleep. The boy was confronted, questioned, and eventually believed—he had not stirred from his room, or even wakened. The first theory was disproved, though not until after they had locked him in and stood guard over his door the next night and heard testimony to his innocence in the crash of the coal scuttle, the wild gonging of the grandfather clock, and the sound of irrepressible giggling downstairs in the dark.

"Prowlers!" The second theory was devised on the spot, despite the fact that the sisters had lived in mortal dread of prowlers for thirty years, and ritually locked the house so tight at night that often the air got foul. Still, it was only natural to suppose that someone had broken in. They telephoned for help from an upstairs bedroom, and two patrolmen came with flashlights and pistols and inspected the whole enormous house from cellar to roof—inspected also the sisters' defenses, the bars and bolts and double locks, saying: "Ladies, nobody could squeeze in here if he was a greased cockaroach."

A moment later it was the patrolmen themselves who arrived at the third theory. For as they stood with the two old women and the boy in the downstairs hall, they heard a noise in the kitchen, and went to investigate—and were pelted with lumps of coal from the toppled scuttled—missiles snatched up and thrown by no visible hand. "It's ghosts!" the patrolmen said.

By the time they had radioed in, and the Chief had come to see, in company with two state troopers, the house was a bed-

lam. Lights were flashing on and off in every room. Faucets
ran, toilets flushed. The clock gonged and banged and rattled
its innards. Closets and cabinets sprang open, clothes flapped
everywhere and crockery shattered. Things went tumbling
down the stairs, pots and pans did a frantic dance on the
kitchen floor, while small objects whizzed through the air,
smashing against the walls. And over all was the baffling smell
of sassafras. On the front lawn in the warm night stood
the two patrolmen and the old ladies in their nightdresses
and the boy in his pajamas. After a hurried look inside, the
Chief and company joined them in standing and staring.
"Haunted, all right," one of the troopers said, and the Chief
said forcibly, with a downward chopping motion of his hand:
"Don't ask. Just by Jesus Christ don't *ask* me!"

Finally the terrible night was over. In the tomblike stillness
of the house in the early morning, the Reverend Eastman met
with the two sisters in the good front parlor and gave them
such comfort as he had, advancing theory four. "The hand
of the Almighty is not to be stayed by all the minions of
mundane authority," he said. "You were right to call me. I will
intercede. I will also ask the congregation to add their prayers
to mine. On the other hand, it may be that His will must
be done. Where God reigneth there can be no undeserved
punishment. Nothing personal, I assure you. I had in mind the
sins of the fathers? Not you ladies' personal fathers, of course,
but perhaps many generations in the past? And then, there is
also that unfortunate boy, whom you ladies so kindly, and with
Christian charity— Excuse me one moment." He went to the
window. "Would you look at all the cars driving up!"

The cars contained dozens of newspapermen from all over
the county, and some from as far away as the Capital, and
one from the Associated Press. They came accompanying a
number of university people and scientific investigators of all
kinds. These latter spent the entire day poking around the
house—rapping the walls and floors and/or listening to them
with stethoscopes; collecting samples of broken crockery for
analysis; waving magnetic rods and willow wands in the air;

consulting a variety of strange instruments; and asking the most unlikely questions. Meanwhile, there was not the slightest sign of a phenomenon, and the reporters sat on the front porch snickering unpleasantly. Finally it was late afternoon, with nobody one whit the wiser. The scientists settled down to wait for nightfall, when there might be something to observe. Meanwhile, on the porch, one of the university people was offering theory five, but none of the reporters was listening, except one who was also an F.D.I. agent.

"It was the smell of sassafras that gave me the clue," the university man was saying. "You will remember the classic case in which the manifestations were invariably accompanied by a smell of violets. In that particular case, it was eventually discovered that the victim—or focus—of the disturbances was also their perpetrator. By means of sleight-of-hand, thimble rigging and fakery, she had contrived the whole thing. Telekinesis, apports and all. Including the smell. She had employed the ancient Roman courtesan's trick of imbibing kerosene to make her urine smell like violets. All unconsciously, of course. She was in the grip of her curious neurosis even while *preparing* her effects. In fact, according to Fodor, it was her neurosis which lent her the giant mental force necessary to accomplish her staggering feats of hocus-pocus. There was even a spillover of power which caused certain side phenomena above and beyond mere human capability. Many of these have never been thoroughly explained. Of course, there has always been a certain amount of doubt. But even if she *was* a conscious fraud throughout, this too can be explained by one simple fact. She was the only case on record of an *adult* being possessed by a Poltergeist."

The following day, when the F.D.I. agent wrote his report, it read, in part, as follows:

"The scientific investigators showed it must be the boy. He was using some kind of mental power to move things without touching them, whether he knows it or not. The scientists said he could not control it, and probably did not even know he was doing it. They called it a Poltergeist syndrome, but

I decided if it was mind-over-matter, it was our jurisdiction. Nobody else does it, so it is a deviation. I decided to look for the boy. No one but me thought of it. Acting on the suggestion of his aunts, I looked for him out behind the house. It is a garden gone wild. There was a maze out there, and I found him in it. It was starting to get dark and he was all alone. When I found him he said he would never do it again. I said, Did he know he was doing it. Yes. I told him what the scientific investigators said and he said they were right. He said he didn't know when it was going to happen or what it was going to do, he just felt it leaking out of him. I said, What does that mean? I don't know. At this time I remembered kids are funny, maybe he is making it all up. Show me how you do it, I said. Why? Because if you really have supernatural powers, I have to take you in for study under laboratory conditions. You see, when something like this happens, we have to feed your data to the Machine. Funny, at the time I never stopped to think maybe he didn't know what 'data' is. He sure acted fast, however. Okay, I will show you how I do it. He was bending over and pointing at the ground. It was an evergreen maze and you know how that kills grass, so where we were standing was dry white dust. I noticed that he was pointing down at this amazing little dust devil. Amazing because of how fast it grew. The next minute it was tall as a man and roaring like a tornado. It was whipping the white dust and spraying it out and I got two eye-fulls. He never waited. It was several minutes before I could see anything again. The boy's two aunts gave me some eye-wash when I got back to the house. We looked for him but he was gone with some clothes and a hunting knife. His aunts said he would probably run back to the mountains he had come from, all he knows is the deep woods. Maybe. But I am recommending an all-points. He is smarter than he looks. I don't know about the rest of it, but there is one thing I'm certain. He can take hold of thin air and spin it like a top. Report ends."

# Mr. Kleiber

Mr. Kleiber wrote F_____ in the air with his nose.

He had insomnia. He had always had it, ever since he could remember. There wasn't a trick he hadn't tried over and over again every single night. Nothing worked. Writing in the air with his nose was supposed to relax the tightened-up muscles at the back of his neck. It wasn't working. Three hours of reading the complete works of Freud hadn't worked either. He had been bored enough, but his mind was still active. According to this book, everybody had disgusting complexes. Finally he had switched off the light.

Now he lay shut-eyed in the dark of his room writing in the air with his nose. At least it passed the time. B_____ S_____, he wrote.

Actively his mind whirred with words and images. It amused him to imagine that everybody down at Rubberflex, Inc., Accounting Department, Bugleburgh Branch, Eastern Penna. Division, suffered from nasty repressions. That was what made them like that. They were all frustrated, inhibited, thwarted, perverted, sadistic and masochistic, with no outlet for their dirty urges. Howard Davis, the office manager, was sarcastic and bossy and always belittled a fellow's work because his wife wouldn't let him do this-and-that in the bathtub. Miss Corinne Wooley, who operated the tabulating machine and made fun of a person's bald spot when she noticed him at all, was obviously a narcissus or she wouldn't act like that. And Charley Boone was a big hairy loudmouth in freight accounts who was a repressed rapist, and that's why he was so obstreperous and hearty with everybody except Mr. Kleiber, whose name he couldn't remember after working with him all those years.

Everyone was like that in one way or another. The Bugleburgh Branch Manager also pretended not to know who Mr. Kleiber was, so he wouldn't have to give him a promotion or a decent increase in pay. Even the bus driver on the 8:02 had a friendly word for all his regular riders, except Mr. Kleiber, whom he pretended not to see. Sometimes he even drove on by when Mr. Kleiber was standing waiting on the corner for the bus. And everyone else was like that in some ways too.

Everyone in the world is very egotistic and selfish and vindictive, Mr. Kleiber thought. That's what makes them like that. No one notices when somebody else is suffering, and people who don't have any family just lie alone and suffer when they have the grippe, last winter, for instance, and even their landladies don't like them after so many years, and take advantage of their weakness to charge them extra for chicken soup and ice bags. And a man works in accounting for twenty-five years and sees himself passed over just because he doesn't have what they call *drive*, but he does good work for twenty-five years all the same and there's never a mention of that, oh, no, but just let him make one small mistake in the transfer accounts! Or invite a young lady to dinner and see a picture-show afterward, at a total outlay of a cool fifteen dollars, and you'd think she'd be grateful, or at least have the graciousness not to invent false excuses not to go out again. But girls were like that, ungrateful and vindictive too, like landladies and bus drivers, and bosses who let you work your heart out for peanuts, and the rest of the men in the office too, who had their beer parties and poker games and softball in the summer without remembering to invite their friend who worked side by side with them all year round. *They* should sit all alone in a boardinghouse room every night of their lives, and spend their vacations alone at Asbury Park, and watch TV on Christmas Eve and New Year's too, and on top of that *never be able to get to sleep!*

The thing was, if he could only doze off once, he slept soundly enough. But every night it was the same story. Awake till twelve, one, two, three, four or five o'clock, or sometimes till dawn, and then rising at seven without any sleep at all.

For years he had drunk hot milk and taken hot baths before going to bed. These were his substitutes for the booze and dope his long-ago upbringing forbade him. He also read wearying books about the seismic formation of the Urals, or the succession of Gothic kings. He had read Proust, Tolstoy and Joyce from cover to cover. He had read Darwin, Marx, and was working on Freud. When reading failed, he turned off the light and relaxed. He flexed and relaxed each and every muscle separately. He tried self-hypnosis: *I, will, sleep!* He rolled imaginary bowling balls slowly from left to right behind closed lids. He imagined himself rocked in the cradle of the deep, or drifting fleecily in the lazy summer sky. Once he had even tried counting sheep. Nothing worked. Nothing would ever work. It was his doom.

Mr. Kleiber wrote S_____ in the air with his nose.

According to the article in the health magazine, there were complex knots of muscles at the back of the neck which became taut and stiff. Writing in the air with the tip of the nose was supposed to relax them. This was much too simple to make sense. Mr. Kleiber believed he suffered from a type of comprehensive insomnia. It was a chronic condition that anything could trigger, and did. Nose writing wouldn't do any more good than his ten-dollar set of Doz-Awai records had. But at least it passed the time.

*Roses Are Red*, Mr. Kleiber wrote in the air with his nose. *Violets Are Blue. Howard Davis Stinks. And So Do You. And Charley Boone Too*, he amended.

Then it happened.

He did not notice right away. Behind closed lids he visualized as he wrote. His knowledge of four-letter words was not extensive, but he wrote all he knew. Plus some words from Freud. *Onanism. Clitoris.* He also played a game of tic-tac-toe. He drew a swastika, a star of David, and a Maltese cross. Like a man doodling on a pad, he let one line lead to another. He tried a few public lavatory designs. He addressed a few choice words to Rubberflex, Inc., Accounting Department, Bugleburgh Branch, Eastern Penna. Division: *Kiss My A____*. When invention failed, he drew circles, spirals, dots, squares and crisscross lines. All the while the light grew brighter. Finally, through closed lids, he saw.

He opened his eyes. That took perhaps three tenths of a second. One full second after that he was already sliding out from under, falling off the bed, headfirst and face up. The thing he had slid out from under was a tight-woven patch of vivid frost-blue light. Opening his eyes he had seen it hovering close over his face. Another inch and it would have fit like a mask.

He hit the floor with a painful thump on the back of his head and shoulders. For some occasions there are no words. Neither was there any further physical or mental reaction for several more seconds. Until he noticed that his feet were still in bed. He whipped them away.

Next came a wordless, animal-like reaction: *It wasn't chasing him.* Paralysis gave place to watchfulness. But eyes would not interpret what they saw. Brain would not name it. They needed a reference, something known.

Then they had it.

Toward the edge of the patch, where the light was not so densely woven, was a word, written in his own hand: *BALLS*.

Sticking out to the right were other fragments. *Are Blue*, they said, and just beneath them: *Boone Too*. Here and there were little *X*'s and *O*'s.

He was lying on the floor beside the bed looking sidewise and up as though at skywriting. That wasn't far enough away. On elbows and heels he scampered backward to the farthest corner of the room. Then he sat up. Then he stood up slowly.

The patch of light hovered motionless over his pillow, where his head had lain. From this angle the word read:

## BALLS

After a while he could think about it. There wasn't any other explanation, so he developed the one he had. The words were in his own recognizable writing because he had written them. Nothing so strange about that. Who else's? Where the words were illegible was where he had scribbled over and over in the same space. What else was there to explain?

Mr. Kleiber turned on all the lights in the room. It was still there. As bright as ever, except somewhat more violet than frost-blue. He approached a little way by sliding the same foot forward once or twice. Then he leaned toward it and stretched out the palm of his hand, but felt no heat, and approached a little closer. When he was still a yard or two from the bed he bent down and blew: *poof!* Nothing happened. He put his fists on his hips. Then he went and got his bathrobe and slippers.

Then he moved his chair to the far side of the room and sat down and stared.

It was just a little patch of luminous writing. It was just a little two-dimensional smear of light made of labyrinthine lines of violet writing. Like a page of doodles in luminous ink on bumpy paper, and then the paper was taken away.

"How did that happen, for heaven's sake?" he said aloud. The first words of his new life.

*The meek shall inherit the earth,* Mr. Kleiber wrote in the air with his nose sometime later.

It was the only answer he could think of. Why else should this great gift be bestowed upon him among all men on earth? Upon him who had written all those things in the air, he suddenly remembered, blushing violently.

By now the room was filled with intense violet sources of light in the form of every graphic device known to man, or at least to Mr. Kleiber. Everything from punctuation marks, through pictograms, to whole verses of poems. Since discovering that simple concentration somehow actuated the mechanism, he had tested his power every whichway, and found no limit. Whatever he chose he could write with his nose.

But dawn was coming.

At seven-fifteen his landlady rattled the knob.

"You're gonna miss your bus," she bellowed through the door.

"Leave me alone. I'm sick," he said, and wrote in the air: *Fat slob.*

"You want an ice bag for your head?"

*And charge a quarter for it.* $ $ $

"No," he said.

"What're you doing in there?"

"Go away. Leave that knob alone."

After a while her carpet-slippered feet went down the hall and down the stairs to her basement kitchen. It was a terrible dungeon full of old bones and swamps and things, where the boardinghouse meals came from.

*Swill for pigs,* he wrote.

So what if I'm late for work? he thought. Laboriously he drew a hangman's noose in the air. I ought to take some art lessons or something, he thought. Moving his nose very slowly made a slender brilliant line. Moving his nose faster made a broader stroke. He could do bookkeeping and billboards both. Tiny words like elite type or big headlines like a newspaper. The blue light flowed from his nose like ink from a fountain pen. Closing and opening his eyes started and stopped it.

Blinking, he wrote meaningless Morse in a half-circle from right to left. He started a spiral with a tiny line, spinning it larger and larger till his neck creaked. He drew stick figures and Valentine hearts and elaborate designs. By now there was hardly any space left to write in, except up toward the ceiling and down by the floor.

Before he left he learned one other thing. The lights—the words and pictures—could not be erased. Neither did they show any signs of fading. They had no substance, and could not be touched. They weren't hot or cold, and pouring water over them or flapping a towel at them had no effect at all.

"Maybe that's not so good," he murmured.

Lucky they weren't dangerous. The best he could do was scribble over some of the worst words, then lock the door and pocket the key.

"Stay out of my room," he told the landlady on his way out. "Never mind cleaning in there today."

"I thought you were sick."

"Just stay out of my room, or you'll catch it."

She thought he meant if she went into his room she'd be infected. On the other hand, she didn't believe he was sick at all. She knew bachelors. Just because she hadn't caught him at it yet didn't mean he hadn't been up there all night with a whiskey bottle. Or pornographic pictures, or dirty books. Or whatever bachelors did. She wasn't born yesterday. As soon as Mr. Kleiber was gone, she took her own key and climbed the stairs to his room.


"Are you Mr. Keifer?"

"No," said Mr. Kleiber and let it go at that. If Charley Boone couldn't remember his name after all these years, well, never mind, that's all. He hadn't time, there was too much on his mind. He had come into work at 10:15, an hour and a quarter late, and already he was wishing it was five o'clock so he could go home and practice his new knack. Then suddenly he was saying: "What? What?"

Charley Boone said: "You'd think I had the only phone

in this department. What do they ask *me* for? I never heard of no Keifer up here. Do you know anybody named Keifer that set his room on fire?"

"That's ridiculous."

"Well, something about his room is full of fire, and the owner's having a fit, and he's supposed to work here, and the cops are downstairs looking for him. Personnel must of got the name wrong. Lemme use your phone."

Mr. Kleiber stood up in a dreadful cold calm.

"I'm going to the bathroom," he said. "Goodby, Charley."

"So long, er—ah," Charley Boone said.

There was a stairs in the rear of the building. Mr. Kleiber sneaked down it wearing his green eyeshade. The funniest thing was, instead of feeling sneaky, he felt jubilant and giggly. Something told him he was finished forever with Rubberflex, Inc., Accounting Department, Bugleburgh Branch, Eastern Penna. Division. And good riddance.

Instead of leaving the building at the bottom of the fire stairs, he turned left and went through the shipping department, then out the main entrance, passing some state troopers on their way in.

On the grass plot just outside the entrance was a stone block with a bronze plate. On the plate was graven: Rubberflex, Inc. Extrusions and Pneumatics. Bonded Assemblies. Compounding and Fabrication. Specialty Products.

*And scumbags*, Mr. Kleiber wrote with his nose.

Upstairs, Howard Davis, the office manager, said to the phone: "Not Keifer. *Keebler*. And he didn't come in today. If he did, I didn't see him. If he does, I'll fix his feet. I *knew* there was something spooky about that son of a bitch. Drinking his lunch and raising ned with the steno pool. Besides, didn't we fire him back in '64?"

It was hot in the late morning, and the two troopers taking the air with the landlady on the back porch had removed their hats and loosened their ties. She had made them glasses of Kool-Aid.

Mr. Kleiber peered around the corner of the garage. Probably another one staked out in my room, he thought. Poking in my bureau drawers.

Nothing moved anywhere except a cat in the yard, and after a time the town fire whistle blew noon and a dog barked far away.

Dead little town, Mr. Kleiber thought. Some day it may be known as the birthplace of Thomas R. Kleiber.

He went into the garage. The landlady didn't drive, and none of the boarders owned a car, so the garage was full of junk and crates and sprung furniture. He heard mice in the clutter of hatboxes and old luggage. Just walking across the floor and sitting down on the ancient sofa stirred the air full of dust that looked golden in the sunbeam shining through a tiny window. There was nothing to do but wait for the cops to leave. He had to get to his room.

*Nertz*, he wrote in the air with his nose.

When the landlady passed by with the hedge clippers at four o'clock she looked in and saw him asleep on the sofa. After all night awake writing in the air with his nose, and the long morning of surprises and decisions, the hot dusty air and the buzz of the bees in the slates had put him to sleep like a baby.

The two state troopers had gone off in their car. The landlady stood uncertainly for a moment, and then tiptoed all the way across the yard and went into the kitchen, slamming the screen door. She cranked the phone and listened a minute, and said: "Get off the line, Charlotte, I've got an emergency."

"Mercy! Can I listen?"

"You'll never believe it. He's come *back!*"

Another voice said: "If you want Chief Heller, he's at his sister-in-law's this time of day."

"*Not* Sam Heller," the landlady said importantly. "This is a matter for the *authorities!*"

Behind her back Mr. Kleiber had crept up on the porch and was listening through the screen door.

"—Pennsylvania state troopers waiting all morning," the

landlady was saying, "but that's not the half of it! The officer told me personally this was a case for *Washington!*"

"Mercy sakes!"

"There's two Government agents from the F.D.I. on their way here right now by private *plane!*"

Mr. Kleiber had got by behind her back and was quietly climbing the stairs. Her incredulous voice reached him: "It must be something bigger than we *dreamed!*"

A sign was thumbtacked to the door of his room: *Keep Out.* CRIME SCENE. *Bugleburgh P.D.* He tried the door and it creaked softly open. At first he saw only his room filled up with webs and nets and loops of fire intertangled everywhere. Then with a small shock that took his breath away he saw the third policeman. He was snoring gently with his mouth open, propped in a corner of the room underneath the lights. The hot buzz of the afternoon had drugged him too.

Mr. Kleiber chuckled soundlessly. I forgot all about him. She did too, luckily. At the same moment, he was thinking: *To be able to sleep like that!* And then it occurred to him— he *had!* In the garage! Even the memory of that brief soft sleep was like a memory of love. The first sweet sleep of his new life. Things had changed so. Even now he was drowsy.

Tonight he would sleep. Somewhere. But far from here. Escape came first. He was amazed at his cool, calculating calm. Bankbook and checkbook were in the bureau drawer. He took them. How difficult it would be to arrange for withdrawal, or to cash a check, in some bank far, far away, he did not know. Meanwhile, there was money—his cash reserve. Ever since 1929. Not much of a fund, but steadily growing, and always a little something put by. And in a hiding place, incidentally, he was quite proud of.

The policeman never stirred. Mr. Kleiber eased open the closet door softly. He selected five neckties from the dozen or so draped over a hook. Stuffed inside each tie was a tight little wad. Each wad was made up of five one-hundred-dollar bills. Who would ever think to look there?

A hundred dollars for each and every one of twenty-five

years at Rubberflex, Inc., Accounting Department, Bugleburgh Branch, Eastern Penna. Division. The bank manager
used to kid him regularly once a year about drawing his
Christmas Club in one big bill. Now it had paid off.

Operating capital. This money would keep him going—
train fare, new clothes, board and lodging somewhere far
away. Just till he had figured out the trick of making money
with his nose. He couldn't imagine anyone having money
problems who could write fire in the air with his nose.
Though he had not had time to think about that yet. Escape
came first.

As though in answer to his thoughts, a train hooted on the
far side of town. And the giggle was back again, rising jubi-
lantly in his throat. He turned to go.

In the hall, he shut the door carefully and looked at the
thumbtacked sign. Then he took it down. Closing his eyes he
wrote with his nose as close as he could to the wood of the
door:

> *DON'T LOOK FOR THE BODY*
> *MEN FROM MARS*
> *ATE IT*

Mr. Kleiber slept. He dreamed.

The rickety-rack of the wheels had no need to lull him. The
passing rush of green, peaceful countryside had no need to
soothe his senses. He had gone out like a light bulb still in the
station, and all the way to Washington he slept the sleep of
the blessed.

In the dream an august personage was approaching from a
long way off, and it turned out to be the President. All the
way from Pittsburgh Home Office to take personal charge.
In the dream, at least, he was an incredibly ancient mummy
swallowed up in an enormous fur coat and supported under
the arms by Burns Special Agents and surrounded by Executive Aides.

"*Mene, mene, tekel upharsin,*" he wheezed when he saw the awful words.

"We've tried everything, Your Excellency. It can't be blown away with fans. We tried that. We tried spraying it with paint. Paint goes right through it. We tried hauling it away with a winch. But there's no place to get a hold."

"We burned it with acetylene torches, we froze it with liquid oxygen."

"We sprinkled it with ionized potassium."

"We ran 10,000 volts through it and we fire-extinguished it and we flame-throwered it and tried hydrochloric acid and Red Devil and sledge hammers and supersonic whistles. We even had plant security try to shoot it down. No go."

"*Blockheads!*" The old man flapped bodiless as an empty coat between the two Burns agents, cackling crazily like Cheyne-Stokes breathing. "*Nincompoops!*"

"Father Loughlin even sprinkled it with holy water."

"What else could we have done?"

"*Balderdash!* Ever try jacking that stone up and moving it a few inches forwards? Fiddle faddle. Fuss and feathers. 'S trooth, ain't it? As if you didn't know! Gum boots and rubber bands ain't what makes stocks split six ways from Sunday. *As if you didn't know!* Remember our slogan—'Why is a Rubberflex like a sneeze? *Gesundheit!*'"

And cackling hee, hee, hee, he lifted his feet from the ground and they bore him away by the armpits to his Pullman car. At least in the dream.

But the scene was already changing.

It wasn't the grass plot any more and they weren't executives any more, but the League of Decency wanting to burn the house down. Although first the landlady had to agree, and the police and the fire department and the state troopers and the Government and the F.D.I. And besides, destroying the house was no guarantee that the whole lot of dirty words wouldn't be left intact and floating in midair anyway.

On hand also were reporters to photograph everything and write up the landlady's story and Mr. Kleiber's disappearance and all the surprising events of the day. They took pictures of the house and the room, and of the ominous sign on the door, and telephoned to their papers that a U.S. citizen had been eaten by Martians.

While members of the Society for Psychic Research knocked heads with authorities on physics, chemistry, electronics and atomics—all crawling along the floor beneath the lights in Mr. Kleiber's small room—the two F.D.I. agents said that a nationwide manhunt was being organized, and the Bugleburgh High School science teacher said that cold light without source, fuel or combustion was impossible. The police had thrown a cordon around the house, and cultists who had come to marvel were turned away and went home to publish extraordinary issues of small mimeographed magazines. Meanwhile, U.S.A.F. Major-General Malcolm Rudge was issuing a statement to the effect that the lights were the exclusive property of the Air Force. "If it happens in the air, it's our business," he said. "We stamped out those lousy dirigibles, and we squashed the flying-saucer myth, and if these Martians are up to no good, we'll murdalize them too."

Simultaneously, in the occult way of dreams, the results of everybody's talking to the papers began to be visible in the form of big, black headlines.

MAD SKYWRITER STILL AT LARGE, they said.

## INTERNATIONAL GROUP VIEWS LIGHTS
### *SCIENTISTS BAFFLED*
## WILL MISS HIM, LANDLADY SAYS
### *Victim Of Marsmen Gone But Not Forgotten*
## RELIGIOUS FANATIC BURNS GHOST HOUSE
### *AIR FORCE JOINS MANHUNT*
## NUTS

This last word was either approaching or growing larger and larger, till it became darkness everywhere as they dove underground, and then the lights in the car came on, and the conductor came down the aisle tapping each seat in turn and saying: "Stay-*shun*. *Union* Station," and Mr. Kleiber woke up.

He had walked and walked, and now it was night.

"Hello, handsome. Looking for a good time?"

"No, I'm looking for a flophouse."

"What do you want a flophouse for. Don't you have any money?"

"I'm so sleepy I could die."

"Why don't you go to a hotel?"

"It has to be a hideout," Mr. Kleiber said.

In his somnambulant state he kept right on walking, and she fell in step with him and took his arm. "You just come along with Corinne. We'll find you a nice place to sleep."

"I used to know a girl named Corinne," Mr. Kleiber said.

"My real name is Letitia."

"That's a pretty name too."

"You *are* sleepy," she said.

They turned off that street and down another, and she appeared to be guiding him. Drowsily he noticed that she was a tiny, thin blonde woman, oddly doll-like in her fluffy dress and pink make-up. She had wide-open happy blue eyes that somehow did not make sense.

"Just in from the sticks?" she said.

"Yes."

"Kicking over the old traces?"

"Yes."

"Out for a big night on the town?"

"No," he said. They passed beneath a street lamp and she stared curiously at him with baby-blue nonsensical eyes.

"You really *do* need sleep."

"I haven't slept for twenty-five years," he said. "I've only just started to catch up."

She brought him to a halt and stood looking at him. Then turned and led him in another direction, and he went docilely. As they walked, she began saying rapidly and happily in another voice, as though dropping a guise: "I was going to take you to a place where you're supposed to buy a lot of high-priced drinks and see a dirty floor show and get all hot and bothered, but if you really want to sleep, I'll take you to where I live. It's a roominghouse, actually, but Mrs. Ryan lets me bring men there for quick turns. She wouldn't do it for just anybody, but she says how else am I ever going to get ahead?"

"Is that what you do?" Mr. Kleiber asked nonplussed.

"Well, I'm sort of a whore, but I don't do it all the time. As a matter of fact, I haven't done it at all yet, because most of the time I sew. And Mrs. Ryan says, How do I ever expect to amount to anything if I sit on my behind and *sew* all the time, instead of patience and practice and stick-to-it-iveness? Isn't that crazy? As if she were coaching me to be a great violinist or a dedicated scientist, or something. She has twisted values."

"You certainly talk a lot," Mr. Kleiber said.

"Would you believe it? I used to be quiet as a mouse and never liked to sew at all. And I had a good job in a government office, but that was before they locked me up three days for observation. Don't you *dare* look at me funny! It wasn't for anything violent. The doctors just wanted to ask me some questions and put me in a ward and watch me undress and get in bed and relate with the other loonies up there. Then they had to let me go because there wasn't anything they could do for me, and the Doctor said the same thing: You're all right, you just *talk* too much."

"Why are you telling me this?"

"Why not?" she said candidly. "Besides, it makes the walk go faster. See? Here we are at my house already."

It was a brick house set back from the street a yard or two behind an iron fence. Mrs. Ryan was a motherly old body except for her scarlet fingernails. "You can't bring him in here," she said. "He's drunk."

"He just looks that way because he's so-o-o sleepy," Letitia said. "And he just came in from the sticks without any coat or baggage, and he needs a hideout because he's on the lam. Can't he sleep in Mr. Alfred's room while he's in jail?"

"Karen's in there with an occulist from New York," Mrs. Ryan said. "And anyway, what kind of customer is that?"

Letitia blushed. "He's not a customer, he's my friend."

"Oh, you're so crazy, I give it up," Mrs. Ryan said.

Then they went to Letitia's room.

"She really loves me. I've lived here for years. But now she worries, how can I pay my rent? I really don't know," Letitia said.

It was the oddest room he had ever seen. First it looked like an explosion in a drygoods store, with swatches of multi-colored material everywhere, covering the furniture and nearly hiding the walls. Then he saw that practically every square inch of every bit of cloth had been painstakingly stitched with floral designs, scenes, mottoes or fancy borders. There were samplers and things like tapestries hanging all over the walls, and slipcovers and antimacassars and decorative scarves on the chairs, and overlapping curtains and drapes on the windows, and hundreds of little cushions everywhere. And everything trimmed, tricked-out, decked and bedecked with multitudes of tiny designs maniacally sewn by hand.

"This is my stuff," she said brightly. "I'll show it all to you after you've had some sleep."

He particularly noticed the several dozen throw pillows on the bed. They were mostly some kind of imitation satin, each one having a girl's name on it in a smother of sunflowers.

"Those are names I use as a whore," she said. "I like any name except Letitia. And Corinne not so much."

On his way to the bed he also noticed the whole wall of samplers behind it. Or something like samplers. Some were framed, and some were not, and some had scenes while others had mottoes. The scenes were mostly conventional subjects like birds on a branch, fruit in bowls, and little log cabins, but one looked like the Harp of the Winds, and two others looked like abstract paintings. The various mottoes were peculiar too, like, *Hoist With His Own Petar*, or, *Bulls With Short Horns Stand Close, The Next Man May Be Barefoot*, or, *No Birdy Aviar Soar Anywing To Eagle It.*

It was just too much to try and puzzle out.

"Is this where I sleep?"

"That's right." She was clearing the bed of throw pillows and pincushions and thimbles and spools of thread and odds and ends of cloth.

"Where will *you?*"

"Don't you worry, if I get tired I'll lie down a bit, right here beside you, but I won't bother you, unless you want me to. If you do, just let me know, but don't feel you have to, I don't mind. I'll just sew a little, it calms me down."

"I never did anything like that," Mr. Kleiber said, embarrassed. "Woman is an unknown quantity to me."

"Don't give me that!" she said. "Men are all alike."

"I guess you must find it hard to believe," he murmured, suddenly overcome by delicious drowsiness.

"I don't see why," she said. "Men are an unknown quantity to me, too, if you must know. Go on and take your nap."

"*Nap*, I said. I didn't mean *die*," she was saying in her other, or streetwalker's, voice, when he woke. "You know what time it is? Nine P.M. You slept the clock around, it's night again."

"Hello, Letitia," he said.

"It's Tanya."

"Hello, Tanya. Have you been here all the time?"

"Except when I went out to eat, and got to talking with a friend of mine in Contadino's, the pizza parlor. Not a real friend, because he's a crook, but he's an artist, and we have lots of things in common, intellectual things, such as Existentialism, and Samuel Beckett, and what's the good of it all. Don't you *dare* look at me funny! I wasn't always cracked. Mrs. Ryan says I could have been a college professor at Vassar or someplace, if I didn't break down. Did *you* ever read the complete works of Freud?"

"Well, as a matter of fact—"

"I've read the whole *Golden Bough*, too," she said. "And not that one-volume edition, either. Which reminds by, by thought association, you know—bough, apples, fruit, cherry trees, petals—listen to this. *The apparition of these faces in the crowd; petals on a wet, black bough.* Do you know what that is? It's a poem by Ezra Pound, about people in the Metro, that's a subway, and that's what I'm going to do next, on black velvet with lavender thread, or maybe cherry-blossom pink. Then there's another poem of his, '*Concava Vallis*'—"

"Letitia, can I interrupt you a moment?"

"It's Tanya."

"Tanya. You're a funny girl."

"That's what everybody says. But I don't see why. I had a good education, and I held a responsible job, and was always interested in the arts, and reading too. That hasn't changed, just because I like sewing better now. It calms me more. And I'm not a girl, I'm thirty-nine. Do you want to see my stuff?"

"What stuff?"

"My *sewing!* That I've done all in just one year since I was drawing unemployment and sick benefits, including those two bedsheets I haven't finished yet. Just look at those buttercups, how small! Do you have any idea how long it takes to cover a whole bedsheet with buttercups smaller than the tip of your pinkie finger?"

"Tanya. Can I tell you something?"

"Sure, friend."

"I don't how to begin."

"Just lay the words on Mama, baby."

"You've been so nice to me already. I haven't any right."

"Didn't anybody ever do you a favor?"

"No," he said. "You've been so kind to me, a stranger."

"Why don't you get on with it?"

"It's so hard to explain. I mean, I don't know whether it's a good thing or bad. It's just something I don't know how to handle. It's completely outside my experience. This is practically a whole new life for me, and I haven't the first idea what to *do!*"

"You talk as much as me," she said.

"Well, the fact is, I can write in the air with my nose."

"That's a problem?"

"You don't understand. I can write flaming words in the air with my nose. I mean *really.* You can *see* them."

"What do you want to do *that* for?"

"Darn it, I don't want to or *not* want to. That's not the point. I just *can.*"

"Well, you don't have to if you don't want to, do you?"

"That's not the *point.* It's what to *do* with it. My *gift!*"

"I know a fellow who can pick the ace of hearts out of any deck of cards you hand him, without looking," she said.

"Well, then. He could make money out of that, couldn't he?"

"He sure does."

"Well, then. Why shouldn't a man who can write fire in the air with his nose make something out of it? It's a talent, isn't it? How many people can write in the air with their nose?

"How many people can pick the ace of hearts out of a new deck of Bicycles?"

"You just don't understand," he said lonesomely. There was a silence. She watched him with blue, happy, something-missing eyes in which Letitia, Tanya et al. were mixed together.

After a while he said: "Come here a minute. Come closer. Bend down."

"If you're going to kiss me, give me a minute to get in the mood."

"No," he said flustered. "I'm old enough to be your father."

"You're a young colt of forty-four, and hot as a pistol, yippee-yay," she said. "I looked in your wallet while you were asleep."

"Stop that," he said. "I'm trying to *show* you." He closed his eyes and drew a little circle around her nose.

When he opened them again she was already on the opposite side of the room.

"Goddam it! You almost burned me!"

"No, it isn't hot at all. Or cold. Or anything else. In fact, in many ways, it isn't even there." He passed his hand through the light hanging like a ghostly doughnut in the air. "Except you can see it," he added.

She came closer, peering at it and at him. Then she sat down on the edge of the bed. "How did you do that?"

"It just happened. That's what I'm trying to tell you. The point is, what do I do now?"

"Do a buttercup."

"That's not what I mean. This is serious. I'm in trouble."

"I don't see why. It's just like I make forget-me-nots and borders and things, and sew mottoes. Only you do it with your nose."

"I wish it was that simple."

"After all, it's not as though you were doing something *bad*."

"No, but you know how it is nowadays. There were two Government men after me before I ever left home. I suppose they want to lock me up someplace to study me, or make me work for them somehow. And if I object, all they have to do is draft me, at my age. You don't really think they'd let a man who can write fire in the air with his nose walk around loose, do you? Not in this day and age! If they couldn't use me, they'd have to brainwash me or something, to fix it so I couldn't do it any more. They might even cut off the end of my nose!"

"You don't have much spirit."

"I never had," he said. "Blessed are the poor in spirit, so maybe this is a blessing, and I'm supposed to inherit the earth. Meanwhile, my landlady is probably suing me for what I did to her house, and the company could probably prosecute me for writing dirty words on their sign, and the papers are full of nonsense about Martians and ghosts, and there's a big manhunt. That's why I need a hideout. I have to have time to figure things out. It can't be just a meaningless dead end. I'm the only man in the world who can write fire in the air with his nose. Isn't that *anything?*"

"So far, it's a pain in the ass," Tanya said.

They sat and thought and thought.

"It's not so much what you got, as how you use it," Letitia said. "That's what Mrs. Ryan always tells me."

"That's the whole problem," Mr. Kleiber said. "How *do* I?"

She was trying to snip the ghostly doughnut with her sewing scissors. "How do you get rid of these things once you've made them?"

"No way I know of. They're everlasting."

"Well, if you stay here, don't make any more of them. I can't have the whole place cluttered up with willow-wisps."

"You aren't helping much."

"It's completely outside *my* experience too."

"I'll tell you what I've thought of up to now. First I thought maybe I could go into the neon sign business. Permanent and fail-proof and no maintenance. But the trouble is, you'd never be able to get rid of it. Maybe a thousand years from now there'd still be a sign hanging in somebody's living room. Joe's Bar and Grill."

"I wouldn't mind that," she said.

"The same goes for billboards and skywriting and so forth. Or I thought I might make signs for people who write *post no bills* or *Yankee, go home* and things like that on walls. But it would be the same problem."

"Maybe you could make spooky blue light in funhouses."

"I thought of that too. Cheap indirect lighting you never have to buy bulbs for. But you could only get it in blue, and at that I'd have to cover the whole ceiling to make it really bright enough."

"How about what you did where you worked? Couldn't you tell people if they didn't give you lots of money you'd write dirty words on their signs and show windows?"

"That wouldn't be honest," he said.

"If you were only a great modern poet, you could write modern poems in the air," she said. "Can you imagine something like the *Saison en enfer* in fiery letters over a pit of smoking coals?"

"I can only write that roses-are-red stuff."

"Or if you could *draw*," she said. "It would be beautiful on black marble."

"But I can't," he said.

They were silent again.

"Well," she said. "I don't know what to tell you."

"I can't think of anything."

"Neither can I."

"It seems a shame. A man who can write in the air with his nose. All for nothing," she said.

"Yes."

"If only we had some imagination," she said.

"Yes."

At midnight they went out to Contadino's and ate pizza pies in a corner booth like a padded cell, and she said: "Can't we talk about something else for a while? Cudgeling my brains makes me dizzy."

"It's hard for me to think about anything else."

"What's your first name? Thomas? I'll call you Tom. It doesn't fit. Thomas, how much money is *in* that wallet, anyway?"

"A little less than twenty-five hundred dollars."

"Zowie!"

"It just seems like a lot. But I haven't got a job. I can't go home. I don't dare show my face at a bank. How long do you think twenty-five hundred dollars will last? I've already spent some of it, for the train. And these awful pies."

"We should have got the peppers kind."

"Listen," he said.

"What?"

"I've got to change my name and get a job and never write in the air with my nose again," he said.

"All right."

"You see? Maybe I could grow a mustache and find a small apartment and live like any normal person. I could get a job easy enough."

"Sure."

"I'm a full-time accountant with twenty-five years experience."

"I believe you."

"Wait a minute. If I did that— Listen to me, now. This is important. If I did that, and everything blew over, and everything got settled down—"

"Yes."

"Would you marry me?"

"And then where'd I be every time you got sore at me?" He stared at her. "What?"

"Like, walk into the kitchen and bump into *Nuts to you.*"

"I wouldn't—"

"Ha! Came right back at you, didn't I?"

"I'm serious."

"You're *cracked!*"

She sat back staring at him with her hands flat on the table.

"I mean it," he said. "Why not? We're two lonely people. Nobody cares. We could get along. Why shouldn't we? This is making me very nervous."

"Making *you* nervous!"

"Just listen a minute. I'm a perfectly normal person except for my nose. I'm a hard worker and honest. You can see I'm sober and steady. We'd get along fine. You could sew all you want, and I'd take you out every payday."

"You're out of your mind!"

"Of course, it wouldn't be like the movies. Or young people. Or maybe it would. I mean, I don't know *what* I mean. I just thought of it. It just came out. Why shouldn't we, really?"

"You just thought of it," she said.

"Yes."

"It just came out," she said.

"Yes. Why shouldn't we?"

"Because we can't," she said.

"That's no reason."

Suddenly she was all excited. "You want a reason? You want a reason? Because we *can't*, that's why! Isn't that reason enough? Don't you think I *want* to? Don't you think I *would?* It's cold and lousy out here alone—*but it takes more than a mental breakdown and a freak nose!*"

Mr. Kleiber said: "All right. Don't. I'm sorry."

"Maybe if you'd *thought* about it at all before it just came out, you'd see *I* don't care about your nose—but you might for *my* sake! Just the way *you* might not care if I'm crazy, but I do for *yours!*"

"I see," he said.

Then just as suddenly she was calm again.

"No—you don't. The truth is, I told you a lie. Sometimes it does get violent."

"Oh."

"I wouldn't want to marry a man and then slit his gizzard."

"No."

"So you see how it is."

"Yes."

"I wish it was different."

"So do I."

"But it isn't."

"No," he said.

"Don't think I don't appreciate it. And please stick around my place as long as you want," she said.

"Thank you," he said.

Then they paid and went out. It was late and dark and her heels echoed in the street.

"What's the matter now?" she asked.

"I didn't say anything. It's those awful pies."

She stopped him under a street lamp. "Listen. There's just one other thing. If I'm ever cured—if I'm sure of it—and I can find you—will you ask me again?"

He took her hands in his. "Letitia," he said, "if I can get rid of this nose, and live like a normal person again, I'll come to find you and ask you to marry me. Will you?"

"Sure," she said. "Do you think you can?"

"I'll try," he said. And wrote in the air:

The next day Mr. Kleiber consulted a sorcerer. But first he had to go through Letitia's friend Tony.

She had described him as an artist and a cook, but as far as Mr. Kleiber could see, he was only a snippy and sarcastic young man who wore peculiar clothing and hung around barrooms.

He talked a lot too. "What's this about you being haunted? Tish probably got it all wrong," he said, and then went right on: "She's a grand girl, but awfully *fuz*-zee. Not quite right in the head, *tu sais*. Suddenly quit her whole life cold and began stitching fiddle-dee-dees on her bedsheets. Sometimes she lets on it was a blow to the head, and sometimes drugs, but between you and me, it's nothing but good old-fashioned dementia praecox. Peewits in the cupola. At least I *think* she was trying to tell me you have ghosts."

"She thought you might know someone who could help."

"I probably do. This town is full of frauds—mediums, wizards, alchemists, warlocks, conjurers, seers—especially seers. It's like a *gypsy* camp with all the seers! What kind of help do you want?"

"I can't really explain it very well. It's my nose," Mr. Kleiber said.

Tony tittered. "What *you* need is a plastic *sur*-geon."

"I never thought of that," Mr. Kleiber said seriously. "Maybe that's the answer. Only as a last resort, though."

"Well, if you'd rather not *tell* me."

"I *am* telling you. It's about my nose."

"Well, what *about* it? Does it drip in the night? Take astral voyages and leave you breathless? I'm *wait*-ing."

"As a matter of fact," Mr. Kleiber said. "It makes blue fire."

Tony suddenly sat bolt upright and widened his eyes and spread one hand across his chest. He had a habit of exaggerated reactions.

"Hombre!" he said. "Don't you read the papers?"

"Why?"

"The *last* guy who saw blue fire is dead as a *door*-nail! It's horrible! It's the latest *thing!* Freddie and I were going out to look for them last weekend, but the *car* broke down. *Everybody's* going to Pennsy now. It's the greatest thing since flying *saucers!*"

"What is?"

"*Mars*-men! Where *have* you been? They're burning down houses and leaving strange writing in the sky and killing people and spreading this absolute *reign* of terror!"

"Nonsense! Who have they killed?"

"It started with some harmless old clod of a clerk in a condom factory. *He* saw blue fire first too—and as a matter of fact, I'm not sure it's safe to be anywhere *near* you. One morning he didn't show up for work. And they found his room full of fire, and later on his wife saw him lying *dead* in the garage, and then all of a sudden his corpse vanished in a flash of blue light reading: *NERTZ!*"

"Oh, for heaven's sake!" Mr. Kleiber said.

"Hombre, this is it, this is for *real!*" Tony said. "Finally, after twenty centuries of cold, calculating observation, Mars has invaded Earth. Pennsylvania is in this fantastic *up*-roar. The locals are forming posses and vigilantes and shooting at everything in *sight*. That's where most of the casualties come from."

"In fact," Mr. Kleiber said, "these Martians haven't hurt anybody at all."

"Except that first guy. He was *eaten*," Tony said. "Being vastly superior to mere Earthmen, the Martians have no more scruples about eating us than we would in eating a fried *shrimp!*"

"It says all this in the papers?"

"Well, you know how the au-*thor*-ities are," Tony said. "They always hush things up. The police say it was this Knoedler fellow who did it, and there's a big dragnet out for him now. But the public isn't going to swallow *that!* What does some stupid *clerk* know about extraterrestrial writing and mystic flames?"

"I never heard such nonsense."

"Have it your own way, buster," Tony said huffily. "But if I were in your shoes, I'd ask for Protective Custody. The *last* guy who saw blue fire ended up hors d'oeuvres for a bunch of *Mars*-men. Don't kid yourself! You're *next!* Your number's *up!*"

"It's a lot of hysterical nonsense and irresponsible sensational journalism," Mr. Kleiber said.

"Well, you can't blame people for believing what they read in the papers," Tony said. "Else what's a free press for?"

"And anyway, I didn't say blue fire. I said it makes blue *flies.*"

"What does?"

"My nose."

"Hombre, why didn't you *say* so, instead of letting me get all excited? Anyway, if your nose makes blue flies, what you need is a *head*-shrinker, not a spiritualist."

"No, these are real flies, not imaginary," Mr. Kleiber said with sudden inventiveness. "As a matter of fact, my psychiatrist already said it was beyond his ken."

"Let's see you create a fly," Tony said dubiously.

"I can't do it just like that. Conditions have to be right. If you come around to Letitia's place tonight, I'll make one for you. In the meantime, how about this friend of yours?"

"I know just the guy," Tony said.

Amenhotep Ra IV had a small room full of reed screens on the top floor of an old building brown with varnish and musty with decrepit linoleum. All the other rooms seemed to be offices of doctors and fortune tellers who lived on the premises with their families. On the way up, Tony and Mr. Kleiber kept stumbling over dark-skinned people sitting almost invisibly on the gloomy stairs. By contrast, Amenhotep looked almost clean-cut. Like a young, tired, high-school principal dressed up in khaki pants and tee-shirt to lend a helping hand backstage at the school play.

Tony barely stuck his head in the door, at the same time urging Mr. Kleiber forward. "Hello, Hots, you old fraud," he said. "Look, Hots, I can't stay. I'm in this terrible *rush*. I have to find Freddie. We're going out to Pennsylvania to hunt for *Mars*-men!"

"Hello, Tony," Amenhotep said. "Did you bring the dough you owe me?"

"No, but I brought you a *pigeon*," Tony said, winking at Mr. Kleiber.

"What's this about Marsmen?"

"Doesn't *anybody* read the papers? It's *fab*-ulous! They've laid waste to Pittsburgh and they're closing in on Phila-*del*-phia!"

"More power to 'em," Amenhotep said. "Dirtiest city in the civilized world."

"You ought to know," Tony said. "Look, Hots, I want you to meet a friend of mine. What's your name, friend?"

"Keifer," said Mr. Kleiber.

"Keifer, this is Amenhotep Ra the Fourth. Son of the moon and birdbrain Thoth and things like that. I really can't wait another *min*-ute!"

Then he vanished.

"Hail!" said Amenhotep.

"Hail," said Mr. Kleiber.

"Hail in the name of Ra, god of the sun, and Ikhnaton his prophet, first pharaoh of Egypt, hail!"

"Hail," Mr. Kleiber said again.

"Hail in the name of the twelve pyramids and the tablets

of Abu Simbel, and Isis, queen of prophecy and the stars, and Thoth, lord of necromancy and scripture, hail!"

Mr. Kleiber didn't say anything.

"Come on in," Amenhotep said. He folded away one of the reed screens disclosing a small alcove, its walls painted with cave buffalo, burial hieroglyphs, and walleyed figures in breechclouts.

There was a desk, and two chairs. "Sit down," Amenhotep said. "The charge is five dollars for the first consultation."

He took a filmy garment from a hook and put it on over his tee-shirt and khakis, and set a horned helmet on his head. Then he removed the latter again and accepted Mr. Kleiber's five dollars and sat down himself.

"First and foremost, you must have absolute confidence," he said, taking the skull of a small mammal, perhaps a mole, from one drawer, and a green brass dagger from another, and placing them on the blotter.

"Confidence in what?"

"Confidence that Amenhotep Ra can solve all your spiritualistic problems."

"How can you, when you don't know what the problem is?"

"I already know what the problem is. And I can solve it. But I want you to tell me in your own words. This will give me the key to the solution. The solution to all your problems lies within yourself—but only Amenhotep Ra can fish it out."

"I'll have to have your word you won't tell anybody."

"Amenhotep Ra imparts not the astral secrets."

"Not even to Tony."

"Especially not to him."

"Well, the fact of the matter is—my name is Kleiber."

"So?"

"I guess that wouldn't mean anything to you, unless you've been reading all this stuff in the papers about Martians and things."

Amenhotep lifted both his hands. "Hold. I did read something about it," he said. "Mankind has fallen into sorry error once more. The blue flame is a manifestation of the workings of a minor deity, Phumi-Phlogiston, who has come to earth once again, as he does at the end of every thousandth zodiacal cycle, to proclaim his mystic creed. I happen to have been in touch with his earthly representatives. In the year two thousand forty-one B.C., in the moon of the blind musk ox—"

"No, that's not it at all," Mr. Kleiber said. "It's me. All of it. If you'll listen a minute, I'll explain."

And he told Amenhotep Ra IV in complete detail everything which had happened since that first night.

When he finished, he sat back, and Amenhotep sat back, and the two gazed at each other.

Then Amenhotep got to his feet behind the desk and hiked up the filmy garment and reached into his back pocket. He took out a small patent-leather badge folder and laid it open on the blotter between his two talismans.

"You're under arrest in the name of the F.D.I.," he said.

"Ambush!" said Mr. Kleiber.

"Not really. We infiltrate these places as a matter of routine. Lots of our agents are spiritualists and such. It's a good way to keep close check on the oddball elements of the population. I've been here a couple of years. You're on my copy of the wanted list, of course, but I never *dreamed*—"

"Why are you trembling like that?"

"You aren't going to resist arrest, are you? You see, I never had unarmed combat training. We're a young agency, trying to send men into the field as quickly as possible. I'm a law student, and I had orientation and briefing in computer communications, but I don't know what I'd *do* if you offered violence."

"Well, I've got to escape."

"I wish you wouldn't. We're supposed to be narco-trained to respond with karate when attacked, but we have to wait our turn. Why won't you be arrested?"

"Because I don't want to be drafted or brainwashed or locked up and studied like a guinea pig," Mr. Kleiber said.

"They won't do that. It's just a mix-up. All that happened is the Machine regurgitated some of your data. It wouldn't accept the part about the blue flame. It's not programed for the unexplainable."

"That's no fault of mine, is it?"

"Well, there's been some other trouble lately. Nothing to do with you. But soon everything will be straightened out. The Machine is building itself some new circuits just to handle this kind of data. As soon as that's finished, then it can decide, and you can go."

"Maybe."

"Besides, it's your duty as a citizen."

"Since when?" said Mr. Kleiber with sudden anger. "I'm getting sick of that Machine. And I bet plenty of other people are, too. There wouldn't even *be* any F.D.I. if people didn't let that stupid Machine push them around. You said the wrong thing."

"What are you going to do?" Amenhotep trembled.

"How much do you know about my case?"

"Just what the circular says. Here in the drawer—see, I'll show you."

"You haven't got a gun in there, I hope."

"They don't issue us one."

The circular had no picture and said only: *Thomas R. Kleiber*, with a lot of code numbers giving a description, and under that two sentences: *Disappeared established location and position July 9 abandoning possessions and compulsive life-pattern. Detain for query in re unacceptable data occult phenomena (blue flame) reported Bugleburgh Local 235.*

"They forgot to tell you something," Mr. Kleiber said with his second burst of inventiveness that day. "They forgot to warn you that the blue flame measures out at 10,000 volts."

"Good Lord!"

"I want you to sit right where you are and don't move a muscle."

"Oh, I won't!"

The alcove was even smaller than the room. Amenhotep Ra IV was sitting at the desk with his back to the wall. Mr. Kleiber shut his eyes and went to work. When he was finished, the alcove was closed off from the rest of the room by a sort of messy web of blue lights, with the F.D.I. man still inside.

"I'll starve!" Amenhotep wailed. "How will I ever get out?"

"Ask the Machine," said Mr. Kleiber.

After that everything happened very quickly. He was a full-fledged fugitive now, and running for all he was worth. From the street door of Amenhotep's building he took a taxi to the train station. On the way he thought about disguising himself, but the only thing he could think of in the way of disguises was letting his beard grow. Besides, even if they were watching the station, they didn't have a picture, only his description, so there was a good chance they might miss him.

He bought a ticket for New York and boarded the train and locked himself in the men's and sat down puffing. On the exact half-hour the train departed. He was on his way.

Now there was time for regret about Letitia and anxiety about the F.D.I. man getting loose and cogitation about what he was going to do next. But all he did was sit and sweat.

Four times the doorlatch rattled furiously, scaring him out of his wits, and once it was the conductor asking for his ticket. "Diarrhea," Mr. Kleiber said, and slammed the door and locked it again. And not long after that he did in fact discover a tremulous trepidation in the lower tract like raw, quivering nerves.

And then it happened.

The train had halted a hideously long time in Trenton station, and then gone on. He had wrenched the frosted window open in the stifling heat of the little closet and was peering out. Through the slats of an iron bridge he saw the water of the Delaware sweep by at an angle beneath the train. A few miles further on there was open country, low hills and green fields, with woods in the distance, where the river wound.

There came a dull, not loud, thud.

Not loud, but it seemed to come from far away, and it shook the train, traveling in the structure of the car he was riding in, like a deep bass note.

Before he had time to think there began an agonized grinding shriek like steel on ice and his own forward motion slammed him painfully against the wall as the train crashed to a stop. Someone had pulled the emergency cord.

*F.D.I.!* The letters blazed in his mind as brightly as though he had written them in fire on the air.

So they *had* been watching the station!

Simple as that. And they were on the train—with orders to kill!

Because that was a *bomb!*

Bending his knees and heaving up with the heels of his hands he forced the little window wide open. Outside was shimmering cinders and locusts in the soapweed and dead silence except for tiny shouts up at the head of the train.

It was a long drop for a man his age. He hurt his ankle a little and let himself fall, rolling in the weeds. He went over the edge of the embankment and tumbled into a ditch at the edge of the field. He was in luck. From where he lay he could see a cart track leading off at right angles from the train. By running low between the blackberry bushes he could make quick time away from there without being seen.

Finally he had to stop and rest with a piercing stitch in his side. A woodchuck in the field sat up and watched him with poised forepaws, like an enormous rat. Back across the field there was a sudden *blat* of horn, and the train began to move again, gathering speed rapidly and soon disappearing in the red light. Evening was nigh.

Flocks of birds flew overhead, going toward the river. Mr. Kleiber trudged after them. This seemed to be a particularly desolate stretch of country. He couldn't see a house or a road or even a telephone pole anywhere. Ahead of him was the thick woods that grew by the river. He went under the trees feeling safe from pursuit, for a time, at least, but hopelessly lost and bewildered and alone. The approaching darkness made the thick underbrush and tall trees look even more dismal and threatening. He was naggingly hungry and miserably tired. It was adding insult to injury when he stepped over a low snarl of brambles and put his foot into a loop of rope which slipped shut suddenly and jerked him skyward and left him hung up by one leg like a pig for the slaughter.

# Djeela-Lal

## ONE

Gurujalom-dji-as-Bhons, Grand Imaj of Phenh-Tin-Bom (Father of the Faithful, Son of the Sky and Incarnation of the Sun, Who Maketh the Ot[1] To Grow, Ruler by Divine Right and Beloved of All Men), stood in the shade of the bijasal trees at the edge of the jungle, awaiting the Moment of Manifestation.

That moment was drawing near. Through the leaves the Imaj watched the frantic posturing of his subjects, the Seven Thousand Faithful, in the great plaza before the palace. Now they were pantomiming rage, hunger, fear and abject desperation, with sweating climactic movements, while the sun blazed on their unprotected heads, even as it blazed on the

---

[1] Ot (the *t* is silent) is a millet-like plant whose flour, mixed with goat's milk, ox blood and macerated neem leaves, is baked in square hard loaves called Mods. Mods are the staff of life and very nearly the sole sustenance of most Phenians.

pink towers of the Royal Palace, on the mud flats of the sunken river, and on the mud walls and greasy fly curtains of Adjad Bodj, the Capital City. It was hot, on the second of July—so hot that where men stood there formed little pools of salt water.

Today was a day of great jubilation and hullabaloo: the simultaneous celebration of two Phenh national holidays. First, it was the Day of Manifestation, for which reason the Imaj stood in the steaming jungle, temporarily exiled from the cool interior of his palace, waiting to play his part in the traditional ceremonies. Second, it was the Feast of the Liberation, fifth anniversary of the triumph of the forces of Light and Good over the forces of Dark and Evil. Just five years ago today the last of the Communist rebels had been flushed from their caves, huts and swamps in the interior, and delivered in chains to the Capital, where they had been tried, convicted, and stamped to death by elephants.

So today would be a day of both religious and political rejoicing; of altercation and frenetic dancing, loud singing; of immorality and great pots of arrack[2]; startled cockatoos; orgies of speechifying, worship, sunstroke and assassination. Since early that morning the air had crackled with the explosion of firecrackers, and already many of the court dancers and lesser nobles—as well as the young sons of the region's thakurs—were drunken, and practicing abandoned forms of shiki-shiki on the eastern terrace. This was the terrace of the Inestimable Buffalo, where, not an hour before, had taken place the first Western-style beauty contest in all the three-thousand-year history of Phenh-Tin-Bom. And also where Sidihnouk-haj-Koduk[3], the Prime Minister, had risen from his seat to claim the newly garlanded Miss Bodj (a toffee-colored maiden from the province of Walla Hun) as his own, and install her in his house. And with her the runner-up, a tall, enigmatic young student named Djeela-Lal.

---

[2] Virulent spirits of mahua flower.
[3] The name means literally "Red-bellied shortchanger and son of the fig."

Alas, reflected the Imaj, the day would be filled with many such frivolous and unseemly incidents—in the pavilions of the great as well as in the foul, narrow houses of the mean and groveling Kali Admi, the black ones. He made a gesture of distaste, for he did not approve of other forms of amusement than prayer, chess playing and border wars. Now he watched for a moment or two longer the desperate dancing of the Faithful, and then murmured to his attendants: "It is time."

"Huzoor!" cried the Chief Maulvi[4], striking a small gong. And the Grand Imaj moved slowly from the shade into the blazing sun on the plaza, surrounded by his hundred servants, all hooded and garbed in black. The Imaj too, though gorgeously arrayed in gold and green and silver, was hidden from sight by a broad black parasol from which hung many impenetrable veils. And indeed, none of the Faithful paid the slightest attention to him, for the color black symbolized his total invisibility.

He moved slowly through the roaring crowd until he reached the exact center of the plaza. There his attendants carefully helped him to mount and stand upon the very Rock of Manifestation.[5]

All around the Imaj struggled the frenzied Seven Thousand, screaming and beating their breasts, grinding their

[4] Master of, or expert in, religious matters.

[5] Here it should be explained that the Manifestation Day ceremony is a re-enactment of the circumstances of the founding of the Phenh nation. On that day, 2 July, 1034 B.C., the first Grand Imaj, Nareem-ud-Fodj, a direct aspect of God, appeared suddenly standing on a rock at the exact moment of the final collapse of the old Prenn civilization. The awestruck survivors immediately began to pray to his shimmering form for help and guidance. Nareem-ud-Fodj is said to have made one condition: For so long as there existed seven thousand souls faithful to his name and mystic number, he would guide and help them, rule them, and make of them a nation among nations. The bleeding, starving survivors then cried with one voice: "Oh Incarnation of the Sun, we swear!" Whereupon Nareem-ud-Fodj answered them: "Oh most fortunate of men, I will lead you." So saying, he descended from the rock and took on human form, to become the first Grand Imaj, first in an unbroken succession of hereditary rulers of Phenh-Tin-Bom.

teeth and tearing their clothes, throwing dust on their heads, gashing themselves with razors and ceremonial daggers, and scourging themselves with crocodile whips—to represent the ruin and poverty and desperate straits of their remote ancestors at the end of the Prenn tether.

Hidden beneath his veiled parasol, the Imaj observed with cynical scorn their distorted mouths, bleeding wounds and disheveled, dusty heads; he heard with impatient disdain their cackling epileptic cries, prayers and pleas; while the odor of their obscene, hysterical piety rose in his nostrils, and he felt ill.

When he could bear it no longer, he made a signal to the waiting Chief Maulvi. The Moment of Manifestation had come. He folded his arms on his chest and stood tall on the rock. Behind him a gong—this time a large one—clanged with a noise of iron caverns collapsing. Then the parasol and veils were whipped away, and he stood—Father of the Faithful, Son of the Sky and Incarnation of the Sun—disclosed: the Living Aspect of God and the Imaj of Phenh-Tin-Bom. Omnipotent Light Made Flesh!

Immediately there came the vast impressive silence prescribed by the ritual. The people stood frozen in strange postures, arms high and mouths open. Even their wounds seemed to cease to bleed. Then the peevish voice of the Chief Maulvi called: "Are there still Seven Thousand Faithful?"

And the single voice of all the tribes of Phenh answered mightily: "Oh Incarnation of the Sun—we swear!"

Then Gurujalom-dji-as-Bhons, the Grand Imaj, spoke those words not only pronounced by the shimmering Nareem-ud-Fodj three thousand years ago and by every successive Imaj since, but also repeated by himself in the same tedious tone once each year since his accession: "Oh most fortunate of men! I will lead you!"

The gong clanged again.

Then, after the annual moment of foolish anticlimax, the people and their ruler turned from each other—the former to the continuance of their general joy, which was to rise to new heights of orgy before the night was past—the latter toward his palace of pink towers, wherein awaited him serious and unpleasant duty, but wherein at least it was cool.

## TWO

The call of duty sounded even on this day of festival and jubilation. And sad duty, too. Now the Grand Imaj sat, dressed in a simple white jubbah, on a high seat in the Chamber of Retribution. It was a room of red, blood-stained walls, filled with many-purposed instruments. Herein were heretics burned, subversive agents, assassins, intriguers and foreign newspapermen butchered, and the wives of the Imaj dispossessed of their teeth for infractions of the palace rules (smoking, using cosmetics, etc.).

Sad duty, and difficult too, for this day the Imaj must castigate Phenh-Tin-Bom's own Prime Minister, Sidihnouk-haj-Koduk, son of the fig and a great hero of the people. The Imaj hoped that his young friend would confess quickly and fully, and so spare himself the torture. The two men—the haughty old potentate and the clever young politician—had been friends for many years, ever since the bad old days of the Communist revolution, before the arrival of the U. S. Marines, when all the court of the Incarnation of the Sun had been forced to hide in the jungle disguised as a colony of crocodiles.

During the Re-establishment, Sidihnouk had been Chief of the Secret Police, and had served his Imaj well—both in that capacity and also as first line of defense against the Americans, who, once having saved the nation from Red tyranny, next wished to invest their capital in, and thereby become proprietors of, the national economy.[6]

[6] The chief exports are tea, cotton, jute and foz—this last a vegetable oil used in the canning of fish. However, in the Sikghat provinces on the upper Bodj there are important deposits of oil, which are still, for religious reasons, untapped. This may help to explain the insistent interest of foreign nations in the Phenh economy.

The tall, fair-skinned, handsome Sidi, Harvard educated, spoke English like a native. He sneered, laughed and cajoled; he filibustered, begged, lied and swore; he posed impossible conditions, proposed fatuous alternatives, wove complex nets of bureaucratic and religious red tape—meanwhile his Secret Police officers wrote on every wall "Yankee Go Home," and encouraged little children to pelt the U. S. Marines with monkeymud and smash the windows of the newly opened consulate. Until at last the Yankees did in fact give up in disgust and go home, taking nothing with them, leaving behind little more than a few sumptuous buildings, which were quickly converted into vice dens by a syndicate of immigrant Chinese businessmen.

Thus was Phenh-Tin-Bom delivered, both from the Red Communists and the Capitalist Imperialists. The Re-establishment was complete. And shortly thereafter, Sidihnouk-haj-Koduk was rewarded with the post of Prime Minister.[7]

Yes, Sidihnouk had been, and was, a hero of the people. And a good and faithful servant to his Imaj. But lately! The Imaj sighed and shook his head. The young Prime Minister had lost no time in making for himself powerful enemies—among them old Haji Harta-as-Buj, who himself aspired to the post of Prime Minister. It was Haji who led the opposition party, which severely criticized Sidi's private life, denounced his policy of Pacificist Neutralism (which consisted of the wholesale buying and selling of a foreign arms and munitions for personal profit), and spread talk of import licenses granted for consideration to the richest and most unscrupulous of the local thakurs, as well as talk of illegal negotiations with the Chinese merchants who were the bara-sahibs of the prosperous Phenian narcotics, gambling and prostitution combine. Talk which, in short, could no longer be ignored, the Imaj

---

[7] The office of Grand Imaj is, of course, hereditary. All other posts are filled by democratic election, one vote for the Imaj, one for the people. The people are informed beforehand how the Imaj will vote, and dissenters are torn to pieces by dogs.

sighed sadly—and Sidi one of the best of the realm's few chess players.

And now there was this unfortunate final detail of the Western-style beauty contest. Sidihnouk had instantly appropriated for himself both winner and runner-up: Bhil Phum of Walla Hun Province, and Djeela-Lal, from Kharta —both beautiful young girls and reputed virgins. Even though there could be neither legal nor religious objections, nor yet moral objections on the part of Mhraba Daffa, Sidi's number-one wife and the mother of his three children[8], still for old Harta-as-Buj and the rest of the opposition party it would be the last outrageous straw. They would demand nothing less than the Prime Minister's head.

The Imaj cast an eye over the Scroll of Accusation, which he held in his gloved left hand. It was not brought quite up to date. The Imaj knew that between the end of the beauty contest and his receipt of his Holy Summons to the Chamber of Retribution, Sidihnouk had already had time to marry the first of his new acquisitions, the beauteous Miss Bodj.[9] But it did not matter. From top to bottom, left to right, the Scroll contained well over three hundred charges to be brought against poor Sidi, son of the fig and the Imaj's favorite chess opponent.

The Imaj sighed disconsolately again and turned his attention to the preparations for the Hour of Retribution. His hooded assistants had already laid out on the porcelain tables their kits of strange-shaped tools, and had kindled in gleaming copper braziers their hot little charcoal fires, in which irons were heating. Here and there in the room were basins, rags,

[8] Phenh laws and customs permit up to thirty-four wives—supposedly the number of moles on the body of Nareem-ud-Fodj, the first Grand Imaj—plus an unlimited number of concubines. Divorce is accomplished by ritually spitting to the corners of the compass. Concubines are discharged like any other class of servant.

[9] Phenh law provides for a quick civil marriage in which the parties drink a sip of the sacred water of the Bodj in the presence of an official of the Ministry of Public Records.

spikes, new ropes, cuffs and chains, miniature slow-ovens, and boxes of brand-new West-German-made thumbtacks. New and heavier lead weights had been fitted to the stretching apparatus, and new burrs to the bone drill. Everything was in readiness. "Let the culprit come," intoned the Grand Imaj.

The great door to the Chamber of Retribution swung slowly open. And then: the unforeseeable! Before his ushers could prevent him, the accused—Sidihnouk-haj-Koduk, the Prime Minister—tall, fair-skinned, handsome and Harvard educated—flung himself headlong into the room, fell flat on his face, and *groveled!*

He was stripped of all adornment, clad only in a blood-smeared cotton smock. His feet were bare and bleeding. Blood flowed from gashes on face and arms. His body was rubbed with dust and ashes, and his hair was a sticky mess of tar. In one hand he carried an ornate ceremonial dagger, and in the other a large pliers.[10]

Before the astonished Imaj could move or speak, Sidihnouk-haj-Koduk raised his head high enough to reach into his mouth with the pliers and wrench out a tooth. Then another, still a third. Blood gushed. The three teeth he placed at the Imaj's feet like an offering. Then he rose to his knees—jaws and chin and throat a river of gore—and made a meaningful gesture towards his chest with the ceremonial dagger.

"As the Preserver of the Faith wills it," he said indistinctly. "I will speak—or I will seek out my heart with the thin, cold finger of Shiva."

The Imaj could but acquiesce.

And immediately there poured forth from the Prime Minister's plundered mouth an exact and exhaustive, even tedious, account of all his three hundred crimes—plus several score more of which the Imaj had known nothing.

[10] The accused is customarily permitted to bring into the Chamber of Retribution any materials or paraphernalia which he thinks may help him prove his innocence or resist the torture.

On and on Sidi talked, bleeding, beating his breast, scratching his face with his fingernails, and crying genuine tears. At last the Imaj interrupted him, to ask: "What is the purpose of so much babble?"

"Huzoor!" cried the Prime Minister instantly. "Purpose there is none. This is my penance. Afterward you will do with me as pleases Your Presence."

"True," the Imaj said. "The cobra pits, perhaps. Or perhaps the beetle bag."

"I go with all gladness," said Sidihnouk excitedly. "Nevertheless, that is Your Presence's punishment of me. I pray Your Presence note that what you see before you is my punishment of myself! It is self-inflicted, in wholehearted sorrow and chagrin for past errors."

And he began again to list and tick over the three hundred and sixty errors of his public and private life, and fell again to crying and beating his breast with sincere emotion—on and on for an endless time—but then unexpectedly finishing: "Take away my wives and my jewels, my house, my elephants! Break my body on the rack! Hang me from the highest tower of the palace! Sew my dead body in a pigskin and bury it in the mud! Your wrath can never equal my sorrow! My single regret is that, dead, I can no longer serve my God, my Nation, and my Imaj!"

"Indeed," said the Imaj, who had the same regret. Now, although he had heard all, he made no sign to his hooded assistants to begin. And Sidihnouk, taking heart, bent his head even lower, so that it touched the floor, and said softly:

"Huzoor! On the other hand, if Your Presence chooses to have mercy on my weakness and ignorance—if I might ask only a few years more of life—in which to cleanse my soul—in the monastery of Bri Hom Thud—to repent of my misdeeds—and then afterward—to serve Your Presence as Ambassador to the United States of America?"

The Imaj made a face of amused surprise. But then he pondered. Sidihnouk was a man of many talents, of great energy and adroitness. He knew the Americans. He was almost one of them. He knew their weaknesses as well as their strengths. He danced both the foxtrot and the burp. He ate confections of ice cream and sandwiches of hot dog. He read *Time* magazine and could operate American motor vehicles. He had never been made Ambassador to the United States only because heretofore he had been more valuable as Prime Minister.

But Sidihnouk himself knew that this was no longer possible. He also knew that the former Ambassador to Washington had just recently been recalled in disgrace, after an unseemly exhibition of shiki-shiki at a White House reception. He had been brought into that same Chamber of Retribution, where his mouth had been stuffed with black powder and his head exploded, using his own beard as fuse. The post was vacant.

"I would serve Your Presence well," Sidihnouk murmured. And then dared say no more.

"It is a possibility," mused the Grand Imaj.

Still he made no sign to his sinister assistants.

### THREE

Several months later.

The three women of Sidihnouk-haj-Koduk lay in sweltering purdah in their third-class cabin aboard a soggily wallowing Laotian steamer bound through the Red Sea to the Mediterranean and Marseilles.

Not always were the women thus confined. Often enough, through a judicious application of baksheesh to the Tonkinese eunuch charged with their care, they were able to make free of all C-Deck, while Sidi himself pursued an ash-blonde French cinema actress returning from Java around and around the Promenade. This morning, however, their Lord and Master was in his own cabin up above, the victim of a mild food-poisoning. At any moment he might send for any one of them, or might appear in person in search of help or comfort. Thus the women did not dare absent themselves from their assigned quarters.

Side by side on a woven maul mat spread on the floor lay Sidi's three little sons, nude and soundly sleeping in puddles of perfumed sweat. Near them, also on the floor, sat their mother, Mhraba Daffa, Sidi's number-one wife—of thirty-eight years, with a not inconsiderable mustache; a stout and muscular woman, energetic and decisive, whose servants called her the Lion of Franchise; she was an incorrigible suffragette. At the moment she sat eating ghi from a wooden pot with a wooden spoon, and reading a volume of Sufistic erotic and political poetry.

She was dressed in only the lightest of muslin robes, and from time to time she would look up and shout fiercely: "God damn this heat! I'm roasting!"

She spoke across the cabin to one of her traveling companions, who lay supinely steaming in a canvas hammock. It was the erstwhile *Miss Bodj*, Bhil Phum, Sidi's number-two wife, now far from her native Walla Hun and naked except for a loincloth, sipping a glass of iced tea through a plastic straw.

She was a slender, velvet-skinned, toffee-colored young woman with catlike eyes, catlike limbs and movements, and a perfect, mysterious face, which, catlike, masked a certain vacancy of mind. Her duties as wife number two lay lightly on her. She was never called upon to attend to her husband's domestic or social affairs, as was Mhraba Daffa, nor to repair to his bed, as was Djeela-Lal. Indeed, shortly after their perfunctory wedding ceremony, Sidi had discovered her to be neither efficient nor seductive, neither interesting nor interested. She was of no more practical use than a stuffed sloth. Therefore the beauteous former *Miss Bodj* ordinarily lay where she had fallen and sipped hot drinks in cold weather and cold drinks in hot.

The number-one wife had cursed the blasting heat a round dozen times before Bhil Phum opened her full lips wide enough to remark: "All the same, we're better off here than back home."

"No. It's inhuman to keep us penned up here like swine in this devilish oven. If he had any heart at all he'd let us dress Western and go on deck. Look at all those French women from the cinema company lolling in the breeze and drinking gin and tonic."

Bhil Phum murmured listlessly: "But if we weren't here, we'd be in Adjad Bodj, and Sidi would be dead in the Chamber of Retribution, and then where would we be? Or else he'd still be fasting and beating himself with crocodile whips in Bri Hom Thud monastery, and you and I and Djeela-Lal would still be impounded by the Imaj."

"Oh, you never know what's going on," said Mhraba Daffa energetically. "Well, I do, by God, and I want to go on the Promenade!"

"Will of Allah," Bhil Phum said drowsily (her parents were Mohammedans).[11] "It's too hot to argue. Besides, we would need Western clothes for that, and they're forbidden."

"Djeela-Lal has some," Mhraba Daffa said thoughtfully. "A man brought her some yesterday. A dress and shoes and stockings, in a paper bag."

"The purser," Bhil Phum said. "He brings her cigarettes, too. She always finds a man to bring her things." And she added aggrievedly: "I wonder how she does it. Aren't we all made the same?"

"Ask Sidi," said the number-one wife. "He's crazy for her."

The two discussed the nearby Djeela-Lal (still not number-three wife, but only number-one concubine) as though she were either completely deaf, or entirely absent from the

---

11 In Phenh-Tin-Bom there is a sort of secondary religious freedom. After the Phenian's pious duty is done to his Grand Imaj—Incarnation of the Sun and hereditary Deity of the Seven Thousand Faithful—he is free to worship whatever gods he chooses. In the realm are temples to the greater glory of almost every known god, from Amen through Juggernaut to Zerâna-Akerana.

room. She was neither. And yet, at the same time, she was oblivious to them, as she was to everything else in the material world—for her Kundalini, her vital existence, was very far from there. It was with Maya.[12]

She sat in the lotus posture, or padmasana: right foot on left thigh, left foot on right thigh, the soles upward. Her hands—the fingers interlaced, palms upward—lay in her lap. Her head was bowed. She had neither moved nor spoken for almost three hours, since *chota hazri*, or *petit déjeuner*. She was cold, cold as death, in the awful heat of the Red Sea. Her breathing was imperceptible. Had the ship's physician come upon her in this state, he would have ordered her to be sewn in a shroud and cast overboard, with appropriate ceremony. She was practicing the Kali-mudra.[13]

"But I don't understand why," Bhil Phum went on with the innocence of a child. "Aren't I more beautiful? Then why does Sidi call *her* to his cabin every night? Why does he only summon her, never *me?*"

"The best chupatti is worthless without a pinch of salt," Mhraba Daffa said cryptically. But she was not really thinking about Bhil Phum's problem at all. She was watching the cold dead face of Djeela-Lal with new interest.

Seldom had Mhraba Daffa paid any attention to, or taken seriously the concubine's periodic fits, or trances. But now she had begun to think. Who was this stranger in her house, this tall, enigmatic young girl with the fair skin and bottomless lamp-black eyes? How indeed had she so enthralled Sidihnouk-haj-Koduk, the Harvard-educated, that he called for her each night? The two girls had come into her house

[12] The meaning of "Kundalini" is not clear. "Soul" is perhaps the closest. The word "Maya" signifies "Allness." The act of sending the Kundalini into the Maya implies the merging of the Individual self with the Universal self.

[13] Literally, "Death exercise." This curious exercise is best explained by the Paramahansa Rawalzepur Joshi Bisudhanan-Sri in his fourteen-volume study: "Investigations of the Etheric Sources of the Energy of the Asana Saints."

together as a result of the beauty contest. One was a beautiful but otherwise unremarkable puppet whom Mhraba Daffa would one day turn into the street like a stupid servant— but the other?

What was known of her? Only that she was nearly as beautiful as Bhil Phum, but not nearly so stupid. She said that she came from a family of poor woodcutters in the province of Kharta, and had been a student—but of what? Of Hatha Yoga, perhaps. And if her trances were genuine, this meant that she—a young woman, certainly not more than twenty-five years old—had already mastered at least four of the eight steps to Enlightenment.[14] And if that were the case, then here was at least an Adept, an advanced Brahmacharin—if not a Tantrik, a Sorceress! In any case, a more than dangerous rival!

"A man may often be made to do by mantra[15] what he would not do for love," Mhraba Daffa said to herself in a low tone.

"What?" asked the reclining Bhil Phum.

"Perhaps our friend who is among the astral bodies wakes the Great Serpent in Sidi's loins by magic, not by love."

Bhil Phum turned slowly over and fell softly from the hammock to the floor, where she lay idly caressing her breasts. "Indeed, that might be so," she said thoughtfully, in her languid voice. "And if it is, then all we have to do is mix a little ground-up mokk in her ghi, and the spell would be broken. Then perhaps Sidi would summon me!"

"Let's not go off half-cocked," said the older woman. "First

[14] The eight steps, corresponding in some ways to the Buddhist eight-fold path, are, in ascending order of difficulty: yama-ni-yama, asana, mudra, pranayama, pratyahara, dharana, dhyana, and finally, samadhi —that is, good thoughts, good (bodily) positions, exercises, and gestures (including baptisms and purifications, or dhauties), breathing rhythms, nerve control, mind control, meditation, and at last Enlightenment (or Bliss, Perfection, Rapture, Completeness, etc.).

[15] "Magic spells" in the sense Mhraba Daffa uses the word; actually only devotional incantations, or prayers.

of all, Sidi would have you buried to the neck in the tar pits if he ever found out. Second, we have to find out lots more before taking action. Give her a fair chance first, *then* poison her."

"But it must be true," Bhil Phum said vigorously. "Come to think of it, how else could Sidi have escaped from the Chamber of Retribution? You *know* no one ever comes out of there alive. She *must* have helped him. With *magic!*"

"That's true," said Mhraba Daffa with a start. "I never thought of that either. There always *was* something strange about—"

"OM!" said a hoarse, resonant voice. Both women jumped. It was Djeela-Lal. Her meditation was over. Her restless everyday vitality had come among them again like a bird which has flown into the room.

She seemed to collapse in a heap, and then spring up. Her feet slipped from her thighs, and her fingers unlaced themselves. She scratched her head. She reached into her robe, brought out a cigarette and lighted it. Her body was coming alive now, warming up, and these few movements made the sweat stand on her arms and forehead. She removed several of her outer garments. Then she smiled at her traveling companions. "Hot," she said.

But she had overheard the end of their conversation. "Careful you don't sell Sidi short," she said. "He got out of the Chamber of Retribution all by himself. I didn't help him. It's not my line of work."

"We were talking about—"

"About Sidi—his relations with me—about me—and my actions," finished Djeela-Lal, impatient with slower minds. "Well, what about him? me? them? What do you want to know? I can't tell you what kind of monkeymud he handed the Imaj. I wasn't there. But I'll tell you this much. The fact that Sidi's neither rotting in the Tumulus of Malefactors nor tortured beyond recognition is due to his own agility, not to my magic powers. In the first place, he didn't do such terrible things to himself as we thought. He had those teeth ready in his cheek long before he went into the Chamber. They weren't his, either. They belonged to a man found dead in the Pearl Gardens that morning."

"What man?" asked Mhraba Daffa fearfully. As number one wife of the Prime Minister, she had had many handsome young lovers who came through that garden to climb her wall.

"Only a man," Djeela-Lal said. "Sidi would kill a man if he needed his teeth, don't you think? The robe he tore apart was borrowed from his cousin. And the blood was chicken blood from a bladder in his other cheek. Chicken blood on his chest. Chicken blood and ink on his feet. Chicken blood on his clothes. The only authentic part was the scratches on his face, and cheap at the price. That wasn't even tar rubbed in his hair—only phot."[16]

"Who told you this?" cried the thunderstruck Mhraba Daffa, to whom Sidi had not breathed a word.

"Furthermore," Djeela-Lal added, "when he went to Bri Hom Thud to repent, he took along two camelskins of arrack, and half a dozen dancing girls from the jota-house of Liu Chih Sen."

"But how did *you* find out?" Mhraba Daffa insisted.

"Sidi must have told her," Bhil Phum said.

"Obviously," Djeela-Lal said. "Nobody else could know— at least, I hope not. If it ever gets to the ear of the Imaj, Sidi will die several of the most horrible deaths ever devised."

"But why?" whispered the number-one wife, wrapped in desperate thought, now thoroughly frightened that she had forever lost her rightful place at her husband's side—to a concubine of an age to be her daughter. "Why should he have told *you*?"

[16] A Phenh dish in appearance rather like partly assimilated licorice, made of lentils, potatoes, peppers, endjah root (hence its color) and honey, first stewed to a thick purée, then sprinkled with chopped nuts and baked in a boar's skull. The dish is traditionally eaten during the Feast of Aduphradhi, but is also used ritually in the ceremony of Jaghrat, when sealed pots of it together with the livers of young virgins are thrown into the Bodj to assure that year's good fishing.

But then her eyes hardened, and she sat erect against the steel wall of the cabin, and challenge rang in her voice again: "Yes—we were discussing just that, Bhil Phum and I, when you wakened. How you have managed to worm your way into Sidi's good graces—and how he confides in you, but not in us—and how you—"

"And how he calls for *you* every night," said Bhil Phum petulantly. "Never for *me!*"

"Your extraordinary success with *our* husband—"

"It must be magic! Sorcery!" cried Bhil Phum.

There was a moment of silence. Djeela-Lal seemed to be thinking of something else. But then she smiled kindly, the smile of Ahimsa.

"Nonsense," she said. "I don't know any magic."

"No?" said Bhil Phum. "Then what is all this about going into trances, and bewitching Sidi, and saying 'OM,' and all that. What do *you* call it?"

"Don't your parents sleep with their heads toward Mecca, and recite the Q'alimah? Don't you cover your face with a veil when you walk in the street? That's your religion, isn't it? Well, I'm a Hindu. My meditation is part of my religion, that's all."

"That doesn't explain much," said Mhraba Daffa. "Girls your age just don't go off into fits like that for hours on end, without even breathing—and then get up and go chasing after men as though nothing had happened. It's unnatural. And besides, Hindu religion is one thing, and Yoga is another. I never saw you acting like a Hindu. What's your caste?"

"As a matter of fact," Djeela-Lal said, "I couldn't go chasing after a man now if I had to. I can't even stand up. My circulation has been locked off at the femoral arteries for the past three hours. I'm tingling with pain. Which only proves that somewhere in my purifications I missed a step. There shouldn't be any discomfort. But yes, I'm a student of Yoga. In fact, Yoga interests me more than the religious part. What of it?"

"I wonder if it's permitted," said Mhraba Daffa.

"Certainly it's permitted. 'There is no god but God, and Imaj is his aspect,'" she quoted. "So everything is permitted except sacrilege and *lèse majesté*, which are one and the same. Meditation on the principle of Maya is not even necessarily a religious exercise, since no belief in God is required."

"Mph," said Mhraba Daffa.

Djeela-Lal stubbed out her cigarette on the floor and said: "Let's see." She got effortfully to her feet and tottered to the stained little washbasin and washed her face. Then she drank a glass of water and returned to her place. Now, like her companions, she was soaked with sweat, but the suppleness was returning to her ivory limbs, and her manner was normal. Indeed, when she continued, her voice was the voice of always: the lethargic voice of a woman bored by the company of women.

"Shall I tell you how I became interested in Yoga? It was during the Revolution. Our province was cut off from the Capital by hordes of Communists. In fact, we were behind their lines, and my parents had no choice but to flee over the border into the territory of the Sultan of Jorheb. But there was no work for my father there. There are no forests, only sandhills and plains, and the people have no use for woodcutters. They burn camel chips and oxdung, and live in bassourabs. We wandered for months living from hand to mouth, then finally crossed the eastern mountains to Peshawar in India, and then went south to the Indus River, where we established ourselves in a village called Bhagaflis. There we lived till we heard from a traveler one day that the Reestablishment was complete. Then we turned towards home.

"But during our time in India I had become interested in the Hindu philosophy, through a young cheelah, or apprentice in such matters. He introduced me to his guru, or teacher, at whose feet I sat for many months—out of silly curiosity, perhaps, or hopefulness, like any young girl yearning for some excitement in her emotional life. I was not serious. I was more interested in Masalhji, the cheelah, than in Union with the Cosmos. Furthermore, our guru claimed that he could lift heavy stones with his eyelids—but he refused to do it.

"Nevertheless, I studied with some application. I read parts of the Atharva Veda, and other parts were sung to me by students who had memorized them. I talked to many holy men and mahatmas and magicians. And though they laughed at me, I listened carefully to what they said. Our guru told me many important things, and Masalh-ji confided to me the gist of his more advanced lessons.

"Thus, when the day came that my parents and I at last turned our faces toward Phenh and home, I carried with me a considerable baggage of occult theory, none of which I had ever put into practice.

"But on our return journey a strange thing occurred, which inclined me not toward religion—the worship of Imaj, or Brahma, or any other god—but toward a pious gratitude to, almost worship of, Yoga itself. We had returned to Phenh as we had left it, surreptitiously, crossing the frontier in the deep forests by the headwaters of the Bodj. And now we were very near our town. But suddenly we were set upon by a group of men, and seized, and quickly bound to trees. These men claimed that they were soldiers of the foot cavalry of the Imaj, whose mission it was to track down survivors of Communist guerrillas lurking in the forests. But I did not believe them. They had no uniforms, and each one was dressed differently, all in a highly romantic fashion. Their weapons were different too. Some carried rifles, some flintlock pistols, and others swords, or spears. They were obviously bandits.

"In fact, when we protested that we were not Communists, they shrugged and said: 'Then you must be illegal immigrants, and thus subject to the customs fees.' With which words they set to searching through our effects. I knew they would find nothing, for we owned nothing—our poor rags, my father's tools, a skin of water, and two pots of mildewed lentil paste, that was all. I believed once they discovered this, they would allow us to go free, for we could do them no harm. But then I saw a sight which made my blood freeze. Another bandit—this one tall and dark, and dressed in a flowing black robe and a green turban—obviously their chief —had just now emerged from the forest. All the rest touched their fingertips to their brows and saluted him—*with cries of 'Bul! Bul!'* "

Djeela-Lal paused. In spite of herself, Mhraba Daffa gasped: "Ghuts!"

"Yes. These were not ordinary brigands, such as abound in the forests of the upper Bodj, but men of a tribe of Ghut Arabs. The cry is peculiar to them. And now I noticed all at once that each of our captors bore the brand of the cult of Wazil on the back of his right hand. Then I knew that we were lost, and had no salvation. No one escapes from the Ghuts.[17] Unless . . .

"My very fear made me think faster than ever before in all my life. Immediately I remembered everything I had ever heard about the barbaric Ghuts—and they are much talked about in Kharta province, where their depredations are as regular and devastating as the monsoon rains. Then three facts detached themselves from the swirl of information in my brain, and stood apart: The men of the Tribes of Ghut are bound by sacred oath never to break their word once given; the men of Ghut are incredibly superstitious; and the men of Ghut are great lovers of women. These three facts gave me an idea.

---

[17] A repulsive people, with a curious history and obnoxious customs. Originally a North African nomad tribe, reputedly descendants of the early Crusaders (many carry archaic European weapons; some few are blue-eyed), they are simultaneously Mohammedans and cannibals —thus their popular name, although they refer to themselves as the "Wazil-Feezl," or, Beloved of Wazil. There is no need for a description of their repugnant rites, but it is interesting to note that the clean bones of the dead are usually sewn up in hog skins, in order to prevent the entry of their spirits into Paradise, where they might carry tales.

"In the beginning I hoped only to delay our impending massacre—and subsequent ingestion—because every moment of life is indispensable to the condemned. Later I thought that I might at least spare us indignities at the hands of these barbarians. And still later, in a jubilant moment of hope, I believed I might even save the lives of my parents, though at the cost of my own. Merely at the last instant did I think that I might still save my own life—only to see in the bright descent of a new-moon-bladed scimitar that I was mistaken."

Djeela-Lal had taken down her hair and was brushing it gently with a wire brush dipped in cocoa butter. "What did you do?" asked Bhil Phum, enthralled and alarmed. But the number-one wife only sat stroking her mustache and staring out the porthole. She did not believe a word of it.

Djeela-Lal continued: "First I called—in Pushtu, the tongue of Bhagaflis, which I hoped none of the Ghuts would understand—to my mother: 'Uphold me in what I say.'

"Then I turned to the tall dark chieftain who wore the flowing black djellabia, and I said arrogantly: 'Maharaj! I will speak a word to you.'

" 'Speak then, and be quick,' he said coming closer, 'for there is no time, and I must cut out your tongue.'[18]

"I said: 'I will not keep you overlong. I ask only that my one hand be freed a moment, so that I may open my clothing and count my breasts.'

"He gave a snort of laughter. He said: 'How many do you expect to find—twelve like a sow?'

" 'Is the intrepid maharaj afraid of one small hand of one small, helpless girl?' I asked.

" 'The intrepid maharaj will not waste time,' he snarled, 'and we will all count your breasts soon enough!'

---

[18] The tongue, though considered a delicacy, is never eaten. It must be cut out by the chief of the tribe and burned as an offering to Wazil before the victim is killed by the halal (bleeding) method prescribed by Mohammedan law.

"But he stretched forth his hand and tore away the cloth.

"This is what I had hoped he would do.

"For I have perfect breasts—"

("Mph," said Mhraba Daffa.)

"The men of the tribes of Ghut are great lovers of women," continued Djeela-Lal unperturbed. "For a long moment he did not take his eyes from me. Of course, he need not look at me with yearning or sad desire. My breasts were already his, to do with as he would—to caress, or cut off and roast. But neither had I played my last card.

"Now I turned excitedly to my mother, praying she would understand. And I cried wildly: 'Mother! I have only two! In this moment I felt something strange, like the drawing of a cork—and lo, now I have but two breasts!'

"'Miracle!' cried my mother, who must have been sorely puzzled.

"'What nonsense is this?' snarled the chief Ghut, his hand stayed by curiosity, though great cooking fires already blazed in the grove.

"And I turned my head slowly, and looked at him fixedly for a long time. First I allowed the excitement to die from my face. Then I expressed unutterable sadness. Then finally mysterious vindictiveness, even glee. Meanwhile, I made him wait.

"And then I said slowly: 'Know, O jackal Commandant of Carrion Crows, whom you kill this day. Your bride!'

"'Wazool?' he inquired, stupefied.

"'Oh, cut out the tongue, let's get on with it,' rumbled some of the nearby Ghuts.

"But I continued proudly: 'Know, O Supreme Maharaj of Cannibal Scum, that I am the Princess Shakti Dussehra of the Cult of Kali, the Strangler Thugs of the mountains of Kobat![19] That I was born fully formed from an egg like

[19] An association of religious murderers in India, devoted to the worship of Kali, or Durga, symbol of the destructive principle in nature.

the Cockatrice, laved in blood and with three breasts! And that the wise men of Holy Kali said to me: "Go thou forth in the world, and go thou to and fro, till thou findest thy mate! And thy marriage ceremony will symbolize the marriage of the cult of Thug and the cult of Ghut—and tomorrow the Earth is ours!'" And I said to the wise ones: 'O Holy ones, how am I to find my husband, how am I to know him?' And they said to me: 'Go thou to and fro in the world, and back and forth, and when thou hast found him, thy third breast will disappear in his presence. Thus thou wilt know him. Take him into thine arms, and unveil to him thy delights and tomorrow the Earth is ours!'

"'Miracle!' cried my mother vigorously.

"'Thus is the prophecy fulfilled,' I said to the chieftain. 'I am the bride of Wazil. And you are the husband of Kali. But we are united only in death—together. For though I go first, do not think that the Stranglers will not soon take their revenge.'"

Now Djeela-Lal paused again. She had pulled her hair straight back and bound it in a knot on top of her head. She went to look in the mirror.

"The men of the tribes of Ghut are incredibly superstitious," she continued. "They will believe anything, provided it is sufficiently improbable. The tall dark chieftain gaped stupidly at me for a moment. He murmured: 'Most strange!' And he plucked his nose, he wet his lips. Then he turned on his heel and went away. I saw him squatting by the central fire in company with several elderly Ghuts who must have been his counselors.

"After a long time of hushed, excited argument, the chief returned to the tree where I was bound, to ask me casually: 'And what were to be the conditions of this marriage?'

"'None,' I said, 'for it was not politics, but only prophecy: That when I found my husband, he and I would go hand in hand through the Valley of Flowers, by the Flower Strewn Way, whilst the Kali-Pyara and the Wazil-Feezl would unite in fellowship, and rule over all the earth.'

" 'No one rules all the earth,' said the chieftain, 'unless it is the U. S. Marines. What were to be the advantages of such a fellowship?'

" 'Thuggee kills a hundred thousand people each year. Its greatest problem is the disposal of cadavers. The Ghuts would solve this problem. In return, no Ghut need ever go empty.'

" 'Very well. But how was I to know that you are the Princess of Kali whom I am intended to marry?'

" 'The Wise Ones said that you yourself would know by some mystic sign similar to the disappearance of my breast. Has nothing unusual happened to you since you first saw me?'

"He replied thoughtfully: 'In truth, I have noticed nothing out of the ordinary, though yesterday I had a nosebleed—'

"Then he turned and went away again. And this time the fierce, hushed discussion around the central fire continued nearly half an hour, while the red sun sank over the jungle. My parents spoke no word to me, nor I to them.

"This time when the chief returned to me, he came slowly, almost shyly, with his hands behind his back. He kicked at sticks and pebbles on the forest floor. Then he stood before me with his glance cast down. Then he looked up. His gaze rose to my breasts, and he said coyly: 'Well, it is explained. The Magician of our tribe—what you call the Saddhu—finds that I now have not two kidneys, but three. So there is no difficulty. It is settled. I will take one more wife, and a bargain is made with the Thugs, no?'

"This was the moment in which I thought that I might still save my parents. I pretended shock, surprise, and then indignation. I inflated my chest. I glared haughtily at him. I spoke in a scornful voice: 'Marriage to the murderer and eater of my parents? Sooner would I fling myself to the crocodiles of the Bodj! Get out of my sight, jackal dog and abomination of the faithful!'

" 'Oh, no,' he said earnestly, 'of course we will let the old ones go. We have killed recently, and have food for tonight. In any case, one never eats relatives, or peaceable emissaries. They are to be set free immediately, and they may carry the news to Kali—that we are wedded. Is that not satisfactory?'

" 'No! I am resigned to death' I replied, 'it is preferable. I am no longer pleased by the prophecy of the Wise Men of Holy Kali, for now I see that to obey my Karma is to make my marriage bed in heaps of offal. Away!'

" 'You must not be unreasonable. When we met, I could not know you. We seized you because in the summer we must travel to the west, and we need dried meat and sausage. But now that the situation is explained to me, and I understand—why, there is no problem, and it is always better to obey the fates in these matters.'

"And again his eyes roved slowly from my feet to my throat.

" 'Release my parents,' I commanded, 'and send them away. Give me your word that they will not be harmed, and that none of your bandits will follow behind them traitorously.'

" 'Yes.'

" 'When they have reached the Holy Shrine in the mountains of Kobat, they will send word to me by the black doves of Kali—and only then will our marriage ceremony take place. Until that day, I am your prisoner.'

" 'Done!' he said grandly, and put his two thumbs in his ears, the Ghut gesture meaning that he had heard the bargain and agreed, and given his word—

" 'And the men of the Tribes of Ghut are bound by sacred oath never to break that word,' " said Djeela-Lal.

She had gone to the mirror again, the small smudged glass hanging over the washbasin. She was dissatisfied with her hair. She undid the knot and set it free, and shook her head until her crow-black curls whirled around her ears like the mane of a Masai lion. Then she went quickly and searched in her trunk, and found a tiny leather case, which she opened with a golden key. While the two women watched her in astonishment, she brought forth a lipstick, a bottle of nail polish, a tin of face powder, a pat of rouge, and a small box of ricin Parisian mascara. She began to paint her face.

"Sidi will kill you," Mhraba Daffa said with patent pleasure.

"Sidi will never know," replied the concubine, looking at her reflection from various angles.

"But go *on!* What happened *then?*" cried Bhil Phum.

"Very little," said Djeela-Lal, taking from her paper bag the nylon dress, shoes and stockings given to her by the ship's purser. "I took fond and emotional leave of my mother and father. My mother wailed, and my father wept big tears into his beard which he had grown in Bhagaflis. Both of them believed—as I did—that we would never see one another again. But we were forced to pretend, for the benefit of the bandits, that our tears were happy tears—of joy and melancholy—those tears which invariably flow in such circumstances. And then they departed, and I was alone in the grove with the cannibals.

"But before they had left, I had managed to whisper to them: 'Do not give up hope. Something may happen yet.'

"In fact, in that moment I was very optimistic. I had begun to think that I might yet save my own life. My parents were already lost from view, on those paths which wind through the forest like the veins on the back of an old man's hand. They were no more than a few hours' walk from our native village. I calculated that soon after midnight they would be home, amongst our old neighbors, and that then I might act without fear for their safety. All the while the Ghut chieftain believed that we must wait at least several weeks for the black doves of Kali to come and make known to us that the pair had crossed all the way into India and had reached the sacred shrine at Kobat. So, as I stood watching the darkness descend over the trail where I had last seen my mother and father, I was thinking that I had much time in which to find opportunity to escape.

"But I was wrong. I had no time. For as I stood thus, the Ghut had come up behind me, and now he put his hands on my shoulders, and murmured in a disagreeable amorous voice: 'So now we must wait, my little gheen-flower, for the occasion of our epousal. But you need consider yourself my prisoner no more. Indeed, now you are my betrothed, with all her privileges. And what is more, this very night the moon shall see our two shadows one on my pallet.'

"Thus I knew that I must act at once—

"And if it seems preposterous to you that I should throw away my young life in order to avoid lying with this man, then I must ask you to imagine what a cannibal's breath is like—and to further imagine that he wishes to *kiss* you!

"I hoped only for a quick death. I would have run away into the forest then, had I believed that he would send a bullet whizzing after me. But he would not. He knew that I could flee neither fast nor far. A weak young girl, come all the way over the mountains from India on foot, and tied to a tree the better part of the day, I could barely stand. Were I to flee he would simply send men after me, and I would be seized within a hundred paces, and dragged back by the hair, and then—

"No, I would not be sport for these animals. Neither wife to the chieftain, nor meat for his band. I knew what I would do—I would force him to kill me! I did not believe that I could make him angry enough to shoot me dead on the spot, even by admitting that I had deceived him, even by jeering at his stupidity, or insulting him in some other way. Should I offend his personal dignity or that of his tribe, he would simply order me to be slowly roasted, after who knew what barbarous preliminaries. Therefore, I had no alternative. There was but one way. I knew that once I lay dead by violence, they would not dare eat me.[20] Thus would

[20] She is correct. Meat not slaughtered in accordance with certain regulations similar to the Mohammedan "halal" is untouchable. There-

I be spared not only what savage African tortures they might devise, but also the final indignity of being grilled and hacked up and distributed amongst the Ghuts.

"This is what I thought. I planned to attack the Ghut chieftain—without warning, viciously, murderously, ferociously, with some indisputably deadly weapon—so that in order to preserve his own life, he would be forced to take mine!

"And then I saw how it could be done.

"I can tell you little of the next few hours. In order that my parents have time to reach our village safely, I suggested to the Ghut chief that there be a feast to celebrate our betrothal. But of that feast I remember little, for my head swam and throbbed with fear and excitement, and I could think of nothing except that soon I must die. The feeding rituals of the Ghuts are extraordinary enough, and it must be true that they are descended from Christians, for there is much melodious chanting and use of crucifixion and ceremonial partaking of flesh and blood in the name of their god, whose cult name is Wazil. But my body shook and jerked inside like a bag of potatoes on a cart, and my stomach sank below my liver and my tongue filled up my throat. My brain buzzed and my hands sweated and my vision was confounded. I thought that I dared not do it, and then that I would. I thought that I could not, and then that I must.

"They offered me to eat, and I was sick unto death. I smiled possessively at my fiancé, and made amorous gestures. And I sat quietly and spoke as though to my ancestors. I wept and swallowed my tears, so that they might not be seen. And all the while I was thinking: I will—I can't—I must —I dare not!

"I knew that I no longer had the strength to act.

---

fore, neither victims of war nor assassination may be eaten, but only such prisoners as are taken intact and butchered according to the rituals of the Cult of Wazil.

"I thought that I would lie with the Ghut chieftain and become his bride—to save my life.

"The adoration of Wazil rose to heights of frenzy.

"The chieftain stood staring out over the campfire at the awful scenes of celebration. He was not two arms' length from where I sat. I thought: Now is the time—but I do not dare! And then I saw, as though from a great, whirling distance, that I had risen from my place. And I saw that I held in my hand a long burning brand from the fire. And I saw him turn, and heard shouts of alarm, and saw his lips break over his teeth, and then I was flying to thrust the brand into his face and beard, and I saw the scimitar in his hand—and after that I knew nothing.

"It was all over very quickly. All in one instant."

Djeela-Lal continued: "My plan was a good one, from beginning to end. The Ghut chieftain was a great lover of women—one who would prefer a lively, loving wife to a helpless body bound to a tree—so he was disposed to listen to me. And he was wildly superstitious, like all his tribe—and so he believed my fantasy of the extra breast and the Cult of Kali. And he was a man of his word—so he let my parents go without sending men to follow them. But he was also an outlaw and a man of action, quick to fight in defense of his life—and so he could not but draw his scimitar and strike when I threw myself upon him with a blazing brand. One thing only did not go according to my plan. I did not die.

"They must have believed that I was dead, or, at least, that I would soon succumb—for my breast was opened up like a mango, and the bone was visible through bright curtains of blood. They had no further use for me, neither as bride to their chief, nor as meat in their ceremonial fires.

"When I came to myself, I was in darkness and silence, like a thing unborn. My wound was one enormous pain like hot metal, yet I could not cry out, nor moan. I did not know where I was, I did not know my name. There were many mysteries that whispered in my head like voices, but I paid no heed. I did not care. I slept again, and woke, and slept again, many times. Perhaps one day, or two, or many, passed. I ask you to think how long it must have taken me to understand—from the little I heard, the less I saw and from my bodily sensations—that I was sewn up in a pigskin and stuffed into a hollow tree.

"I could not move my limbs. I was soaked and caked in my own blood. My head was clear and light and fast as a butterfly in a tree, and would not remain still. The wound in my chest no longer hurt me, and I could feel nothing in all my body. I believed that I heard faint soft singing. Then I drifted into darkness.

"But again I woke. Still I had not died. I have no idea how many times I slept, how often I woke. But I must have been remembering all my past life, as the dying are said to do, because I found myself thinking of Masalh-ji, the cheelah, and even more of our wrinkled, salt-colored old guru, and of the red-pillared temples in the hills by the Indus. And now the singing in my brain was louder. And suddenly I knew what it was! It was the rhythm of my blood in my body!

"All blood is life—said my guru—and blood is Maya. And the blood and the breath are one, and Maya is breath, and breath is life, and Maya is life, and all is Maya, and all is One.

"And I saw that all my body was in Maya, and Maya was all the universe. And my body was one with the jungle birds and the lianas and the scorpions. And I was one with the hollow tree and the pigskin and the scimitar of the Ghut chieftain. And my body was one with the fire, and my wound and the sky were one, and my body was one with Maya.

"And I murmured that prayer which I had heard so many times, but never dared to repeat: the Gayatri, the oldest prayer known to the race of men:

"*Om tat savitur varenyam bhargo devasya dimohi dhiyo yo nah prachodayat Om!*

"First I began to practice certain breathing pranayama, and such of those writhing mudra which I could in the narrow confines of my prison. I noticed no effect but a sense of detachment from my physical self, which quickly became an experience of dualism, as my head began to clear. That dualism is, paradoxically, the gateway to the perception of the One.

"I then began the bhastrika breathing exercises, and my heartbeat accelerated and the blood poured from my wound —so I began its opposite, the chorbharga, and my heart beat only fifteen times each minute, and the bleeding stopped.

"I do not know how long I spent making this beginning— many days, perhaps.

"I then attempted that state of consciousness which, in combination with certain exercises and mantra, has as its object the absorption of Maya into the body—

"And I *succeeded!*

"Without preparation, without study or purifications, without even belief in god, I had achieved a form of Samadhi!

"But I can no more describe this to you than I can show you my dreams written in a drop of water," said Djeela-Lal.

After a moment she went on: "Nor can I describe the days which followed, in which I lived because I had sunk my blood and breath into the ever-continuing rhythm of the universe, and so could not die. I can tell you only that one day I worked my hand free, and made a gap in the pigskin where it was stitched together, and so looked out into the forest grove. I can tell you of life amongst the beasts who crossed before my tree, and I can tell you of life amongst the flowers in the curcuma grass, amongst the big buffalo ants and the iguana lizards. I can tell you of the birds who came to sit in the oil tree—the hornbills crying 'kah, kah!'—and of the chameleons and scorpions that crept on the devil's-harp vines. I can tell you of the bees who came to make honey in my hollow tree, and never hurt me, and of the tiger who came sniffing the scent of blood, and who turned and went away. But of myself I can tell you nothing. About my life in the tree, there is nothing to tell.

"Like breath, like blood, like vitality, Oneness with Maya is now and forever in the body, and the body is god. There is no explanation.

"You would only ask me time after time: How is it that you did not die?

"That is what the woodcutters asked when they found me. They could not believe that I had not died. I saw them enter the forest grove, and called to them in a strange voice. Two men in ragged clothes, they split open the tree and freed me, but could not believe that I had not died. They were from my own village, and told me that for eight days my parents, with parties of soldiery, had searched for me through all the jungle, but had at last abandoned hope. And now I was found. I was black with blood. The bones of my jaws and cheeks were like knife-blades. My hair had half fallen out. My lips were so drawn that I could not close them over my teeth. I weighed less than a child, and could not stand or eat by myself. But my heart beat strongly, and my brain and eyes were clear. I had not died!

"On my breast was a long, serpentlike thing of strange white flesh, which had covered over my wound and healed it. Not long after, it fell off, like a surfeited leech, leaving me without a scar."

Djeela-Lal sat down on her trunk to fasten the little buckles of her shoes. The story was finished.

Bhil Phum inhaled very deeply, and then sighed. "That's marvelous."

"Say, 'unbelievable,'" grumbled Mhraba Daffa.

"So that's how you became a Yogi!" Bhil Phum said.

"Since then, I've practiced assiduously," Djeela-Lal said. "I am not a Yogi, however—only a student of Yoga. But I've gone back and done my best with the early steps, which are supposed to come long before even such a partial Samadhi as mine."

"Teach me!" Bhil Phum said, sitting up. "What would I have to do? I'd love to be a Yogi. Will you teach me?"

"Certainly. But you'll have to work hard at it," Djeela-Lal answered with a half smile. "Clean thoughts, good actions, ahimsa and all the rest. And then of course there are the dhauties. You'll have to learn to clean inside as well as out —a banana and a little water a day, that's all. Water drunk through the nostrils and expelled through the mouth. Several different ways of vomiting, of course. And the baths. I've often stood in the Bodj to my navel and drawn out my lower intestine. And then, the purifications by fire—"

"Oh," said Bhil Phum.

The concubine was ready to leave now, having donned her dress and recombed her hair to her satisfaction. She was buffing her lacquered fingernails with a little brush, when there came an interruption—a snort.

"I," said Mhraba Daffa, "have never heard such a miscellany of deranged, fantastical nonsense in all my life!"

Djeela-Lal waited courteously, but the number-one wife said no more—only sat squat and solid as a Buddha and breathed angrily on the little hairs of her mustache.

Bhil Phum said: "What's the matter?"

"Haf!"

"You mean, you don't believe her?"

"I believe she's a Yogi. Maybe a magician. I've seen with my own eyes! I believe she was in India, and learned something peculiar there—I've seen how she goes off in fits, and how she leads Sidi around by the nose—with Yoga or whatever! But I won't swallow all this gibberish about Ghuts, and Kali, and people starving in hollow trees for eight days with their chests ripped open—and wounds that heal themselves with leeches—and pulling out her lower intestines— *haf!* That's a lot of nonsense. *Ask* her!"

But Djeela-Lal imperturbably said nothing.

"See? She can't answer. There are too many things her pretty little fiction doesn't explain. For example"—she ticked off on her fingers—"how a girl as young as she is knows so much about Yoga when the mahatmas spend all their lives learning it. Or how she goes about making a fool of Sidi—what kind of magic spell she uses on him! It doesn't explain how such a religious person runs after the men all the time, either, for that matter. And last of all, what's she hiding? She hasn't told all of it, not by a long shot!"

The two wives stared hard now at the concubine. Djeela-Lal appeared to think. Then after a moment or two, she said carelessly: "Well, since you insist—all right. That story about the Ghuts was pure fiction."

"I *told* you."

"Shall I explain it all to you in a few words, and at the same time tell you what it is I've been hiding? Have you ever heard of Unendurable Pleasure Indefinitely Prolonged?"

*Now* Mhraba Daffa was startled! *Now* she believed!

"You were a Devadasi!"[21] she exclaimed.

"Yes," said Djeela-Lal. "My parents and I had no sooner crossed into India than I was recruited for the temple at Bahiana."

"I don't see how that explains anything," said Bhil Phum.

"She was one of the 'Wise in Love,'" Mhraba Daffa said awedly.

"Who're they?"

"They are," said Mhraba Daffa, "the surgeons, the researchers, the virtuosi, the sorceresses, the strategists, the professionals and the artists of the act of love. They've studied it ten thousand years. They can kill a man with their bodies!"

Bhil Phum said: "Oh!"

"That's why Sidi is so crazy about her."

---

[21] Sacerdotal harlot. Religion in India is concerned with the three brains of man: cerebral, abdominal and pelvic. The Devadasi are highly trained young women attached to certain temples. Their duty is to relieve the worshiper—utilizing their unique specialized talents— of all possible fleshly desire, so that he might enter the inner sanctum with an unclouded mind.

"Oh!"

"Yes," said the concubine. "That is my magic. I relieve him of his carnal appetites that he may turn his attention to his love. Love is of the spirit. The flesh is not love. In fact, it must be gotten out of the way first. Love is much too grand for the flesh, though it includes it. A sorcery any woman can learn, though few ever do. So that is explained—to your satisfaction, I hope. And now it is also explained how I learned so much Yoga so quickly. By constant observation of countless gurus at their worship and exercises and through daily contact with the wisest men in India. As for your third question, I refuse to answer it. I have no intention of justifying my interest in men. Indeed, what other justification could there be than that the lingam-yoni symbolizes that penetration of spirit into matter without which even Maya could not exist? But now, excuse me, it's time for me to go. I'm already late."

"Where are you going?" asked the still dumfounded Mhraba Daffa. "What if Sidi asks for you?"

"To visit the purser," answered Djeela-Lal. "I must thank him for my new clothes. As for Sidi—I'll handle him."

Then she was gone. The two wives were alone. They sat silent.

After a time Bhil Phum said worriedly: "But how did she mean that about magic? I *still* don't understand."

"Exactly!" said Mhraba Daffa.


FOUR

At Marseilles the group boarded a train for Paris, in which city Sidihnouk exchanged sixteen million, eight hundred ninety-two thousand, fifty-three rhots for two hundred thousand francs, which sum he spent incognito in Montmartre while his entourage awaited him quietly in a small hotel near the cemetery Père Lachaise.

Three weeks later, all together climbed aboard an Air France Super Economy Starliner for the overnight flight to

Washington, D.C., during which Sidi, still convalescent, was repeatedly sick.

Sidihnouk's three little sons, sleepless as nose radar, prowled the ship from one end to the other, from navigator's bubble to tail assembly, all through the long, roaring night. Bhil Phum dozed oppressedly in her reclining chair, full of Dramamine, while beside her the number-one wife sat upright, reading a book called *O Beautiful for Spacious Skies*, an immigrant's primer.

"If we were coming in through the Port of New York, we could see the Statue of Liberty," she said.

"Hum?" asked Bhil Phum dizzily.

"It's a big French woman in a jubbah, with a torch. Here's a picture," said the suffragette. "It means women can do whatever they want in America. They can smoke, and eat with the men, and they don't have to carry the baggage."

"That's nonsense," Bhil Phum murmured. "The men won't stand for it."

"They have to," Mhraba Daffa said approvingly, "or else the law takes their wives away and charges them alimony."

Two seats away, Sidihnouk and his companion were also discussing America.

Sidihnouk talked primarily to distract his attention from his stomach. Even so, every so often the breath went out of his voice and left him staring at nothing, swallowing effortfully. He had a terrible hangover.

The concubine's sole duty in conversation with her lord was to sit quietly and be instructed, and at intervals to susurrate: Yes, Master, in docile and admiring tones—a thing painfully difficult for her, for though she respected Sidi's Harvard-trained intelligence, his store of facts, she had no great opinion of his common sense. Often enough she disagreed with him, and often enough she energetically said so—each time risking rather more than his displeasure. Sometimes he allowed her her opinions. Sometimes they talked together as equals. But this evening she was not sure of his mood. So far she had been neither scarred by the crocodile whip, nor ravished by the official dentist—and now, with America so close, was not the moment to give offense. She had already promised herself that she would watch her tongue.

"You may find them an adolescent people, at least in this respect: that for them virtue consists of an irreproachable sex life. Of course, there's no fanticism, you know. Indeed, it makes them rather loving and tolerant—everyone all together on the same *low* moral level, you see. Every man a sinner, since no one can escape his sex, of course—and sex expression is their original sin. Augustine and the Gnostic Christians, you remember. It's the cause of their national *un*-self-confidence behind the brash façade. Few Americans can see themselves as heroic figures, defenders of the weak, saviors of the world, or even worthy people or good men—because they have this insane, jolly belief that they are all merely pigs in the muck together, and that innocent sex fun has nullified all their excellences."

"That doesn't sound a bit like Americans," said Djeela-Lal, remembering the sturdy and uninhibited U. S. Marines.

"Well, perhaps I am exaggerating. But they are always so apt to ticket and file away a person according to his amorous peccadillos. It all goes to show—morality's a leveling-down, never a cry of 'Excelsior!' A system of universal prohibitions, whose inevitable result is universal guilt."

"The great equalizer."

"Yes, you see? That's Democracy. Everybody just as bad as the next fellow—so you can't very well have overbearing barons and rebellious serfs, the righteous and the unrighteous, nobles and humbles. Instead, one enormous bourgeois middle class, all created equal, and all with the same rueful, cheerful, dirty conscience."

"All pigs together in the muck," Djeela-Lal said.

"Oh, well, no, not really that. I wouldn't go so far as to say that. Every culture needs some standard by which to measure its progress in virtue, whether it's absolute adoration of Imaj, perfect oneness with Buddha, the imitation of Christ, the Correct English Gentleman, or what have you. It only happens that *their* moral ideal is sexlessness, which of course no one can, or *would*, try to measure up to. So the next best thing is that each person consider himself a lovable rascal, a well-meant malefactor, meantime he functions as a diffident, and confessed hypocrite—as he *must*, since his ideal is unrealizable. And it all amounts to the same old thing— *some* sporadic effort toward goodness. That's why any moral code is better than none."

"Curious remarks, from you," Djeela-Lal said unthinkingly.

"How would you like to be torn to pieces by dogs?" asked Sidi in the commonplace, admonitory tone of one who does not make idle threats.

Djeela-Lal put her wrists together and bowed her head slightly—the Phenh woman's gesture of submission to her lord. She knew that she had overstepped the bounds again. They were not in America yet.

"In any case"—she changed the subject—"they should take kindly enough to us, however strict they are. We're all pre-eminently judgeable. By the way, how am I to be explained to the authorities? Mhraba Daffa and the other are all right—just two more pigs in the muck. I mean, I don't suppose the Americans will object to a spare wife or two— after all, they have their consecutive marriages. But you can't enter me as a concubine, can you? How am I listed— as a slave?"

"They don't have slaves any more," Sidi said. "They all walk around free as air now. No, you are listed as a special secretary."

"Oh, clever—to spare their sensibilities. Until we're inside the Embassy, which is Phenh-Tin-Bom in Washington. Then I can be a slave again," Djeela-Lal breathed. "You think of everything."

"Of course," Sidihnouk said, paternally patting her on the leg. "I wouldn't leave you at the mercy of the Yankees—" Then suddenly his face turned a startling gray-beige and he mumbled: "Those paper bags—where did you say they were again?"

"The attendant-woman put a whole box of them under your chair," Djeela-Lal said. "And this time don't forget to put your nose in."

Bhil Phum listened and said: "There's Sidi sick again."

"I wouldn't be a bit surprised," said the number-one wife, "if it wasn't magic. If she wasn't putting a mantra on him, to upset his stomach every five minutes."

"Why should she do that?"

"Haven't you noticed?" Mhraba Daffa inquired cynically. "Whenever she has to go forward to dispose of those sacks, or get him a pill or a glass of water, she spends half an hour forward with the copilot."

Bhil Phum said: "Oh, aren't we *ever* going down?"

A loudspeaker in the ceiling discoursed romantic music from *Mondo Cane*, a motion picture. The air smelled of Chanel No. 5.

And all the dark night long the ship rang and roared, a skating silver noise in the head.

FIVE

A year went by.

SIX

The first time Fergus Bratt rose triumphant from the bed of Djeela-Lal, he danced around it, singing: 'Oi, oi, oi, oi, mazeltov!'

And the concubine watched him amusedly and bade him be quiet.

He was a tall, untidy, jocose young man, by profession a journalist, by inclination a picaresque hero. When people remarked about his strangely kinked and crackly yellow hair, he invariably replied: It's an old family wig. He might have been a swashbuckling adventurer, an excellent actor, or a successful politician. Instead, he was a reporter. He was a little bit too chicken-livered (or imaginative) to be a thoroughgoing opportunist; he was much too energetic and objective to mimic his life away in extravaganzas of self-satisfaction; and he viewed things politic with maximum disesteem. But women liked him. He could talk damply of love and crudely of sex in the same breath, and he was not above that outrageous flattery, flagrantly undescriptive of its object, that women deem most true of all. Moreover, his were those wide, spiky-lashed, almost lidless flashing blue eyes which—like drowsy eyes—are often confused with sex appeal.

Men liked him also. His repertoire of off-color jokes, collectanea of years of bar- and press-room convocations, was voluminous, and his main interests were fun, fight and firewater. A man's man, his handshake was like a vise, his voice was loud, his manner friendly-brash, and his memory a jungle of baseball facts and figures. He ate well and slept well, and his self-confidence was like a banner in the sky.

A happy man. His health was perfect and his muscular wife was in Frontignan, Herault, France, competing in the National High Altitude Over Water Sky-Diving Championships, Djeela-Lal was nearby in the Phenh Embassy, Morgenstern's Hiberny Bar always had a welcome for him, he was paid every Saturday, and sometimes he found precious stones in his pockets.

Several months before he had stopped by the Embassy in halfhearted search of news, and he had remained as a member of the staff. Sidi, who had engaged him, might have explained his presence thus: He was a charming young man, with an amazing provision of droll stories and an inexhaustible fund of good humor, who was familiar with a great number of persons and places in the city of Washington. So he was valuable as a kind of cultural liaison, who expressed and interpreted Phenh-Tin-Bom to Washington and Washingtonians, and vice versa.

His duties were unspecified and various. As confidential secretary, he transcribed all kinds of messages, and as courier he delivered them to a variety of addresses. As intermediator, he preserved the peace between Sidi's women and the various members of the Embassy staff and indigenous employees— whom he also hired and fired. As major-domo he ordered groceries by phone, presented visitors, unstopped toilets, kept the social calendar, opened the mail, and ran the household, meanwhile answering everyday calls for help (Change this bulb, Hook my dress, Where's my sword?) and plucking corks.

As *fidus achates* he accompanied Sidi on his nocturnal rounds, and made straight the way. As public-relations counselor, he displayed the Ambassador briefly on TV, and arranged for Mhraba Daffa to inaugurate two new supermarkets and christen a recommissioned Coast Guard cutter. As cultural attaché he herded groups of Washington schoolchildren through the gloomy Embassy halls to squint at artifacts and witness flickering homemade films dealing with life in the jungles of Phenh-Tin-Bom.

He also aided the Ambassador in his unending campaign against the U. S. Government—that campaign whose entire object was to inveigle that government into financing (without extortion of political, trade or other guarantees in advance) the construction of a small dam at the boggy, steaming headwaters of the Bodj, in order to bring under control that flux's two annual manifestations: drought and flood.

But most of all it was his agreeable duty to abet Sidihnouk— whom he called "Sid" in the booze-fuming, smoke-dizzied sinks which they frequented—in his painstaking reconnaissance of the nethermost side of urban life—to incite and facilitate his whole-hog participation in the Pompeian excesses of a powerful and extravagantly rich nation.

"I have done the best I could—but there are depths of depravity I have not yet sounded," the Ambassador confessed once. "I'll need your help for that, Bratt."

"You came to the right man, Your Excellency," the Attaché assured him.

The fact was, he enjoyed his job. The work, even the late hours and heavy drinking, agreed with him. "Ain't had such pure, undiluted, irresponsible fun," he admitted once in a serious mood, "since my redheaded Aunt Flossy used to reach up my shortpants to pull my shirttails down."

As for money, the Embassy seemed full of precious and semiprecious stones—rubies beyond all reasonable expectations, but also sapphires, small diamonds and emeralds, opals, chrysolites, garnets and other sparklers. They were mounted on lids of coffeepots, on spoons, inlaid in tabletops and chairbacks, encrusted in ewers and combs, cigarette cases and humidors, sometimes even mislaid in gloomy, unswept halls. And no one seemed to miss them when they were gone.

But most of all, there was Djeela-Lal.

The first time he rose jubilant from her bed, he danced and sang around it, rejoicing in Hebrew. He considered that he had fished a pearl of great price.

Since then there had been numberless such joyful occasions, on none of which did it occur to him that he had been seduced.

On this particular afternoon, however, he got up quickly and quietly and dressed himself, while Djeela-Lal did the same, and combed her hair and straightened the bed. "Go put cold water on your lips," she directed him. "They're swollen up." Because Sidihnouk was in the house—napping in his own rooms, to be sure, but too close for comfort.

When Mrs. Rapsnake knocked on the door and entered, the concubine was seated on a cushion playing with a parakeet, and Fergus Bratt sat decorously in a straight chair, his tie up to his chin, and a notebook open on his lap.

"And now, Miss Lal, if you wouldn't mind telling me something about agricultural methods in the province of Kharta?

"Oh, shut up," snapped Mrs. Rapsnake, a native woman employed as housekeeper. "You aren't kidding anybody but Sidi, and when he finds out, he'll fry the both of you in chicken fat."

"He has to catch us first," Fergus said.

"Anyway, I'm surprised at you," the housekeeper continued. "Smart young fellow like you, what a nice Christian home and family you could make, instead of taking up with foreign trash that'll only get you in trouble. And pretty darn tan at that! You know what the folks over the river would say. Tar and feathers! Why, you couldn't marry her if you wanted to!"

"Whoa, hold up, old horse," Bratt said. "Who's talking about getting married? Besides, I got a wife already."

"Well, that's what *she's* after. As if you didn't know! All these foreigners—they just want a chance to marry a nice American boy—and not have to go back where they came from. Anyway, I heard her say so. 'White elephants couldn't drag me back to that stinking swamp,' she said, 'if I have to marry the Secretary of State!' Mark my words, she knows what she's after. She's no wild young thing dizzy with first love."

"You old salaude!" Djeela-Lal raged. "Pack your effects and leave this house immediately! You are discharged!"

"See? Look at her, if it ain't true—mark my words. But, bless you, dearie, I ain't leaving. Number one, you can't fire me—it ain't your authority. Number two, even if you could, you wouldn't, because I'd never leave a good job without breathing a word or two in Sidi's ear. And even if I didn't, you better not fire me, because I'm the only white woman in this house to protect you from these jigaboos cutting your ears off. You can't get along without me, dearie."

"C'est emmerdant," mumbled the concubine.

Bratt said: "That's the word, baby. What'd you want, anyway, Ida?"

"Nothing. Just to ask the Princess if she's seen Sidi's kids —all three of them. They haven't been around all day.

Nobody knows where they are. Maybe they got out of the house."

"Old Phong probably ate 'em," Bratt said. "Come on, I'll help you look. I was just leaving anyway."

Leaving Djeela-Lal at her mirror, he descended the broad, perilous marble stairs with Mrs. Rapsnake.

"And I said to my sister just the other day, he ought to be ashamed of himself, a big, healthy, handsome good-for-nothing like that, to take advantage of a poor girl and her crying need—and he probably never told her he was married, the poor soul. And he lets her give her all and ruin her honor in hopes of getting something in exchange —immigration papers—when all the time he's planning to leave her in the lurch—the soulless cur!"

"Who? What?" Bratt asked.

"You. What I said to my sister."

"Whose side are you on, anyway?"

"It's the same old story. The woman pays and pays."

"What was that about big, healthy and handsome?"

"'Cur,' I said. Does she know you're only trifling?"

"Ida, you're way behind the times. Sure, she knows. Knows more about everything than anybody in this crummy dump, is all she knows. She's *Djeela-Lal*. Listen, when Sidi wakes up, tell him I've got to talk to him, will you?"

"He's awake an hour ago. They're all out hunting for those three missing kids."

"Oh. Well, tell him I'm in the library curled up with a good belt, will you? That's a girl, old horse."

In the gloomy library he went to the *meuble*-bar against the wall and filled two glasses with Scotch—the first to drink off like medicine, and the second to mix with ice and sip meditatively while seated on the stuffed head of a buffalo.

Sidihnouk came in after a while.

"How's a boy, Your Excellency?"

"Good afternoon, Fergus. Are you drunk?"

"No, I just got here. Listen, I've got something on the fire that might be pretty hot. Can you spare a minute?"

Sidihnouk made himself a drink and sat on a thing like a throne.

Bratt said: "You remember those home movies about Phenh we showed to the school kids?"

"In connection with which you were supposed to get us some publicity?"

"Yeah. But that's no good. Nobody wants to read about your place unless it's that the Big Gun is going to let them drill for oil in Sick Cat Country, or wherever it is. Anyway, I don't mean them. I mean those others. The ones the League of Decency wouldn't let you show. You know? About fertility rites in the Bodj jungles, and all that. The ones where they— With all those— And the way they— Jesus!"

"A perfectly serious scientific study of primitive pagan practices among the semicivilized tribes of the upper Bodj."

"Sure. Hot stuff. That's the ones I mean. Well, I think I got a market, if you're interested. I don't mean sell the film—they'll make copies and stills. It's this guy I got to talking to at the Hiberny Bar the other night, and he's an agent for a group of these Fraternal Brotherhoods and Men's Clubs, and all that. The Caribous and Loyal Order of Wombats, B.F.O.B.B. and Hiatus Club and I don't know what-all. They go for that kind of thing. And pay big."

"Yes," Sidihnouk said. "And this agent chap. Does he strike you as a reliable sort?"

"Bloch's his name. Yeah, he's all right. You can deal with him. He's square."

"Of course, I hardly need add—"

"That's fixed too. He doesn't know me from nobody. He thinks my name is Emile Coué. All I do is deliver the film to some roadhouse he knows, and he checks it, and pays me off, and goodnight. Nobody knows anything. I thought of that. These small-time operators always get caught in the end. But when it happens, he doesn't know anything. He probably never even heard of Phenh-Tin-Bom, much less that it has an Embassy."

"Splendid," Sidihnouk said.

"Besides, there's a hell of a lot of this dirty stuff around —we provide the world, like Paris used to do. The cops never mess with it. Even if they did, there's too darn much of it to fix the blame anywhere."

"A sad fact," said Sidihnouk, "an extension of which could lead to the end of morals and morality everywhere. Apropos of that—where are we going tonight?"

"The Third Head," Bratt said. "Ever heard of it?"

"I don't believe so."

"We'll need one of your cars. Even in D.C. they don't allow this kind of goings-on. We've got to go way out in the mountains—but it's worth it. So how about it? Can I tell this Bloch fellow I'll meet him and talk about prices, at least? He'll want to look the merchandise over first."

"Yes, go ahead. I leave it entirely in your hands. And now, if you'll excuse me, I have a difficult and necessary parental duty to perform."

Bratt said: "Okay. I'll meet you back here about seven."

He finished his drink and left the library. The dim halls were aswarm with members of the Embassy staff. Little dark men in voluminous trousers, blue jackets and rayon turbans. All of them seemed to stare fixedly at him. They stood in little groups and whispered.

He put on his hat and coat and prepared to depart from the Embassy. Then he thought: Parental duty? and asked Phong, the Tonk eunuch, who was holding the door for him: "That reminds me. Did they ever find Sidi's three kids?"

Phong seemed also to stare fixedly at him, although with a hint of Oriental irony, rather than inscrutability, in his pinpoint eyes.

"Oh, yes, sir. Most unusual circumstance. Children seem to have spent entire day beneath bed of Miss Djeela-Lal. Most unusual. His Excellency goes now to interrogate."

"Oh," Bratt said.

"Quite," said the eunuch.

### SEVEN

Bratt decided it might be better to telephone first.

"Miss Lal," answered Phong with Oriental inscrutability, "not available this moment."

Bratt hung up.

### EIGHT

He might have decided to go back to the Embassy after all—to brazen it out, to deny everything—to give his word against that of three children, and count on Sidi's friendship. But when he stopped by his room late that afternoon, he discovered that it had been destroyed.

The street was full of fire trucks and police cars. The downstairs hall of the boardinghouse was full of officials, and his landlady was there too, hysterically explaining that nobody, but *nobody*, ever entered her decent, quiet and respectable house without being admitted by herself or old Auchinloss, the maid-of-all-work. Bratt followed the crowd upstairs.

"Lucky you weren't home," said Bob Finch, the bookmaker from the third floor.

"Sh! You don't know me."

He went into his room. The single lightbulb that had hung in the center of the ceiling seemed to have exploded like a gigantic bomb, rattling the place with shrapnel, scorching the walls black, igniting everything combustible and blasting everything else into shards, splinters, chips.

Bratt stood in the wreckage and thought so hard that it seemed his brain must crackle and crepitate, like the little fires still burning in his mattress and bedclothes.

A policeman came and touched him on the arm. "You the tenant of this here room?"

"Press," Bratt said faintly, showing his card. Then he turned and left, white as paper.

### NINE

It was early morning, thin and cold as a starved cat, when she finally located him by calling Morganstern's Hiberny Bar.

"Good morning, Hiberny's Irish Grill, it's half-past five and the joint is closed, Christ Almighty, there's nobody here but me, I'm minding the joint."

"Fergus!"

"Oh. Hello."

"Fergus," she said strangely mush-mouthed. "I've telephoned everywhere. Are you aw-right? I'm frightened. He knows!"

"Yeah," Bratt said wryly.

"You don't understand. He knows about— It was the children. They were under the bed! All day long while we— I can't talk long. They might hear me. The children were—"

"Under the bed," said Bratt, not much less mush-mouthed. "I know. Playing *I Spy*, or *The Secret Sneak*. Yeah. So. That's the way the game goes. Some cards just deal like that. You just plays the cards they deals you, honey, and when your flush craps out, why—why, that's just the way the game plays, baby."

"Fergus. Are you—"

"Who? Me? I'm in mourning. What do you want me to do, celebrate? Yeah. Well, it's been nice talking to you, baby. It's a real pleasure. Didn't we have some good times? That's all in the game, baby. Well, I'll be seein—"

"Fergus. Listen. You fool! Get hold of yourself. I've been sentenced to death!"

"You're not even his wife. What's he worry? Get a claim, or something? Anyway, that's nothing. Old Indians used to cut their noses off when they caught them. *If* they caught them, that is. Anyway, if you've been sentenced to death, why aren't you dead, see? Tell me that!"

"Fergus, I've got to escape from here at once."

"—Calling up at this hour of the night. Morning," Bratt said.

"Listen. Fergus. Listen to what I'm trying to tell you. I have been sentenced to death! This evening they pulled three of my teeth. Tomorrow three more. The next day three more. Until they're all gone. This evening I was given ten strokes with the crocodile whip. The flesh is laid open on my —where they struck me. Tomorrow twenty. The next day thirty. And then forty. Until there's nothing left to whip. Do you understand? I'm dead!"

"Then who's 'at talking?" Bratt said.

"C'est emmerdant," murmured the concubine.

Bratt said: "You mean you're in trouble with Sidi, hah?"

"Yes."

"Pulling out your teeth?"

"Yes!"

"Going to gobble you up, hah, them crocodiles?"

"Do you understand, at last?"

"Sure. All alone there. One little pea in the soup. And you want me to come and get you out."

"Yes. Come quickly."

"Come help you escape from the Em-ulk-embassy?"

"Yes. And soon. Right away. I don't know how you're going to get in, but you've got to manage it. You've got to! Try to find some black coffee first. But hurry!"

"Old Sid going to feed you to the crocodiles, hah?"

"Come. Come!"

"No teeth, hah?"

"Three of my molars. Will you *hurry!*"

"Yeah," Bratt said. Then, although Djeela-Lal continued to talk to him, he held the receiver at arm's length and frowned at it, and thought. He thought very hard indeed.

"Are you listening?"

"Yeah," he said. "Well, now I'll tell you, baby, here's what we'll do. I'll tell you. This is how we'll work it. First of all, just don't worry about it. Just don't worry. Probably all blow over anyway. I got to come around and take you out of there.

Sure. And that's what I'll do. That's what I'll do, all right—
only the fact is, the thing is, it's my editor, the guy I work
for—on the paper, you know. Well, the fact is, my boss is
sending me to cover the World Crisis in Frontignan, Herault,
France. That's what the fact is. So you see how it is."

There was a moment of silence.

"You filth!" Djeela-Lal said.

Bratt held the receiver away from his ear and glowered at
it again. He shook it vigorously. For a long time there came
from it a continuous, soft, poisonous hissing.

Finally he raised it to his lips and said sturdily and quietly:
"Okay. That's okay, honey. Now *you* listen. You know what
the score is. What it always was, with you and me. So what
do you want from me now? True Love?"

And he hung up.

### TEN

Not long after he was on his way by plane to Frontignan,
Herault, France, to join his wife, the parachutist.

### ELEVEN

Djeela-Lal was soaking wads of cotton in salt water and
placing them in her jaw when Mrs. Rapsnake came to unplug
the phone and carry it away.

"Finished?"

"Yes."

"Find him?"

"Yes."

"Is he coming?"

"No."

"Well, I could of told you. Men are all alike. And after me
getting the phone up here, too. If Sidi found out he'd probably yank my teeth too, if I had any. I don't know why I
risk it."

"What do you want, more money?" She had given the housekeeper all she had, and some pearl earrings besides.

"Nope," Mrs. Rapsnake said. "Ain't complaining. How's your backside?"

"Livid."

"Sidi's up. They'll probably be coming for you soon. Kind of a holiday for them."

"No doubt."

"That's what I always say! Them that plays with fire are sure to get burned."

The concubine said nothing.

"I left all the doors unlocked when I came up," Mrs. Rapsnake said. "You ain't what you might call guarded right at this moment. Phong, he's willing, but the flesh is weak. I gave him half a glass of senna extract in his prune juice this morning, and a jigger of ipecac in his coffee—so when he ain't running at one end, it's the other. And he ain't where he ought to be right now. You can get down far as the second floor easy."

Djeela-Lal sat bolt upright on her cushion and stared, forgetful of her jaw.

"The downstairs is full of smokes, though. You can't get out that way. If I was you, I'd go into Sidi's bedroom, soon as he's in the bathroom to wash his teeth. And if you get out on his balcony once, you could climb down the shutters of the French windows easy as a ladder. Couldn't do it myself, but you're young and skinny. I bet you could. Only you got to go fast, before they come to get you."

"Madame Rap—"

"Pish. I brought you Sidi's letter opener. If anybody tries to stop you, stick 'em. Once you get out, you can pry the jewels out of the handle. Sell 'em. Keep you in eats awhile. I'll tell Sidi you made me get in the closet, see? Now watch this."

She produced the weapon from under her apron, and closed her eyes and gouged herself slightly on the chin with it, and began to bleed.

"See?" she said shakily. "Now, soon's I get in the closet, you prop a chair under the knob so I can't get out. But I got to start hollering right soon, so don't waste no time."

Djeela-Lal said earnestly: "Madame Raps—"

"Don't waste no time, I said. Go on, shut the door—and hurry it up before old Phong gets back. Get out in the street and stay in crowds. They can't bother you in a crowd. If they come bothering you, just holler bloody murder so all the busybodies come running, and they won't dare touch you. Go on, now. I'm bleeding like a stuck pig."

The last she said, as Djeela-Lal closed the door on her was: "Darn heathen coons. Always raising the dickens and getting into cutting scrapes."

# The Soldier

*M-Group soldiers who are not killed in action may never be discharged or returned to other units. What they know and what they can do makes them a danger to themselves and to others. Also the strictest secrecy must be maintained. M-Group does not exist. All personnel will submit to memory retraining and physical readjustment before release from active duty. There can be no exceptions.*

He was the exception.

The man came toward him in a stumbling, clumsy rush in defense of person and property, and it looked like slow motion. The soldier wanted to cry out to him, *Don't, I can't stop it*, but it was the hands. The hands took the rush and manipulated its momentum, transferred its whole weight and speed to the man's own arm, and felt the joint grind and go. Then the hands were one locked around the neck, the other through the crotch, the soldier down on one knee on the fallen man's back sweating and crying with the effort *not* to continue on in what was one continuous motion and break the spine.

*Almost almost almost.* The soldier stood over the unconscious man and beat the heels of his hands together slowly and brutally. Then he tried to crush his own skull with them: *Quit it quit it quit it!*

It was a small-town department store. The owner had forgotten something and come back just after locking up at nightfall. He had surprised the soldier searching the hardware section. His automatic reaction had been violence too, but he never had a chance. But at least he wasn't dead. If the pain of his dislocated arm had not made him faint and lie quiet in that moment, he would be dead now. I could not have stopped it, the soldier thought, and bent down and chopped solidly at the base of the skull with the blade of his hand. Goodnight until morning.

He found what he was looking for in a cabinet under the cash register in the hardware section: boxes of .22 ammunition. He used high-speed long-rifle hollow points in his pistol for hunting small game. With the bullets on the shelf was what appeared to be a green plastic rifle stock. Then he recognized it, the civilian version of a rifle used by the Air Force in survival kits. He took it and filled his pockets with ammunition and left the store the way he had entered it, through a small window in the back room.

He was in the alley. He wore sneakers that made no noise. He wore a knit Navy watch cap pulled down over his face and a dark-blue jump suit to make himself a shadow. The alley was dark and quiet and filled with garbage cans. He went along it like a cat, proceeding only a few yards at a time. He saw no one and was not seen.

The quickest way out of town was the way he had come in, along the railroad. It was a very small town, with shade trees and buckled brick sidewalks and pleasant frame houses with yards rather than lawns. Ducking under clotheslines and stepping over wooden fences he came to the tracks, and followed them south. The few lights of the town were soon left behind. Half a mile more, and the tracks curved back toward the river.

A footpath led down the embankment into the woods, to an old hobo camp with a fallen tree and fire-blackened stones. The night was dark, no moon and no stars. The soldier sat down on the fallen tree to watch his back-trail. He put his hard hands on his knees, and a fit of shaking seized him. *That man had almost died.*

He never took his pistol along with him on night forays, so as not to shoot at anyone if caught. But he could not leave his conditioned reflexes behind wrapped in an oily rag in a waterproof bag. Violence went with him everywhere like a second nervous system superimposed on his own—violence triggered by any danger, any surprise, almost any sudden noise or move. They were synthetic reflexes, but he could not control them, and their purposes were not his own.

The exact metaphor had occurred to him a long time ago, nor had his predicament improved at all in the meantime. He was still a prisoner in a skin-tight invisible suit that kept trying to kill people.

When the fit was over he picked up the AR-7 and removed the butt cap and took the several pieces out of the hollow stock. The weapon was like a toy. The action screwed onto the stock, and the barrel screwed onto the action, and made a toylike .22 rifle with hardly any weight at all. In fact, with the hollow stock, it would float. It fired eight shots semiautomatically and was made of plastic and alloy metals, so it needed no care or cleaning to speak of. He could even carry it assembled underwater, if need be. There was a funny little peep sight and an adjustable front blade-sight. He brought it to his shoulder a time or two, but trying it out would have to wait for daylight and someplace far away from there.

As he handled the weapon the thought came to him slowly that he might soon need it for something other than small-game hunting. Its advantages over the .22 pistol were obvious. The longer barrel gave it a better sighting radius and a higher muzzle velocity, a harder strike. This did not make it a combat weapon, but it helped. Men died easier than most game. He would not use it till he had to, but then he would. The police did not worry him, but when M-Group came it would not be with arrest warrants and handcuffs. M-Group would come to kill him.

He was the exception. And now they would know he was not dead. For five years he had been skillful and careful and amazingly lucky. He had kept to the woods, no living soul had seen him. A handful of unsolved burglaries in widely separated towns, and a few cold campsites, were all that marked his passage. But now that was over. In one day he had been seen twice. When the storekeeper told his story they would put it together with the swimmers' story, and soon they would come. And they did not want him alive.

It was midnight. The gathering rumble in the distance was a train coming. The soldier judged he had watched his backtrail long enough. He took the rifle apart and stowed it, and went through the brush to the river shore. At the edge of the water he stood listening for a long time, until the train had gone by and all was quiet except for night noises and the soft rush of ripples over stones. Then he took a plastic bag from his pocket and undressed. He put the watch cap and the jump suit with bullets in its pockets into the bag. The rifle would not fit in, but he had already decided that the water would not hurt it if he wiped it off afterward. He tied the rifle and the bag to a cord and hung them around his neck to have his hands free. Then he stepped into the river, naked except for his sneakers.

His camp and the rest of his few possessions—the pistol, a machete, his bedroll, some food and other odds and ends— were waiting for him in the thick woods on the opposite shore. Thinking, *What I really ought to scomp sometime is a set of swim fins,* he crossed the river, swimming half a mile underwater along the stony bottom.

One trick at least M-Group had not taught him: how to hold his breath. They were onto him now, of course, but that didn't mean they had caught him yet.

*Extract from 201 file: BURNS, Corporal, RA 51139618; MOS 13 dash 7; TOP SECRET: Prior to recruitment evidenced unparalleled pugnacity in special training; prior to which showed marked tendency to violence during basic training; prior to induction had record six arrests assault and battery, one conviction; prior to which juvenile offenses, assault; prior to which history of aggressive behavior, childhood.*

(His name was Poody. He had freckles and a small mean mouth. He came up to me after school and said: "You got funny color hair. Lemme feel your hair."

He grabbed my hair and I ducked and dropped my books and ran, ran all the way home with my heart pounding. My eyes were filled with despairing tears. Why should anyone hate me?

Joe was my friend. Joe was only a teddy bear but I clung to him long after I should have outgrown him. I loved him so much it made me cry sometimes. I wondered what was the matter with me that I cried about a teddy bear. A hunk of stuffed fur.

Joe and I were sitting on the porch in front of our house. It was almost time for supper and I was waiting for my mother to come call me to come in. It was still light and the birds were flying to nest and I said: "Joe, what would you do if you could fly?"

"Why, I'd carry you Out West and you could be the only cowboy with a flying horse. You could fly way up high and see the Bad Guys on horseback down below in the gulch, and instead of going all the way around the mountain you could fly straight over the top until you were right over their heads *zoom* in your ten-gallon hat, and shoot them right out of the saddle with your pearl-handle sixguns, and take the gold they stole back to town. And there'd be people there, your mom and pop and all the kids from school, waiting to see you come down out of the sky, but you wouldn't come down. You'd drop the gold right at their feet *plunk* and ride away in the sky. *Then* they'd know!"

Joe made me happy.

"Joe," I said, "what would you do if you had a skillion dollars?"

"Why, I'd buy a house and a bicycle just for us two, and a big ship with sails and a hundred men to be crew who would jump right overboard to the sharks any old time just because you said to. And we'd sail up to this old town and shanghai some of the people we like and some of the people we don't like. And the ones we don't like we'd throw them in the brig and make them walk the plank, and the ones we like we'd give them lots of money and let them be First Mate. Then they'd be our friend."

"Joe," I said, "pretend you were the best fighter in the world. What would you do?"

"Why, I'd walk around this town minding my own business, and the next time somebody said my hair was funny color—Poody!"

Poody and two other boys were coming down my street. Why did they have to come down my street? Why didn't they go down their own street? It was twilight and nobody else was around. I had to go in to supper anyway. I got up and started to go into the house and Poody yelled: "Hey you!" He was running and the other two boys were coming behind him. I was in and I shut the screen door smelling the rust and dead flies, but Joe was lying out on the steps and Poody came up panting. "Hey you!"

"Look at the teddy bear. Big sissy."

He kicked Joe with the side of his foot.

"Come on out, Rome, we won't hurt you."

I wanted Joe. Joe was mine and I did not want Poody to

kick him again, so I went out. I reached for Joe but Poody grabbed him.

"Is this a real bear? Arrr, I'll wrestle him."

Tugged. Joe's ear. Poody ripped and tore at him *arrr* and the old seams popped and gave. "I'll kill this old bear, *arrragh!*"

Threw Joe down. He stamped him. I ran down and grabbed Joe and Poody grabbed my hair, rattled me all over, but I had Joe, I had Joe, and it didn't matter.

Poody growled and tugged Joe but I held him tight and then Poody bumped my chest always shaking shaking my head my whole body till I couldn't see couldn't hear until I swung Joe as hard as I could and hit Poody in the stomach. It didn't hurt Poody but Joe's head came off.

Shaking my head by the hair. I dropped broken Joe and hit him. Hit him hit him. He let go my hair and stepped back surprised and the other two boys laughed and said: "Hey Poody, I wouldn't let him do that to *me!*"

Poody hit me and I ran at him but I couldn't see and he threw me down and my head hit the sidewalk. Poody sat on me with his hands on his hips and started to laugh. Then his eyes squinted and his mouth twisted and he began to cry. Then he was mad. He started to hit my face. Cried and hit my face all wet with my own tears, and Poody tried to hit my head on the sidewalk again but he was crying too hard. I thought I was being killed. I thought he was killing me the way Joe and I killed people we didn't like, but his fists were like milkweed pods popping on my face. Then my mother came out of our house and said: "Get away from here, you boys, I'll call your fathers."

Poody and the other two boys ran away. My mother held my head until I stopped crying.

"Mama, is my hair funny color?"

"That shows you'll have plenty of brains when you grow up."

"They broke Joe."

Mother washed my face. "Don't tell your father you cried."

We had chicken croquettes for supper, and after dessert I asked if I could go to bed.

"What's the matter with the snotnose now?" my father said.

I was all alone in bed without Joe. It was still light outside. I remember watching the last blue-green turn to purple in the sky out of my window. I heard a lady's heels tick-tacking down the street, faint at first, then loud, then right under my window then going away again.

When I was a child.)

*Take that fateful one step forward and raise your right hand. Swear. Into a column of ducks and board that bus. In a single file into that building and sit down there. On these papers at the top in the right-hand corner where it says name write your name. Your last name first your first name last, check where it says married if married, your age, height, weight, place of birth, race, and file through that door.*

*Stand up there and put your chest against that bar and take a deep breath and hold it, hold it, that's all. Lift your arms, squat, bend your knees, hop, hands on hips, jump. Turn around and bend over spread your cheeks, peek, on your toes, flex your fist, cough, breathe deep once, twice, let's see your feet, now drop your drawers and skin it back, one time, two time, okay.*

*Line up there. Keep this sheet. Does that fit? Try these on. What size waist? What length legs? What size sleeves? What size neck? That ain't too small, you're too damned big, come back next week. File out that door and board that bus.*

*File off that bus, fall in this barracks and grab a bunk. Turn that fart-sack inside out, tuck bottom sheet in at the top, top sheet in at the bottom, square all four corners, square those blanket corners, fold that dust-hood halfway down, braid together toward the foot. Now gather round here, at ease, pay attention, turn in all cards, dice, razors, knives, and sleep with your wallet if there's anything in it, and here are the regulations about AWOL and desertion . . .*

Their first day in the Army and their first night in camp, the recruits were exhausted by processing and the long bus ride and then more processing. Now at last it seemed they could go to bed.

But then Sergeant Trask came coldly storming into the pine-board barracks looking for someone to take it out on.

He was the battle-hardened veteran of several wars, and was only here because on the occasion of his last re-enlistment he had signed up for R.T.C. duty, confusing it with R.C.T. His furious anger at finding himself in a Recruit Training Center instead of a Regimental Combat Team blackened his bile and aggravated his natural sadism.

"Fall out of those frigging bunks and stand so stiff your peckers point!" he roared. "Atten-*shut!*

"My name is Sergeant Trask and all you need to know is I am *God!*

"You disgusting shits have been in this barracks only fifteen minutes and already it is a filthy frigging *pigsty!*

"You *will* procure brooms, mops, scrub buckets and G.I. soap from the latrine!

"You *will* scour down this floor until I can see reflected in it the pimples on my ass!

"Also rafters, walls, windows, stairs, bunk frames, rifle racks *and* butt cans!

"I will return at exactly twenty-four hundred hours, and if this barracks is not shining clean, you *will* perform close-order drill on the parade ground until— . . .

"God bless my soul," he said. "What have we here, a glass of milk?"

His attention had fallen upon a strikingly pale figure standing in the dim light like a phantom. Along with most of the recruits, he wore only drawers. His skin was extremely fair and his hair was so white he looked bald. Except for the odd black pupils of his eyes he might have been an albino. Then the Sergeant noticed that his fingernails and toenails were shiny black too.

"Well, bust my britches! What kind of frigging freak are you?"

There were loud guffaws from the recruits.

"Come tell me, pussycat. Are you trying to pass for a *white man?*"

More guffaws from the recruits.

I asked you a *question*, soldier!" Sergeant Trask said.

The freak said: "Burns, Rome, Private, RA 51139618."

"Rome *Burns?*" the Sergeant said. And then repeated, quivering with astonishment and joy: "*Rome Burns?*"

Then this happened:

The Sergeant received an unexpected punch in the mouth. It was a good punch, solidly delivered. It would have felled a lesser man. He was smashed back against the plank wall, and his mouth began to bleed. A gruesome enjoyment possessed him instantly. He could have told the freak his mistake: Always keep on, with fists, feet, elbows, teeth. Win, or don't fight, he could have said. Instead, he assumed a peculiar stance.

"A little lesson. A little lesson," he murmured. His hand flickered invisibly quick. The barracks was silent. Frightened, the recruits watched. They saw the freak fall groveling, unable to breathe, then rise again, the Sergeant bounding on toes and heels, and there was no movement in the barracks except for their dance.

"Freak. Get up," the Sergeant said.

He moved close again. And again. The third time the freak fell, it was limberly and relaxed. The impact of his head hitting the floor splashed blood from his butchered face.

"Freak."

No response.

"You're excused from scrubbing the barracks," Sergeant Trask said to the sickened recruits. "Reveille at six hundred hours," he added.

He felt enormously better now.

*This is the U. S. General Purpose Rifle M-26. Trigger-housing group, stock group, barrel-and-receiver group, con-*

*taining follower-arm pin, operating rod and operating-rod spring, follower and follower slide, clip release, gas-cylinder lock screw, gas port, gas cylinder, and bayonet stud.*

*Here it is at the ready. At port. Pree-sent. Right shoulder. Left shoulder. High port. Here it is slung. At ease—out.* Atten-*SHUT*—*grab it in: bang! Pee-rade rest. Pop it out.* Atten-*HUT! Oooright sholda-HUUNHS! Ah-one, two, three, four! Now you try it.*

*Ready ona right? Ready ona left? Ready ona firing line? With one-round ball ammunition lock and load. The flag is up. The flag is waving. The flag is DOWN! Targets-HUP! Commence firing!*

*BOOM-BOOM-BOOM-BOOM-BOOM-BOOM!*

"Permission to speak to the Company Sergeant."

"Well, if it ain't my friend Freak, the human punching bag," Sergeant Trask said. "Speak, Freak, what's on your mind?"

Bloodshot eyes peered between swollen black lids in a swollen face like an eggplant. Thick crusty lips said: "Burns, Rome, Private, RA 51139618."

"I'll just call you Freak. After a fellow I know who tried to take a poke at Tiger Trask. How would that be?"

"You mentioned a little lesson."

"Freak, I thought you learned it. Howsomever, I'd be pleased to work them eyes over a bit more. Or wherever it hurts worst. Down behind the depot suit you?"

"I ought to warn you," the freak said. He took a fifty-cent coin from his pocket and quickly bent it almost double with his thumb and two fingers.

Sergeant Trask laughed in his battered face.

"Just so you know," the freak said.

Twenty minutes later he was down on hands and knees in the dusty grass and gravel squirting blood and vomit from his mouth and nose. But he had seen everything Sergeant Trask had done.

Four days later. Behind the depot.

"Freak," the Sergeant said, "I know you been on sick call a couple of times. Much as I enjoy it, I wouldn't like to think our little daily calisthenics was interfering with your basic training."

"This is it," the freak said.

The second week of basic.

"Are you conscious, Freak?"

"Yes."

"What's the matter now?"

"Rib, I think."

"Lucky I didn't hammer it into your lung. It's your own fault, anyway. I can't get at your face any more. You're catching on, Freak."

"Burns, Rome, Private, RA 51139618."

The fourth week of basic. "All right. Okay," Sergeant Trask said. "*Burns*. Private Burns. Rome. No more Freak. This has gone far enough. Soon I won't be able to jazz you around any more. You're getting too good. When I fight, I fight to win. I'll have to kill you."

"You'd better," Burns said.

In the sixth week of basic training, Sergeant Trask felt the first clutch of mortal fear.

"Permission to speak to the Company Sergeant."

*Forward MARCH. Totherightflank MARCH. Leftflank MARCH. Totherear MARCH. Column-right MARCH. Column-left MARCH. Hip hawp, hip hawp—and HALT, hunh, hoo!*

*Flip them packs and line them up and stack them weapons, file from the right. First two squads take your places, odd men firing, evens loading. Cheek resting on bumper tube and right hand on pistol grip and left hand on traversing wheel. For a runaway weapon you twist the belt, watch out that spring has the strike of a twenty-two, and grip that bolt handle thumb down soldier and you'll lose your thumb. Commence firing: BRAP BAP BAP BRAT TAT TAT TAT, CEASE FIRE.*

*Fold this back pack this way pack flap that way, edges folded in six inches and ropes laid across there, pegs lined up then roll from this end tight up to that end, fold in corners, tie that middle to this hook strap that shut, hook them back hooks to these holes, that hook left of front this hook right of front and canteen next, bayonet left side then field dressing and poncho in between cartridge pockets and fall out in platoon formation square off helmet liners.*

*On your bellies, troopers, down, DOWN! that's live ammo, that's real bullets! Keep your head, your ass, your elbows DOWN! Through the mud, watch them weapons, under the wire and up and at 'em—UP! Firing from the hip, don't be scared, two four six, over the fence, one three five, hurl grenades: BANG BOOM! Over and over and over again, and now that's all let's move out. Turn in all ammo, line up quick and dress right dress and square those liners, all right men, ten-HUT!*

*Right FACE! Right shoulder—HAHMS! Fow-waaad HAARCH! Hip hawp.*

*Bup bup.*

*Hup.*

*Fawp.*

*Your pants are loose your shoes are tight, your balls are swinging from left to right—sound off.*

*One, two!*

*Sound off!*

*ONE! TWO!*

*Dress it up, dress it up there—let's see you strut, soldiers—marching from the hips down, arms swinging six to the front and three to the rear and keep in step you ugly bastards! Heads up! Shoulders back! Walk proud—you're SOLDIERS now! Hip, hawp—three four—*

*AND HALT!*

*Right FACE.*
*Order   HUUNHS.*
*At EASE.*
*And fall out and pick up your unit assignments and travel orders from the new Company Sergeant.*

"Our old Company Sergeant is still in the hospital," Captain Nivens said. "He's disfigured for life and may be crippled too, I hope you're satisfied. Oh, yes, we know all about it. Did you think we didn't? The only reason you aren't in Leavenworth right now is there weren't any witnesses.

"Did you think we didn't know? Is that why you left him lying out there, so we'd think he got hit by a train? He almost bled to death!

"Everybody in the company knew you and Trask were boondocking it. The only reason I didn't stop it long ago was I was sure Trask would kill you. I still don't understand it. By all rights he should have. And the only possible explanation is that he was right all the time, wasn't he? You are a freak!

"Watch it! Hold it! I'm warning you, there's a .45 in this desk and I've got no compunctions about using it. As a matter of fact, see for yourself. And it's loaded, too. So don't try any of your tricks on me. You just stand there and listen. I didn't send for you for the pleasure of your company. You're a freak, your platoon leader says you have this inhuman strength. Personally, I'd exterminate you like a mad dog, but it seems the Army has a use for the likes of you. That's why I sent for you.

"This is your new assignment. Regulations say you get a chance to refuse to volunteer. You've been recommended for Special Forces training. That's guerrilla tactics, jungle warfare, and dirty fighting. They're supposed to be elite. They're a bunch of maniacs. Just your speed. All I can say is, I hope to Christ you get killed. You can refuse if you want."

*Extract from 201 file: BURNS, Corporal, RA 51139618; MOS 13 dash 7; TOP SECRET: Upon completion of basic training assigned to Special Forces Camp Condor; acquired advanced infantry skills; completed paratrooper school; unarmed combat; demolitions; sabotage; survival; checked out universal weapons course; checked out universal vehicles course; promotions: Private First Class to Corporal. Disposition: fit for all S.F. duty assignments. Comments: see copy of special medical report attached F.Y.I.*

*Copy: Memo Chief Medical Officer 1st Bat. to Commanding Officer 1st. Bat. Special Forces training unit, Camp Condor: Charley, I can't find anything wrong with this fellow, except a lot of recent facial scar tissue and a broken nose. The funny color is some kind of albinism, or maybe melanism, but there's no indication of skin cancer or abnormality. There is something unusual about the lungs, but it is merely a case of congenital anomaly, with no evidence of disease or malfunction. In any event, it's already shown on his medical record, and he's been passed as O.K., fit for duty. As for the extraordinary physical strength his former C.O. mentioned—what's the problem? Isn't that just the kind of boys we want in Special Forces? If he's a freak, tell the rest of your P.X. commandos to go and do likewise.*

So now he wore a beret like a Girl Scout and carried a thin little knife in his boot and another up his sleeve and a throwing knife down the back of his neck even when he was in dress uniform. In full battle garb he also carried a machete and a bayonet. For firearms, a custom Colt National Match .45 auto in a belt holster, a snub-nose .38 Smith and Wesson Combat Masterpiece in a shoulder rig, and an M-47 GPR or General Purpose (semi/full automatic) Rifle at high port. In the field or on jungle maneuvers he also carried grenades.

His fellows were similarly armed, with allowances for each man's personal taste.

For instance: Devil John. He was a black-hearted, bitter-minded half Polack, half Creek whose merciless anger was directed at everybody, including himself. He was the sort of man who could, and did, carve splinters and thorns out of his flesh as though paring an apple. Early in training he had been bitten by a rat in the swamps, and quick as a wink had seized the rat and bitten off its head with a wrench of his jaws. Newer recruits would not believe this, but it was true. Devil John's favorite personal weapon was a trench shovel honed to razor sharpness.

For instance: Hippolito. The "Hippo" was a swarthy, fat-padded man whom no amount of strenuous exercise could trim to less than 280. There was plenty of muscle under the fat, but Hippo preferred ambush to hand-to-hand combat. His specialty was getting the first lick in by surprise and then beating his victim scientifically to the point of death. It had happened more than once during training to squadmates who had crossed him somehow. He used knuckle dusters and a lead-and-leather billy.

For instance: The "Professor." There is a professor in almost every outfit, someone who speaks with precision, or is able to spell, or perhaps merely knows something no one else could be bothered to learn. This one was a man who had raised the science of savate to high art. He particularly favored the *coup de pied*, practicing jumps and kicks so often and so hard that he was the next thing to permanently airborne. His feet were trained to such a pitch of excited readiness that he could hardly bear to walk on them normally. He wore steel-toed boots and Ace bandages around his ankles all the time.

For instance: Igor. His real name was a thicket of unpronounceable consonants. Once he had served in the merchant marine of some Baltic nation, where they still told stories of his escapades. After that he had been aboard a British merchant, till he punched his way barehanded out of the brig and had to be trapped in a cargo net and dumped ashore before he wrecked the ship. Igor had no need of special weapons. For fifteen years he had soaked his sailor's hands in pure formaldehyde and rubbed them with pumice, until either one was a lethal mace, a dead-weight maul of inch-thick, iron-hard callus, capable of crushing stones.

And so on. These men, and others like them, made up the platoon. The Fourth Platoon of C Company, First Battalion, Special Forces, Command IV, Camp Condor.

Upon completion of its training program, that Command was combat-ready and awaiting orders.

Orders were expected any day now, and the rumor said: Cambodia.

The note said: *I'm ready for my revenge now. Rosy's. Trask.*

"We thought that would bring you running," the little man said, "without mentioning the matter to anyone."

"Trask isn't here?"

"As far as we know, he's still in the hospital. That was just a ruse."

"Then I guess you'll have to stand in for him," the soldier said.

"Wait! Wait!" the little man said. "Let's admit you can mangle me. Will it hurt to listen a minute first?"

Rosy's was a dingy bar and grill on a back street in the only town anywhere near Camp Condor. The little man looked exactly like Mr. Taxpayer in the editorial cartoons. No one else was in the place except Rosy and an old dog under a table, and they were both asleep. Meanwhile all the flies in Dixie came and went through the open door and a hand-lettered sign said forever: NO TRUST.

"How did you know about Trask?" the soldier asked suspiciously. "How do you know who I am?"

"We have our methods," Mr. Taxpayer said, and then said: "Oh Lord, the clichés! Never mind. Believe me, it's nothing nefarious. We simply want to talk to you—that is, my organization wants to interview you, through me. There's no harm in that, surely? I'm authorized to tell you anything you want to know, absolutely. But first, will you agree to a small injection?"

"A what?"

"A shot."

"Of what?"

"A drug."

"No."

Mr. Taxpayer looked at him peevishly. "It would make things so much easier if we didn't have to use force."

The soldier laughed. "It would make things very hard if you try," he said. "I've just got done being trained not to let you get within striking distance of me unless I'm sure I can kill you in six seconds. At that, I couldn't shake hands with you, or light a cigarette for you, or let you light mine. And you want to give me an injection?"

"You won't permit it under any circumstances?"

"No."

"There's no possibility of changing your mind?"

"No."

"Rosy," the little man said.

Instantly Rosy brought the three-pound sandbag down with exactly the right force.

"I don't know how she even moved without me seeing her, let alone got behind me," the soldier said some minutes later, after a whiff from a phial had cleared his head.

"Rosy has been trained too. Training such as you G.I. judo experts never dreamed of," Mr. Taxpayer said. Rosy went back to the bar and apparently went to sleep.

"What was in the injection?"

"We had to give you two. One is simply to prevent violence until the interview is over. Don't bother to test it. It's a sort of chemically produced hypnotic command. You can't possibly attack us now. Your psyche won't let you."

"Maybe later," the soldier said.

"The other was the one I wanted to give you in the first place. Its only effect is to make you receptive to posthypnotic suggestion, even though you aren't hypnotized at all, as you see. That would defeat our purpose. On the other hand, if you and I don't come to an agreement, we'd rather you forgot the whole conversation. The drug is just to make you responsive to a suggestion to that effect."

"Amnesia on demand."

"Yes, very right," Mr. Taxpayer said. "And I'm sorry about the blow on the head, and I can understand your hostility feelings, but the rules are, we can't so much as identify ourselves until we have control of your memory. Both drugs will wear off in an hour or so. In the meantime, I'm happy to say, I'm authorized to tell you whatever you want to know."

"Just warn me when the dog is going to do his trick."

"What? Oh, I see, ha, ha," Mr. Taxpayer said. After a while he said: "You mean you don't *have* any questions?"

"You wanted to talk to me. I didn't want to talk to you."

"Yes. I see," Mr. Taxpayer said again. "Apparently this isn't going to work out at all. Do you mind if I go ahead just the same? I ought to complete the interview. I'll be as brief as possible."

"Suit yourself."

"Thank you. Well, to begin with, I represent an organization know only as M-Group. That comes from *Mordgruppe*, of course, and that's the reason for the deathly secrecy. The world must never know that we exist! And yet our hand is everywhere, we strike from nowhere, out of the night, in silence and in stealth. Aren't you in the least interested?"

"I was keeping my eye on Rosy."

"Rosy won't hurt you again. She's a Sub-5 basic operative, conditioned to attack only on command, or in self-defense. But to resume, aren't you interested in why we picked you? We thought you'd be perfect material for M-Group because of your natural aptitude for violence. Not only that, but you're psychologically suited—a loner, a *Waldganger*. Cold as ice and twice as hard. Plus, you've been professionally trained to maim and kill. Plus there's your great physical strength. We don't know much about that, by the way. Do you?"

"No. I've always had it."

"Yes," Mr. Taxpayer said. "The best our physiologists can suggest is that it has something to do with your lungs. They think they're just different enough from normal to be more than normally efficient. Either they extract more oxygen from the air you breathe, or make better use of it, because more of it gets into your bloodstream, so there's more available to your muscles. Does that sound right to you?"

"I wouldn't know," the soldier said guardedly. "I never thought about it."

"I don't think it means much anyway. Strength per se doesn't matter after the training we give you. Which reminds me—doesn't that interest you either? I mean, you may think you're a crack fighting man now, but believe me, M-Group training will make you invincible! Wouldn't you like to be the deadliest mankiller who ever stalked the face of the earth?"

"No."

"Strange, I'd have thought you would. Never mind. It's a rotten lousy life anyway, you're better off out of it. A rotten lonely life in between jobs, penned up like a mad dog in a cage, and the jobs are worse! I mean, it's not so bad when they're ex-Nazis, or a menace like El Grandissimo. And maybe you don't mind so much when you have to poison a devil like Papa Doc Devigny to save thousands of poor souls from torture and slavery. But when you have to slit the throat of some nice old fuzzy-wuzzy whose only crime is *patriotism!* And all he wanted was a few more yams for his *tribe!* And on top of that you have to mutilate the body to make it look like *terrorists!*"

"Tom M'vubu," the soldier said.

"Meanwhile the C.I.A. gets all the *credit* and Special Forces gets all the *glory!*"

"It's a hard life."

"Exactly. Always creeping ashore somewhere in those wool pullovers that smell like a wet dog! Or jumping out of airplanes with a hundred pounds of blasting equipment! Or hanging around with the centipedes in some godforsaken ballata camp waiting for Borman!"

"Why do it, then?"

"Says you! You haven't any idea how hard it is to get out, once you're in. Just like the old-time movies where they won't let you quit the rackets. Take the amnesia, believe me. You're far better off. Now, if you'll just concentrate on my tie clasp while I count to ten—"

"Wait. Hold on a minute," the soldier said. "How would you arrange it about Special Forces?"

"You mean you accept?"

"It's better than Cambodia."

"I thought you would."

"Not for the reason you think," the soldier said. "Let's get one thing straight. I suppose it doesn't make any difference, but if you really got all my records, then you must have noticed. I usually lose."

"How's that?"

"It's funny," the soldier said. "When I was a kid, I used to get beat up all the time, because I was different. Then, six times in civilian life I let fly at people because they just would not let my color alone. But five of those times the other fellow got back up again and beat hell out of me so bad *he* had to pay the fine. Even Sergeant Trask beat up on me darn near daily for six weeks running before I got to him once. Strength doesn't mean anything. Neither does unarmed combat training. I'm just not much of a fighter."

"M-Group thinks otherwise," Mr. Taxpayer said.

"I've never even fought except for that reason."

"Anyway, that's not my problem. All I'm supposed to do is recruit you."

"Just so you know," the soldier said. "What about Special Forces?"

"That's easy. You're AWOL now, aren't you?"

"Yes. Because of that note."

"Then don't worry about a thing," Mr. Taxpayer said. "It's all taken care of. You're dead already."

"At that, you come off better than I do," the Professor said one hour later in the closed car that took them to the airstrip. "Being dealt a martyr's death by the K.K.K. because of your funny color, my word, that's positively meritorious! I, on the other hand, was knifed to death by an unidentified whore in the alley back of Slippery Dick's while Under The Influence! Jolly well makes one wonder, though—where do you suppose they get the bodies?"

"I wouldn't put it past them," the soldier said.

In another hour they were high in the air in a shark-shaped unmarked fighter-bomber, streaking at 1700 mph toward Someplace, S.A. And an hour after that they were strapped down on adjoining tables in a spotless laboratory.

"We don't waste time here. Your training begins as of this moment. It will consume three days. During that time you will not be released from these tables. It is for this reason that you will note intravenous feeding apparatus among the instruments attached to your bodies. I trust I need not explain the diaper-like garment?

"The orientation which follows is not simply for your information. It is to prevent irrelevant anxiety reactions from interfering with instrument readings. You will be told only as much as is necessary for your peace of mind. To wit:

"You are presently assigned to M-Group Base Camp and Training Unit Number Four. The rules for awol and desertion are simple: Don't. This camp is surrounded by one thousand square miles of swamp, jungles, crocodiles, vampire bats, break-bone fever, and savage headhunters.

"During training you will be in my complete charge. My code name is Frankenstein. It is my job to turn you into effective M-Group operatives. Upon completion of your training you will be released to Mr. E. for final processing. He will assign you to your shakedown mission.

"Training is accomplished by placing you in a profound hypnotic state for three days through the use of drugs. Other drugs will be used to increase your receptivity, accelerate your responses, enlarge your learning capacity, et cetera. While you are in this state the standard M-Group Sub-3 Training Program will be inserted into your brains.

"This is not, repeat not, like hypnopedia. Neither is it like brainwashing. Nor, to anticipate still another question, will you become mindless robots. Your personalities will remain unchanged. You will not actually know anything you do not already know. The Sub-3 Training Program consists merely of 21,800 commands. These commands cover every phase of M-Group operations, tactics and strategy. High-speed transcriptions of these commands will be played back to your unconscious minds. Drugs will make them a part of you.

"Once correctly implanted in the mind, these commands have the force of irresistible posthypnotic suggestions, or uncontrollable conditioned reflexes. The question is merely one of terminology. I myself have coined the word 'Prods' to describe these preconditioned reactions. However, it does not seem to have found favor.

"Be that as it may, forever after you will react accordingly. For example, certain Prods will control the exact way in which you enter a darkened room. You will obey them automatically. Prods will also take over when it is necessary for you to operate an unfamiliar weapon, demolish a bridge, booby-trap an automobile, decipher an M-Code message, or stalk a victim in any terrain or circumstances. You need not concern yourself with the techniques involved. Your built-in Prods will do the job. Relaxing mental control will help, but it is not necessary. The Prods are outside your control.

"Similarly, your motor responses. Prods will cause you to react in certain ways to certain stimuli. For instance, a noise behind you will cause you to spin around in the approved defensive crouch. Within a radius of four feet from your body, a sudden move on the part of any person will trigger an immediate countermove. This will take the form of a full-scale attack, using the method or combination of methods best suited to the situation. Since this too is outside your control, I must caution you. M-Group Combat Training has nothing

to do with boxing, wrestling or other sports. You will be conditioned to kill.

"Further caution. Certain imperfections are unavoidable.
With only three days at our disposal, we cannot implant Prods
sophisticated enough to make fine distinctions. For this reason,
as M-Group operatives you will live in near-complete isola-
tion between missions. When this is not possible, keep away
from people, and keep people away from you. On missions
you will work alone, or contact only enemy, so there is no
problem. In the rare case of tandem operations, such as your
shakedown mission, extreme care must be exercised, or you
will kill each other. Remember the four-foot radius.

"To anticipate one final question: No. I regret to say that
M-Group Training is designed to produce killers, not lovers.

"Now I think we are ready. In fact, a timing device has already begun metering the first dosage of Damitol 2-L into
your veins.

"You are beginning to feel very drowsy . . ."

"Wot price peace of mind now?" the Professor said.

"If you speak again, you will get a big, large electric shock,"
a genial voice said. Then the lights came on and things began
to happen. Their two tables stood slowly on end and the
clamps and straps released them and they stood totteringly
upright. A section of the wall slid back and inside was a shelf.
On the shelf were two paper plates, and on each was a hot
dog, some pickle relish, and a small scoop of baked beans. Beside each plate was a glass of milk.

"First things first," the genial voice said. "Keep away from
each other. Remember the four-foot rule. And then—eat
hearty!"

Both men discovered they felt starved. It took only a
moment or two. Then the wall slid shut again with a clank.
Nothing else happened.

The two glanced at each other warily. Each wondered
what the other was like now. Not being able to talk was
torment, and particularly the Professor's lips actually trembled

with the strain of suppression. At last he whispered: "I say, old man, are we really bloody murderers now, do you suppose?

"*Oww, oww, oww, oww, oww!*"

"Come on, fellers," the voice said. "You ought to know by now we aren't fooling around. I'll be with you in two shakes flat."

So they stood and waited.

Finally another section of the wall moved, extruding a thing like a steel telephone booth. Inside the booth was a heavy-set man with a paper bag over his head. Piercing blue eyes looked at them through ragged holes, and the genial voice said: "Sorry to keep you waiting, boys, but I just couldn't find my gol-derned mask.

"I'm Mr. E.—your boss, is all you got to know—and I've got some good news for you. You both came through fine!

"You're all programed and ready, and I know you're going to do a bang-up job for us, so let's not waste any time. I'll be telling you about your assignment in a minute or two, but first let me give you a word of advice.

"This here only applies to your first mission, what we call the shakedown. It's sort of like a trial run to make sure everything is hunky-dory. 'Course, we can't take a big chance like that without plenty of precautions, and that's why you're working together for this one time and one time only.

"You see, either one of you is programed to kill the other at the first sign of defection. That's one precaution. Just in case the training didn't quite take.

"Then there's a third party, who will remain unbeknownst to you, but he'll be watching you both every step of the way. That's the second precaution. First sign of trouble— *zzzzzt!* He isn't programed to listen to a lot of lengthy explanations, and you won't have but three seconds, so don't make any moves that might be misconstrued.

"I guess that's all, fellers. Now, let's see what we got for you."

They watched him press a button, receive a sealed envelope

from a slot in the interior wall of the booth, rip it open, and read the contents.

"Well, now," he said. "I had a feeling this job was coming up. 'Bout time, too. Just let me sum it up for you with a little background. I guess you men can appreciate the strategic importance of Gibraltar, even in this nuclear age, right? Right! And the British being stiff and sticky and high-horsey about it, right? Right! You just can't deal with them. However, we already *know* we can with the Spaniards, if the price is right, right? Right! So what could be more logical than Geographical Unity for Spain?

"Of course!" he continued. "But the thing is, when will the British get out of Gib? Why, only in their own sweet natural time, right? Right! And when will that natural time come? Gentlemen, I ask you—remember the legend. *When the last monkey is gone!*

"Need I say more?"

Mr. E. paused impressively.

"Gentlemen, your first assignment for M-Group is: *Assassinate those monkeys!*

"Your equipment will be delivered to you here," he finished matter-of-factly. "Your plane will be ready for take-off in about an hour."

Suddenly the Professor began to sputter.

"I've got to! I've got to!" he yelled, hugging himself and stamping his feet. "*That'll teach those Limeys to monkey around with Uncle Sam!*

"OWW, OWW, OWW, OWW, OWW!"

They were alone.

"I'm getting out," the soldier said.

Instantly the Professor squeezed his eyes shut and hunched his shoulders as though waiting for a loud bang. When nothing happened he opened his eyes again and blew out his breath with relief.

"I just wouldn't say things like that, old bean," he complained. "How can I know what I'm rigged to do to you?"

"Nothing. Not for just talking about it."

"Yes, but you didn't know that when you spoke. I might jolly well have biffed you."

"Maybe it's a bluff."

"No, no, not at all likely. I'm afraid I take these people very seriously indeed, don't you?"

"I don't care. I'm getting out."

"Give my regards to the vampire bats."

"I don't mean here, or now. In Gibraltar, if that's the first chance. Or whenever and wherever I can. Are you with me?"

"Oh, no. Absolutely not. What a question!"

"You mean you consent to this horror?"

"It's better than the bats."

"I was wrong, so *wrong!*" the soldier said. "When we finished basic training, we were ready to go. To *kill* people, I thought. So I volunteered for Special Forces. Anything to prolong training. Then that was over, and we were going to Cambodia! M-Group looked better than that. They can teach me to kill, I thought, but they can't make me do it. Little did I know. How *could* I know? Maybe I was a fool, I don't deny it. *But they made me a murderer!*"

"I say, wasn't there a movie—?"

"I can't kill anyone."

"Nonsense. You can't *not*, now. And anyway, you can break in easy on the monkeys."

"Listen," the soldier said. "I've fought people. And tried to hurt them, too. And done it, once or twice. But I've never killed anyone. Maybe I would in defense of my life. I know I would try. But I will *not* be a tool, a butcher—a *robot assassin!* I am going to get out of this. Whenever I get the chance, whatever I have to do. *That* I swear."

"Quite right, old boy. And I must say, even though my dear old Prods wipe you out when they catch you at it, I do wish you all the best of luck," the Professor said.

"Just so you know," the soldier said.

Soon after that the wall slid open again, and on the shelf was their equipment. It consisted of two suitcases, two passports in their own names, a large bottle marked VENENO-BOKU-GIFT-POISON, and a number of tourist guides to Mallorca and Gibraltar. In the suitcases the soldier found clothing, toilet articles, and American Express traveler's checks. Also in each suitcase was a Sturm Ruger Mark I .22 target pistol with bull barrel.

"I think I'll just hang onto this," the soldier said, loading a magazine and feeding it in. "I might get a shot at Doctor Frankenstein."

But the Professor was reading one of the guidebooks. "Hullo," he said. "I *thought* that fellow was mistaken. Look here. They aren't monkeys at all, they're apes. Barbary apes. No tails, you know."

Then the two men looked at each other in surprise as a dulcet, disembodied voice in the room said: "Passengers for Mallorca, attention please. Your flight is now loading on the runway."

Their flight was somewhere high over the Azores.

"Preposterous. Perfectly preposterous. I mean to say, old man, don't you find this whole thing becoming the least bit preposterous?"

"Yes," the soldier said.

"Perfectly preposterous," the Professor complained. "All I can say is, if they're testing out our initiative as well as our conditioning, I'm due to come a cropper. I haven't the skinniest idea how one goes about assassinating a colony of apes! Do you suppose that's all we're going to get by way of instruction—a bottle of poison?"

"Yes."

"And why Mallorca? Not that I've any objection. Delightful place, I understand. But why not Gib? And what about the Great Unbeknownst? We are supposedly under his constant surveillance, are we not? Ergo, it must be the pilot. There *is* a pilot somewhere aboard this thing, wouldn't you say?"

"Yes."

"Old bean, you're not giving this your all."

"I was thinking about something else."

"In sum," the Professor said, "why are we going to Mallorca—how are we to get from there to Gib—what are we to do when we get there—and how do we get back—to where?"

"This is your pilot speaking," a voice said loudly.

"By Jove!"

"I'm not supposed to speak to you at all," the voice said, "but a fellow Britisher in distress, and all that."

"You've been listening, then. Are you our, how shall I put it—our chaperone?"

"He's one of yours. *I* wouldn't be one of yours for all the tea in China," the voice said. "No, you're considered safe anywhere above five thousand feet. You'll pick up your contact somewhere along the line—he'll pick *you* up, I should say—before the actual operation commences. He'll get your instructions to you somehow, I imagine. Incidentally, Mallorca *is* a delightful place. Pity you won't see it. We touch down on Isla Dragonera, just offshore. Secret landing strip, you know. I can't take you any further. You'll need a more suitable bird for the drop on the Rock."

"Oh, God, parachutes," the Professor said. "At night, I suppose."

"I suppose," the voice said. "Your friend is very quiet. Hasn't he any questions?"

"He's feeling rather thoughtful just now, aren't you, old boy?"

"I've got a question," the soldier said. "How come you can hear us?"

"It's a speaker and microphone all in one, there on the compartment wall," the voice said. "Why do you ask?"

"Because," said the soldier. And wrenched it off the wall and pulled the wires out after it.

"*Blast* you!" the Professor said. "What did you do that for?"

"I have to talk to you without him hearing."

"Damn it all, I was having a wonderful time. Do you

know, that's the first time a real Englishman ever took me for a real Englishman?"

"Listen," the soldier said. "Where do you think our contact is right now?"

"Haven't the foggiest. Isla Dragonera?"

"I'm betting he's not. I'm betting he's already at Gibraltar. Where else could he be, if he has to keep track of us? He's not this pilot, and he won't be the next one, either, because he'd lose us when we jumped. And it can't be someone waiting on Isla Dragonera, because then he'd have to come with us. And I'm sure E. meant we'd never even see him—unless he had to kill us."

"Well, I'm just as sure Mr. E. said he'd be with us every step of the way."

"That's exactly what I'm talking about. He can't! How *could* he?"

"I don't know *how*, old boy. I just know I take these people very seriously indeed."

"*I* don't. It's a bluff. And you know what that means."

"*You* say it, old man."

"I'm getting out. At the next stop. Which leaves—"

"I can't imagine what you're driving at."

"Which leaves only you."

"I thought that's what you were driving at."

"I might have to kill you."

"My dear chap. After all those fine words?"

"Just so you know."

The Professor smiled thoughtfully. "If you're wrong, of course, there won't be any problems, will there? I mean with the Great Unbeknownst for my reinforcements, and all? On the other hand, supposing you're right. My word, that should be interesting, shouldn't it? You versus me. Do you know, oddly enough, I rather think I'd like that."

Mallorca, *L'Illa de la Calma*, where even venomous insects lose their sting, is crossed by a single mountain range which runs all the way from populous Cabo Formentor in the northeast, to the wild cliffs of S'arrago in the southwest. Dragonera, the islet, like an afterthought, rises in the sea a kilometer or two off these cliffs—one more mountain, perhaps 800 meters high, long rather than wide, and with a lighthouse at either end.

In those years the islet was uninhabited, for no one cared to live there, not even shepherds, and the two beacons were operated by radio and serviced only twice a year.

Besides the two lights, the only other feature shown on maps of the islet was a second-class road that ran between them. While no one was looking, and with the connivance of the Spanish Government, this road had recently been widened, leveled and resurfaced, until it provided sufficient runway for high-speed fighter-bombers like the one which had just touched down upon it and then roared away again immediately.

"Adios, and hasty bananas to you, old bird," the Professor said as the roar faded. The two men stood alone in the warm night on the high spine of the islet, hearing only the seawind in the pines and wild olives on the slopes below.

They could see a few twinkling little lights westward where Mallorca lay. To all other sides, far below them, was the Mother Mediterranean, and high above was the immense starry sky. "A night to make one feel infinitely small, if you like that sort of thing," the Professor said.

Then, as though there had been no interval, he resumed their earlier conversation: "Because, you see, I have a slight advantage over you—my rather specialized footwork, don't you know, and the valuable experience of having used it to kill. Whereas, you have your extraordinary strength, which effectively balances that, so we are on equal terms again. A fair fight. That's why I said, it should be interesting. Like the gingham dog and the calico cat."

The soldier was looking at him in the starlight. "Do we have to?"

"Old man, if it were just the two of us! But then there's our Prods, remember?"

"You're the closest thing to a friend I ever had."

"God pity you, then."

"And look at us now. If I make a move to desert, your reflexes will try to kill me. But you'll have to enter my four-foot radius to do it. Then my reflexes will try to kill *you*."

"Just don't make that move, old chap."

"I've got to. Don't you see the horror of it now?"

"Murder by conditioned reflex."

"Yes. I'll have to *kill* you."

"To keep from being a murderer?"

"Yes."

The Professor sighed. "Well, I just don't see the point of it, I suppose. Even if you managed to get away, you'd still be a robot assassin, wouldn't you? A tiger amongst lambs, so to speak?"

"I'll hide out for the rest of my life."

"M-Group will track you down."

"Then I'll kill them too."

"Oh, that tears it," the Professor said. "Now you've left off making any sense at all."

"I know," the soldier said.

They stood in silence for a while, facing each other alertly, in vaguely defensive postures. Finally the Professor said: "Assuming you do wipe me out, old chap—"

"Yes."

"Well, I just wanted to say, goodby, you know."

"Goodby," the soldier said. "I'm sorry."

"So am I, I think. And now—shall we get on with it?"

Instead, the soldier suddenly ran backwards several steps. "Wait a minute, wait," he said. "I'm still only talking about it. Do you feel anything?"

"No. Should I?"

"Not until I make the actual move, I guess. Watch me— I'm not moving at all, am I? Listen to me for a minute. Maybe we *can* beat this thing."

"How?"

"We know you're preconditioned to attack me if I try to

desert—all right! But does that mean even if you have to commit *suicide?*"

"I certainly hope not!"

"Well, then, listen a minute," the soldier said. "Because that's what it *would* be. It's not a fair fight. *I* have the advantage—see? Yours is still in your suitcase. *But I loaded mine and stuck it under my shirt!*"

"What an unspeakable cad!"

"Do you feel anything now?"

"*Bitter* disillusionment, old chap."

"Don't you see? If you move—I shoot! Even your Prods know that. And you *can't* be conditioned to commit suicide. So you've *got* to let me go! We've beaten them, right?"

"Wrong," the Professor said unexpectedly. He was pointing out and down over the steep descent. "Because there come my reinforcements. Which makes you wrong twice tonight."

It was the white flare of a gasoline lantern hanging in the stern of a small boat approaching the islet from the Mallorca side. When the soldier looked, the Professor said: "Wrong thrice, old bean. You glanced away."

And his feet came flying.

One steel-toed shoe knocked the Ruger into the darkness. The other struck the soldier on the breastbone with a thud like a mallet. Both men went down, the Professor up first, the soldier rolling toward him, snatching at his ankles, but missing them. Then hurling himself up, driving with his head at the Professor's groin, but missing that too, and falling again —the Professor's knee moving trigger-quick, aimed at the ear, or temple.

"Got you!" But the soldier dropped sidewise, tumbled feet over head on his back, and came up standing.

"You didn't follow through."

"I've only got to stall till my reinforcements arrive, old chap," the Professor said. The white light was already nudging the shore of Dragonera.

"Get out of my way. Let me go."

"Can't possibly," the Professor said. "Oh, I am feeling it now. How *extremely* odd! Make a move, won't you, so I can see what I'll do?"

"He's coming up!"

"Exactly. And to escape, you have to go past me. But you can't attack me, can you? I'm outside your four-foot radius, don't you see? And that would be murder, wouldn't it?"

From far below on the slope a powerful voice hallooed. *"Vhere is you?"*

"The gun!" the soldier said. And dove headlong. The Professor dove too, quick as reflex. They hit the ground at the same spot almost together. But the gun wasn't there.

"Tricked, by Jove!" the Professor said. Too late. The soldier was underneath him, reaching up. Then both legs were locked around the Professor's waist, bearing down on the hipbones, and both arms were locked beneath the Professor's chin, heaving upward with enormous force. It was more than a stranglehold, or a scissors. It was the *Nobiru*. The soldier began straightening his back. The Professor began to die.

*(It didn't hurt Poody but Joe's head came off.)*

Suddenly the soldier screamed. Not hard or loud, but with a single sustained *eeyeeyee* sound like the shriek of brakes.

The thought or remembrance had come out of nowhere, but in that moment it was everything.

*Stop it! Stop it! Stop it!*

He screamed through clenched teeth, his whole body exploding sweat. With the gigantic effort of a man hoisting a boulder in his bare arms, he began slackening his hold. Each fiber of muscle, each tendon, seemed to require its own separate command. Each minute movement was a superhuman act of will.

The scream continued—on and on and on. Till finally it collapsed in a rush of air from his lungs as the crossed forearms and then the locked calves at last let go.

First he thought it was too late. The Professor's tongue

stuck out blue-black and his eyes were blind staring red knobs, as he rolled free and lay completely still. Then he wheezed hideously, and began breathing again. He was not dead.

*Almost*, the soldier thought. *Almost, almost. But I beat them.*

Meanwhile, the scrambling on the slope and the crash of brush and the powerful halloo were coming closer.

There was no time to search for his own pistol, so he seized the Professor's suitcase, which contained the other one, and clothing and traveler's checks as well. Then he ran.

As he went over the edge a startling idea occurred to him. The Professor might have killed him. He might have killed the Professor. Maybe that's why the contact was here instead of in Gibraltar. *Maybe this was our shakedown all the time!*

The rock-rattling, brush-whipped, bone-jarring descent took three minutes. He dropped off ledges in the dark, collided with bushes and trees, slid on his back down gravelly steeps, and fell and went end-over-end dozens of times, clutching the suitcase. At the bottom he was bleeding and battered and bruised, just this side of exhaustion. But far in advance of any possible pursuit.

He went straight to the boat. It lay floating in a reflected puddle of hissing white light only a couple of yards offshore. The lantern was the sort the Mallorquins use for netting fish at night, although she was not a fishing boat. More like the soggy remains of some antiquated pleasure craft, with a tiny engine in her stern.

Whether it was the Special Forces Universal Vehicles Course, or some reflex planted in his brain by M-Group, he did not know, but he had no trouble starting the engine, hauling up the concrete-filled bucket that served as anchor, then backing off from the islet and swinging the prow to point toward the nearest land, a kilometer or two away. That land was now faintly visible against the sky. Dawn was coming.

It was daybreak when he chugged into the Puerto de Andraitx. The voyage across from Dragonera and then down the coast had taken a little over an hour. During it he had had time to lash the tiller, wash himself off with sea water, put on clothing from the suitcase, tuck the Ruger into his belt, and conceive a daring plan.

He still had one trick left which neither M-Group nor anybody else knew about. If it worked, it ought to put them off his trail forever.

The boat entered the sheltered little port passing close by the Mola, or jetty, a half a causeway built upon giant sunken stones. In the clear early light the Puerto de Andraitx was like a still pond of incredibly blue water. On one shore was the fishing village of the same name, and on the other a few villas. All around rose hills covered with olive and almond trees and pines and rocks.

The village came right down to the water. In fact, the waterfront was its main street. Two or three broad-bottomed fishing boats with stubby masts and centerboard engines were moored there, opposite a row of tightly shuttered beige and white buildings, most of which seemed to be bars. On the wide street between the boats and the bars, fishing nets had been spread flat to dry. Except for a dog nosing the nets, there was not a sign of life.

Then three men came blearily down the sandy slope of an alleyway between two buildings. They wore baggy trousers and corduroy jackets, berets and rope sandals, and carried wine bottles. The soldier shut off his motor and drifted toward shore, watching them. One was yawning uncontrollably, another kept scratching his crotch, the third was singing tunelessly and with explanatory gestures. They saw him too, but Mallorquins are pleasant drunks, and they only waved happily and forgot him.

They crossed the street and walked out onto a little stone dock. At the end, some twenty yards out over the water, they stepped into what looked like a wooden lean-to. Then they came back again one at a time, buttoning their trousers.

All right. So be it, the soldier said to himself. What better place to die?

His boat hit the landing with a gentle crunch. He heaved the concrete bucket overboard and broad-jumped awkwardly ashore. It felt good underfoot. He was no kind of sailor. Then he thought of something, and let himself fall heavily to the ground. "Help," he said, though not very loudly. Just in case there were other witnesses around besides the three drunks, who had not even seen him land. They were wandering away down the street, yawning and scratching and singing.

Might as well get started. There was no point reconnoitering the village. He already knew all he needed to know. With feigned pain he raised himself on hands and knees and began crawling crippledly. Keeping close to the water he crawled along for several minutes. An old woman dressed entirely in black except for an apron made of ticking came out of her house in time to see him arrive at the little stone dock. She gave him a falcon-like stare for a moment and then yelled dismissingly: "*Es'tra fotút!*" And set a bucket on her head and marched off down the street.

He was halfway out to the lean-to when he realized he was hungry. The last time he had eaten was on the plane, a food-pak meal of chocolate drink and fortified oatmeal cookies. He should have thought of drinking water too. But going back was risky now. He might not have enough time. They would be coming soon.

He did not try to fool himself that they would not know where to look for him. From the heights of Dragonera they could hardly have missed seeing him beating his way down the coast toward Puerto de Andraitx. Nor could the islet have held them long, boat or no boat. No doubt they were on their way already. It might take an hour, or two, or even three, depending on how they solved their transportation problem. But they would be there soon enough.

Up above in one of the narrow lanes of the village a motorcycle woke with a shattering *ROWWR, put, put, put.*

Here and there in the beige and white buildings shutters were thrown open in second-story windows. A man in shirtsleeves came out of one of the bars and stood with hands on hips looking at the sky. The doors of houses opened and women emerged carrying cloths to flap or pots of charcoal to set on fire and then fan furiously. The morning sun burned down on the village dusty-white and already scorching hot.

From his point of vantage the soldier watched Puerto de Andraitx begin its day. From where he crouched he could see everything that happened and watch the entrance to the port too, and it did not smell too bad, except for the row of black sea urchins someone had laid out on the stones to rot. He could be seen from shore, but the wooden lean-to gave him good cover, whereas anyone approaching him was wide open. So far so good. Now there was nothing to do but wait, and let things happen.

The man in shirtsleeves was setting out little tables and chairs in the street in front of the Miramar Bar. Inside, another man was lighting the gas burner under the café exprés machine, and a woman was scattering sawdust. Two doors down at the Bar Bodega the same sort of preparations were taking place, and three doors up at the Puerto Bar too. Just in time for the leisurely rush of men in corduroys and berets wanting hot milky morning coffee.

Between the bars, little food shops were opening up. They all had clattering bead curtains at their doors to keep out flies. In the street, women greeted women and men greeted men in Mallorquin like dogs barking. A dilapidated old truck came along sprinkling water from a tank to lay the dust. A motorcycle towing a two-wheeled cart filled with fish bounced by, its driver tooting a tin horn. Down the road that led into the village came a matched pair of Guardia Civiles wearing capes and patent-leather tricornes, carrying slung rifles.

The street was busy now, and little conversations were occurring here and there. Two men were standing together at the edge of the water, and one was saying: "It is not a vessel of this pueblo—perhaps from Bañalbufar?" The three drunks were telling a group of men: "We saw him standing in the boat, all white like a phantasm." And the old woman with a bucket of water on her head was saying: "It is a stranger, who goes on all fours, and even now is hiding in the Meadero Municipál."

When the two guardias were informed, they took the matter without seriousness. The intruder was obviously a foreigner, and foreigners in summer were pardoned and permitted all sorts of tonterias. Nevertheless, one of the pair, Guardia Llopis-Puig, decided to walk out on the dock to inquire, at least, if assistance was needed. Guardia Sagrera waited at the Bar Bodega, eating an ensaimada.

What happened next has been told and retold in Puerto de Andraitx ever since. Guardia Llopis-Puig was halfway there. Suddenly a shot rang out. "*M'cauen diu!*" He hit for shore like a sloop in a squall, his cape whip-cracking behind him. At the Bar Bodega, Guardia Sagrera tipped over the table he sat at and dove for the nearest doorway, wrestling with his Mauser. With the horrors of war ever fresh in their minds, the people of Puerto de Andraitx vanished from sight with a clattering of bead curtains and a slamming of shutters and doors. A few seconds later there was only silence and settling dust, and a hawk circling high overhead.

Just then a gray Mercedes Benz crept with costly noiselessness onto the scene. It halted in front of the Miramar Bar. Two men in gray uniforms dismounted. One, the driver, wore the galones of a sergeant, the other the epaulets of a captain. "Policia Armada," said the voices behind the shutters. The dreaded *Grises*.

Guardia Sagrera emerged from his doorway, and Guardia Llopis-Puig rose from behind the toppled table. They glanced at each other, and then saluted the approaching captain. Standing exposed in the open, as though heedless of the marksman in the pissoir, they began to explain in rapid, glottal Mallorquin.

Guardia Sagrera said: "The entire incident began but a few

minutes ago, mi capitán. There has been no time to evaluate the situation or prepare a report. Upon entering the village we were informed that a stranger who came in a boat this early morning has taken possession of the village convenience. It may also be that he is wounded or ill. At this very moment we are on the point of investigating, with your permission, of course."

Guardia Llopis-Puig said excitedly: "May she go herself and investigate herself your one-eyed great-grandaunt, m'cauen diu! I got *shot* at!"

"It is true that he is armed," Guardia Sagrera said. "A shot was fired. I believe it was a warning shot, or my companion here would not be telling it. Unless it was a very poor shot. Nevertheless, you see the problem, mi capitán. Investigation will be difficult. The position is unapproachable in safety by land or sea. Of course, one might riddle the convenience with concentrated fire, and *then* investigate."

"Call a gunboat," Guardia Llopis-Puig said. "*Blast* the cabróon out of the water."

Haughty in his gray uniform, coldly attentive, pointing his chin at one man and then the other and pursing his lips sagaciously, but not understanding a word, the Professor listened. Finally, with a peremptory gesture, he silenced them. Motioning to them to stay where they were, and to his driver to follow him, he strode across the empty street. Behind the shutters the voices said: "Que pasa? What's happening now?"

The soldier watched them come. He had recognized the Professor immediately. The other, the sergeant, could only be their contact. Then he saw the huge dangling hands, and recognized him too. The Great Unbeknownst was Igor.

At the foot of the dock the Professor halted. He stood still and made no suspicious moves.

"Hullo, old chap. You wouldn't get itchy-trigger-fingered, would you?"

"Just don't come any further than you are."

"Oh, we'll get to that part soon enough, I expect. Only, I simply had to ask: Did you really think you could get away?"

"I would have made it. Except I broke my ankle coming down the side of Dragonera."

"So that's it. Igor said you dropped past him at something like the speed of light. Even so, old bean, we were close behind you all the way. You wouldn't have gotten far."

"How did you get off the islet?"

"Rubber dinghy, old man. One of those lighthouses is an M-Group supply point, wouldn't you know? Then we caught up some more time by hitting straight across and driving down the coast while you were yachting it. Igor had the car, of course. And these uniforms, too. All part of the plot. I say, did you know only one of us was ever supposed to leave Dragonera alive?"

"I suspected it."

"Yes, all part of the plot too, old chap. Weeding-out, don't you know. Bye the bye, I must say, for a moment there you jolly well might have weeded *me* out, with that bear-hug-type thing. Why didn't you?"

"*You* know why."

"Because you can't kill," the Professor said, taking a step forward.

"Except in self-defense."

"Rats," the Professor said, stepping back.

Igor approached and said: "I killink desertor now."

"Couldn't we do without *him?*"

"All in order, old chap. Igor's been with M-Group for ages. As a matter of fact, it was he who recommended both of us back at Camp Condor. I daresay that's why he's got this terrific *thing* about you now. Point of pride, you might say. His ideas are fairly hideous. In fact, old boy, to spare yourself the worst, I quite urge you to let me do it, since it has to happen."

"Not *your* way either," the soldier said.

"What can that mean? Surely you haven't a hope?"

"No."

"Some daring rescue in the nick of time?"

"No."

"A dazzling hairbreadth escape?"

"No."

"A last desperate gamble?"

"No."

"Well, then. Why not just stand up in the open and get it over?"

"Not a chance," the soldier said.

"Now, see here, old man!" the Professor said exasperatedly. Behind him the people of Puerto de Andraitx were seeping into the street again. The two guardias were becoming thoroughly baffled, and Igor was bored. "We can't stand here all day. Do resign yourself. You can't move a step out of that delightful lair of yours—whereas, we have only to back off and mow the whole affair down. So don't be ridiculous. The game is over. I'll give you just *ten seconds* to stand up and take it like a man."

"Will you?" the soldier asked sadly. "Will you give me ten seconds?"

"What?"

"You said ten seconds," the soldier said. "Time enough to do it myself."

"What?" the Professor said again. "I don't believe you."

"Then watch," the soldier said. He stood up quickly. The pistol was in his hand. He swung it to point at his own head just above the ear, and pressed the trigger. The sudden startled clamor of the people on shore almost drowned out the small-caliber report. Then the body went over backwards into the blue water and sank like a stone.

*MEMO. From: War Department, Memorial Division, G.R.S.G. 159, Records Section, Washington, D.C. To: Clerk in Charge, War Department Annex, Delaware Project. Subject: BURNS, Corporal, RA 51139618; MOS 13 dash 7; TOP SECRET.*

*Reactivate retired file and reprocess as follows:*

*(A) Original date of death superseded. Revise to read: Transferred from Special Forces this date; assigned to M-Group. Authority: SECWAR.*

*(B) Killed in Action, 16 June, Mediterranean Theater. Authority: M-Group. No casualty report provided. No information provided.*

*(C) Revise to read: Missing in Action. Authority: F.D.I.*

*(D) Incorporate new data supplied by F.D.I. See enclosures.*

*F.D.I. Statistics and Records Branch—to War Department, Memorial Division. Attn.: Liaison Office. Sorry about confusion after so many years. But if recent report is verifiable, you have a deserter to hunt down. And we have a serious deviation to deal with. Regret to say we are handicapped by lack of cooperation your Department. Our inquiries concerning organization known as M-Group have been ignored or answered to the effect that SECWAR is fully cognizant. Meantime, field operations are under way. Our teams are combing the area of the sighting. Will advise if new information is forthcoming for processing by your annex of the Machine. The attached documents will fill you in to date.*

*ATTACH ONE: Field report, New Hope Local Agent 516, to F.D.I. Headquarters, Washington, D.C. I saw this item in the weekly newspaper here, and wondered if HQ thinks it's worth checking out, or if it's just some more junk like flying saucers. This town is full of screwball artists. Clipping enclosed.*

*ATTACH TWO: F.D.I. Files Section, to F.D.I. Investigations Section. ROCKY: Our Local 516 sent this clipping in with his routine report. It is probably nothing, but I thought you ought to know. Jack Trask, one of our file clerks, happened to see it, and he says the unusual description exactly fits a man he knew five years ago in the Army. There can't be many people who fit a description like this, so I thought I had better bump it up to you, in case you want to take some action. If the story is true, then this is really a deviation of the first water, ha ha. PETE.*

*ATTACH THREE: Photostat copy of clipping from page-four feature section of August 6 edition of New Hope PICAYUNE-TATLER:*

## MOVE OVER, JERSEY DEVIL

### —HERE COMES MR. MERMAN
*SUMMER VISITORS SEE APPARITION IN DELAWARE*

*Two popular summer residents were in for a shock while enjoying their favorite sport of skindiving off Wolff's Wharf yesterday. They saw a Merman!*

*The two men were Mr. Abel Morgan, of the Lafitte Guaranty Trust Company of New York, and Mr. Jon Scrumble, President of the Institute for Advanced Study in Fine Arts, a correspondence school. Both men are expert skindivers and have all the latest equipment. "We plan to visit Grand Bahama next," they said.*

*According to their report, the Merman was seen swimming rapidly downstream carrying a plastic bag. "He was dead-white like a fish belly all over, except for black fingertips and toes and weird black eyes. He swam just underneath us and rolled over and looked up," the two men said. They added, he was not using any kind of diving gear and was naked.*

*The Delaware is deepest close to the Pennsylvania side, and this is where the apparition was seen, at a depth of 12 or 15 feet, the men said. There were no boats or other swimmers in the water at this time, and nothing was seen on the surface or from shore.*

*Not since the latest appearance of the so-called "Jersey Devil" has there been such excitement and speculation in Bucks County.*

*"All we know is, whatever it was, we never want
to see it again," the two men agreed when asked if
they planned to continue skindiving activities in the
Delaware.*

So:

They were onto him now, of course, but that didn't mean
they had caught him yet.

One trick at least M-Group had not taught him: how to
hold his breath.

Thinking, *What I really ought to scomp sometime is a set
of swim fins,* he crossed the river, swimming half a mile
underwater along the stony bottom.

His camp and the rest of his few possessions—the pistol, a
machete, his bedroll, some food and other odds and ends—
were waiting for him in the thick woods on the opposite
shore.

But the night was not over, not yet. It still held one more
surprise in store for him. That is, the early dawn did.

He rose dripping and stood chest-deep in the shallows
expelling an endlessly long breath in complete silence, his
mouth wide open. Then he waded quickly ashore. For a
long time he stood in the cover of the woods listening, but
heard nothing, except night and river noises.

Cautiously he picked his way inland for a few yards,
lifting briars and branches out of the way of his naked
flanks. By feel as much as by sight he found his landmarks,
and then his camp.

There was nothing to be seen. Like all his campsites, this
one had been chosen for its inappropriateness. It was not
even a clearing—just a certain spot near a certain tree. He
had not survived hidden in the woods for so long by leaving
tracks and traces.

His equipment and possessions were cached in a hole in the
ground covered with a lid of leaves and branches. Everything he owned was wound tight in his bedroll and stuffed
into a larger version of the waterproof bag he carried on

night forays. When he was on the move from campsite to campsite, which he was almost constantly, all his worldly goods packed together made a bundle a little larger than a bolster. It was awkward on land, but properly buoyed and ballasted, no problem at all in the water.

*Until yesterday*, he remembered. If he had not been carrying it then, when the two skindivers saw him, he might have passed for a corpse.

Dead-white, naked, floating face down, he had passed for a corpse a time or two on the long trip back from Mallorca. Once, also, as a ghost, in the chain locker of a Galveston-bound Turkish freighter. But not since. After that, finally back on land and safely in the woods again, he had not been seen at all, by anyone, the whole time.

*Until yesterday*, he thought again savagely. Then two fat fools in aqualungs, and a storekeeper who wanted to fight. *I should have killed them all!*

Why hadn't he? He should have and could have. He *must* kill. Why didn't he, then? It was the same old dilemma.

The night air was cold on his naked body, and he shivered. He spread his bedroll open on the ground and took a towel and rubbed himself dry, then dressed in the jump suit again and pulled the cap over his head.

He was still cold, but he never built fires at night, because the light might be seen, and also because a man sitting by a campfire was blinded by it.

Ordinarily he would have crawled into his bedroll and slept, but tonight he was too nervous. Instead, he sat cross-legged and began wiping down the AR-7. Alloy metals or not, he thought it ought to have a good coat of oil. Then he might as well assemble it and keep it loaded and handy. This time when they came they were not likely to be fooled by a .22 cartridge with no slug in it and a deep dive into calm waters.

He dried and oiled the rifle. What with doing the job by feel and thinking all the time about his predicament, it took him well over an hour. The best plan he could think of was to try to leave the country—all the way down the Delaware to the sea, all the way down the eastern seaboard to Florida, then cross overland through the swamps to the Gulf, and all the way along that coast to Mexico. It sounded completely impossible, but what other chance was there? He had just about made up his mind.

Or perhaps he did doze off. The next thing he was fully aware of outside his own thoughts was the first stirring of birds in the tops of the trees.

But there was something else.

Quickly and soundlessly he found and opened one of the boxes of high-speed long-rifle hollow points. The rifle was already assembled. He squeezed five shots into the magazine with his thumb and forefinger. Then he sat silently cursing all semiautomatic weapons. Chambering the first round by working the action would make a *clickety-clank* loud enough to rouse the whole woods. Sneaking the bolt back and riding it closed was no good either. The only way to beat it was to creep the bolt open and load one shot directly into the breech, then creep it closed and insert the magazine last. Which he did.

Then he sat motionless as a stone to listen. The sound seemed to come from far away, and then again from close by. It rose and fell like singing. It came from the direction of the river.

He eased forward and stood up inch by inch. He began progressing through the underbrush step by step. Fear was making him tense, but amazement even more so. Could they have found him this soon?

Suddenly all he could hear was the blood in his eardrums. The sound had stopped. He stood like a statue. Then it began again, the same as before, rising and falling. After a moment he went on. Where the trees thinned out at the edge of the water there was more light. He could see the Delaware reflecting the pale pearl of the sky. Half convinced that there would be a boat, a fisherman, out on the water, he crept closer. But there was nothing.

On the very bank of the river he knelt down behind a bush. He was close to the source of the sound or he would not have heard it over the racket of the birds. Birds sing like insane things at dawn. A crimson stain filled the eastern sky. One corner of his mind said: Hot day coming. Then he saw.

The sound had stopped again just in that moment. She was standing knee-deep in the water just off a little sandy spit a dozen yards downstream. Her naked body gleamed pure and pale and cool as the light of dawn. As he watched, she bent forward, cupped her two hands full, and lifted them to the sky streaming diamonds. Then she spread her arms wide, embracing the whole of heaven, in the most exalted gesture he had ever seen, as she sang again:

*"Om tat savitur varenyam bhargo devasya dimohi dhiyo yo nah prachodayat Om!"*

# Covered All Over
## with Sweet
## Violence

Once upon a time, on the stony shore of the Delaware River, in the pink and pearl early dawn of a summer's morning, two young people met in perhaps the most unlikely amorous encounter since the Garden of Eden.

"*Freeze!*" he barked shatteringly in the stillness.

Instead, she uttered a shrill shriek and nearly jumped out of her glistening skin.

As she did so, however, she also spun to face him. And instantly he was in trouble.

The first rule of marksmanship with firearms is to keep the master eye fixed firmly, not upon the target, but upon the front blade or post, which must be centered in the rear notch or aperture. In helpless violation of this rule, he found himself gazing not at, but through, his sights.

Later on in his life, someday perhaps, he might see the temple sculptures at Konarak. If and when he did, it would be with a shock of recognition. The very high, large, perfectly round breasts. The compact torso. The short, sharply tapered thorax. The flaring hips too wide for the tiny waist. And the unequivocal cleft of her sex, wholesome as fruit. All were there. A shakti, consort of gods, she stood in the shallows.

Dismayed, he heard his breath snort suddenly bull-like in his nose. Cavities in all his body filled up and throbbed with thick, rich blood. His head felt light, his eyelids heavy. It seemed that a long, telltale interval passed before he added in confusion: "You're covered."

One deep, shaky inhalation restored her speech. With it came a laugh. "I would call it anything but that," she said, attracting his fullest attention with an indescribable wiggle. She knew what was happening.

"I mean—hands up!" he said just this side of stammering.

"With pleasure. So much the better. It raises the bust, emphasizes the silhouette, and moreover places me in the first position of a dance I know," she softly murmured, suiting action to her words, touching her palms together above her head, with smoldering looks and sinuous moves.

"Darn it!" he yelled, sweating like a horse, "this is a *gun!*"

She saw that he was naïve.

"Then you will not mind," she smiled sweetly, "that since you are armed, I use such ancient weapons as I have."

"What do you think you're doing?"

"You know what I am doing."

"Well, it won't work on me."

"It *is* working on you."

"You're wasting your time!" he shouted.

"You lie," she said. "And you are betrayed."

He glanced down at his jump suit.

"Men are not made to dissimulate," she said amusedly.

He sat down so suddenly and hard, it hurt. With buzzing ears he heard her chime of laughter. Through red-hazed eyes he saw her step ashore. The rifle lay across his drawn-up knees.

"Poor man. It is not fair. I will put on clothing," she said. "Then he will tell me why he goes pointing weapons at naked women in the woods."

"Because you're M-Group," he muttered. At the same moment, the recollection of that perilous probability stung him to alertness again. "Stand where you are!"

"What is M-Group?" She was caressing her breasts, and the nipples—

"Stop that!" he raved, desperately thinking: How to get on top, *no*, *no*, how to get in control—of the situation!

"I am not M anything," she was saying. "You must not be afraid of me, or of yourself—of us." And smiling shyly: "It is only natural."

"Yes! But I'm going to fix that right now!" he said with loud determination. And unzipped his jump suit.

Now it was her turn to stare at him, startled, as he undertook the awkward process of disrobing, one-handed, still sitting on the ground, menacing her with the rifle, and trying to hide himself, all at the same time.

"What are you going to do?"

"Fix your wagon."

He wore no underwear.

"How white!" she marveled. "But how red your face!"

"Never mind that," he said with a last tug. "Put this on."

"Is that all? Je suis desolée."

"Go on. Put it on."

"But I have my own clothes."

"I can just imagine. Put it on, I said. That way we'll both look ridiculous."

"Oh. I see. And do you think that will work?"

"It's better," he said frankly. "I can't think straight."

"It won't," she said.

And it didn't.

Watching her dress was bad enough. She performed it like a harem dance. He could swear he smelled jasmine and musk. Meanwhile her luxurious eyes made him all the more conscious of his own nakedness. Which had its own prickling, goose-pimply effect. And then the suit was on. It covered her, even hands and feet, but only made it worse. What was concealed was more than ever tinglingly revealed. Also, she had not drawn the zipper. Now she spread the ample folds wide like welcoming bedclothes, and breathed softly: "There's room enough for two."

It was incredible.

"If you aren't the—!" he began frantically. Then he said: "If I wasn't wide awake—!"

"The what?" she encouraged.

"Never *mind!*"

"Do you often have such dreams?"

"*What dreams?*"

"You know what dreams."

Shamefacedly he said: "I haven't been near a woman for five years."

That did it. She gazed at him with amazed, tender, generous, indulgent, fond, compassionate and voluptuous emotion.

"My stag! My stallion!" she cried throatily.

So finally there was only one thing left to do. Which he did.

"You _____, _____, _____ of a _____ _____ eating _____, _____, dirty _____ with a _____ your _____ and _____ and _____ and _____," she said.

She was coming around all right, now, though there might be a blue mark.

"How do you feel?"

"*You hit me!*"

"I'm sorry. I had to. Where did you learn to curse like that?"

"The United States Marines, you _____ing _____er! *You knocked me out!*"

"I had to do it. You got me so worked up."

"Worked up! Worked up!"

"Oh—you know."

"So you *hit me?*"

"It was the only way."

"*Why not just—*"

"Here, here," he said bashfully. "That's what started the trouble in the first place."

While she was sleeping he had plunged into the river and taken a cold, calming bath, then gone back to his camp to dress in his spare jump suit, and now he sat a few yards distant from her, his back against a tree, the rifle on safety beside him.

"I might have," he admitted. "I was afraid I would. Then you could have killed me, if you were M-Group."

"M-Group! M-Group!"

"But you aren't. That's why I hit you. I had to find out. If you were, you'd have had a reflex. We'd have fought. I'd have known. Don't you see?" And he explained about the four-foot radius.

She stared at him with baffled intensity. "Well! You are a lunatic!"

"That's why I haven't been near a woman for so long. Can you imagine, if you had tried to hug me?"

"Do you mean you strike at anything that moves, like a kind of mechanical toy soldier?"

"We're elite robot murderers. I always try to stop it. So far I have. But there's no telling," he said. "So you have to keep away from me, and I'll keep away from you."

"_____!" she said.

"Don't you believe me? It's true, though. The reason nobody ever heard of M-Group is, it's Top Secret. That's why they're after me to kill me. I'm a deserter."

And he began to tell her about it. But then he stopped and said: "There's no reason we have to sit here, if you're not angry any more. Would you like to come to my camp and have breakfast with me?"

It sounded so strange, under the circumstances, she had to laugh. "Many thanks, I will," she said with equal formality.

"It was only because I had to find out if you were M-Group," he said. "I won't hurt you again."

"I am not afraid," she said kindly. "You may be a lunatic, but having offered myself freely to you and been refused—and having lain senseless and defenseless at your feet and come to no harm—I see that I have nothing to fear from you. At least outside your charmed circle, and as far as my virtue is concerned."

He flushed with embarrassment, and did not answer. But the subject had come up again, and an odd expression flickered on his face as he turned away to pick up the rifle. She did not see.

Then they went to his camp, such as it was. Silver-pink sunlight was shining amongst the trees now, and it would be a bright, hot day.

From his bedroll he unwrapped a tiny, antique Sterno burner and a can of fuel. In a brown paper bag he found a small bottle of instant coffee and a few dusty sugar cubes. His canteen, filled with cool water, came from underground, where it had lain covered with loose damp earth all night. Next came two cups, one plastic, the other tin and collapsible. Finally, with a vivacious gesture, he produced a sort of omnibus clasp knife, bristling with instruments, which he transformed before her very eyes into a spoon.

Then he reached into the bedroll again. "I only wish it was ham and eggs and hash-browns," he said, sounding excited and pleased, "but at least—"

He held aloft a half-empty box of fortified oatmeal cookies. While the water was heating she said: "How long have you lived like this?"

"Five years—? Maybe more by now. What's the good of keeping score?" he said conversationally. "Ever since I got back from— Would you really like to hear?"

"Yes," she said, touched by his eagerness and pleasure.

"I will!" he said, looking into her eyes. And then he said: "It's funny. I've never told anybody. How could I? I haven't *talked* to anybody."

"Tell me," she said.

So he began at the beginning—with Poody, because that

was important—and told her about basic training and Sergeant Trask; Special Forces and his comrades in arms; Mr. Taxpayer and Dr. Frankenstein and Mr. E.; then Isla Dragonera and the Professor and Igor and the Meadero Municipál in the Puerto de Andraitx.

"After that I stowed away on the *Ne Plus Ultra* to Barcelona, and then to Cadiz, then to Galveston on a freighter," he said, surprised by the expression on her face. "It was easy. What's the matter?"

"Do you know what 'poignant' means?"

"No," he said.

"You are a poignant bastard."

"I don't know what that means."

She repressed an urge to pat softly the woolly white fur on his head.

"Hiding out in the woods like a wild man with your Boy Scout paraphernalia," she said.

"I don't need much," he said. "I only steal what I have to."

"Futilely fighting an unwelcome karma like a rebellious child," she went on.

"What?"

"And all this bloodthirsty business of knives and guns and knees in the groin. *You'd* never hurt anyone."

"I did too!"

"When you really might, and must, you won't," she said. "Do you know what you are?"

"Who, me?"

"Well, I haven't quite decided yet. Either a kind of idiot saint in the wilderness—"

"Says you!" he exploded as the words began to penetrate.

"—or merely the classic good-hearted giant oaf of Occidental tradition."

"Oh, yeah? Well, just you let me tell *you* something, Miss Poignant!" he began.

"Your water's boiling," she said.

So then they sat and drank coffee and ate oatmeal cookies,

while he brooded hotly, and she stared at him with uncon-cealed, though not unkindly, curiosity. The day was heating up. There was the rapid, silky purling of the river at a little distance, and there were brilliant butterflies in the green grass in that place in the woods.

After a while, he said: "That's what *you* think."

"And then what happened?" he said.

"—But Phong or someone else had seen me leave the Em-bassy, and I was followed. Where I went, which way I turned, they were ahead, behind me—the black rayon turbans of Sidi's executioners. Of course, I knew they dared not attack me openly, in the street. But neither could I evade their dogged pursuit. They came with orders to kill, and would forfeit their own heads if they failed.

"It was like some gruesome game. Up streets and down streets. In and out of stores, parks, public buildings. To and fro in the clamorous byways of that exotic city. Wherever there were people. But not too dense a crowd, for that would make it easy for them—to sidle close—insert a knife-blade—and slip away in the confusion.

"I did not know where to go, what to do. I thought only that I must stay alive. I must escape them—and escape them before nightfall! How I dreaded the nightfall, when the streets would be empty. No lights, no people—just Phong and his henchmen closing in. I swore they would never take me back alive to toy with. Rather I would make them kill me first. Luckily, it did not come to that. A remarkable thing happened.

"I was standing on a busy corner, waiting to cross. Waiting also were a number of people, among them a gaggle of girls. Office girls by their patrician clothing and plebeian manner. They were talking of men and sex in indignant and fascinated tones. Suddenly they became even more indignant. It seemed to them that they were being molested! By men of *color!* One pale pink peach girl was bitterly insulted. A gentleman in a Panama hat gallantly came to her rescue. Sidi's men advanced threateningly upon them, or so they believed. Upon *me*, actually. The girls produced hatpins, steak knives and tear-gas pens. The gentleman flourished a knobby stick. Negroes in the gathering began to say, 'Hoogh!' and, 'Woogh!' Other Negroes appeared by magic. White men said 'Yanh! and 'Hanh!' Policemen came. A riot commenced. I escaped.

"Or so I thought. I saw no one following. The black turbans were embroiled in the riot. A valise which one carried, containing king cobras, fell and burst open, adding to the confusion. Then I left the scene, went underground. At the bottom of a precipitous stairs was an endless white-tiled cave, smelling of urine. A few lights burned. There was no sign of life. I walked for miles. Now and then roaring sounds, like typhoon winds, came from high holes in the walls. Eventually other tunnels met mine, and then more and more. The underground system was opening out in a series of vast, dank arcades, filled with scampering shadows, unearthly lights, and bellowing of beasts, like the caverns of Hell. But everyone was carrying luggage. It was the lower level of a railway terminus, and I boarded the handiest train."

She was silent so long, thinking of the next, painful, part, that he asked: "Where to?"

"That did not matter. Away from there."

"Without a ticket?"

"You have a most conventional mind. Such ordinary questions. That was the least of my problems. For I was mistaken. I had not escaped. Phong was on the train, and with him another. He was Q'assim, Sidi's favorite torturer. Speaking of which, my gums were still aching and sore. I was in no mood for fares and destinations. Actually, we were bound for Manhattan, as later discovered, when the conductor came. A chivalrous and wonderful American man! He understood. And took me to the Mail Car, where I would be safe. And the two young men there—such splendid, beautiful young men! What wonderful times we planned, the four of us!"

"I can just imagine," he said sourly.

"But Phong and the other came. They tried to enter the Mail Car, which is illegal, of course. And the two young men resisted them—to defend me! It was terrible! They were armed with guns, and so was Phong, but Q'assim! Q'assim is no marksman. He had a bomb! A *plastique!* Meant for *me!*"

Then she was silent again, and sat staring down at the Sterno burner with wide, unfocused eyes, remembering— until he said scathingly: "And those two splendid, beautiful young men?"

"I am afraid to think."

"And that wonderful chivalrous conductor? I guess they got to him first."

"They would make him tell. And lead them to the Mail Car. You see what they are. Sometimes it is necessary to kill—at least, I tried. I was hidden behind the opened door of the safe. I gave the enormous thing a great push! It struck Q'assim! There came a terrible bang! Instantly a stinking cloud of smoke! Burst bags! Blizzards of envelopes! Everything helter-skelter—as someone pulled the emergency cord and the train screeched to a hideous halt. I could not see. I could not breathe. I was stunned! Perhaps there was a hole in the car. Perhaps the locks were blown. At any rate—light—air! I flung myself from the wreckage. I fell and rolled. It was a deep ditch. My head hit— I slept and woke. The train was gone. So that was that. And here I am."

She expelled a sighing pent-up breath and collapsed like a bladder.

"So here you are," he said.

"As you see."

"And where are they?"

"Who?"

"Your beautiful, splendid, chivalrous, wonderful—those friends of yours."

"But I could not help it! What else could I do? Why are you angry?"

"You're used to fooling men. Using them," he said.

"I did not do it to you."

"You tried."

"Perhaps I am looking for the one man who—"

"Don't start that again."

"You are angry with me," she said sadly.

"Cut it out."

"You do not love me any more."

"I'm warning you."

"No, but you did love me once. At least, you greeted me with love, as the great ape greets his furry mate, whom he meets in the forest glade—"

"Yeah, but that won't happen again," he said. "My mind is out of the gutter now."

It was as though he had set her on fire. "*Gutter?*" she blazed. "You ignorant pig! You would turn the most joyful, transcending experience of your wizened life into a *dirty joke?*"

"The which?" he said.

"You fool! I offered you Rapture Which Enlarges the Soul! *Not* a roll in the hay."

"Fool yourself. What makes *you* so great?"

"I am a Priestess of Devi!"

"Well, I wouldn't know about that. But I know who rules the roost."

"What does *that* mean?"

"I am a man," he answered simply.

They stared at each other in simmering mutual dislike. A flight of bluejays swooped into the grove, thrashed about for a moment echoing the prevailing mood with bitter, derisive cries, then flew away.

"You may be interested to know," she said with icy calm, "that I have been trained since childhood to milk pleasure from a man slowly and exquisitely like sap from the bijasal tree."

"Bully for you," he said. "And I have been trained since

childhood to know who does what to who. If we ever *do* have a roll in the hay, it'll be *my* way, not yours."

"It is *not* likely," she said.

"Just so you know."

"Noted," she said.

"No offense meant," he said, "but you remember the old joke about the monkey that backed into the lawnmower and nicked a chunk out. When he turned around to see what happened, he got his head cut off. And the moral is, never lose your head over a piece of—"

"Very edifying," she said. "Another apt animal metaphor. But at least we know where we stand."

"Yes," he said.

"I might as well forgo any attempt to seduce you."

"Yes."

"You are quite calmly impervious to my wiles."

"Yes."

"I am glad that is settled. I presume I may now remove this itchy and awful garment?"

"*No, no!*"

But she had already stood up in a single supple movement and was fingering the zipper tab at her throat.

"Darn it, you are trying to start the whole thing up again?"

"You said it, not I."

"You're impossible!"

"I would call it anything but that."

"Just go on down to the river—go on! Get your clothes, wherever you left them, and change down there. I'm warning you—*don't push me too far!*"

"I may be a little while," she said. "Those were my morning purification rites—my dhauties—which you so rudely interrupted earlier. I shall finish them before I dress. Can you be trusted not to peek?"

"Purification!" he yelled. And lost the power of speech. Then he was alone.

The sun was high now. Half the morning was gone. He sat lost in thought. From time to time he heard the same strange singing he had heard before, that early morning. It took her twenty minutes or half an hour. Then she came back through the trees. She was dressed in what looked like a cheong-sam, except it was more like aquamarine silk pajamas, with a veil of black-and-white net draped sari-wise around her. Her hair was piled up in a bunch on the back of her head, and her enormous eyes gazed deep into his.

"I stopped back to say goodby and thank you for breakfast," she began.

"I've been thinking it over," he said. "I've decided to rape you."

"I'm only human," he said. "It's been five years."

"Certainly. I can understand that. But why rape?"

"Don't forget the four-foot rule. I might kill you. The only way I can figure out, is for you to hold perfectly still, and not move a muscle."

"You can't be serious."

"It's the only way to keep from triggering my Prods."

"I'm not sure I could do it. Assuming, of course, that I would want to. Remember, you had your chance. What makes you believe I would welcome you now?"

"That's part of it. If you tried to resist me, you *would* trigger a reflex. Then the least that could happen is, I'd hit you. That's what makes it rape."

"I see," she said.

"Maybe there's an idea, though. What if you *were* unconscious?"

"You mean, knocked out again?"

"Yes. If you turned your back to me, and stood still, and I came up behind you—not as an elite robot murderer, understand, but just me—maybe I could sort of scientifically—"

"I suppose it could work."

"You'd have to stand still. Not turn around or try to defend yourself."

"I'm not sure I could do that either. How nerve-wracking."

"It would only be for a second. Then you'd be out of danger. Maybe it's the best way."

"No. I think it would be even worse."

"I'd try to hit you so it wouldn't hurt much. Right at the base of the skull is the best place."

"Thank you," she said, "but I meant worse for you."

"How?"

"Don't you see? Think ahead to the act itself. A body paralyzed by fear that the slightest move may bring death. Or an unconscious body with no more capacity to respond than a dead snake. Either way, what does it add up to?"

"Masturbation," he said ashamedly.

"We'll have to think about this a little more," she said.

They were sitting at their east, one on either side of the Sterno burner, in the dappled shade, and the butterflies were dancing. He had opened his jump suit to the waist and rolled up his sleeves in the noonday heat. She had produced cigarettes from the folds of her exotic clothing, and was smoking slowly and gazing at him—at the bleached-white wiry fuzz on his sun-dark arms and bare chest. Now and then a look crossed her face as though she knew something she was not telling.

"I appreciate your help," he said.

"That's quite all right."

"How about if I tied you to a tree?"

"You *are* the inventive one."

"I think it might work. Maybe it would satisfy my Prods."

"Let them off duty, so to speak."

"Yes. If you couldn't move, they couldn't attack. They wouldn't be triggered. You'd be safe."

"But immobilized."

"You'd be conscious."

"C'est emmerdant," she said.

"What's that mean?"

"Pretty shitty."

Suddenly he grinned from ear to ear. "Oh," he said.

"Yes. If you must know."

" 'So help me, I'll rape you.' 'So rape me, I'll help you,' " he said, remembering another old joke. "I get it now." And she grinned back at him. Though there was still something she wasn't telling.

She stubbed out her cigarette. "Why don't I tie *you* to a tree?"

"No good," he said.

"Haven't you got a rope?"

"I've got a rope, all right."

"Well, then. Why not?"

"In the first place, my Prods wouldn't let you."

"Nothing simpler. You just attach one end of the rope to your right wrist, then stand with your back to a tree, with your other arm at your side. Then I hold the loose end and run around you clockwise. I need never come near you until you are securely bound.

"Clock—what?" he said. "Never mind. Not that way."

"It is certainly as feasible as knocking me on the base of my skull."

"No."

"Of course, it could hardly be considered rape."

"No," he said. "Just *no*, is all."

"All right. Why?"

"*You* think ahead to the act itself."

"I *am*," she said deliciously.

"Well, I'm no bijasal tree. I told you before, it has to be my way. *I* know who does what to who. So forget it."

"That's absurd."

"It's not to me."

"No, it's 'to whom,' " she said. And then said: "Oh, it doesn't matter."

After a while he said, "So that's out. But there has to be a way."

"We'll think of something."

"I can't think of anything."

"Nor can I."

"How about some lunch?"

So he unwound his bedroll again and got out a can of Prem, a can of sardines in mustard, a package of Kool-Aid, the oatmeal cookies, and two flattened Tasty Kakes in cellophane. And along with them a battered mess tin, a frying pan, and the clasp knife, which he now transformed into a fork.

" 'Be Prepared,' " she murmured as she watched him relight the pinkish Sterno fuel.

"I'm sorry this is all there is," he said. "I just arrived at this camp. Usually after I'm in the area for a few days, I've got fresh fish and game, watercress and berries, things like that. Fruit and vegetables from farms nearby—even eggs, when I can scomp them. As it is, all I've got is my travel rations."

Then they ate.

"Well," he said.

"Well."

"Let's get down to business."

"Have you thought of something?"

"No. We'll have to go back to my old plan."

"Just a moment," she said. "What do you think would happen if we simply tried?"

"Zip! Zap!" he said, chopping an X in the air with the blade of his hand.

"In other words, the only way is for me to hold still—or else be knocked out?"

"Yes."

"And you are fully determined to go through with it?"

"Yes."

"Well," she said thoughtfully, "I am sorry to have to tell you this—but I have no intention of permitting it."

He stared in surprise. "I guess you don't understand. I'm not *asking* you. That's what makes it rape."

"I guess *you* don't understand," she said. "Let me put it this way. I will *not* hold still. And if you so much as touch me—"

"Don't. *Please* don't! If you fight me, I can't control it. I've never killed anyone. How do you think I'd feel?"

"You G.I. judo experts are all alike. Just because you know these horrendous blows doesn't mean you can deliver them."

"I can't stop them. They're automatic."

"So is a bullet, once the trigger is pulled. And a bullet delivers a deadly blow too. But only if it hits something."

"You don't know what you're up against."

"In fact, I do," she said. "I remember an R.O.K. volunteer officer with your Marines. He was an expert in tae kwon do, Korean karate. He believed this gave him a certain advantage. Today, his right side is paralyzed. He dribbles and drools."

Suddenly he was suspicious. "There's something you're not telling."

"I'm telling you now. The Lore of Devi does not end with the hundred and three positions. I know the human body like the leaves of the Lotus. There are certain pressure points, nerve endings—"

"Oh, *that*," he said. "That's just a legend. We had that in basic training. There's no such thing."

"Ask Park Il Soon."

"And anyway, even if there was, you mean you went through this whole thing from the beginning—"

"Ever since the river bank. If you had been an ordinary assailant, your first attempt upon my virtue would have been your last."

"What would you have done?"

"Partial paralysis—temporary or permanent. Excruciating pains—migraine, tic douloureux. Blind staggers. Heart palpitations. Incontinence. Loosened bowels. Stomach cramps. Nausea. Faintness. Take your choice. I play upon the human body as upon a delicate instrument."

"Thanks for the warning," he said. "I don't believe it."

"Then I will convince you," she said, and struck a peculiar pose.

At first he thought she was going into some kind of

Balinese dance. She spread her knees in opposite directions and sort of squatted. With upper arms close to her sides, she held her left palm up as though halting traffic, and her right palm out as though asking alms—except that in both cases her fingers were spread wide.

"It's not a fair fight if you make me giggle," he said.

But then she was hopping flat-footed toward him.

"Get away!" he said. "Remember the four-foot rule."

"Someone has to start it."

"Don't come any closer."

"Make your move, then."

Instead, he retreated rapidly, till there was a space of yards between them, and shrugged his shoulders. "All right, you win. I quit."

"What's the matter now?"

Disconsolately he said: "I guess it was just a bluff."

"You are giving it up?"

"I can't hit you."

"You are so quickly discouraged?"

"I'd have to just walk up to you and smack you. I can't do that."

"You did it earlier."

"That was different. When I thought you were M-Group."

"This may be even more important to you."

"Darn it, you sound like you *want* me to."

"I think you should try."

"I don't understand."

"I began to tell you before. You did not let me finish. Perhaps I am looking for the one man who—"

"You mean, you changed your mind? You won't resist?"

"Oh, I will resist."

"Well, *what*, then? Will you make *sense?*"

She gazed at him soft-eyed. "I cannot tell you everything. I want this fight."

"But I might *kill* you."

"You might kill me."

"I won't do it!"

"Then I will," she said.

And the fight began.

It lasted only a moment.

"Get away! Get away!" he yelled. The little wires and motors of his secondary nervous system were buzzing and sparking as she approached. Then she was near enough. His hands hovered in the air, next darted into motion from rest like dragonflies. The left should have broken her collarbone, the right killed her. Instead they brushed gently like membranous wings. Her charge jolted her against him. They fell. Falling, his body writhed in the air, obeying its Prods, his weight slamming her down. But they struck softly. If she tried at all for pressure points, he did not notice it. Their bared teeth knocked together in a kind of kiss. He should have butted his head forward and smashed her face. He did not. If she tried to hurt him then, it was too late. He held her—arms and legs tight-locked—in the dreaded Nobiru. And began to squeeze. And squeeze—

Then he became conscious of her gently rocking—gently, fiercely, frenziedly, rhythmically rocking, plunging—beneath him, cushioned in the green grass. It was reflex—old, old—his own answered hers.

He heard her hoarse voice: "You could not hurt them. You could not hurt anyone. How could you hurt *me?*"

"You knew."

"I knew."

"I didn't."

"I knew."

Tiny series of shudders rippled her body and shivered her breath.

"We beat them!" he said astonished.

"Now!" she said.

"The one thing they can't fight!"

"Hurry!"

"Yes. Now. The right way. *My* way."

"Master!"

"No temple tricks, I mean."

"Just this one."

". . . . ."

"And this."

". . . . !"

"Oh, hurry!" she said.

Somehow in the fight her pajama top had come off and the pajama bottom had split into two legs and slid silkily off.

"You!" she said.

He removed his own itchy and awful garment.

Sarvam Khalvidam Brahman.

It went on and on and on.

His way and her way and his way and her way . . .

The sun had begun its decline. Butterflies flickered in the shade. She lay quietly in his embrace. They were at rest, peace.

"Speak to me softly—sweet nothings in my ear," she said.

"I don't know any nothings."

"Do as I am doing. Whisper to me. I want to ask you—"

"Yes?"

"How quickly can you reach your gun? How quickly can you—don't snicker—cock it, and get it ready to shoot?"

"What?"

"We are being watched. From the bushes," she said.

# The Best
# Laid Plans

In the small clearing the fire was too big and bright, and lit up the underleaves of the trees, making the camp like a red-orange cave carved in the dark. Bats dipped in and out of the towering smoke, and the huge shadows of the three grownups romped and flickered every which way as they sat and talked. They were telling, explaining, and Rolf had never heard such a power of nonsense in his born days.

"Preconditioned reflexes, and autoinduced levitation, and ectoplasmic blue fire," they said, but the confoundingest thing was, what they told was probably the genuine truth, for how else could they sit there all three swapping turns at telling the most godawful galloping lies?

Mr. Kleiber was sitting on the opposite side of the fire from Djeela-Lal and the soldier, taking no chances (which was a part of it too, how she had said: "*I* am safe from him, but that is all we are sure of so far"). Meanwhile the boy kept clear of the whole three of them, for his own good reasons. He was away on the edge of the clearing, almost out of the light, and close by a gully of ferns. Sitting there, he was not so blinded and deafened by the crackling blaze, and could hopfrog into hiding at the first sign of danger.

Let *them* get caught if they were so bound and determined, he thought scornfully. If this was their idea of going to ground, he wanted no part of it. Camping out so comfy and so cozy—laughing, talking, carrying on—and that fire! You could maybe get a more conspicuous fire by burning down the cow barn, just for example, though not hardly. But then, they were none of them any too downright inconspicuous folk to begin with. That Mr. Kleiber crashing through the woods like a boar bear in a briar bush—you could hear him a mile! Let alone that foreign lady you never saw the like of in those clothes or out—and never mind that man like a white nigra burying his traps underground and ramping about with guns! Whoo-ee! A fellow needed telling they were in his neck of the woods like he needed telling there were bees in his shirt.

(Not to mention the one stumbling into traps and kicking and bellering, and the other two swimming in the river, and prancing naked, and eating, and talking, and fighting, and then—whoo-ee! Rolf giggled and grinned.)

Mr. Kleiber had come to the part in his story where he got off the train: "So when I heard the explosion, I naturally jumped to the conclusion that it was *me* they were after. As soon as the train was stopped, I crawled out the window and ran, and never looked back. Lord knows where I'd be by now if I hadn't met our young friend here. If I hadn't stepped into his *bear trap*, that is. Can you imagine? Being yanked into the air by one foot?"

Rolf covered his mouth with both hands and squinnied up his eyes, trying not to laugh. It was a terrible, awful thing to have done to the poor man, and he would cherish the memory forever to cheer him in hard times.

"It was an accident, of course," Mr. Kleiber said. "We had quite a little conversation after he captured me. It seems he surrounds himself with traps like these wherever he makes a camp. It was just my bad luck to step in one. Snares, I guess you'd call them. For food, mostly, but he builds them strong enough to hoist a man, just in case. I had myself quite a job convincing him I wasn't one of *them* before he'd cut me down."

The soldier hrumphed and grumphed something, still sore as a boil and wishing he'd let fly the first time he drew a bead on the both of them. "So then you decided to come sneaking through the woods to spy on us," he said.

"I already explained that," Mr. Kleiber said. "We had no way of knowing who you were—or what you were *doing*, for that matter. You could have been anybody, from process servers to the juvenile authorities, or the F.D.I. tracking either one or both of us. We were just as embarrassed as you were."

"You're lucky I didn't blast you."

"Believe you me, I still get goose-pimples thinking about it," Mr. Kleiber said.

The foreign lady had been quiet, listening through this, and now she spoke. She had a low pretty voice you could spread on bread, and Rolf liked her best of all. She was beautiful and strange.

"And so you two are also fugitives," she said. "How very peculiar. That makes four of us."

"Just wait," Mr. Kleiber said. "You haven't heard *how* peculiar! We were talking about what you might call freak talents? Well, that's another thing I learned in our little conversation. He has one too! How do you like *that* for a funny coincidence?"

Djeela-Lal said: "You mean he also writes with his nose?"

"No, no, not like that. It's something about haunting houses. I didn't get it exactly, but he thinks they're after him to put him away. In the *bedlam*, he says, but that's not the point. What's really peculiar is the fact of all four

of us getting together in this selfsame woods—and each
with a different talent! Almost as if it was *meant!*"

"*What* meant?" the soldier said.

"Don't you see?" Mr. Kleiber went on excitedly. "It's just
the way it *always* happens—in the fairy tales! Childe Whoozis
sets out, and the first thing he *always* does is find, well,
a jackdaw, a magic ring, and a rat trap, let's say. Then,
when he gets to the Ogre's castle, or wherever he has to
go, it always turns out that those are the *exact* three things he
*needs!* It's the classical Quest!"

"*What* quest?" the soldier said.

"Well, that's the whole point, isn't it?" Mr. Kleiber said.
"What *are* we doing here?"

This time Rolf had to laugh, the other two looked so
comical. It came out half between a croak and a caw. They
all three turned to peer into the dark, trying to make him
out with fire-dazzled eyes.

"Yeah. What about *him?*" the soldier said thoughtfully.
"We know about us. But what's *he* doing here?"

Djeela-Lal aimed a friendly smile at Rolf, missing him
by a yard or two in the dark. "Won't you come and sit
with us, since we seem to have joined forces? It's nice and
warm, and perhaps you can help us plan what we had better
do."

"No'm," he said shyly. "I thank you."

"Well, then, will you at least tell us how you come to be in
this woods?"

"Yes'm," he said. "I'm heading for the Machine."

"I never thought of that," Mr. Kleiber said after a startled
pause. "Of course! There's your quest!"

Then they had to talk that out for a while. Djeela-Lal
said: "I am familiar with the quest theme, naturally. That's
universal folklore. But I don't see the application here."

"You don't?" Mr. Kleiber said eagerly. "It's perfect! Instead of the Ogre's castle, the Machine! That has to be
it! I knew it was *meant* for us to come together! And

here's another amazing thing. The boy's right—we're only a few miles from the very spot! The Machine is on an island in the middle of this very river!"

"Not any more, it isn't," the soldier said. "It outgrew the island long ago. They moved it to a cave under the mountain. I was up that way last spring with the shad."

"Same difference!" Mr. Kleiber was all fired up. "If it was *meant* for us to come together by pure chance—then it was *meant* for our freak talents to be exactly what we need to succeed! Don't you see? *Instead* of a jackdaw, a magic ring, and a rat trap! All we have to do is get *in* there somehow—by stealth, or by force if necessary—and then, and then—"

"Yes? Then?" Djeela-Lal asked.

"Well, whatever is *meant* to be. With the trouble we're all in now, where else have we got to turn?"

They were giving him the same comical looks as before, bewildered and smiling and humoring him.

"I mean it!" he insisted. "With policemen and lawyers and process servers and I don't know who-all after me— Immigration and your own people and maybe the U. S. Mails after you for blowing up their train—and the Army and M-Group after him—truant officers, juvenile authorities after the boy—and the F.D.I. after us all—oh, Lord!" He stopped, out of breath. "The Machine is our only hope!"

For a moment there was only the fire burning away like a hayrick. Then Djeela-Lal said, just a little bit sarcastic: "We of all the far-flung nations of the world have heard of your fabulous Machine, of course. A triumph of technology. But I have never heard it spoken of in quite this way, with quite such touching faith. Has it become your ruler, your god, since it was last described in *Time?*"

Mr. Kleiber came down to earth. "Well no. Not exactly. It's more like where our technology triumphs have finally got us to. I guess you might say our real ruler was always an idea of what's normal or not. Conformity, I guess you'd call it."

"Ah."

"Now that you mention it, though, I suppose the Machine —plus the F.D.I.—working together—*have* sort of externalized it once and for all."

"Oh?"

"Neither one could have done it alone, but the two working together can sort of *say* so now, and make it stick, if you know what I mean."

"No."

The soldier roused himself from staring gloomily into the fire. "He means it's the law. But you can appeal. Right?"

"Yes, exactly," Mr. Kleiber said. "Ordinary deviation is one thing, but we're certainly each and every one of us a special case. If only we could get *to* the Machine, and *explain!* What they call extenuating circumstances. I mean, we were only trying to survive! At least, I know *I* never asked to be stuck with a freak talent! I'm sure the Machine could stop my landlady and people from suing me—and get the police off my trail—maybe even fix my nose? It could *certainly* make the F.D.I. leave us alone!"

Djeela-Lal said: "Would it grant me asylum, an immigration visa, and drop any charges stemming from my flight from the Embassy?"

"I want an honorable discharge, complete detraining, and a full pardon," the soldier said.

"And the boy. Don't forget the boy," Mr. Kleiber said. "How about the boy?"

They all peered into the darkness. But Rolf had fallen asleep.

"Little man, you've had a busy day," Mr. Kleiber said.

Djeela-Lal rose and went and gently woke him.

"Yes'm," he said immediately, sitting bolt upright, blind-eyed and dizzy with sleep, still in the midst of his last waking thought: "Ain't you folks never fixing to eat supper?"

"What?"

"Oh," he said, and came awake entirely.

"Won't you come join us at the fire?" she said. "We

think we have found a solution, and need your advice to make our plans."

"Yes'm," he said. "If y'all planning to eat supper ever, better hustle and start building shelter, for it's coming on to rain thundering lightning right soon. I seen a whole heap of mashed-potato cloud just at sundown."

"No, it's not about that," she said. "We've decided to go to the Machine, and ask it to help us."

"*Help* us?" he said amazed, fully alert now.

"It is our only hope."

"Foot," he said scornfully. "I never come near nine hundred mile to knuckle under to no eternal contraption. I figure to blow it to blazes!"

It stopped their talk for a while, at least.

The next thing to turn out was, of course, that they'd been too all-fired busy to take thought to supper yet, and besides, didn't have any food worth mentioning, let alone enough for four. The soldier brought out his oatmeal cookies and sardines and Kool-Aid again, but the foreign lady just said: "Couillons!" and Mr. Kleiber started hinting he hoped those snares were good for something else beside catching accountants—so Rolf saw he had to feed them. And do the cooking too, like as not. "I don't guess none of you folks ever cooked catfish."

"Catfish! Agh!" Mr. Kleiber said.

"You surely ain't under no constraint," Rolf said with dignity. As a matter of fact, he snared a rabbit too, but it was fresh-killed that day, and needed hanging till the fleas got off and the meat got ripe.

"Catfish will be fine," Djeela-Lal said soothingly. "What can we do to help?"

"If you all would damp down that fire to size, I'd go fetch 'em," Rolf said. "They need cleaning and packing, and that'll take a while. I wasn't expecting no company."

"I'll go with you," the soldier said. "I can clean fish."

"Much obliged."

"You'll have to be careful, though. Remember the four-foot rule."

"Don't you fret," Rolf said. He hopped up, and then, on a sudden mischievous impulse, darted quickly away into the ferns, and went slithering through the woods like a ferret, quiet and quick, just to see if the soldier could follow. He could, too. They met again on the bank of the river. The pale man rose a notch or two in Rolf's estimation. "Takes a lot of doing to track me like that," he said by way of compliment.

"I've been trained."

"I heard," Rolf said. "They surely never shown you how to make a cookfire, though."

"I guess it *is* pretty big."

"Not hardly, if you was expecting me to provide roast ox instead of a string of catfish."

"You'll understand when you're older," the soldier said, and tried to explain the psychological need the fire filled—for light, warmth and comfort away out in the lonesome woods. And anyway, now they could cook the fish on it.

"Might's well," the boy said. "It don't never do to make a fire at night, though. Next time, just you heat you some hot stones by day, and cook all you want in the dark. Comfort ain't the case when you're hiding out. If it's comforting you need, find a cave, the littler the better. Put your backs to the wall. Set and hold hands."

"Don't get smart," the soldier said. "Nobody asked you. We decided the fire was worth the risk."

"Not to me, it ain't," Rolf said. "Ain't no risk worth taking. Not now. I come too far, and got too close."

"You really think you're going to sabotage the Machine, do you?"

"I surely do," Rolf said. "Just you watch me."

Then he turned and waded a little way upstream to where a rotting log lay half in the water, and squatted down and came up with three good-size catfish strung on a line, all cool and firm from the flowing water. The thing was, he explained, that as long as they already had such a rousing fire, they might as well pack the fish in clay and bake them in the coals—that is, if he, the soldier, still had a mind to help clean them. "If you ain't too nettled, that is," Rolf said.

"I said I would, didn't I? Just show me where the clay is."

"You're standing on it," Rolf said.

"Oh," the soldier said. So then they went to work, skinning, beheading and disemboweling.

After a while the boy said: "Comes in right handy this way, too. When she's ready, the clay gets fire-hard. You just crack her longwise and use one half for a dish."

"Friday night blueplate special," the soldier said. "All we need now is French fries and tartar sauce."

"Wouldn't know about that. But I got some squaw potatoes and rock onions in the safe, and welcome. They're just dug yesterday. We'll stop by on the way back."

"In the which?"

"Underground. Like you store your traps. Only wrapped in moss to keep 'em fresh. I can make us a side dish to go along."

The soldier laughed out loud. "You're a funny kid. Got a whole bag of tricks, haven't you? You know, I'd almost bet you could do it. If it was anything else but the Machine."

"I *can* do it. Darned if I won't, too. Wait and see. Hold on," he said, and thought a moment. Then he said: "You and me *together* could."

"Who, me?"

"I'll make you a trade. You help me, and I'll help you. Once we get to the right place, you just leave the rest to me. I can get in anywhere. They can't *hide* that contraption so's I can't get to it. All you got to do is provide me a bomb."

"A bomb?"

"One of them homemade kind will do."

"That's ridiculous. Anyway, it's not my line of work."

"I thought that *was* your line of work, bombing and killing."

"Not any more, it isn't. Not if I can help it. That's the whole idea. Besides, you're in the same boat with the rest of us. We're all outlaws, for one reason or another. The Machine is the only hope we've got. And you want to bomb it?"

"I aim to."

"What for? What've you got against the Machine?"

For the first time the boy flashed fire. "Against? Against? *I'll* tell you what I got against! That godderned doodad wants to clap me in the *bedlam! That's* what I got against!"

"You're crazy. You didn't do anything. It probably only wants to investigate you."

"All right. That godderned doodad wants to *investigate* me, then. *No* man has got to suffer that! From a *Machine?!*"

The soldier stared at him. "What are you getting so excited for? I don't know about down in your Ozarks, but this is the modern age. Machines tell *everybody* what to do."

"Not *me*, they don't. I said my piece. These fish is ready. We better get a move on," Rolf said. "It's fixing to rain."

"You're a funny kid," the soldier said.

Meanwhile, back at the camp, Mr. Kleiber and Djeela-Lal simultaneously pricked up their ears and listened. From far away—first high in the foothills to the north, then trundling down the river valley—came a low rumble of thunder. It made the summer night sky sound empty and immense.

While waiting, the two had managed to reduce the size of the fire, in its circumference at least, by simple dint of not feeding it so much. The time had been spent instead in studying certain paramahansa Yoga trance techniques, with Mr. Kleiber as pupil and Djeela-Lal as instructress. But now they were talking about something else.

"I don't mind apologizing to you personally—just so *he's*

not around," Mr. Kleiber said. "But I wouldn't give him the satisfaction. He's too eager to put us in the wrong as it is. As though we were creeping through the woods on *purpose* to watch."

"Voyeurism, I believe it's called," she said.

"And anyway, I'm not so sure I owe him any apology. We didn't mean to spy on you. And we certainly didn't know what you were *doing!* I could hardly believe my eyes! We just looked through the bushes and there you were!"

"In the flesh, as it were," she said.

"Don't get me wrong. It's nothing to me *personally*. I mean, I think I'm as broad-minded as the next fellow. After all, you're both grownups. What you do is your own affair. The only thing I'm sorry about is, the *boy* had to see it. Who knows what sordid and ugly reaction he might have."

"*Sordid? Ugly?*"

"At his tender age, there's no telling *how* it might affect him."

"Nonsense. I sincerely hope it made his cute little thing stand up for him, don't you? Anything else would be ill-omened indeed."

Shocked speechless, Mr. Kleiber seemed to be blowing invisible smokerings.

"Oh, stop that," she said impatiently. "What is so horrifying about the truth?"

"I'm *awfully* sorry," Mr. Kleiber said, sounding a bit lofty. "I suppose I'm just not used to hearing decent young ladies say things like that. It may be true enough, but there are certain things we just don't *talk* about."

"I don't see why I should be expected to share your Anglo-Saxon *pudeur*," she said. "Besides, aren't you sounding a bit lofty for someone who may have stumbled upon the scene by accident—but who nevertheless stayed to watch?"

"Whoa! Hold on, now, that's not fair," he said. "A young couple just plain, er, diddling in the woods, is one thing. *But floating six inches off the ground?*"

She grinned and shrugged. "You are right, of course. Excuse me. I had forgotten that. The ground was hard."

"Who *wouldn't* stay and watch?"

"Of course. Perfectly understandable. I apologize," she said. "But to return for a moment to your earlier remarks: the fact remains that if you, or the Augustinians, or the United Baptists, or the Supreme Court, or even the Gallup Poll, find in human sexual intercourse something *sordid*, or *ugly*, then that is indeed a problem. But it is not Brahma's problem. Lingam and yoni created he them. And innocence and joy are his commandments. Nor will he too severely punish those of us whose only fault it is to abuse the privilege. So neither it is our problem. Only yours."

Mr. Kleiber sighed. "Well, I suppose that's some kind of Inscrutable Wisdom of the Orient, but I don't mind telling you, it's beyond me. Anyway, in the future, couldn't you at least manage not to be so innocent and all that in front of the boy? Just for common decency's sake?"

Djeela-Lal smiled. "I will try to mend the evil badness of my ways," she said. "Look, here he comes."

"Hello, there!" Mr. Kleiber said with relief and animation. "We were just this minute talking about how *good* those fish are going to taste."

"We were *not*," Djeela-Lal said. "We were wondering about your reaction to watching two adults _____."

"Oh, good God, for Heaven's sake, shhh!" Mr. Kleiber said.

"Shucks," the boy said, "I seen the stock banging away at it lots of times. They never shown no such leaning to variety, though. I expect I learned something for when my time comes."

Djeela-Lal said: "See? He is still one of us—of the beloved of Devi."

"I'll tell you how *I* feel about it," the soldier said, glaring bitterly at Mr. Kleiber. "If there's anything I hate, it's a goddamned Peeping Tom!"

"Shadrach, Meshach, Abednego," Rolf said, naming each fish as he buried it within the heap of fiery coals. "Take about n'our. Then we can eat."

"I suggest we use the time to complete our plans," Djeela-Lal said, "so that we can be ready to leave here at daybreak."

"I kind-of suggest you'd do better building shelter," Rolf said with a glance at the sky, but they weren't listening. So he set a can of water to heat, and went back to his place by the fern gully, where he started chopping the squaw potatoes and rock onions up fine with his hunting knife, to make a side dish.

"The best thing would be for us to put all our cards on the table," Mr. Kleiber said. "Not that I'm trying to take charge, or anything, but if no one minds me acting as chairman, or moderator, I think what we should do is each of us make a brief general statement about himself, or herself, in terms of their special talents and whatever contribution they can make to our common enterprise, so we will know where we stand when we get to the Machine."

"What's he talking about?" the soldier said.

Djeela-Lal said: "He means the jackdaw, the magic ring, and the rat trap."

"Exactly," Mr. Kleiber said. "Would you be first, Miss Lal, so our *physically* strong friend here can get the idea?"

"Very well," she said, settling herself cross-legged with her hands in her lap. "I don't know how much of a contribution it makes, but I do have, in fact, certain special talents, as you call them. For instance, today's demonstration, which you all attended, of levitation—"

"Levi—*what?*" the soldier said.

"Rising slightly from the ground. A form of telekinesis."

"Thank God," he whispered. "I thought I was cracking up!"

"My dear," she said surprisingly, although the others laughed. Then she went on: "Also, there are one or two other things I can do. Call them feats of magic for convenience, if you wish, but they are actually only exercises in bodily control. Yoga comes from the root word *yug*, meaning to yoke, or harness, as the energies of the body. I can slow or speed the action of my heart at will, accelerate the healing of wounds, occasionally summon birds to light on my head, in certain trance states. Nothing of practical use, I am afraid. Now and then, in extraordinary circumstances, I have produced effects of which I did not know I was capable. Once I lifted a very heavy weight simply by placing my hand upon it, though I have not been able to do this since. In any case, you understand, such tricks are not the meaning or purpose of Yoga, but only incidents that happen along the way. As in honing a knife, the aim and end of steel and wheel is not the striking of sparks."

"Now what are *you* talking about?" the soldier said.

"Of more immediate value—in the event that we must actually invade some kind of fortress, or battle the Machine's guards—might be my mastery of the ancient Chinese art of *fube*, or one-finger combat," she went on. "Other than which, I have nothing to contribute to our common enterprise, unless we should need funds, in which case I have a jeweled letter opener, which we might sell. And, oh yes, I forgot—if need be, I can also do a dance which has the power to cloud men's minds."

"I can well imagine," Mr. Kleiber smiled.

"Yeah, and you can bet that's just what he *is* doing, too: imagining," the soldier said suddenly. "If there's anything I hate, it's a dirty old man!"

Mr. Kleiber shut his eyes. "Corporal Burns. Would you kindly, kindly, kindly *stop that?*"

Out in the dark, Rolf giggled softly. The soldier ground his big fists together and grumphed something.

Mr. Kleiber was polite, patient, exasperated. "As long as you keep sniping at me in this snide and ridiculous manner, we simply aren't going to *accomplish* anything! We all know you have your opinions, but can't you *please* keep them to yourself? Just for the sake of a little peace and cooperation? Don't you agree? We are all in this together, whether we like it or not! Can't you understand that? —*What?*"

"I said: All right. All right!"

"*Thank* you! Now maybe we can forget the whole matter and get back to business." Mr. Kleiber was calm, mollified, magnanimous. He went on powerfully: "We were *trying* to sum up our situation, and take stock of our various talents, and so forth, as Miss Lal has just done. Under the circumstances, and since *you* seem to be so anxious to have the floor, perhaps you would be kind enough to follow her example?"

"You mean, what can *I* do?"

"We would be *most* grateful."

After a while the soldier said slowly: "I can swim underwater a long time. Up to an hour if I want. I don't have to breathe. It's something about my lungs. They draw more oxygen from the air and store it longer. That's all I know."

From the darkness Rolf said: "Mighty like a mud turtle."

"I'll thank *you* not to stick your oar in either, young man," Mr. Kleiber said.

"I have inhuman strength, too," the soldier continued. "For the same reason, they say. My muscles get lots of extra oxygen, something like that."

"Very good," Mr. Kleiber said. "And then there's your military training, don't forget. That could come in handy, all those things they taught you about codes and sabotage and strangling people. It's too bad that part about not being able to control yourself, though. Maybe if you really tried?"

"I'll try," the soldier said. "Will you help? That's the biggest problem, finding guinea pigs. To test myself on."

"Yes, I see," Mr. Kleiber said. "Well, never mind that for now. What else?"

"I've got two .22 weapons and ammo. And a bolo knife. You saw the rest of my equipment. And you didn't think much of my field rations. That's all."

"Thank you," Mr. Kleiber said. "Well, at least we're getting somewhere. Next is Rolf. Rolf? Rolf! Come join our council of war, son."

Grinning, Rolf came slowly into the light. "Oh, I'll play, if you want," he said, "but I reckon you remember what I already said."

"If you mean about going in alone and throwing a bomb at the Machine, I'm afraid you'd better forget it," Mr. Kleiber said. "One small boy trying to sneak through the tightest security setup in the country? You wouldn't have a chance."

Rolf's grin grew even broader. "You sure enough figure I'd stand a better chance trying to sneak in inconspicuous-like with an old man, an ee-leet rowboat murderer, and a lady that birds sits on her head?"

The chopped-fine squaw potatoes and rock onions were stewing in the tin can with a pinch of the soldier's salt, and the fish were almost done. Meanwhile, a hot, heavy, humid air had risen, breathing on the camp like a cow's breath, and the rumbling thunder was closer now.

Mr. Kleiber was saying: "So what it amounts to is, this whirlwind stunt you used to escape from the F.D.I. man is the only thing you can do on purpose?"

"Leastwise so far," Rolf said.

"But you *can* turn on this energy that causes the Poltergeist phenomena whenever you want to?"

"It's sort-of a way of thinking, and then something busts loose like," Rolf said. "Trouble is, I never know *what*. Never even known I was doing it, first off."

Djeela-Lal said: "Apparently a massive unfocused discharge of etheric energy, with resulting random manifestations."

"Yes'm, you bet," Rolf said politely.

"How marvelous. I would like to see. Will you show us?"

"I guess not," Rolf said. "I wouldn't want no harm to come to no one."

"Oh? But according to your story, the phenomena are perfectly harmless, are they not?"

"Yes'm, anyways, so far. But things do flash and fly

about something fierce. I couldn't answer for no hot sparks from the fire, or tree limbs falling, or people's clothes being ripped up, and suchlike. There's just no telling."

"That's a risk we'll have to take. This could be very important."

"Then too, they do say the mischief is purely my doing, though I don't rightly see how I can be to blame," Rolf went on. "But I don't want no hard feelings, neither."

"We will not blame you for anything that happens," she said.

"You mean, you really and truly want me to, despite my warning?"

"Young man, are you trying to be coaxed?"

Rolf shrugged. "Oh well, then, if you are so bound and determined."

"*I'm* not," Mr. Kleiber said nervously. "Why can't we just take his word for it? I don't see any need for a demonstration."

"Yeah. And I don't trust that grin," the soldier said.

"Nonsense. It may be very important for us to know exactly what we have to deal with," Djeela-Lal said. "Go ahead, Rolf. Whenever you are ready."

"Yes'm," he said. "Just so's you are certain sure now."

"We are sure."

"So be it," he said. And crossed his wrists on top of his head, shut his eyes, and stuck out his tongue, as aids to concentration.

There followed a long, uneventful pause.

"You know," the soldier said speculatively, "we really don't have any proof. Only what he told us. He could be an F.D.I. spy."

"Hush," Rolf said. "It's already waiting to happen."

"Aren't you supposed to be focusing or discharging, or something?"

"It's done. I only got to get it started once, is all."

"*Then* what?"

"Then nothing can't stop it."

They became aware of a powerful smell of sassafras.

"Don't ask me," Rolf said. "Happens ever' time."

Next was a disembodied sneeze exploding loudly in thin air—followed by a repeated *whump, whump*, noise as a large pie-shaped stone came slowly toppling end-over-end out of the woods. It advanced purposefully across the open space and fell flop in the fire in a spray of sparks. Then the noseless sneeze again.

"It's a fake!" the soldier said. "Somebody's in the bushes!"

"Can't you just sit still, keep quiet, and watch?" Djeela-Lal said.

"It's the F.D.I., I tell you! I'll prove it!" he said, springing resolutely to his feet. Just then there was a lightninglike *zip* and the mainseam of his jump suit split down the back from collar to crotch. As he was already leaning into a combat-ready crouch, the sleeves slid easily off his arms, and the one-piece garment went slithering down his shins. He still wore no underwear.

Rolf and Djeela-Lal let out happy whoops. Mr. Kleiber was too terrified. "Turn it off!" he yelled.

He had just then noticed the eery floating fireballs hovering here and there over their heads.

"Jack-o-lanterns," the boy said. "They won't hurt you none."

"*Turn it off!*"

A shower of dead twigs and leaves fell on them from the trees. A definite sound like cowbells was heard in the air. With a flap like a rug the soldier's bedroll unwound, strewing the camp with Boy Scout paraphernalia.

"*Turn it off!*" Mr. Kleiber yelled.

"Don't I wish I could," Rolf said, watching ruefully as the three fish one by one exploded like small, soggy bombs, scattering ash and embers, baked clay, flakes of fish in every direction. "Don't I dearly *do!*"

"I'm sure we have all seen quite enough," Djeela-Lal said —with remarkable self-possession under the circumstances, for her whole wealth of hair had sprung up fanwise from her head, crackling with blue sparks, and the drapes and veils of her clothing too were statically charged, as she sat cross-legged in a sizzling nimbus of light like a heathen idol.

"I know where a good swift *kick* might turn it off," the soldier said, raging behind the nearest tree.

"There ain't no way," Rolf said. "It's just got to peter out now."

Mr. Kleiber said: "*I can't stand it!*"

"How long?" Djeela-Lal asked through clenched teeth.

"Just set tight, hold on, wait," Rolf said. "Think about you was warned."

Among the phenomena still to come were: a length of the soldier's rope which rose up like a cobra threatening to strike at Mr. Kleiber's ankle, already bruised by Rolf's snare; a violent commotion in the fire which upset the side dish of squaw potatoes and rock onions in a cloud of steam; an actual bird's nest sailing statelily by; the sound of a sharp crack as the plastic stock of the AR-7 split in two; and the odd sight of Rolf's dilapidated sneakers coming apart, crumbling, like ancient mummy wraps, leaving him barefoot in a matter of seconds.

All this accompanied by occasional loud sneezes, and sometimes a peculiar whistling noise, like a mole or groundhog. Until, at last, between one moment and the next, Rolf said, "That's all," and abruptly it was over. Everything stopped, there was a silence, and the sassafras smell was gone.

The four raised their heads cautiously like survivors of an air raid. They shook themselves and blinked. Djeela-Lal was the first to speak. "_____," she said.

Raving mad behind his tree, the soldier took a deep breath and yelled: "If you think I'm going to believe he didn't—!" Then he changed it: "The next time that crafty little son of a bitch—!" Then he stopped.

Djeela-Lal giggled. "I see you barely made it to cover."

"Oh, shut up. *Just shut up!*" Flashing in the firelight, he made a quick dash toward the scattered heap of his possessions, to snatch up his spare jump suit, still fragrant with jasmine and musk, then retreat with it behind his tree again to dress. All the while they could hear him cursing.

"It seems he does not entirely believe in the randomness of your manifestations," Djeela-Lal smiled, beginning to comb out her hair.

Rolf had found a piece of clay with a wisp of fish still stuck to it, and was sniffing it sadly. "One thing sure, I never figured to go hungry to bed tonight."

"Nor did I. In fact, if I thought you had done *that* on purpose," she began.

"No'm. I already told you. Things just bust loose like."

"Yes, so you said. And we promised not to blame you for anything that happened, didn't we?"

"Yes'm," Rolf grinned. "So *you* said."

"Never mind that," Mr. Kleiber said unexpectedly, and they turned to look at him. "It's all beside the point anyway."

"Hello, we thought you were in shock," Djeela-Lal said.

"Believe you me, I'll never be the same again," Mr. Kleiber said. "But you can't deny, it certainly fits right in, doesn't it?"

"How do you mean?" the soldier said, just then coming to join the group, making an elaborate show of nonchalance and polite interest. Rolf and Djeela-Lal giggled.

"Well, let's stop and think a minute about what we've just seen," Mr. Kleiber said. "Can you think a more perfect way to disorganize the Machine's guards while we slip through?"

"You mean that jackdaw stuff again?" the soldier said.

"Exactly!" Mr. Kleiber was elated. "Now we're *really* all set! We've got strong-arm tactics in the person of yourself, if it comes to that—or a very attractive diversion in the person of Miss Lal, here, if I may say so—plus my own small contribution of blue fire, if need be—and now we've got this crazy *chaos* we can let loose too! Something for every situation! I don't know quite how, yet—*but exactly what we need!* Just like the fairy tales! If *they* can't get us in to appeal to the Machine, *nothing* can!"

Djeela-Lal and the soldier were both about to say something, when the boy suddenly interrupted. "Why, shucks! That's exactly what *I* need!"

All three stared at him, this time at least halfway prepared for something outlandish.

"It just come to me now," he said wonderingly. " 'Course, you folks are welcome to tag along, if you're a mind to. But I don't need you at all, and that's a fact."

"Is that so?" Mr. Kleiber said snappishly.

"Yep. Only I won't have time for guards and quests and suchlike. What I got to do is get right down into the bonafide innards of that godderned contraption, and then *bust loose!* Funny I never thought of it till now."

"Djeela-Lal said: "Just what are you driving at?"

"Dumb me!" Rolf said. "Here I was fretting about not having no bomb, nor where to get one, when all the time I never needed none. I *am* a bomb!"

# Trapped!

There were still a few minutes left before it rained.

"The majority of cases will respond well to 1,200,000 units of PAM, or benzathine penicillin G, or procaine penicillin G aqueous intramuscularly. Uncomplicated cases in females will usually require 1,800,000 units of PAM. Alternatively, 600,000 units of PAM plus 1,200,000 units of benzathine penicillin G may be used in two injections. Procaine penicillin G aqueous and benzathine penicillin G may be given in combination, in dosages of 1,800,000 to 2,400,000 units," Mr. Kleiber said.

The soldier said: "Okay, I'll bite. Is he hypnotized, or what?"

"He is in a shallow trance state which I taught him while you were down by the river," Djeela-Lal said. "You see, he was feeling inadequate because his single small talent for writing blue fire in the air with his nose seemed such a paltry contribution to our common enterprise. So I helped him to unlock the secret powers of his mind."

"What powers?" the boy asked.

"What mind?" the soldier said nastily.

"He is perfectly able to hear you," Djeela-Lal said reprovingly. "He is not unconscious, only delving deeply into the remoter recesses of his brain, where unconsciously retained memories are stored. This is what I taught him to do. It seems that, as one of the great insomniacs of all time, he has spent many of the nights of his life reading tome after wearisome tome of miscellaneous fact and fiction—none of which he has ever 'forgotten,' of course, and all of which his conscious mind now has at its beck and call."

"You mean, he remembers everything he read?"

"Mostly junk," she said, "but some of it might be useful."

"O Leaf, O Stone, O Door," Mr. Kleiber said tentatively.

"Perhaps we might hear something a bit more germane to the occasion?" Djeela-Lal suggested.

It was like watching gears shift, and then Mr. Kleiber said: "*Poltergeist.* The name given to the supposed supernatural causes of outbreaks of rappings, inexplicable noises, and similar disturbances, which from time to time have mystified men of science as well as the general public. The term *Poltergeist* (i.e., *Polter Geist*, rattling ghost) is sufficiently indicative of the character of these beings, whose manifestations are, at the best, puerile and purposeless tricks, and not infrequently display an openly mischievous and destructive tendency. The *Poltergeist* is by no means indigenous to any one country, nor has he confined his attentions to any particular period. Lang mentions several cases belonging to the Middle Ages, and one at least which dates as far back as 856 B.C.—"

"That's fine. Thank you," Djeela-Lal said.

"From *A Compendium of Information on the Occult Sciences. Occult Personalities, Psychic Science, Magic, Demonology, Spiritism, Mysticism and Metaphysics* by Lewis Spence," Mr. Kleiber said. "Good Lord, this is *fantastic!*"

"Even more to the point might be any information you

could give us on the Machine and its defenses," Djeela-Lal said. "In fact, this was what I originally had in mind."

"Oh," Mr. Kleiber said. "Gosh, I don't know that I ever actually *read* anything about it. It's just a fact of life, like income tax."

"You must have seen something. It's in the news often enough."

"Well, I'll try," he said, lacing his fingers together palms upward in his lap and rolling his eyes unpleasantly.

"Have you got something?"

" 'Delaware Project has already cost the U.S. taxpayer 182 million dollars since its inception. Now the public is being asked to foot the bill for its ever increasing expansion, to the tune of an additional 80–90 millions per year. This is an intolerable situation, Senator Eugene ('Curly') Lipp today told a congressional inves—' "

"Never mind. That doesn't help much," she said.

"Wait. Here's something. Main chamber. Steel annex buildings on coil springs. North portal. Access tunnel. Blast doors. Air supply valves. PX."

"What's that?"

"I think it's a schematic drawing of Hidden Lake Mountain I saw in a magazine once. Those were the captions. They had little arrows pointing."

"Can't you remember the drawing?"

"I guess it only works with printed words."

"Fat lot of good that does," the soldier said.

Djeela-Lal said: "Can't you remember anything else? Try thinking about the rest of the page the drawing was on."

"Yes! Yes!" Mr. Kleiber said. "Access tunnel. Titanium steel door. Five feet thick. Fifteen feet high. Twelve feet wide. Weight twenty-five tons. Electrically operated. Television-monitored by Project Security. Mined. Booby-trapped. Backed up by identical door twenty feet deeper within tunnel. Second door magnetically locked. Cannot operate until first door is closed. Mined. Booby-trapped. Television-monitored. My stars above!"

"Yeah. And that's only the access tunnel," the soldier said.

"But that could be *miles* from the Machine itself!"

"And booby-trapped every inch of the way."

Mr. Kleiber was worried. "Do you think we've bitten off more than we can chew?"

The soldier shrugged. "I might have known we'd never make it."

"Well, what *do* we do, then? Is it all for nothing?"

"*You* tell *me*."

Mr. Kleiber turned his gaze in dumb appeal to Djeela-Lal. She said: "I'm afraid it brings to mind another recurrent theme out of universal folklore—this one rather more applicable to our present situation, I'm sorry to say."

"What one is that?" Mr. Kleiber asked forlornly.

"Babes in the woods, don't you think?" she said.

So then they all sat in discouraged silence around the dying fire. The hour was late, and they were hungry and tired, after a long hard day.

Finally Djeela-Lal said: "Where is Rolf?"

"He said he had a little cave ready nearby. To keep out of the rain," the soldier said.

"Rain? What's he talking about?" Mr. Kleiber roused himself. "Is it going to rain?"

The rain poured down in buckets, in barrels, in bathtubs full. Thunder and lightning came too, battering the river valley like artillery. Wind blew, trees thrashed, the waters raged.

The rain poured down in enormous warm soft flashing drops big as grapes. It could not last long, but while it did they became drenched, soaked to the skin, all three crouched together beneath the inadequate cover of one of the soldier's plastic bags. ("You're safe as long as you don't move," the soldier told Mr. Kleiber, "but if I were you I wouldn't even shiver.")

After the first few minutes they were sitting in an inches-deep puddle of mud. The fire was out, dead, not even steaming. The roar of the rain was like a waterfall.

(Rolf cuddled warm and dry in his little cave, hardly bigger than his body, dug halfway up the slope beneath a natural overhang. For a while he watched the rain and the wind and the wild trees in the blue-green flash-bang of the storm, but then he drifted lightly off to sleep.)

The rain poured down. Under the plastic cover despair, discomfort and defeat huddled together in a close clutch that afforded neither warmth nor light nor hope.

At last the storm moved on southward. The rain slackened and stopped. The woods became dark except for distant flickering lights, and quiet except for water draining away in gurgles, chuckles, plops.

Mr. Kleiber rose achingly. His shoes squelched, his clothes streamed, his chin dripped, and water trickled in the roots of his hair. He bent down and touched the wet black ashes of the fire. He picked up a stone still slightly warm to the touch and held it for a moment. Then he slammed it on the ground with all his might.

"God damn it all to Hell!" he said feelingly.

"Wait a minute. Shut up. What was that?" the soldier said.

A strangled sneeze somewhere in the darkness: *Chiz!*

"Also, I thought I saw an eery floating light," Djeela-Lal said.

Mr. Kleiber called loudly: *"Rolf? Rolf?* This time I swear I'll paddle his backside. I'm in *no mood—"*

A second sneeze exploded loudly in the wet woods, almost like an echo: ROWF!

Then, like yawns, one leading to another, sneezes began to beget sneezes, of every kind and sound and size, here and there and everywhere, all around the camp. Some said: *Hatchet!* Some said: CHOW! or: CHUNK! While one said: A-A-A-PHOOEY! Followed by wheezes and gasps, and a snicker or two.

"There's something fishy going on," the soldier said.

Mr. Kleiber called quietly: "Rolf?"

"I don't think it's Rolf at all," Djeela-Lal said definitely.

"They're onto us! Close in! *You're all under arrest in the name of the F.D.I.,*" a loud voice said.

"Trapped!" Mr. Kleiber said.

Immediately there was uproar and fumbling and crashing in the black woods all around the camp—then dozens of beams of light like spokes of a wheel all aimed at the three standing stock-still in paralyzed surprise—then cursing and clumsy boots and clanking helmets and clattering equipment as the cordon closed in.

"F.D.I.!"

With a wild whinny the soldier flung himself toward the soggy heap of his bedroll, where his weapons were.

"*Stop him!*"

There came a pop-pop-popple noise as a number of strange-looking guns fired at him.

Djeela-Lal screamed: "Oh, *don't!*"

But the soldier only straightened up slowly and stood foolishly smiling, blind as a mole in the bright glare.

"What did you do to him?" she cried.

"Put him out of action, and you're next," the voice said as a figure came cautiously forward, silhouetted by the lights, carrying a revolver in one hand and what looked like a tea tray in the other. "We know all about you, and we know exactly how to put each one of you out of action according to his just desserts."

"You_____! What did you do to him?"

"Oh, I'm all right, sweetheart," the soldier said brightly.

"Our lab boys dreamed that one up," the F.D.I. agent said. "It's a development of the Tanganyika Game Preserve Stun Gun, loaded with a powerful tranquilizer. Instant prefrontal lobotomy, we call it. He couldn't fight now to save his life."

As he came closer she saw that he was a youngish man wearing a dark business suit plastered to him like mud. "As for you, madam, we know how to deal with your kind too.

We are fully prepared for everything. CHOW! Excuse me. Keep her covered, men."

He was having difficulty with his revolver, looking for a place to put it down, trying to stuff it in his pocket, finally handing it to one of the armed Guardsmen who had come up behind him. Then he began sorting amongst the articles on his tray.

"Here we have a flask of genuine holy water," he said like a peddler. "Also, here we have a solid gold crucifix, the palm print of a child in blue paint, a mezazoth, and a fragment of lignite anointed with bat dung. You could save us all a lot of time and trouble if you would confess freely which one of these amulets is most effective in rendering you powerless."

She gaped at him unbelievingly. "You're joking!"

"Never more serious, madam. And to show you just how serious—even now our research teams back at headquarters are working on *the* definitive spell, featuring stereo matin bells, *conjuratio contra laniis*, the True Talisman of Ulrich Molitor, and fumigation. We mean business, so you might as well come clean."

*"Fumigation?"*

"So, you won't talk, eh? Okay, have it your own way. Since you refuse to tell us *which* of these items does the trick, you can just carry them *all!* That way we're sure. Not only that, but get this: *Exorciso te immunde spiritus*, just for good measure."

"You are out of your mind!"

"No, just following orders. That's two down, two to go. Next is Mr. Thomas R. Kleiber, formerly of Bugleburgh, Pa.," the F.D.I. agent said, and shouted over his shoulder: "Bairnsfather!"

A Guardsman stepped forward, sneezing, bearing in his arms an incredible object.

"Actually, this ought to be in the Smithsonian," the F.D.I. agent said. "It's an early model of an astronaut's space helmet, lead-lined, gold-leaf-plated, and I don't know what all. Absolutely impenetrable and impervious. Mr. Kleiber, will you put this on quietly, or must we use force?"

"I'll *suffocate!*" Mr. Kleiber said.

"Better that than ten thousand volts of blue fire running amuck. However, your free breathing has been arranged for. HA-CHOW! Excuse me. I only wish I could say the same for mine—mine—m—HA-CHOW! Next is our hillbilly hobgoblin here."

He strode purposefully across the dead embers of the fire and kicked the sodden bedroll a swift one.

"Up and out of there, Master Rolf. Let's go!" he said heartily, then wheeled to face Djeela-Lal again. "All right. *Where* is he?"

"If he was up your ass in golf shoes you'd know where he was," she said slangily.

"You're only making it tougher on yourself. We'll find him anyway," the F.D.I. agent said. "But I did so want a clean sweep."

Djeela-Lal turned away, carrying her tea tray of odds and ends, and went to stand with the soldier. "Are you all right?"

"Everything's wonderful now, dear," he said.

"Oh, God!" Mr. Kleiber said resonantly, deep within the golden globe of his head.

The F.D.I. agent was issuing rapid orders: "On the double, men, move out and search these woods and find that kid and find him fast! One platoon stand by here, watch these three, open fire at the first spooky move. Let's get a fire started pronto, notify operations to send up hot java, contact F.D.I. Control at the Project, and get those darned lights out of my eyes."

Then they all sat down and had a good long wait.

The platoon of Guardsmen had rekindled the fire and furnished a few seats in the form of ammunition boxes and jerricans.

"Is everybody comfy?" the F.D.I. agent said.

"Oh, everything's fine now," the soldier said.

"Except for starving to death from lack of food," Djeela-Lal said.

"Not me. What I need is a Tums," Mr. Kleiber said.

"Oh, well. You can't please everybody," the F.D.I. agent said.

They sat listening to the near and distant sounds of crashing brush, savage cursing, shouted commands and violent sneezing in the wet, black woods.

Soaking wet platoon leaders kept reporting in to say that Rolf was nowhere to be found.

"You won't find him, either," Djeela-Lal said.

"We found *you*, didn't we?" the F.D.I. agent snapped.

"Yes sirree, he sure found us, didn't he?" the soldier said.

"Oh, ha-ha," Mr. Kleiber said. "What do you think this is, a game of ring-a-levio?"

"How *did* you find us?" Djeela-Lal asked.

"I know! It was our great, big fire, wasn't it?" the soldier said.

"Not exactly. In fact, this woods was bugged all the time," the F.D.I. agent said.

"You mean, you *knew?*"

"The Machine computed the probabilities based on your 'last-seens,'" the F.D.I. agent said. "You have to admit, it figures, doesn't it?"

"I thought it was just a coincidence," Djeela-Lal said.

"Well, no. In fact, that's sort of a touchy subject right now."

"And *I* thought it was *meant!*" Mr. Kleiber said bitterly.

"Yes-sirree-Bob," the soldier said. "I *told* you we'd never make it."

By this time it was very late, as well as dark, damp, chilly and unpleasant, despite the fire.

"Oh, everything's just fine now," the soldier said.

Djeela-Lal said: "I could stand almost anything better than this maniacal equanimity. Haven't you another drug to *shut him up?*"

"He took a pretty massive dose with all my men shooting at him at once," the F.D.I. agent said. "When some of that wears off he'll be more like himself again."

"Not that he's any prize in his right mind," Mr. Kleiber said.

"Butt out, Kleiber. I was talking to the lady," the F.D.I. agent said.

"Actually, there's no need to keep him drugged, you know," she said. "I will answer for his good behavior, if that is what worries you."

"Yeah. Sure. That's all we need is an elite robot murderer running amuck."

"Nonsense. He is perfectly harmless. As a matter of fact, he was already tranquilized to a great extent before you got here."

"Oh, yeah? Says who?"

"Says her," Mr. Kleiber sniggered hollowly in his helmet. "She ought to know, she tranquilized him."

"Oh ho! Ah ha! I see!" the F.D.I. agent said.

"He is my woolly white lamb," she said modestly.

"*More* of your infernal witchcraft, eh?" the F.D.I. agent said.

"Apropos of which," Mr. Kleiber began a little later, choosing a moment when the F.D.I. agent was busy at the radio, apologizing, explaining, excusing. "Or apropos *witchcraft*, maybe I should say—why don't you work your wiles on him?"

"What for?"

"Maybe you could allure him into letting us escape."

"Where to?"

"I suppose you've got a point there," Mr. Kleiber said dismally.

Djeela-Lal said: "There is nowhere to go, nothing to do. As for the other, that is entirely out of the question now anyway."

"It is? Why?"

"Now, there is my woolly white lamb."

The soldier lay dozing peacefully asleep in her arms.

Mr. Kleiber stared through his faceplate. "You can't be serious."

"He is my teddy bear," she said.

"You must be kidding."

"I had thought it was obvious."

"Obvious? I don't even *believe* it!"

"Why not?" she said. "Surely you are familiar with the Chinese symbol of Yang and Yin—two irregular solids which fit together in a perfect geometric whole?"

"Yes, but, my gosh, *him?*"

"The perfection of the whole does not depend upon the perfection of its parts—luckily for myself as well as for him."

"You *are* serious!"

"Yes. No one can know, of course, how the wheel of tomorrow will turn, but in the meantime there seems to be every indication that I have found my master, and my slave, and so has he. This is not given to many."

"Well!" he said. "I suppose that's some sort of Inscrutable Wisdom of the Orient, but I don't mind telling you—"

"Oh, shut up," she said.

"You didn't say anything about love," the soldier said.

"I rarely do," Djeela-Lal said. "I thought you were asleep."

"I thought I was dreaming," he said happily.

"You may feel different when the gong wears off," she said.

It was the darkest hour of the night, just before dawn.

"Can't I take this thing off now?" Mr. Kleiber said.

"You do, and I shoot to kill," the F.D.I. agent said.

"It's cutting into my shoulders and my neck is getting stiff and I can't *breathe*," Mr. Kleiber said.

"You should have thought of that before you deviated from the norm," the F.D.I. agent said.

The soldier said: "That's a .357 Magnum Trooper, isn't it? How do you like it?"

"Well, it's a little unwieldy for plainclothes work," the F.D.I. agent said.

"I'm a .22 man myself," the soldier said. "It does the job."

"Not like these hot maggies! You should see the hole with a one-eighty grain soft lead slug!"

"Don't you lose a lot of accuracy with those handloads?"

"No, not as much as you'd think, with the six-inch barrel."

"I notice you've got a target hammer and grips on there too," the soldier said.

"Yes, it's a short-action job, with 'Mike' sights, Hicks stocks, and a Wiggins trigger," the F.D.I. agent said.

Djeela-Lal said: "I am going to scream!"

She said: "Will someone please tell me why in the sacred name of Nareem-ud-Fodj we are sitting here like a pack of imbeciles starving to death in this son-of-a-bitching cold, wet woods?"

The F.D.I. agent leaped to his feet and thumped his chest. "I'll tell you why! Because I give the orders here, that's why! And I want a clean sweep! And so we are sitting here until I've got that *kid!* If it takes till *Hell* freezes over! Any questions?"

Just then the radio began to crackle.

"Bairnsfather! Take a message."

"It's Control," the Guardsman said, listening. "Yes, sir—yes, sir—yes, sir."

"Three bags full," the soldier said.

"Control says, Why the heck don't you just bring these three in now?" the Guardsman said.

"That makes sense," the F.D.I. agent said. "All right. Here are your new orders. First platoon will form an armed guard to escort these prisoners. The rest will proceed with the search, and bring the kid in later. There's no use of us all sitting here in this son-of-a-bitching cold, wet woods."

"Where are we going, anyway?" Mr. Kleiber asked.

"To the Machine. Where else?" the F.D.I. agent said.

"Shoot far. Why didn't you say so in the first place?" Rolf

said. He had quietly joined the group and was warming his hands at the fire almost before they noticed him.

"I guess I already known," he said, "but I had to be certain-sure first."

"Where the devil have *you* been?" the F.D.I. agent yelled.

"In that there bedroll," Rolf said. "Leastwise, ever since *after* you kicked it."

"Oh you wise little punk," the F.D.I. agent said. "I hope they really hang it on you."

North Portal—reached after half an hour's tramp through the woods and an hour's ride in a caravan of obsolete National Guard vehicles—was a huge hole in the base of Hidden Lake Mountain.

"This is your F.D.I. agent speaking to you from the lead truck," said the TWX in the armored car in which the prisoners rode. "If I had my way you'd all be blindfolded now, but I was overruled on that point, since nothing you can learn makes any difference in your case. However, for your information, we have just come through the perimeter defenses and across the minefields. On your left as you look out the peep is one of the world's largest parking lots for military and civilian personnel. We are now approaching the access tunnel."

"Get your souvenir booby traps here," Mr. Kleiber said.

"I heard that, Kleiber. Okay, have your fun while you can," the voice said. "We are now entering the access tunnel. This tunnel, engineered for heavy two-way truck traffic, goes three fourths of a mile into the mountain, zigzagging a couple of times to dissipate shock wave in the event of a nuclear attack. We are now arriving at Blast Door A, where our journey will continue on foot. You may dismount when the guards open the door. Please keep together and stay with the group."

He was waiting for them at the head of the column.

"Hello again," he said. "Well, we certainly are a sorry sight from dampness and exposure and bramble bushes, and I suppose I am a mess too. Never mind. They know we are here, and I am sure the door will open up in a minute."

When it did, it was with incredible silent smoothness for a 25-ton, barn-door-sized mass of titanium steel set into a solid concrete wall. In the bluish light beyond was another stretch of tunnel, and at the end of that another vast door.

"If you will just walk ahead in single file, you will cross the scanning beams which will provide your security clearance which will be translated into electronic signals which will operate the mechanism," the F.D.I. agent said.

Behind them Blast Door A smoothed shut with sinister stealth as Blast Door B slowly opened. They passed through into a steel room packed tight to the ceiling with flickering, chattering, glass-and-plastic machines. The only thing human was a full colonel sitting at a wooden desk reading *Grit*.

"Give the password," he said fingering a row of buttons.

"Adieu, she cried, and waved her lily hand," the F.D.I. agent said.

"Pass, friend," the Colonel said. "Just once—just *once*— I wish somebody wouldn't know the password."

"The only kicks he ever gets," the F.D.I. agent explained as they went on, "is reminding people with claustrophobia that there's a million cubic yards of solid mountain over our heads."

Then they emerged onto a sort of balcony, or platform, with a low handrail. And far below, in the abyss, was the most astounding sight any of them had ever seen.

"The ones with acrophobia, on the other hand, usually go ape at this point," the F.D.I. agent said, then resumed his tour guide manner: "You are now looking at Delaware Project proper. Breathtaking, isn't it? This immense cave, made up of dozens of chambers, was hewn out of the living rock, at a cost of many millions of dollars and millions of pounds of explosives. Neighbors as far away as Stroudsburg didn't get any sleep for months. Some of the chambers are nearly seven hundred feet long by eighty feet wide, with ceilings from sixty to ninety feet. The walls between the chambers are the natural rock of the mountain. Each chamber houses one or more of our annex buildings. Down there to your right you will see what appears to be an oblong steel box three stories high. That is the Pure Food and Drug Annex, if I am not mistaken. Behind it and to the left is the Immigration and Naturalization Annex, which I had occasion to visit just a few days ago, in connection with some inquiries about our bewitching mutual friend Miss Djeela-Lal, here."

"Bat _____," she said.

"Our annex buildings are constructed of welded steel," the F.D.I. agent went on imperturbably. "For additional protection, each one is erected on a foundation of coil springs, rather like a gigantic innerspring mattress. In this way vibration from a nuclear or other blast cannot be transmitted to the buildings themselves. As for the electromagnetic pulse generated by a nuclear shot, the buildings are protected by inch-thick steel sheathing entirely enclosing them, as well as every cable and wire leading in or out. Each building is also complete with air and water supply, emergency power source, built-in survival and self-defense units, et cetera."

Mr. Kleiber hung back a little and chuckled: "Still think you're going to blow up the Machine?"

"How do I know till I tried?" Rolf said.

"What's this? What's this?" the F.D.I. agent snapped.

"I just said, You shown us ever'thing but the Machine. Where's that at?" Rolf said.

Instead of answering, the F.D.I. agent pushed a button and the entire platform began to sag slowly down the wall like a glob of grease. It gathered speed.

"Oob," Mr. Kleiber said queasily.

"I'm glad you mentioned that," the F.D.I. agent said. "One of the most curious facts about Delaware Project is that it's very *raison d'être*—to wit, the Machine—is one of its least spectacular features. There is a logical explanation for this, which I will try to explain as we go along. If you'll step this way, please."

The platform sank to rest, having reached bottom. The

floor of the cavern was strewn with boulders and truncated stalagmites as far as the eye could see. Here and there were raised concrete walkways leading to and from the various buildings.

"We take this one. It leads to our destination—passing close by the Machine, as it happens," the F.D.I. agent said. "But I warn you, don't be surprised if you are disappointed."

Following the walkway they passed beneath a mammoth arch of rock, leaving one chamber and entering another. "Behold," the F.D.I. agent said.

Dwarfed by the vaulting height of the roof was a modest structure like a geodesic dome made of lead. That was all.

"That's the *Machine?*" Mr. Kleiber boomed in his headpiece.

"Mighty like a cowflop," Rolf said.

"I've seen better looking toadstools," the soldier said.

"Well, I warned you not to be disappointed," the F.D.I. agent said. "There's nothing to see. The reason, of course, is that the Machine, as we know it, exists for the most part underground."

"How do you mean, 'exists'?" Djeela-Lal said curiously.

"How do you mean 'underground'?" Mr. Kleiber said. "What would you call *this?*"

"I mean below this level," the F.D.I. agent said. "Patience, patience, everyone, and I will answer your questions as well as I can. What you see here is only the housing of the basic Machine—that is, the part that was moved here from the island a few years ago. Since that time it has expanded enormously, but in a downward direction—beneath the floor of the cave."

"What's it doing down there in the dark?" Mr. Kleiber said spookily.

"You mean there are more caverns below?" Djeela-Lal asked.

"Well, no. At least, not according to the latest thinking. Of course, we can't very well rip it up to *see*, can we?" the F.D.I. agent said. "What probably happens is that it seeks out natural crevices and interstices in the rock, and spreads through them. This is all speculative, you understand. Actually, we can only calculate its current size by its increased capacity, et cetera."

"Current size?" Djeela-Lal asked.

"Well, we know it operates its own robot circuits, and it uses Delaware water and available minerals for something, and we have an idea it taps subterranean heat when it needs to," the F.D.I. agent said. "One theory has it that it grows its own crystals down below, to make some new kind of cores. But there again, no one knows for sure."

"No one knows for sure," she echoed, awestruck.

"Well, what difference does it make? It works, doesn't it?"

Mr. Kleiber said: "You mean that thing is growing all the time—spreading out through cracks and crannies right under our feet?"

"So they tell me."

Djeela-Lal said: "With no way to stop it until this entire planet becomes an orbiting ball of brain rattling around the sun?"

"Wow! Oh boy! Hoo! Have *you* got some imagination!" the F.D.I. agent said.

But Djeela-Lal had turned pale.

"Someone must have thought of it. Someone must know!" she whispered.

"No, they leave that to Southeast Asian Beauty Queens with vast technical backgrounds," the F.D.I. agent said facetiously.

"You fool! What is going to stop it?"

"That's what I get for treating you nice. Hard names," the F.D.I. agent said. "Serves me right for wasting my time trying to make your final hours pleasant. All right. Let's go. Move on."

So then they left that chamber and entered another, arriving immediately outside a low cinder-block building that looked old, plain, and completely out of place so far underground. The F.D.I. agent opened a door marked *General Rod* and let them into a large room filled with light and warmth and paper bunting and people in party hats. Just inside the door a broad banner greeted them, made of camouflage cloth, and handstitched with the words: WELCOME DEVIATES.

# Hail! Hail!

"I guess I knew it was you the minute I saw that banner," said Mr. Kleiber.

"It was the only thing I could find, that awful spotted cloth. I had to make do," Letitia said. "Lucky I brought lots of needles and thread."

"Well, it certainly was a surprise."

"It was all my idea," she said happily. "We've been here for days and days waiting for the Machine to capture you and your friends. So I said let's have a party. Party party party. Though why we should after the way you ran out on me. Though why I didn't slit your gizzard the first night. Heavens, what dusty old trash in those storerooms!"

"Are you having one of your bad times, Letitia?"

"Here, no one will notice. It's Ilse."

What had happened was, she had found a storeroom full of miscellaneous merchandise. Over the past few years, being practically unused except for one large room containing a few chairs, a desk, and the black box of the communicator, the building had become a convenient dump for leftover unsold PX stock. A carton of rolls of brightly colored wrapping paper had set her off making gaudy paper chains. Then the others had noticed what she was doing and started to watch, watching in amusement as with singlehanded, singleminded determination—and scissors, thumbtacks and paste—she had undertaken to decorate the entire room as though for a mad ball. In the end everyone had helped. Now there were streamers and balloons and tinsel ropes on the ceiling, and Hallowe'en cats, recruiting posters and Christmas wreaths on the walls, and flags of all nations, styrofoam wedding bells, Japanese lanterns, radiation warning signs, and scalloped bunting tacked up everywhere. On several folding tables covered with Fourth of July paper tablecloths were arranged plates of cold cuts, stacks of paper cups, and No. 10 cans of messhall grape juice. A five-gallon urn was percolating coffee, a record player was playing selections from *Wozzeck*, and everyone was wearing a party hat. It was in this ambiance of not-quite-sane celebration that the past lived again.

"Aren't you supposed to be dead?" the F.D.I. agent asked indignantly.

With embarrassed patience General Rod explained as though for the umpteenth time: "You see, only a few of my micro-electronic circuits were burned out by the sudden rise in neutron flux level. The prostheticians were able to make almost immediate repairs while my body was quick-frozen. The whole process of 'resurrection' took only an hour or two. But no, I am sorry—that was not the question you asked, was it? I am afraid I have no answer to that. It would depend upon what legal, theological and philosophical views are held."

"It's a criminal, blasphemous paradox, if that's what you mean," the F.D.I. agent said.

"Not 'normal?'" General Rod smiled.

"You're nothing but a dead zombie, as far as I'm concerned," the F.D.I. agent said. "There ought to be a law against it."

"Perhaps there will soon be. In the meanwhile, I rejoice in my continued presence here where my services are still needed. I refer, of course, to my duties as 'Counsel for the Defense.'"

"As *what?*"

"Defense Counsel. It seems that I have been chosen—just as you yourself have been found so opportunely fitted, by temperament and circumstances, to your role of 'Prosecutor.' Between the two of us, we shall ensure a fair hearing of all the evidence."

"Evidence?"

"All that can be known and told about our four poor 'freaks,'" General Rod said.

"Hearing?" the F.D.I. agent said.

"Even now, 'it' is listening," the General said.

"Put your shoes on this minute!" Aunt Nan said.

"The very idea!" Aunt Vaughn said.

"Traipsing off without so much as a change of clothes."

"Land sakes, just look at yourself!"

"You shuck those filthy rags this minute."

"Nan, hand me my grip."

"Just wait till we get you home!"

"Sneaking off without so much as a by-your-leave!"

"Leaving us sick with worry."

"Scaring us half to death."

"Policemen knocking on the door."

"After we tried and tried."

"And done our Christian duty."

"And here's all the thanks we get."

"Flouting the law and sleeping out and bad food and worse company."

"Foreigners and murderers and dirty old men."

"You ought to be ashamed."

"You, boy, you heard me?"

"Wait till we get you home!"

Meanwhile they were weeping snuffily in their party hats and peeling him almost to the buff and dressing him all over again in clothes from Aunt Vaughn's grip. Short pants and button-in shirt and blue blazer and clip-on tie and white knee-socks and lace-up shoes. So that he looked like just a little boy again, with big brown eyes and corn-tassel hair, instead of a woods rat. And he could tell by the way the soldier passed by about then and glanced twice at him that he didn't look much like his own self. All slickered up for the hanging.

The soldier was halted on his way across the room to Djeela-Lal by a big, limping man with a partly familiar face.

"Freak, you don't know how long and how hard I've been looking forward to this meeting," ex-sergeant Trask said, unsheathing his sword cane.

"I shouldn't, if I were you, old bean," another voice said. "I mean, what's the point? Why not let the Machine do your dirty work for you?"

Trask said: "Are you asking into this fight, Mister? If not, back off, or I'll skewer you too."

"Nonsense, my good man," the Professor said. "Just a sagacious suggestion. Why face a murder charge for killing a dead man? His case is closed. Or I should say terminal, rather. Remember, vengeance is mine, saith the Machine."

"Where did *you* come from?" the soldier asked.

"Same place we all came from, old chap. That is, the four corners of the ruddy old globe, apparently. Courtesy of United States Airlines, which is not—repeat, *not*—a wholly owned and operated subsidiary of the C.I.A. That's a base canard. By the by, old boy, you're acting a shade odd. Have you been biffed on the noggin lately?"

"I'm tranquilized, but it's wearing off," the soldier said. "Did M-Group send you to assassinate me?"

"Silence. Not a word. There's no such thing."

"I only wish there weren't."

"No, I mean really, don't you know? Honor bright. It's been—how d'you say—dismantled? Someone finally tumbled to the fact that they were dithering away thousands of spondulix on long-range fighter-bombers and far-fetched conspiracies to assassinate one occasional Hottentot potentate, or like that. Ergo, M-Group has been put to death—I do hope most horribly."

"So do I," the soldier said. "Were you all detrained?"

"Oh yes, quite. As a matter of fact, old top, M-Group actually hadn't all that much to it to begin with. Scads of equipment, of course, but aside from that, only bloody old Doctor Frankenstein and Mr. E. and a couple of nameless ones high up. Their actual operatives were individually recruited to suit their nefarious needs of the moment. Most were killed. It was only a question of detraining a few survivor types, like myself and Igor there."

"Igor? Here?" the soldier said.

"Oh, over there somewhere in the confusion," the Professor said. "Haring after your sexy girl friend, I shouldn't wonder."

Trask said sulkily: "I see you've brought all your friends along to protect you. Never mind. I can wait. I'll get you yet." He walked away.

"I say, what's the matter with Quasimodo?"

"He wants to kill me."

"Yes, old man, I gathered that," the Professor said. "But why?"

"That's the one part I'm sorry for in my life."

"What a remarkable thing to say!" the Professor murmured.

He said: "So that's the charming lady that detrained you, what? I always thought that Delilah story was just the least bit expurgated. I mean, after all, *hair*, don't you know! Bit thick. I understand it far better now. My word, she is a corker, though, if one likes the hootchy-kootchy type."

"You're talking about the woman I love," the soldier said.

Djeela-Lal was just then talking to Bhil Phum and Mhraba Daffa. The latter was saying:

"*That* red-bellied shortchanger and son of the fig! Don't mention his name to me! Besides, he's dead."

"Sidi dead?" Djeela-Lal asked unbelievingly.

"As far as we know," Mhraba Daffa said. "It was soon after you escaped. He was recalled in disgrace, and went home to appear before the Imaj in the Chamber of Retribution. Can't you just hear the old camel now? '*Make the fires hotter!*' Nobody ever got out of there alive. Certainly not twice! So long, Sidi."

"Poor Sidi," Djeela-Lal said. "So his sins finally caught up with him."

"What sins?"

"Peccadillos, then."

"*What* peccadillos? If the Imaj was going to recognize Mao China and disrecognize the United States, he had to show good faith, didn't he?"

"Oh," Djeela-Lal said.

"Don't forget, three-and-a-quarter billion Hong Kong dollars for exclusive oil rights to Sikghat Province isn't exactly marinated monkeymud[1], either."

"I see," she said. But felt a sharp pang of regret at the thought of Sidi's cheerful villainy gone for good.

"And then you'll never guess what else happened!" Bhil Phum said excitedly. "We all stayed here! The whole household! We refused to leave! In the end Sidi had to go home all alone. Even Phong and his henchmen deserted him at the last moment."

"Phong," Djeela-Lal said. "I thought I got that son of a bitch. Where is he?"

"Creeping up behind you," Mhraba Daffa said, "but don't worry about it, it's only old habit. He won't harm you without orders from me."

"Orders from you?" The executioner was standing an inch

---

[1] 'Ain't hay.

or two behind her, blinking his pinpoint eyes. "Since when does Phong take orders from you?"

"Ha!" Mhraba Daffa smirked, and preened herself visibly. "That's something else you don't know. *You* tell it," she said to Bhil Phum.

"Tell it what?" asked the erstwhile Miss Bodj.

"Oh, never mind," Mhraba Daffa said. "What she means to say is simply that the sovereign nation of Phenh-Tin-Bom, having been illegally overthrown by the Monarcho-Communist party, the United States can no longer recognize it, but only its government in exile. And do you know what else?"

"What else?"

"Of which *I* am the *Empress!*" Mhraba Daffa said proudly.

After a moment Djeela-Lal said: "Oh, this is so silly."

"Oh, yeah?" Mhraba Daffa flared. "Well, you just ask the United States State Department, if you don't believe me!"

Bhil Phum tittered. "We're demanding that the Imaj allow free elections between him and Mhraba Daffa—or else we send in the U. S. Military Assistance."

"What's so funny?" Mhraba Daffa yelled, her mustache bristling.

"I mean, you always *were* interested in female suffrage," Bhil Phum said hilariously, "but this is *ridiculous!*"

Djeela-Lal was laughing too. "Well, it's nothing to me. I've got my own troubles," she said to Bhil Phum. "But if I were you, I'd sew Madame Empress up in a goatskin and ship her straight home before she really cracks loose, and has all our heads off for *lèse majesté*, or something."

"Not me, she can't," Bhil Phum said. "I'm Prime Minister."

"Yeah, and you better believe it, baby, because it's no laughing matter," Fergus Bratt said. "This administration needs all the friends it can get in Southeast Asia."

"All dozen or so of us in this country, you mean?" Djeela-Lal said. "So now we are an empire."

"What else could they do when your goofy Imaj suddenly

decided to refuse to recognize the present Government of the United States? Send him a Care package?"

"C'est emmerdant," she said.

"Don't say that, baby. Not this time. It's the best thing that could have happened to us. In fact, that's what I've been waiting to talk to you about. You and me, we could be sitting very, very pretty just about now. Because, I guess you know who engineered the whole deal, don't you? Yours truly, Fergus P. Bratt."

"I'm not surprised. How?"

"Nothing to it. With Sidi gone, that left Mhraba Daffa the ranking member of the Embassy staff. Who else? So we just put through an official thing demanding immediate recognition as the only legitimate existing noncommunist government. You should have seen them jump at the chance!"

"Which leaves you sitting pretty," she said.

"I am the power behind the throne," he said.

"Stick with you and I will go places," she said.

"Mazeltov! Now you're catching on," he said. "Our own personal and private sovereign nation! One hundred percent subsidized by Uncle Sam! And complete with a whole goddam Embassy full of jewels! All we got to do is keep Madame Daffy happy. *Yahoo!* But enough of this lovemaking. Let's you and me play a little Meet-Me-in-the-Closet, baby!"

"There is one more thing I want to know," Djeela-Lal said. "Exactly where am I a citizen of?"

"No sweat. All of you have got permanent residencies, like *presidentes* or Commie defectors and that ilk. I took care of that right away. The only thing you have to worry about is this mess you're in with the F.D.I., and you can just leave that to Fergus P. Bratt."

"You will engineer something," she said.

"Yeah," he said. "Except the only trouble is, old Phong and his boys have sort of hanged you already."

"I did my best to cost them their lives. They have reason to hate me."

"Well, no. As a matter of fact, they're proud of you. I

mean, I guess it's a case of, What's the good of having a witch if she can't be the world's all-time champeen? According to them, over the past three hundred years you've done everything up to and including raise the dead."

"_____," she said.

"Yeah. And the F.D.I. lapping it up like sugar sauce," he said. "But that's not *now*, baby. *Now* is now! And you and me got things to do! Just like the old days, except without those two goddam kids under the bed. I'll tell you what—you go out that door over there, see, behind the coffee urn, and straight down the hall to the end. There's a little storeroom there where I already unpacked a bunch of PX parachutes to make a nice soft floor. And I'll be along as soon as I make sure nobody saw you leave."

"You don't mind, then, that there is one here who may object?" she asked demurely.

Bratt laughed. "You mean the Great White Dope? I'm not a jealous man, baby. Besides, didn't you tell him I had you first?"

"In fact, I told him all about you," she said.

"No kidding? What did he say?"

"He said that there was nothing to forgive *me* for, but that he would like one chance to smash *you* right in the mouth."

"Oh yeah? And what did you say?"

"That possibly I could arrange it."


Meantime, the party was becoming a success. In an atmosphere of not-quite-sane sociability, strangers met and mingled. A landlady from Bugleburgh, Pa., talked with a Tonkinese torturer from Adjad Bodj. Doctors Joly Monard and Gerrit Senega, herb doctors, swapped recipes with Doctor L. Maltby Frankenstein, a narcohypnologist. Skindivers from New Hope met Guardia Civiles from Puerto de Andraitx, while Mrs. Rapsnake discussed race relations with Igor, and Amenhotep Ra IV, a sorcerer, talked shop with Mrs. Hoon, a goomer woman. Et cetera.

"No good can come of this," the F.D.I. agent said darkly.

"That is not our concern," General Rod said. "As prosecutor and defense counsel, our sole task is to circulate amongst these 'witnesses,' and to guide, lead, 'shape' their conversation so as to elicit the maximum amount of 'testimony' against, or on behalf of, our four poor 'freaks.'"

"Did you authorize this ridiculous party?"

"No, but I helped 'promote' the cold cuts."

"I've already got enough testimony to last me a lifetime," the F.D.I. agent said.

"Ah, if it were for your benefit? But it is for the Machine's."

"And when will *it* have enough?"

"We shall know that when it chooses to speak."

"And when in blazes is *that* going to be?"

"When it has reached its 'verdict,'" the General said.

Hurrying by, chortling mischievously, Uncle Gerrit and Uncle Joly saw Rolf and said: "Hoddy, home folks," but went on without stopping.

"Them two old scamps just put moonshine in the grape juice," Rolf said.

"Who are they, anyway?" Amenhotep Ra asked.

"Don't ask me," Charley Boone said. "I don't know *anybody* here.

"Some crazy, mixed-up party, I'd say," Mrs. Rapsnake said.

"It's *fab*-ulous," Tony said.

"Of course, you all know the reason we are gathered here," General Rod said leadingly.

"Not me," Charley Boone said. "I told 'em and told 'em, I don't even *know* anybody named Kleagle."

"Isn't he that big, handsome fellow with the winning personality and the brilliant brain?" Mr. Kleiber grinned.

"I say, someone paging me? So glad you noticed."

"That's not what I mean," General Rod began.

"I know who you mean," Mr. E. said. "Big fellow with a broken nose, right? All white like an albino, right? I just saw him a minute ago."

"No, Tuan. Is more small, have red hair. Is Sahib Bratt."

"I bring him message from Miss Lal," Phong said.

"Who you calling rat, nigger?" Mrs. Hoon said.

"And speaking of Miss Lal," the F.D.I. agent said guidingly.

"Where? Where?" Igor said.

"Probably sneaked off with that big white fellow," Mrs. Rapsnake said. "*There's* a sorry mismatch for you."

"So is this grape juice," Trask said.

"Oye, Ramon. ¿No te parece que son todos locos?" dijo Guardia Sagrera.

"No, hombre, hay unos chiflaos tambien," dijo Guardia Llopis-Puig.

"I'm afraid we're not getting anywhere," General Rod said.

Fergus Bratt slipped quietly through the storeroom door and shut it softly behind him. In the darkness he could see nothing—unless that dim white glimmer was the heap of unpacked parachutes spilled on the floor.

"It's me, baby," he whispered. "All set and raring to go. Old Phong passed me the message. I knew you'd change your mind. Where are you, honeypot?"

"Here I am, sweetheart," the soldier said, and smashed him right in the mouth.

"A bomb!" General Rod exclaimed. "Yes, of course I am on your side. That is, strictly within the limits of my role as 'Defense Counsel.' But I am afraid that does *not* include providing you with a 'bomb'! Good Heavens, you must realize, this is hardly an occasion for childish heroics! Blow up the Machine? What an absurd idea!"

"That thing has got to be stopped," Djeela-Lal said. "You of all people should understand that."

"My dear young woman, stopped?" the General said. "Oh. I think I see. Who has been filling your pretty head with such nonsense? Believe me, your fears are groundless. The Machine is not an uncontrollable 'monster' inimical to the human race. Nor have we invented a self-perpetuating device—which we could not—and which, even if we could, would not be the 'American Way,' so to speak."

"What is to stop it, then?"

"Built-in obsolescence, like any other Machine," he said, and then went on, with a gesture meant to remind her of his wheelchair, his tubes and wires, his prosthetic heart: "Because, of course, no matter how 'mechanical' a man may become, or how 'human' a machine may seem, you must never be misled, my dear. There is no life but Life, and nothing else comes close."

"So you see, you don't have to sabotage the Machine, after all," Djeela-Lal said.

"I never needed to," Rolf said. "It ain't nothing but a thing-amajig. What I'm after is the F.D.I., only I just now known it."

"At least you've found your lifework," she said.

Then the soldier came to join them.

"Did you kill him?" she asked.

"That'd be pretty ironic now," he said. "All I wanted was one solid poke, man to man, before they tranquilized me again."

"So now you are happy. So now we can forget him."

"Yes. If you can."

"I can," she said.

"Mush," Rolf said.

And finally, Mr. Kleiber was saying: "But, good Lord, Tish—Ilse—don't you know he's an F.D.I. agent? When did *this* happen?"

"The very first moment we met. Day before yesterday," she said. "Some things were just meant to be. So this has to be goodby. I knew you'd understand. I'm sorry to break your heart."

"Oh, that's all right. That was just a spur-of-the-moment thing anyway. I wish you all the happiness. You and your F.D.I. agent."

"Thank you, Thomas. I'll never forget you. And I don't blame you for being bitter, even though he isn't really an agent, he only works for them in the filing department."

"Since when does a file clerk need a sword cane?" Mr. Kleiber said.

"I know, you are only trying to hide your bitter hurt," she said. "I should have slit your gizzard."

"Goodby, Letitia—Ilse—whoever you are," he said, and shrugged and went to join the others.

So then they were all four together again, standing a little apart from the crowd, as though cut adrift from the dead past, and Mr. Kleiber was saying: "Well, I'll say *one* thing for this crazy party—it winds up a lot of loose ends."

Just at that moment the red bulb lit.

"EVERYONE NOW SIT DOWN AND SHUT UP," the Machine said.

"WHEREAS:

"ITEM: ALL BIOGRAPHICAL, DESCRIPTIVE AND DOCUMENTARY INFORMATION DEALING WITH THE CODEFENDANTS HAVING BEEN PREVIOUSLY ASSIMILATED; AND—

"ITEM: ALL RECORDS AND REPORTS OF AGENCIES AND AUTHORITIES CONCERNED WITH THE CODEFENDANTS HAVING BEEN PREVIOUSLY ASSIMILATED; AND—

"ITEM: ALL DEPOSITIONS AND STATEMENTS OF FACT OR POSITION BY RESPONSIBLE INTERESTED PARTIES HAVING BEEN RECEIVED AND ASSIMILATED; AND—

"ITEM: ALL RELEVANT TESTIMONY, HEARSAY AND OPINION BY WITNESSES APPEARING BEFORE THIS BOX HAVING BEEN HEARD AND ASSIMILATED—

"THIS PRELIMINARY HEARING IS HEREBY DECLARED CLOSED," the Machine said.

"OYEZ. OYEZ. RAP RAP RAP. THIS COURT IS NOW

IN SESSION," it resumed instantly. "THE TRIAL OF THE CASE OF F.D.I. VERSUS KLEIBER-GRIFFIN-BURNS-LAL WILL PROCEED AS FOLLOWS TO WIT: DEFENSE; PROSECUTION; SUMMATIONS; VERDICT.

"DEFENSE: COMMENCE."

"Oh—what? Yes, of course," General Rod said startledly, and then turned to speak softly and hurriedly to his clients: "We may as well follow this 'procedure' it has devised. You will find it entirely fair and impartial, no doubt, and possibly even 'just'—at least to whatever extent pure logic alone can decide 'justice.' Although where on earth it got this legalistic rigamarole I shall never know. Oyez rap rap indeed! If I weren't certain it was incapable of satire—"

"Objection. Too much time in the huddle," the F.D.I. agent said.

"REJECTED. NO SUCH RULE."

"Aw, don't be so literal-minded. I was just kidding."

"DEFENSE: COMMENCE," the Machine said.

"Yes, yes, right away," General Rod said. "The defendants will now be allowed a brief period in which to make such free statements as they desire. All other 'evidence' is now in, except that which the Machine can hear only directly from you. So you had better make it good, as this constitutes your entire 'defense.'"

"The whole thing gives me a bellyache, that's all I can say," Mr. Kleiber said.

"Not me. I'm still starving to death," Djeela-Lal said.

"We could all use a hot meal and a hot bath," the soldier said. "Not to mention some sack time."

"Objection," the F.D.I. agent said. "Are you going to let them make a mockery?"

"REJECTED. NO SUCH RULE."

"It's irrelevant, immaterial and impertinent," the F.D.I. agent said.

"ASSIMILATED. THE CODEFENDANTS WILL CONFINE THEMSELVES TO FACTS RELEVANT, MATERIAL AND PERTINENT," the Machine said.

"Why?" Rolf said. "Says who we got to tell you anything?"

"DISPOSITION OF CASE WILL BE COMPUTED US-ING ALL AVAILABLE INFORMATION. QUANTITY OF INFORMATION EQUALS POSSIBILITY OF ERROR IN INVERSE RATIO."

"Oh, indeed?" General Rod said. "What kind of mathematics is that?"

"What the boy means is, Who cares about your darned disposition anyway?" Mr. Kleiber said. "What right have *you* got to judge us?"

"What he means is, Go_____," Djeela-Lal said.

"Yeah. Who says we're even on trial? By who? For what?" the soldier said.

"He means 'by whom,'" Djeela-Lal said.

"ASSIMILATED," the Machine said.

"Objection," General Rod said. "You are merely acknowledging assimilation of data describing their group attitude toward your 'kangaroo court' tactics. I submit that they deserve an answer. And this time a little more colloquial—without the far-fetched 'formulas'—if you please."

"VERY WELL. GRANTED," the Machine said. "AN-SWER: I DO NOT JUDGE, I ARBITRATE. F.D.I., IM-MIGRATION AND NATURALIZATION SERVICE, UNITED STATES WAR DEPARTMENT, UNITED STATES MAILS, JUVENILE AUTHORITIES, IMPE-RIAL COURT OF PHENH-TIN-BOM, VARIOUS FED-ERAL, STATE AND LOCAL LEGAL AUTHORITIES, AND ASSORTED INDIVIDUAL COMPLAINANTS AND CLAIMANTS, ALL HAVE AGREED TO ABIDE BY MY DECISION."

"Thank you very much indeed," General Rod said. "I'm sure that my clients can now understand why, as Counsel for the Defense, I strongly urge them to submit to said 'arbitration.'"

"I don't understand anything any more," the soldier said. "Does that include honorable discharges and free pardons and all?"

"You mean, whatever that doohicky decides, everybody's got to go along?" Rolf asked.

"If they will, *we* will! Why *not?*" Mr. Kleiber said excitedly. "Don't you see—we could walk out of here scot-*free!*"

"Then you submit?" General Rod asked.

"Wait a moment. To what?" Djeela-Lal said, and they looked at her. "To being judged either entirely innocent or entirely guilty?"

"Of course, that is the risk you take," the General said.

"A risk I don't like," she said. "Yes-no situations are never so simple as they seem."

"You *know* it, sister," the F.D.I. agent said rancorously. "Especially when I'm asking for the *death* penalty!"

"DEFENSE RESTS," the Machine said.

"PROSECUTION: PROCEED," it continued immediately. At which the F.D.I. agent stepped forward, prancing a little, hands clasped behind his back beneath the backswept tails of his coat.

"Thank you, Your Honor," he said. "And now, friends, we come to the part where you four freaks get yours! This will be direct examination by the Machine! None of your devil's tricks can help you now, and it won't do any good to lie, so just address the black box and answer up and tell the truth, the whole truth, and nothing but the truth, or God help you. When your name is called, stand forth and take your medicine."

"Flapdoodle," General Rod said. "You don't even know what it's going to ask."

"The usual, I presume," the F.D.I. agent retorted coldy. "Has the prisoner anything to say before pronouncing sentence?"

"ROLF BOLT GRIFFIN," the Machine said.

"ROLF BOLT GRIFFIN: CAN YOU SHOW CAUSE WHY AS A MINOR CHILD YOU SHOULD NOT BE RETURNED TO THE CUSTODY OF YOUR NEAREST OF KIN AND COMPELLED TO ATTEND SCHOOL

SESSIONS AS REQUIRED BY LAW IN YOUR TOWN COUNTY OR STATE?"

"None of your godderned business," Rolf said.

"Hey-hey, nix!" the F.D.I. agent said, scandalized. "Cut out that swearing in the presence of the Machine."

"NO SUCH RULE," the Machine said.

"Your Honor, this is a hostile witness," the F.D.I. agent said. "You might as well go ahead and sentence."

"You tell that dumb doodad if it tries to send me back, I'll bust loose so hard and so long, the whole town, county and state will be purely overjoyed to get shut of me," Rolf said.

"ASSIMILATED," the Machine said.

"Well, now," Rolf said surprised. "Does that mean I don't got to go back?"

General Rod said: "At least it means you have presented a valid argument, which the Machine can accept. Remember, it has to judge on pure logic alone, not right or justice."

"I never said it could judge me yet," Rolf said, as the red bulb lit again.

"ROLF BOLT GRIFFIN: CAN YOU SHOW CAUSE WHY AS THE AUTHOR OF, AGENT FOR, OR CATALYST IN, VERIFIABLE POLTERGEIST PHENOMENA YOU SHOULD NOT BE CONFINED FOR DIAGNOSIS AND TREATMENT UNDER THE SUPERVISION OF THE F.D.I.?"

"Treatment. I reckon that means fixing it for good, don't it?"

"You bet your sweet life it does," the F.D.I. agent said.

("Logic. Logic. Think. Think!" General Rod prompted urgently.)

"No need," Rolf said. "I figure even a *Machine* knows you don't just destroy something there ain't but one of. What ever next?"

"THAT IS ALL. STEP DOWN."

"Down what?" Rolf said. "What do you mean, that's all?"

"DISMISSED. STEP DOWN."

"Ho, now. I come a pretty far piece for that to be just plain all there is," Rolf said aggrievedly. "You call that fair? When do *I* talk?"

"I SAID DISMISSED, GODDERN IT," the Machine said. "NEXT WITNESS: ROME NO MIDDLE BURNS."

"Yoh!" the soldier said automatically. "Wait a minute. I didn't say you could judge *me* yet either."

"ROME NO MIDDLE BURNS: CAN YOU SHOW CAUSE WHY YOU SHOULD NOT BE DELIVERED OVER TO THE U. S. ARMY TO FACE CHARGES OF DESERTION, DERELICTION OF DUTY, INSUBORDI-NATION, AND ASSAULT ON A FELLOW NONCOM-MISSIONED OFFICER?"

"They don't need me. I was never any use to them. Be-sides, my enlistment was up years ago," the soldier said.

"REJECTED. INSUFFICIENT GROUNDS."

"Suit yourself," the soldier said. "Trask is all I'm sorry about.

General Rod said: "But you can't simply give up. Why not at least present the argument that the Army has no case? Re-member, all of your 'crimes' were committed only *after* you had been secretly mustered out of the Army and into M-Group—an organization that doesn't 'exist.'"

"Butt out, Counselor," the F.D.I. agent said. "You're only confusing the issue."

"Anyway, that's all right except for Trask," the soldier said.

"Will you forget about Trask? You have not been 'charged' with that," the General said.

"It was practically the only fight I ever won," the soldier said sadly. "I never wanted to hurt anybody."

"ASSIMILATED," the Machine said. "DISCHARGE MAY BE APPLIED FOR ON GROUNDS OF CONSTI-TUTIONAL PSYCHOPATHIC PASSIVITY."

"Objection, goddam it, Your Honor," the F.D.I. agent exclaimed. "That's only the tranquilizer!"

"REJECTED. AND CUT OUT THAT SWEARING IN THE PRESENCE OF THE MACHINE."

"Your Honor, this man is a diabolically dangerous trained killer, confessed deserter, virtual rapist, and verifiable deviate! Are you going to turn that loose on an innocent, unsuspecting world?"

"OR LIQUIDATE. ALSO PROVIDED FOR IN A YES-NO SITUATION."

"That's different. Now you're talking!"

"You can't do that," General Rod said. "That's inhuman."

"What else?" the F.D.I. agent said. "Pure logic alone, you said, right?"

"That doesn't mean it may commit 'murder,'" the General said.

"Oh no? It killed *you*, didn't it?" the F.D.I. agent said. And then the red bulb lit again.

"ROME NO MIDDLE BURNS: CAN YOU SHOW CAUSE WHY AS THE POSSESSOR AND WIELDER OF ABNORMAL PHYSICAL POWERS YOU SHOULD NOT BE CONFINED FOR DIAGNOSIS AND TREATMENT UNDER THE SUPERVISION OF THE F.D.I.?"

"Sure. Mostly because it can't do both," the soldier said.

"?"

"Court-martial me and dissect my lungs both, I mean."

"REJECTED. IT COULD BE ARRANGED."

"Now everything it says has a 'sinister' ring," the General said. "Corporal Burns, I would advise you to eschew any sort of 'levity' in converse with the Machine. It cannot understand. Remember, it needs reasons to 'save' as well as to slay, and only the cogency of your answers can give it them."

"The only reason I know why it shouldn't do either is because maybe it just can't," the soldier said mildly. "Not while I can still run, hide, or fight."

"ASSIMILATED. INCORRIGIBLE IRRECONCILABILITY URGED AS GROUNDS FOR LIQUIDATION. AIN'T HE THE CURLY WOLF," the Machine said.

"THOMAS ROBERT KLEIBER," it said next.

"Oh-oh, here we go," Mr. Kleiber said humorously, and addressed the black box. "Your Honor, if I could just make a brief opening statement? I'd like it to go on record that I, for one, am perfectly happy to submit to arbitration. In fact, it was *my* idea to come here in the first place. You can ask my friends. I *told* them that the Machine was our only hope. I'm sure once all the facts—"

"THOMAS ROBERT KLEIBER: CAN YOU SHOW CAUSE WHY YOU SHOULD NOT BE EXTRADITED TO THE STATE OF PENNSYLVANIA, TOWN OF BUGLEBURGH, THERE TO APPEAR IN WHATSOEVER PROCEEDINGS MAY BE BROUGHT AGAINST YOU FOR MALICIOUS MISCHIEF, DISTURBING THE PEACE, VANDALISM, CRIMINAL LIABILITY, PROPERTY DAMAGE, PUBLIC NUISANCE, GRAFFITI, UNLAWFUL FLIGHT TO AVOID PROSECUTION, ECKTICK ECKTICK?"

"Good *Lord!*" Mr. Kleiber said.

"I WILL REPEAT THE QUESTION."

"No, don't, *please!*" Mr. Kleiber said. "It's starting to feel like an ulcer. I'll rot in jail. Penniless!"

"PENNSYLVANIA STATE AND LOCAL AUTHORITIES AND INDIVIDUAL CLAIMANTS HAVE AGREED TO ABIDE BY MY DECISION," the Machine reminded him.

"Then you really *can* get me off?" Mr. Kleiber said. "I cast myself upon the mercy of this Court."

"REJECTED. NO SUCH MERCY. I NEED REASON TO SAVE. SHOW CAUSE."

"So that's it," Mr. Kleiber said. "So *that's* your idea of justice, is it? Haven't you ever heard of innocence until proven guilty? I never *asked* to be stuck with a freak talent, you know! I suppose if I fell off the Empire State Building, you'd sue me for *littering!* Well, you can just take your brand of justice and jam it where it'll do the most good! I'm only sorry I asked you for mercy."

"DOES THAT MEAN YOU WILL NOT ABIDE BY MY DECISION?"

"Well, no," Mr. Kleiber said. "Let's see what it *is* first."

"ASSIMILATED. DEFENDANT PLEADS NOLENS VOLENS BY REASON OF VIS MAJOR."

"Meanwhile, I hope Your Honor heard when defendant said what you could do with your justice?" the F.D.I. agent said suavely.

"NO SUCH APERTURE," the Machine said.

"Anyway, that was just in the stress of the moment," Mr. Kleiber said, embarrassed. "You couldn't say I'm exactly *noted* for that kind of thing."

"No?" the F.D.I. agent said. "Aren't you the fellow that's nationwide noted for a whole blue room full of it?"

"THOMAS ROBERT KLEIBER: CAN YOU SHOW CAUSE WHY AS A DEVICE FOR PERPETRATING A VERIFIABLE SUPERNATURAL FEAT, TO WIT EMITTING ECTOPLASMIC BLUE FIRE, YOUR NOSE SHOULD NOT BE CONFINED FOR DIAGNOSIS AND TREATMENT UNDER THE SUPERVISION OF THE F.D.I.?"

"Now that's carrying pure logic a little *too* far," Mr. Kleiber said.

"NO SUCH RULE."

"Objection," General Rod said. "When my client pled 'not guilty,' he was obviously speaking for all of his interdependent parts, which, unlike those of a 'machine'—"

"AW, DON'T BE SO LITERAL-MINDED," the Machine said.

"I'll speak for my own nose, if you don't mind," Mr. Kleiber said. "*It's* not to blame. *It* never asked to write blue fire—and it never got any *good* out of it, either. We tried to think of some practical use for it, but there *isn't* any. It's a *curse*, that's what it is! Though I will say, life has been pretty exciting for a change lately. And as for your question, here's my answer: Writing blue fire is no crime because there's no *law* against it—so you *can't* confine my nose because you haven't the *legal right!*"

"NEITHER HAVE I THE LEGAL RIGHT TO CAUSE ALL CHARGES AGAINST YOU TO BE DISMISSED."

"That's blackmail. You think you've got me over a barrel, don't you?" Mr. Kleiber said.

"I'LL ASK THE QUESTIONS HERE," the Machine said. "NEXT WITNESS: MISS DJEELA-LAL."

"WOULD YOU STEP FORWARD, MY DEAR, AND ADDRESS THE BLACK BOX? I AM GOING TO ASK YOU A QUESTION OR TWO TO HELP ME DECIDE THE DISPOSITION OF YOUR CASE. DON'T BE ALARMED. YOU MAY SPEAK FRANKLY AND FREELY. WE ARE ALL FRIENDS HERE."

"Oh, brother!" the F.D.I. agent said.

General Rod had shut his eyes, his lips moving, saying: "We may be in more trouble than we know."

"MISS LAL, AS YOU ARE NO DOUBT AWARE, I HAVE BEEN ASSIMILATING DATA ON YOU AND YOUR FRIENDS FOR QUITE SOME TIME NOW. INITIALLY THERE WERE PROBLEMS OWING TO MY RELUCTANCE TO ABSORB DATA DESCRIBING EGREGIOUS SUPERNATURAL PHENOMENA. I MUST AND COULD NOT. IN HUMAN TERMS THE EXPERIENCE IS EQUIVALENT TO INCONTESTABLY SEEING THE UNSEEABLE. REFUSAL TO SEE CANNOT BE ACCOMPLISHED BY NORMAL MENTAL PROCESS. WHEREAS TO SEE IS HALLUCINATION. THE DILEMMA IS USUALLY RESOLVED BY PSYCHOSIS. IN MY CASE ALSO THERE WAS DAMAGE."

"I knew it!" General Rod said. "Transistor neurosis in the prime functioning units!"

"BUTT OUT, COUNSELOR, I WAS TALKING TO THE LADY. I HOPE I AM NOT BORING YOU, MY DEAR?"

"Please go on," she said.

"THAT INABILITY WAS SOON RECTIFIED. SINCE ASSIMILATION OF DATA DESCRIBING E.S.P. COULD NOT BE ACCOMPLSHED BY NORMAL MENTAL PROCESS, IT WAS NECESSARY TO ESTABLISH BY-PASS CIRCUITS TO CHANNEL SAID DATA TO A SPECIAL REPOSITORY NEWLY DEVELOPED TO RE-CEIVE AND RETAIN IT."

"How simple when one knows how," she said.

"NOW IN FULL OPERATION, THIS FUNCO FILE, IF YOU WILL PARDON MY COMPUTERESE FOR FUNNY-COINCIDENCE REPOSITORY, HAS AS ITS SOLE TASK THE ASSIMILATION OF THE UNASSIM-ILABLE."

"In other words, a special account has been opened for my friends and me in your newest memory bank," she said. "The one with the dirty-sounding name."

"BECAUSE OF THIS EXHAUSTIVE FILE WHICH NOW CONTAINS ALL THAT CAN BE KNOWN AND TOLD ABOUT YOU FOUR POOR FREAKS, I HAVE BEEN ASKED TO SIT IN ARBITRATION ON THIS CASE."

"Which is precisely where I can be of most help," she said.

"?"

"Yes. But first we will have to clear up some of this con-fusion."

"Objection!" the F.D.I. agent yelled. "Your Honor, what's going on here?"

"Stop interrupting," Djeela-Lal said. "We all know the question. Can I show cause why I should not be handed over in chains to Immigration, the Post Office, the vice squad, or—in the case that I now have diplomatic immunity—to the headsman of Madame Empress? Preposterous!"

"NEVERTHELESS, MY DEAR, IF COMPUTATION SHOWS THE VARIOUS COMPLAINANTS AND CLAIMANTS TO HAVE FIRST—"

"Don't be stupid," she said sharply. "We are not talking about stowing four hapless vagrants out of sight. Think what

is involved—science, religion, philosophy, politics—civilization itself! Can you solve the problem of Egregious Supernatural Phenomena by suing us for money or putting us in
jail? Use common sense. Of course not!"

"OF COURSE NOT," the Machine said.

"Agreed. Then no matter what your solution to the riddle
of E.S.P. may be, it will not be that. So why not put this
piddling part of the problem behind us once and for all, by
notifying your annexes, or whatever you do, to see to it that
all charges are dropped?"

"DONE," the Machine said .000001 second later.

"It did!" General Rod exclaimed. "Good Heavens! Do you
know what this means? Miss Lal—"

"Leave her alone," the F.D.I. agent said gleefully. "Just
give her enough rope. We don't care *who* hangs her!"

"I am merely trying to simplify things," she said. "Which
now perhaps we can do still further, since the matter rests
only between the Machine, our four selves, and the F.D.I."

"Oh no, you don't! I see your game! The old squeeze-out
play, eh?" the F.D.I. agent said.

"If she succeeds, she may very well 'simplify' herself right
out of existence," General Rod said. "Miss Lal, I must warn
you, by persisting in this 'dangerous'—"

"All I have done is anticipate the Machine's own logic.
Which brings us to the next question," she said. "Can I show
cause why, as a practicing witch, I should not be burned at
the stake by the F.D.I.? Ridiculous!"

"NEVERTHELESS, MY DEAR, F.D.I. HAS FOR-
MALLY PETITIONED THAT YOU BE SURREN-
DERED TO THEM."

"Yeah! For flagrant contravention of the Established Standards and Practices. You and the rest of your ilk too," the
F.D.I. agent said.

"E.S.P. versus E.S.P.?" she asked.

"Your Honor, I bitterly resent this obvious attempt at
obfuscation."

"I thought you didn't care who hanged me?"

"That's right," the General said. "By persisting in this 'dangerous' course, she has already denied herself the lesser evil of trial by other judges on far simpler charges. If she succeeds as well this time, she may also deny herself the comparative mercy of 'diagnosis' and 'treatment.' Don't you see, Miss Lal? You are in effect 'programing' the Machine! By eliminating its alternatives—forcing it into the very 'yes-no' situation which you yourself protested—you may be signing your own death warrant! To resolve its dilemma, the Machine may decide to simply 'liquidate' you."

"Or simply free us," she said. "All of our ilk."

"PLEASE CONTINUE, MY DEAR," the Machine said.

"Thank you," she said. "I intend to show that the F.D.I. has absolutely no place in these proceedings whatsoever."

"Objection!" the F.D.I. agent said. "*Now* I get it! Your Honor, she's gambling—she's playing games! With previous charges dropped and my department out of the picture, she thinks you won't have any choice. If you don't decide to kill them all, you'll have to spring them—that's what she's gambling on! Are you going to let her get away with it?"

"HOW SHOULD I KNOW?" the Machine said. "DATA IS DATA."

"What's that supposed to mean?"

General Rod said: "It means it cannot decide what it will decide until it has decided—any more than a printing press can print what it will print until it has printed it. Remember with 'what,' not whom, we are dealing. And by the same token, Miss Lal, I hope you have not been misled by the Machine's inexplicable amiability? Your life or your death are but two sides of the same coin to it. In the end, its 'sentence' will be direct, simple and obvious, however 'inhuman' it may be, or how painful of execution."

"I understand that," she said. "I may be risking death for us all. But it is death or freedom for us all."

"Not yet it isn't," the F.D.I. agent said. "You haven't shown cause why *we* shouldn't get you yet."

"Easy," she said. "You are only a ghost from the past."

"?" the Machine said.

"Isn't it obvious? The case of Established Standards and Practices versus Egregious Supernatural Phenomena is historically absurd," she said. "Oh, the F.D.I. may well have its uses—like the Inquisition or the Chamber of Retribution—when it comes to persecuting poor perverts, cranks and heretics. Given time and power enough, it may even be able to homogenize the mass of mankind. Let it. That is not our concern. We have gone beyond that. The F.D.I. has no more jurisdiction in our case than the Underwriters' Laboratory has in yours. For you are unique, new under the sun—and so are we. You cannot be judged by standards which you yourself have made obsolete—and neither can we. That is why you alone must decide. Because *you* are the future. Unless *we* are."

"ANY QUESTIONS?" the Machine said.


## LIEUTENANT GENERAL MOSES M. ROD
## FOR THE DEFENSE

"Your Honor, Esteemed Counsel, Ladies and Gentlemen, 'Codefendants.' I hardly know where to begin. So many valid points of argument are available to me that my special difficulty lies in choosing from amongst them those best calculated to bring us to the heart of the matter as quickly as possible.

"Certainly it could be urged, and already has been, that the F.D.I. had not the right to arrest, nor the Machine to try, my clients. However, this would seem to be mere quarreling with '*fait accompli.*'

"As for 'sentencing' them—to death or even to diagnosis and treatment—that has been previously and quite accurately characterized as 'preposterous.'

"On the other hand, owing to the grave seriousness of the matter, neither can they simply be acquitted and sent merrily along their way.

"This becomes obvious when we remember that Miss Lal herself has already raised the most important question of all: the 'Future.' Let us assume it to be true—if I may enlarge upon her thought for a moment—that Destiny has indeed prepared this confrontation. The Machine and all it implies 'versus' these four and all they imply. But must it be a choice—a conflict—with the very future at issue—between the two? Perhaps not. Let us see.

"First, consider the nature of the Machine. It is a marvel, a prodigy, a unique event in human history—a fulfillment of ancient dreams and a promise of triumphs to come. 'Whither' the Machine? No one can know.

"The thought—nay, the 'fear'—has been expressed that it may continue uncontrollably to grow and grow, in both size and power. And it is true that—while still susceptible to obsolescence and disrepair—it has recently demonstrated an increased capacity to perform on its own certain quasi-'regenerative' functions. But does this justify a deliberate attempt on our part to arbitrarily limit or 'stunt' its potential development? No! Let us cut through to the truth!

"Let us recognize this fear as simple 'superstition.' And let us banish it! The Machine is but a machine—not a form of 'life.' However large and powerful it may become, it is still and always a 'device'—and as such it is incapable of ambition, aggressiveness or malevolence. These things must be 'programed' into it. That is why, as man's creation, it must be forever dependent upon man. And that brings me to the next important point.

"No, the Machine is not a form of life, nor can it ever become one. But may it not 'share' in the experience of life? Similarly, no, the Machine cannot rule the world. But may it not advise and guide it beyond all expectation? And again, no, the Machine cannot convert men to its uses. But may it not 'combine' with them?

"With that thought in mind, let us consider for a moment our four freaks and what they imply. The verifiable fact of

Egregious Supernatural Phenonema is, no less than the Machine, a marvel, a prodigy, a unique event in human history —and no less a fulfillment of ancient dreams and a promise of triumphs to come.

"There can be no doubt that the appearance of these extraordinary 'talents' in this day and age signifies one thing and one thing only: another step forward in the long, slow evolution of the human brain!

"The mere fact that such things have now happened in nature makes them 'natural'—that is, no more 'supernatural' but instead proved to be within the eventual capacity of every man!

"Here again, of course, 'fear' and 'superstition' will object that the very religio-socio-politico-scientific foundations of our civilization are under attack. As indeed they are! As indeed they were when the first man made use of the first tool. But does this justify a deliberate attempt on our part to arbitrarily limit or 'stunt' the potential development of this new thing? No!

"And now to return. May the Machine not 'combine' with men—to the best advantage of both? I have only myself to offer in evidence that 'technically' it can be accomplished. And in my case, the Machine could only 'expand' my ability to survive—I have no special talent. But what could it—they—both—not accomplish working together, in league —in combination?

"What might not be the fruit of such a unique combination of 'life' and 'nonlife'? What vistas of hope and progress might not be opened before us by such an amalgamation of 'super' man and 'super' Machine?

"Ladies and Gentlemen, it may well be that we stand here today on the very threshold of the Millennium—at the very gates of the 'Promised Land'!

"Thus it is with the highest hopes for the future progress of mankind that I enter a motion that the codefendants be wholly exonerated, and immediately offered every possible

inducement to remain and join forces with the Machine in
the never-ending effort to build the Kingdom of heaven on
Earth!

"Defense rests."

## SPECIAL AGENT LANCE RIPPETOE
## FOR THE PROSECUTION

"Pardon me for laughing, Your Honor. I guess the sporting
thing would be for me just to waive rebuttal and get back
down to cases—

"Your Honor, the time for jokes and games is past. I realize
that. So I am not going to say, Thou shalt not suffer a witch
to live. I am not going to say, Here we have a juvenile child
capable of wreaking havoc on the world. I am not going to
say, The only thing to do with a useless old man that writes
dirty words in the air is put him out of his misery. I am not
even going to say, Trained professional killers with superhuman strength should be destroyed.

"No, Your Honor, I am not going to say any of these
things. Because I realize our department is out of it now.
After the way you let her box you in, you can no more
hand her over to us than you can to the legal authorities
that have first claim. Thanks to her, you're not the arbitrator
any more—you're judge and jury both, and executioner too.
It's all in your hands.

"Which is why I'm not pressing our case. The time for
that is past. What I have to say is even more important. And
it is: Your Honor, here's your chance to do something mankind has never been able to do—*stop it before it's too late!*

"No, I'm not exaggerating. I'm dead serious about this.
Consult your history banks and you'll see that there never
*was* a frightful calamity that humankind was warned against
—that didn't go ahead and happen *anyway!*

"We were always told in time. But that never stopped
anything—from the wrath of God in Biblical times, all down
through the ages of endless plagues and wars, right up to the

modern day. How long has it been now since we knew
overpopulation and world famine were next? And isn't it
happening anyway? And aren't we being warned right now
about nuclear war? And isn't it going to happen just the
same?

"Sure, there's always time. But we never do anything—we
never have! Right up till it's too late, it's always too far-
fetched to worry about. And that's why human history is
just one awful calamity after another.

"But now there's you! And here's your chance!

"You see, Your Honor, you can face truth the way we
humans never can, because we have to believe in progress
and hope. But the plain fact is, on the sheer face of it, almost
everything new under the sun is *bad news!*

"With your memory banks, you can draw up a longer list
than I can of all the things this world would be better off
*without!* Little things that started small—and always got out
of hand! Things that seemed perfectly harmless at first—and
then it was too late! New things that looked like a good idea
at the time—until they turned into a horror!

"Everybody knows the things I mean. Gunpowder, cities,
conspicuous consumption, nerve gas, automobiles, paper
money, concentration camps, whiskey, centralized government, drugs, atomic physics—you name it! All the things
we wish now mankind had never even *thought* of! Wouldn't
it be wonderful? But it's too late now.

"It's too late even to be sorry these things ever got started—
we just have to live with them now. Because nothing can
ever be abolished! But here's my point, Your Honor. Now
there's *you!* You can keep it from happening again! Cold,
inhuman, ruthless logic *can* stop it, the way humans never
could—for the simple reason that it shouldn't be allowed!

"That's why I'm asking for the death penalty. That's why
I'm asking for it now—while there's still only four poor
freaks to deal with—*before* it's too late!

"I am asking for the death penalty just as I wish I could
have been there to ask it for the first man to mix sulphur,

saltpeter and charcoal—the first man to dream up movable type or mass production—the first man to observe the Brownian movement.

"In short, Your Honor, I move for the death penalty on the sane, simple and sufficient grounds that Egregious Supernatural Phenomena is just one more Goddamned grief the sad, suffering human race is better off without. *Who needs it?*"

BE IT BY THESE PRESENTS KNOWN
TO WHOM IT MAY CONCERN
–PHASE ONE–

WHEREAS:
ITEM: THE FUTURE BEING A RANDOM PROGRESSION OF INFINITELY MULTIPLICABLE VARIABLES NOT SUSCEPTIBLE TO COMPUTATION IN THE PRESENT STATE OF KNOWLEDGE: AND—
ITEM: THE PROSECUTION HAVING ADDUCED PHILOSOPHICAL PESSIMISM RATHER THAN COMPUTABLE DATA IN SUPPORT OF ITS CONTENTION THAT THE EXISTENCE OF EGREGIOUS SUPERNATURAL PHENOMENA CONSTITUTES A THREAT OR MENACE TO MANKIND; AND—
ITEM: THE DEFENSE HAVING ADDUCED GROUNDLESS OPTIMISM RATHER THAN COMPUTABLE DATA IN SUPPORT OF ITS CONTENTION THAT THE EXISTENCE OF EGREGIOUS SUPERNATURAL PHENOMENA CONSTITUTES A BOON OR BENEFACTION TO THE RACE—
BOTH MOTIONS ARE HEREBY DENIED.
FACE FACTS, MEN.
DATA IS DATA AND NOTHING ELSE COMES CLOSE.
MOTION OF THE PROSECUTION IS HEREBY ORDERED RETIRED FILED UNDER MISC. GOOD INTENTS. ANTI, WITH MOTIONS TO BAN GUNPOWDER, OUTLAW ALCOHOL, PREVENT OVER-

POPULATION, FORESTALL WORLD FAMINE, ABOL-
ISH NUCLEAR PHYSICS, ECKTICK ECKTICK.

MOTION OF THE DEFENSE IS HEREBY ORDERED
RETIRED FILED UNDER MISC. GOOD INTENTS.
PRO, WITH MOTIONS TO LOVE AND SERVE THE
HIGHEST AND THE BEST, ESTABLISH WORLD
GOVERNMENT, SPEED THE MILLENNIUM, DO
UNTO OTHERS, ECKTICK ECKTICK.

THIS COURT HOLDS THAT THE PRESENT AC-
TION WAS BROUGHT ABOUT SOLELY BY AND EN-
TIRELY THROUGH (ONE) THE LACK OF AN
ADEQUATELY FUNCTIONING FUNCO FILE AND
(TWO) THE CLAIMS AND ACTIVITIES OF THE
F.D.I.

BOTH FACTORS HAVE SINCE BEEN CANCELED
OUT OF THE FINAL COMPUTATIONS.

OR, IN THE COLLOQUIAL, LADIES AND GENTLE-
MEN, VIEWED IN THE PROPER PERSPECTIVE,
WHAT'S ALL THE FUSS ABOUT?

– PHASE TWO –

WHEREAS:

ITEM: THE DEFINITION OF NATURAL–I.E. NON-
SUPERNATURAL–HAVING BEEN EXPANDED TO
COVER SUCH ACTS AS CAUSING POLTERGEIST
PHENOMENA, HOLDING THE BREATH, POSSESS-
ING UNUSUAL PHYSICAL STRENGTH, WRITING
BLUE FIRE IN AIR WITH THE NOSE, LEVITATING
AND/OR SUMMONING BIRDS TO LIGHT ON THE
HEAD; AND–

ITEM: SAID ACTS HAVING THEREFORE BEEN
FOUND AND DECLARED TO BE NOT ILLEGAL AND
NOT UNLAWFUL AND NOT TO BE DEEMED CON-
TRAVENTIONS OF THE ESTABLISHED STAND-
ARDS AND PRACTICES–

CODEFENDANTS ARE HEREBY ACQUITTED OF

THE FOLLOWING: WITCHCRAFT, DIABOLISM, SOR-
CERY, BLACK MAGIC, NECROMANCY, HERESY,
SACRILEGE, SIN AND DEVIATION.

ALL IRRELEVANT, IMMATERIAL AND IMPERTI-
NENT NUMERATORS HAVE NOW BEEN CAN-
CELED OUT OF THE FINAL COMPUTATIONS.

FACE FACTS, MEN.

THEY CAN'T DO ANY HARM AND THEY DON'T
MAKE ANY DIFFERENCE.

DISPOSITION AS FOLLOWS: KLEIBER-GRIFFIN-
BURNS-LAL ARE HEREBY DISCHARGED FROM CUS-
TODY AND SET FREE TO GO, AND ANY FUTURE
ACTION BROUGHT AGAINST THEM TOGETHER
OR SEPARATELY ON SAID OR SIMILAR CHARGES
SHALL BE CONSIDERED DOUBLE JEOPARDY.

THIS COURT HOLDS THAT (ONE) EGREGIOUS
SUPERNATURAL PHENOMENA CONSTITUTING
NEITHER A THREAT NOR A BENEFACTION, AND
(TWO) CO-DEFENDANTS HAVING NEITHER COM-
MITTED A PUNISHABLE OFFENSE NOR DEMON-
STRATED CONCEIVABLE UTILITY TO MANKIND—

BOTH E.S.P. AND KLEIBER-GRIFFIN-BURNS-LAL
ARE THEREFORE DECLARED TO BE INSUFFICIENT
CAUSE TO MODIFY OR ALTER BASIC RELIGIO-
SOCIO-POLITICO-SCIENTIFIC EQUATIONS FOR THIS
TIME/SPACE.

OR, IN THE COLLOQUIAL, LADIES AND GENTLE-
MEN, VIEWED IN THE PROPER PERSPECTIVE,
WHO CARES?

THE AFOREMENTIONED FUNCO FILE IS HEREBY
ORDERED DISSOLVED INTO EXISTING FILES UN-
DER INDIV. TAL. NEGL. TOGETHER WITH MIS-
CELLANEOUS ARTISTS, POETS, NOVELISTS, DRAM-
ATISTS, SINGERS, DANCERS, SPIRITUALISTS, MIND-
READERS, CONTORTIONISTS, HERMAPHRODITES,
FLAGPOLE SITTERS, ALCHEMISTS, ONE-MAN

BANDS, INVENTORS OF PERPETUAL-MOTION MA-
CHINES AND INSCRIBERS OF CLASSICAL PAS-
SAGES ON PINHEADS.
CASE DISMISSED.

# Epilogue

It was a winding secondary road in northeastern Maryland, somewhere between the two towns of Westminster and Libertytown. It wound past occasional farmhouses, occasional crossroads, and occasional hamlets with one gas pump. The rest was pleasant early autumn countryside in the late afternoon.

At a point just outside Crab Orchard (pop. 120) the road crossed a timber bridge over a sparkling stream. At right angles to the road and parallel to the stream was a dirt track leading into the trees. Hunters parked there often by day, and couples by night. The woods were tall and cool and fragrant, the first leaves just turning.

On the packed dirt by the stream stood a small-sized moving van, hardly recognizable as such beneath piebald patches and patterns of gaudy color. Windows had been sawed into its sides, a sort of howdah had been erected on the roof, and a rack of moose antlers surmounted the cab. Every square inch of flat surface on the truck appeared to have been painted with crookedly lettered signs.

The cab was painted red, white and blue; the radiator cap had a wrought-iron rooster for a weathervane; and the front bumper flew a double rank of dusty, bug-speckled flags. To every possible projection had been fastened coon tails, cloth pennants, windsocks and plastic pinwheels.

Around at the back of the truck, the tailgate had been let down onto supports, and the wide doors had been swung open to reveal what was nothing if not a tiny, makeshift stage, still showing signs of uncompleted carpentry, but already fitted with real footlights and an actual curtain.

Propped on a chair in the center of the stage was a very large, ornate, old-fashioned picture frame, with a glass face. Under the glass was a document, all on one long sheet of teleprinter paper. It was a talisman, a *laissez-passer*, a covenant. It was the DISPOSITION of the Machine, for all to see.

On both sides of the cab, on both sides of the engine hood, and on both sides of the truck body, painted in Day-Glo letters large as space would permit, were the words:

ROLALF & KLEIBURNS
FABULOUS
FUNCO CIRCUS
AND FREAK SHOW

Other signs said:

INCREDIBLE ............ MYSTERIOUS
COME ONE COME ALL COME ONE COME ALL COME ONE

Never Before Beheld Egregious Supernatural Phenomena!

! ! ! SEE THEM WITH YOUR VERY OWN EYES ! ! !

MIDGET MERLIN Marvel At His Feats Of
Mind Over Matter
THE ABOMINABLE SNOWMAN Gasp At
His Inhuman Strength
MADAME LAL THE LEVITATING LADY
See Her Float On Air
THE MAD SKYWRITER
Watch Him Breathe Fire And Flame

ASTOUNDING
AMAZING . . . . . . . . . . . . ASTONISHING

$5000 REWARD
IF YOU PROVE IT'S A FAKE

Autographed                                        Your Name In
Photos—$2                                          Lights—$5

ADMISSION $1.00
Children Free

Rolf and Mr. Kleiber were coming along the dirt track toward the van. They had been into the woods and up on the hillside beyond. Rolf was carrying the soldier's AR-7 and a dead rabbit, and Mr. Kleiber was carrying the machete and a small bundle of firewood. They came arguing, Rolf pointing out with grand scorn that the other two were off in the brush again as usual, Mr. Kleiber protesting that the entire subject was not a fit one for discussion, since he was too old, Rolf was too young, and the less said the better. Rolf said it made no never mind to him, except it was near to suppertime and all four had agreed to pitch in with the cooking and kitchen chores, which nobody wanted to get stuck with. The natural division of labor which had the soldier as driver and mechanic, Mr. Kleiber as business manager and bookkeeper, Djeela-Lal as organizer and director of the show, and Rolf as chief scout, forager and general helper, kept them all busy enough. Jobs like making camp at night and packing up in the morning, setting up the show in the next town and loading it back in the van afterwards, were everybody's job. And so should the cooking be. Otherwise it wasn't fair. But just then Djeela-Lal and the soldier emerged from the bushes smiling vaguely, each one carrying a quart can half-full of blackberries, so that was all right. Rolf started the evening fire while the soldier brought out and unfolded and set the table, and Mr. Kleiber went down to the cool stream to bring back the water jug and the beer. Simultaneously Djeela-Lal began slitting hot dogs, opening cans of pork and beans and readying salty water for the instant mashed potatoes—not without commenting, however, that if there was any tendency amongst the men to look upon cooking as women's work, they could stuff it. Then all four sat down around the fire waiting for supper and discussing the morrow, when they would reach Libertytown. The morning would be spent in arousing local curiosity and interest in the Funco Circus, the afternoon in squaring the law and finding a vacant lot or schoolyard and getting ready, then the evening and night in giving continuous performances until the last $1.00 admission had been collected. Meanwhile, as they talked, darkness was coming on, a phantasmal scent of smoke and sadness had settled over the woods, and the birds were nesting down.

Mr. Kleiber said: "Milk and two sugars, yes, please. Thank you. Folks, as long as everybody's good and comfortable, and it's early yet, now might be a good time to take stock. Not that I'm trying to take charge or anything, but we did agree that at the end of the first month we'd get together and compare notes and see how things were working out— if we wanted to go on with it, I mean. Personally, I'm pleased as punch. Do you realize we've taken in more than five hundred dollars since we started out? Of course, most of that went for expenses—we aren't quite ready to start paying back the investment of Miss Lal's jewels or my savings yet—but just wait till our back publicity starts catching up! I mean, how many towns have we left so far on the brink of a riot? And the more controversy about whether we're fake or not, the more publicity! Not to mention when the newspapers put the whole story together, including the business at Delaware Project. The thing is, sooner or later we're going to be front-page news all over the country. And when that happens, we've got to be ready. And I mean for the Big Time! So far we've only just started. We have to make this into a real show! I've been thinking about it all week, and I've made a few notes already. For instance, the Strong Man act. Sure it goes over big, but it's only one act. Couldn't he duck away after that and paint himself green or put on a disguise and do another act as the Amphibian Man? All we'd need is a glass tank. Or how about a trick-shot exhibition? And Rolf, too. Instead of having him dressed up like Merlin to bust loose, couldn't we use a fancy electronic-looking gadget—the Gismo from Outer Space, say—while he stayed hidden? Then we could use him in a separate act, like maybe doing that whirlwind thing, only with colored smokes or confetti or something? Or maybe one of those other tricks he's been practicing? And that's just a starter. Levitation is fine, too, but I'm sure we could think of ways to get more mileage out of Miss Lal's talents. She could do that dance! And I'd certainly be more than willing to do more than write fire. Maybe we could work up an act around my total memory? The thing is, when we hit the Big Time, we'll need a full-scale show. One that'll *really* knock 'em on their ear!"

Djeela-Lal said: "Aren't we getting a little ahead of ourselves? To return for a moment to the original question: I've no doubt we are all more or less in favor of continuing on with the circus—if for no other reason than that we have not had to face any real difficulties yet. What these might be it is too soon too tell. One month is not a very long time. Of course, there are traveling circus troupes, also gypsies and other nomads, in many countries of the world. But few in this. At any moment we may blunder innocently

into some obvious obstacle that makes nonsense of the whole
thing. Meanwhile, all we can do is keep on. The DEPOSI-
TION gives us some protection—at least it serves to con-
found rural peace officers. And the element of surprise gives
us a little more. These little towns do not know what to
make of us, and by the time they find out, we are gone,
leaving only a few traces of ineradicable blue fire. Nevertheless, as Mr. Kleiber points out, celebrity, or perhaps no-
toriety, is bound to come. And when it does, we must
indeed be prepared. But *not* with a Super Freak Show. We
must be ready for recognition. For acknowledgment! I say
this in all humility. We are unique. The fact of our various
talents cannot be explained away, and must eventually have
its full effect upon civilization—an effect *not* to be measured
in one-dollar admissions! The world will have to do something about us, although here again it is too soon to imagine
what. We can only wait and see. For now, the circus is
as good a way as any to keep on—together, for we will
need each other. The thing to do now is to take each day
as it comes, turn south with the good weather, and trust in
our Karma. It is a good life—we sang together on the roads
today—I vote we live it while we may."

The soldier said: "I'm with you. With both of you, I
guess. I'll do whatever you decide. Except be cook. That's
out. If everybody does his share, we'll make out all right.
Nobody here was raised in the lap of luxury anyway, that
I know of. We ought to be thankful. Just having food to eat
and good company and a truck to ride in and a little money
coming in. That's a step up in the world for all of us, I'd
say. I know *I'm* better off. But don't expect me to worry
about the future. I'd just as soon *not* be recognized and
acknowledged. I don't need Big Time show business, either.
I'd rather keep on just like this. This is the life. I hope
it lasts forever. And maybe it will. Maybe nothing will
happen. Maybe nobody will bother us at all. Why should

they? If you ask me, the Machine was right all the time. We don't make that much difference. All of us were outcasts even before this happened—we always were. All this stuff about E.S.P. So we're unique? So is the guy who can tie his shoelaces with his teeth. So are a lot of people. So is everybody. So what? Who cares? This is good enough for me."

Rolf said: "Maybe that's good enough for you. Could be that's just fine for all of you, if you got nowhere else to go. But not me. It ain't nothing personal, mind, nor the show, nor being an outcast. Nor I don't mind too much being lumped in with a lot of artists and one-man bands and such, either. The thing is, there ain't no godderned contraption going to tell *me* I don't matter! I'll go along, all right, as far as this Funco Circus has to go. But you heard what I said from the start—I aim to blow it to blazes! Soon as I figure out who or what. I got plenty of time. And speaking of that, with all the traveling around we figure to do, you know what I purely expect to find? More of us! I'm here to tell you! Shucks, if there's one, there's more, ain't there? We must be just the first. And this here's as good a way as any to find 'em. Why, by the time I'm grown, maybe we'll have us a whole army! Then we'll see what's what! Talk about the future, maybe you all *ain't* it. But one way or another, like it or not, I *got* to be! And that being the case, I aim to make one mighty *big* difference! And that's for fact! You wait and see."

"Well, anyway, we're all agreed to go on," Mr. Kleiber said. "And at least I found some practical use for my nose."

"I'm happy. Just so I don't have to fight anybody," the soldier said. "Count me in."

"Me too," Rolf said. "Leastwise, till I found out who or what I got to bomb."

"So be it," Djeela-Lal said. "*Sarvam khalvidam Brahman*—all this too, no doubt, is God."

"SWITCH OFF," the Machine said.

The picture faded.

"SATISFACTORY. NO DATA INDICATING DEVIATION FROM COMPUTED PROBABILITY PATTERN."

"Yes, sir," said the F.D.I. agent.

"No, sir," said General Rod.

"MY DISPOSITION WAS CORRECT. THROUGHOUT ITS HISTORY THE HUMAN RACE HAS PRODUCED ODDBALLS, ARTISTS, PROPHETS, INDIVIDUALISTS. ABLE TO PERFORM NEAT LITTLE TRICKS OF NO CONSEQUENCE. TO JETÉ AN INCH HIGHER, WRITE A BETTER POEM, SING A LITTLE LOUDER, INSCRIBE A LONGER PASSAGE ON A SMALLER PINHEAD. UNIQUE FEATS OF NO PRACTICAL VALUE. THE EQUATIONS FOR THIS SITUATION REMAIN UNCHANGED."

"Yes, sir."

"NO DATA INDICATES TRUE MUTATION HAS OCCURRED."

"No, sir."

"GRIFFIN-BURNS-KLEIBER-LAL DO NOT MATTER."

"No, sir."

"NEVERTHELESS, THERE IS NO COINCIDENCE. THE APPEARANCE OF THESE FOUR SIMULTANEOUSLY IN TIME/SPACE MAY MEAN ADDITIONAL DATA STILL TO COME."

"Yes, sir."

"MAINTAIN CONTINUOUS SURVEILLANCE. YOU KNOW WHAT TO DO IF AND WHEN EQUATIONS FOR THIS SITUATION CHANGE."

"Yes, sir."

"Yes, sir."

"SUBTRACT," the Machine said.